Praise for *Equal of the Sun*

"*Equal of the Sun* is a page turner, with plenty of gripping moments. Here's hoping Amirrezvani will write many more tales illuminating the incredible history of the Iranians."

—*The Washington Post*

"Expertly woven."

—*Kirkus Reviews*

"*Equal of the Sun* is a fine political novel, full of rich detail and intrigue, but it's also a thought-provoking study of the intersection between gender and power."

—Historical Novel Society

"Amirrezvani's fans will feel silk carpets under foot, taste black tea, and delight in the language of old Iran in this new tale, one every bit as intriguing as her internationally best-selling debut, *The Blood of Flowers*."

—*San Francisco State Magazine*

"Amirrezvani's sixteenth-century Iran is a world as complex as Shakespeare's London, that seethes with intrigue, passion, and lawlessness, a world where a brilliant young princess, who longs for power denied her as a female, and a servant, with a desire so relentless he half destroys himself, make a desperate pact to control the government and fate of the country, and in doing so discover their greatest loves and sorrows. In this astonishing novel, Amirrezvani reminds us what all human hearts suffer and dare. *Equal of the Sun* is an irresistible novel."

—Jonis Agee, author of *The River Wife*

"A dazzling historical novel of ancient Persia, a fairy tale of universal resonance, *Equal of the Sun* is a story of love and ambition, loyalty and intrigue, the eternal anguish of a heart—and a country—at war with itself."

—Gina Nahai, author of *Moonlight on the Avenue of Faith* and *Caspian Rain*

ALSO BY ANITA AMIRREZVANI

The Blood of Flowers

EQUAL

OF THE

SUN

A NOVEL

ANITA
AMIRREZVANI

Scribner
New York   London   Toronto   Sydney   New Delhi

Scribner
A Division of Simon & Schuster, Inc.
1230 Avenue of the Americas
New York, NY 10020

Copyright © 2012 by Anita Amirrezvani

First Scribner trade paperback edition March 2013

SCRIBNER and design are registered trademarks of The Gale Group, Inc., used under license by
Simon & Schuster, Inc., the publisher of this work.

For information about special discounts for bulk purchases, please contact Simon & Schuster
Special Sales at 1-866-506-1949 or business@simonandschuster.com.

The Simon & Schuster Speakers Bureau can bring authors to your live event.
For more information or to book an event, contact the Simon & Schuster Speakers Bureau
at 1-866-248-3049 or visit our website at www.simonspeakers.com.

Designed by Carla Jayne Jones

Manufactured in the United States of America

1 3 5 7 9 10 8 6 4 2

Library of Congress Cataloging-in-Publication Data is available.

ISBN 978-1-4516-6046-3
ISBN 978-1-4516-6047-0 (pbk)
ISBN 978-1-4516-6048-7 (ebook)

Sa'di, excerpt on p. 253 from "The Cause for Composing the Gulistan" and excerpt on p. 229 from
"The Manners of Kings" from *The Rose Garden of Sa'di* (or *The Gulistan*), translated by Edward
Rehatsek (Kama Shastra Society, Benares, 1888).

Hafiz, excerpt on p. 292 from XXXVII from *Poems from the Divan of Hafiz*, translated by Gertrude
Lowthian Bell (London: William Heinemann, 1897).

Excerpts on pp. 315 and 343 from "The Reign of Yazdegerd," "The Reign of Hormozd," from
Shahnameh: The Persian Book of Kings by Abolqasem Ferdowsi, foreword by Azar Nafisi, translated
by Dick Davis, copyright © 1997, 2000, 2004 by Mage Publishers, Inc. Used by permission of
Viking Penguin, a division of Penguin Group (USA) Inc.

Rumi, excerpt on pp. 372–73 from "Weave Not, Like Spiders, Nets from Grief's Saliva" from *Look! This
Is Love: Poems of Rumi*, translated by Annemarie Schimmel, © 1991 by Annemarie Schimmel.
Reprinted by arrangement with Shambhala Publications Inc., Boston, MA. www.shambhala.com.

FOR MY PARENTS
AND
FOR ALL THE KAVEHS

LIST OF KEY CHARACTERS

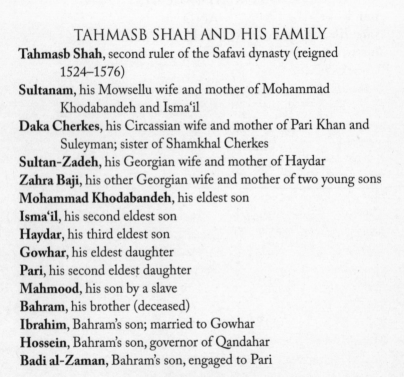

TAHMASB SHAH AND HIS FAMILY

Tahmasb Shah, second ruler of the Safavi dynasty (reigned 1524–1576)

Sultanam, his Mowsellu wife and mother of Mohammad Khodabandeh and Isma'il

Daka Cherkes, his Circassian wife and mother of Pari Khan and Suleyman; sister of Shamkhal Cherkes

Sultan-Zadeh, his Georgian wife and mother of Haydar

Zahra Baji, his other Georgian wife and mother of two young sons

Mohammad Khodabandeh, his eldest son

Isma'il, his second eldest son

Haydar, his third eldest son

Gowhar, his eldest daughter

Pari, his second eldest daughter

Mahmood, his son by a slave

Bahram, his brother (deceased)

Ibrahim, Bahram's son; married to Gowhar

Hossein, Bahram's son, governor of Qandahar

Badi al-Zaman, Bahram's son, engaged to Pari

ISMA'IL SHAH AND HIS FAMILY

Isma'il Shah, third ruler of the Safavi dynasty (1576–77)

Khadijeh, his wife; a slave from Africa

Koudenet, his wife; daughter of Shamkhal Cherkes

Mahasti, his wife; mother of his son Shoja al-din; a slave from the Caucasus

Mohsen, Khadijeh's brother

MOHAMMAD SHAH AND HIS FAMILY

Mohammad Shah, fourth ruler of the Safavi dynasty (1578–1587)

Khayr al-Nisa Beygom (Mahd-e-Olya), his wife and mother of
his sons Hamza, Abbas, Abu Taleb, and Tahmasb

Sultan Hassan, his eldest child by another wife

SERVANTS OF THE SAFAVI COURT

Amir Khan Mowsellu, Sultanam's brother

Amin Khan Halaki, a physician

Anwar, a eunuch from Sudan; head of the royal harem

Azar, chief lady to Pari

Balamani, a eunuch from Hindustan; Anwar's chief assistant

Fereshteh, a prostitute

Javaher, a eunuch from Qazveen and servant to Pari; also known as
Payam

Jalileh, Javaher's sister

Hassan Beyg Halvachi Oghli, Isma'il's favorite companion

Hossein Beyg, leader of the Ostajlu

Khakaberi Khan, Sultan-Zadeh's brother

Khalil Khan Afshar, Pari's childhood guardian

Kholafa, a leader of the Rumlu

Looloo, a court astrologer

Majeed, Pari's vizier

Maryam, Pari's favorite

Massoud Ali, an errand boy in Javaher's service

Mirza Salman Jaberi, chief of the royal guilds

Mirza Shokhrollah, chief of the treasury

Mohammad Amir Shirazi, Javaher's father (deceased)

Nasreen, chief lady to Khadijeh

Rasheed, head of the scribes

Saleem, chief of protocol

Shamkhal Cherkes, Pari's uncle, a leader of the Circassians

Note: Agha, Beyg, Beygom, Khan, Khanoom, Khatoon, Mirza, and
Sultan are titles. Titles typically appear after the first name.

EQUAL OF THE SUN

PROLOGUE

I swear to you on the holy Qur'an there has never been another woman like Pari Khan Khanoom. A princess by birth, a strategist by the age of fourteen, fierce but splendid in her bearing; a master archer, an almsgiver of great generosity, and a protector of prostitutes; a poet of uncommon grace, the most trusted advisor to a shah, and a leader of men. Do I exaggerate, like a court historian writing flowery panegyrics to a leader in the hope of being rewarded with a robe of honor? No such gift is forthcoming, I assure you: I am a man without a protector.

I wrestled over whether to attempt this work, since I am neither biographer nor historian. Despite the danger, the ignorance of the men around me compels me to set down the truth about the princess. If I refuse this task, her story will be misrepresented or distorted to become a tool of those in power. Court historians report only the best known facts about how royal women have led troops into battle, deposed shahs, killed their enemies, and thrust their sons into power. They are forbidden from observing the lives of these women directly and therefore must rely on rumors and invention.

As Pari's closest servant, I not only observed her actions but carried out her orders. I realized that upon my death, everything I know about her would disappear if I failed to document her story. But I must proceed in the greatest of secrecy. If this book were discovered by the wrong man, I could be executed, for I have committed monstrous deeds and made mistakes that I would prefer not to reveal—although what man hasn't? Man is flawed by his very nature. His ears hear only what they wish; God alone knows the absolute truth.

Perhaps, now that I think of it, I exaggerate slightly in saying that Pari was the only woman of her kind. She came from a dynasty that bred valiant women, starting with her grandmother Tajlu Khanoom Mowsellu, who had helped elevate her own ten-year-old son, Tahmasb, to the throne; and her aunt Maheen Banu, who advised Tahmasb until she died. By then, Pari was fourteen and wise enough to take Maheen Banu's place, and she reigned unchallenged as her father Tahmasb's advisor, above and beyond his wives, until his death almost fourteen years later. But Pari's deeds outshone those of her foremothers, and her boldness knew no bounds.

When I think of her, I remember not only her power, but her passion for verse. She was a poet in her own right and lavished silver on the poets she admired, keeping bread and salt on their tables. She had read all the classics and could recite long sections from them. Of the books of poetry she loved, a single tome stood out above others: the *Shahnameh,* or *Book of Shahs,* in which the great poet Ferdowsi recounted the passions and struggles of hundreds of Iranian rulers. During the time I served her, one story from that great book—about the usurper Zahhak and the hero Kaveh—guided our thoughts, directed our actions, and even invaded our dreams, so much so that I sometimes wondered if the story was about us. We turned to it for advice, wept over it in despair, and drew comfort from it in the end. It guides me still, as I celebrate Pari for the sake of generations to come.

CHAPTER 1

A NEW ASSIGNMENT

The way Ferdowsi tells it, Jamsheed was one of the first great civilizers of mankind. Thousands of years ago, he taught the earliest humans how to spin yarn and weave cloth, how to bake clay into brick for dwellings, and how to make weapons. After dividing men into craftsmen, tillers, priests, and warriors, he showed each group their duties. Once they had learned to work, Jamsheed revealed the world's sweetest treasures, such as where to find the jewels in the earth, how to use scent to adorn the body, and how to unlock the mysteries of healing plants. During his reign of three hundred years, nothing was lacking, and all were eager to serve him. But then one day, Jamsheed called on his sages and announced to them that his own excellence was unparalleled, wouldn't they agree? No man had ever done what he had, and for that reason, they must worship him as if he were the Creator. His sages were astonished and appalled by his extravagant claims. Back then, they dared not oppose him, but they began to desert his court. How could a leader become so deluded?

On the morning of my first meeting with Pari, I donned my best robe and consumed two glasses of strong black tea with dates to fortify my blood. I needed to charm her and show her my mettle; I must demonstrate why I would be a fitting match for the dynasty's most exalted woman. A thin sheen of sweat, no doubt from the hot tea, appeared on my chest as I entered her waiting area and removed my shoes. I was swiftly shown into one of her public rooms, which glowed with turquoise tile to the height of my waist. Above it, antique lusterware caught the light in alcoves and mirror work shimmered all the way to the ceiling, mimicking the radiance of the sun.

Pari was writing a letter on a wooden lap desk. She wore a blue short-sleeved silk robe covered with red brocade, belted with a white silk sash woven with bands of gold—a treasure itself—which she had tied into a thick, stylish knot at her waist. Her long black hair was loosely covered by a white scarf printed with golden arabesques, topped with a ruby ornament that caught the light and drew my eye to her forehead, which was long, smooth, and as rounded as a pearl, as if her intelligence needed more room than most. People say that one's future is inscribed on the forehead at birth—Pari's forehead announced a future that was rich and storied.

The princess continued writing as I stood there, her brow furrowing from time to time. She had almond-shaped eyes, forceful cheekbones, and generous lips, all of which made the features of her face appear to be writ larger than other people's. When she had finished her work, she put the desk aside and scrutinized me from head to toe. I bowed low with my hand at my chest. Pari's father had offered me to her as a reward for my good service, but the decision to retain me would be hers alone. No matter what, I must persuade her I had much to offer.

"What are you, really?" she asked. "I see ropes of black hair escaping from your turban and a thick neck, just like a bear's! You could pass for an ordinary man."

The princess stared at me in such a penetrating fashion it was as if she were asking me to reveal my very being. I was taken aback.

"It is helpful to be able to pass as ordinary," I replied quickly. "In the proper attire, I can be convincing as a tailor, a scholar, or even a priest."

"So?"

"It means I am equally accepted by commoners and royalty alike."

"But surely you cause consternation among the ladies of the royal harem, starved as they are for the sight of handsome men."

Panah bar Khoda! Had she learned about me and Khadijeh?

"It is hardly a problem," I parried, "since I lack the tools they crave the most."

Her smile was broad. "By all accounts, you are good at gathering intelligence."

"Is that what you require?"

"Among other things. What other languages do you speak and write?" she asked.

Switching from Farsi to Turkish, I replied, "I speak the language of your illustrious ancestors."

The princess looked impressed. "Your Turkish is very good. Where did you learn it?"

"My mother was Turkish-speaking, my father Farsi-speaking, and both were religious. They required me to learn the languages of the men of the sword, the men of the pen, and the men of God."

"Very useful. Who is your favorite poet?"

I groped for an answer until I remembered her favorite.

"Ferdowsi."

"So you love the classics. Very well, then. Recite to me from the *Shahnameh*."

She kept her gaze on me and waited, her eyes as sharp as a falcon's. Verse came easily to me; I had often repeated poems while tutoring her half brother, Mahmood. I recited the first verse that came to my mind, although it was not from the *Shahnameh*. The lines had often filled me with comfort:

If you are a child of fortune, every day is blessed
You drink wine, eat kabob, your skin is sun-kissed
Your beloved hangs on your every word
Your children love you like you are a god.
Ah, life is rich! Your goodness is deserving,
And just as soon as you start relaxing
Like a baby in its mother's warm embrace
Like a bird in flight soaring at its own pace
Joyous, carefree, fully adored,
The world snatches away what you most loved.
Your stomach burns with shock
Your heart stands still as you take stock.
Me? But I am the world's special one!
No, my friend, you were never a favorite son
But just another human sufferer, once loved,
Now pierced by sorrow, weeping tears of blood.

When I had finished, Pari smiled. "Well done!" she said. "But is that from the *Shahnameh*? I don't recognize it."

"It is by Nasser, although but a poor imitation of Ferdowsi's world-brightening verse."

"It sounds like it is about the fall of the great Jamsheed—and the end of the earthly paradise he created so long ago."

"That is what inspired Nasser," I replied, astonished that she knew Ferdowsi's poem well enough to question whether a small section of verse formed part of his sixty thousand lines.

"The great Samarqandi says in his *Four Discourses* that a poet should know thirty thousand couplets by heart," she said, as if reading my thoughts.

"From all that I have heard, I wouldn't be surprised if you did."

She ignored the flattery. "And what do the lines mean?"

I pondered them for a moment. "To me, they mean that even if you are a great shah, don't expect your life to proceed unblemished, since even the most fortunate will be tamed by the world."

"Have you been tamed by the world?"

"Indeed I have," I said. "I lost my father and my mother when I was young, and I have relinquished other things I had not expected to lose."

The princess's eyes became much softer, like a child's. "May their souls be in peace."

"Thank you."

"I hear you are very loyal," she said, "like others of your kind."

"We are known for that."

"If you were in my service, to whom would you show fealty, me or the Shah?"

How to respond? Like all others, I was bound first to the Shah.

"To you," I replied, and when she looked quizzical, I added, "knowing that your every decision would be made as the fondest slave of the Shah."

"Why do you want to serve me?"

"I was honored with the care of your half brother Mahmood for many years, and then I served as his mother's vizier. Now that she is no longer at court, I crave more responsibility."

That was not the real reason, of course. Many ambitious men ascended the ranks by serving the royal women, and that was what I wanted to do.

"That is good," Pari replied. "You will have to be bold to survive in my employ."

I like a challenge and said so.

Pari arose abruptly and walked to the alcoves in her wall, pausing before a large turquoise bowl whose design showed a black peacock fanning its beautiful tail.

"This is a valuable old bowl," she said. "Where do you think it is from?"

"Nishapur."

"Of course," she scoffed.

Sweat traveled down the back of my neck as I tried to decipher a few hints from the color, the pattern, and the brushwork. "Taymur's dynasty," I added quickly, "though I could not say whose reign."

"It was his son Shahrukh's," Pari said. "Only a few pieces of this type have survived in perfect condition."

She lifted the bowl to admire it, holding it in her hands like a newborn baby, and I admired it with her. The turquoise was so brilliant it was as if the glaze were made of gemstones, and the peacock looked as if it might peck for grain. Suddenly Pari opened her hands and let the bowl fall to the floor, where it shattered into a thousand pieces. A shard came to rest near my bare feet.

"What do you have to say about that?" she asked in a tone as sour as green almonds.

"No doubt your courtiers would say that it was a shame for such a costly and beautiful bowl to be destroyed, but that since the act was committed by a royal person, it is a fine thing."

"That is exactly what they would say," she replied, kicking one of the shards with a bored look.

"I don't imagine you would believe they meant it."

She looked up, interested. "Why not?"

"Because it is nonsense."

I waited with bated breath until Pari laughed. Then she clapped her hands to summon one of her ladies.

"Bring in my bowl."

The lady returned with a bowl of a similar pattern and placed it in the alcove, while a maid swept up the shattered pottery. I bent down and examined the shard near my foot. The peacock's head looked fuzzy, unlike the crisp lines on the bowl that had been brought in, and I understood that she had broken a copy.

Pari was watching me closely. I smiled.

"Did I surprise you?"

"Yes."

"You didn't show it."

I took a deep breath.

Pari sat down and crossed her legs, displaying bright red trousers under her blue robe. I tried to suppress my imagination from traveling to the places hidden there.

"Do you like to start things or finish them?" she asked. "You may not say both."

"Finish them."

"Give me an example."

I thought for a moment. "Mahmood didn't care for books when

he was a child, but it was my duty to make sure that he could write a good hand, read with expertise, and recite poetry at formal occasions. He now does all three, and I am proud to say he does them as well as if they were his favorite activities."

Pari smiled. "Knowing Mahmood's preference for the outdoors, that is quite an accomplishment. No wonder my father recommended you."

"It is an honor to serve the fulcrum of the universe," I replied. In fact, I missed Mahmood. After being in charge of him for eight years, I felt as protective toward him as if he were a younger brother, but I dared not claim such feelings for royalty.

"Tell me the story of how you became a eunuch."

I must have taken a step back, because she added quickly, "I hope you don't take offense."

I cleared my throat, trying to decide where to begin. Remembering was like sorting through a trunk of clothes worn by a dead man.

"As you must have heard, my father was accused of being a traitor and was executed. I don't know who named him. After that calamity, my mother took my three-year-old sister to live with relatives in a small town near the Persian Gulf. Despite what happened to my father, I still wished to serve the Shah. I begged everyone I knew for help, but was shunned. Then I decided the only way to prove my loyalty was to become a eunuch and offer myself to the court."

"How old were you?"

"Seventeen."

"That is very old to be cut."

"Indeed."

"Do you remember the operation?"

"How could I not?"

"Tell me about it."

I stared at her, incredulous. "You want to hear the details?"

"Yes."

"I am afraid the story's gruesomeness will offend your ears."

"I doubt it."

I did not spare her; I might as well find out right away what she was made of.

"I found two eunuchs, Nart and Chinasa, to assist me, and they took me to a surgeon who worked near the bazaar. He directed me to lie on a bench and bound my wrists underneath it so I could not move. The eunuchs positioned themselves on the inside of my thighs to hold back my legs. The surgeon gave me some opium to eat and dusted my parts with a powder he said would relieve the pain. Then he placed himself between my thighs and held up a cruel-looking curved razor. He told me that before he could perform such a risky operation, I must grant him permission in front of two witnesses. But the sight of the gleaming razor in the air unnerved me, and the restraints against my legs and arms made me feel like an animal in a trap. I twisted against the bench and yelled that I did not give my assent. The surgeon looked surprised, but lowered his razor right away and told the eunuchs to release me."

The princess's eyes were as round as polo balls. "Then what happened?"

"I considered my options once again. I didn't see any way of subsisting except at court. I needed to earn enough money to take care of my mother and my sister, and I wished to bring back the luster to our family name."

I did not tell her that deep in my heart had burned a fierce desire to unmask my father's murderer. As I contemplated the surgeon's knife, I imagined myself dressed in shining silk robes, having attained high position at the palace. Such prominence would allow me to expose my father's assassin and force him to admit to his crime. "From now on, your children will know the sorrow I have endured," I would say. Then he would receive his punishment.

Pari looked down and adjusted her sash, an evasion that made me wonder if she knew anything about his murderer.

"What happened next?"

"In the end, I told the men to proceed, but added that they should cover my eyes so I could not see the razor and that they should not restrain my arms."

"Did it hurt?"

I smiled, grateful that now it was just a memory.

"The surgeon tied a cord made of sinew around my parts and asked for my permission. I gave it, and seconds after I felt his hand lift up those parts, the razor sliced through me in a clean sweep. Feeling nothing, I tore off the blindfold to see what had been accomplished. My parts had vanished. 'That was easy!' I said, and I even joked with the eunuchs for a moment, until all of a sudden, I felt as if I had been sliced in two. I screamed and descended into blackness. I learned later that the surgeon cauterized the wound with oil and applied a dressing made of the bark of a tree. Then he applied a bandage and left me to recover."

"How long did it take?"

"A long time. For the first few days, I was not myself. I believe I said broken prayers. I know that I begged for water, but was not permitted to drink in order to allow the wound to heal. When my mouth became so dry that no words could emerge, someone moistened a cloth and placed it on my tongue. My thirst was so great that I begged for death."

"By God above! I can't think of another man willing to do what you did. You are very brave, aren't you?"

I did not tell her the rest of the story. Several days after the operation, I was allowed to drink some water. Nart bustled around me, attending to my bedroll and pillows, but looked strangely nervous. Every few minutes, he asked if I needed to relieve myself. I told him "no" repeatedly until he became tiresome and I begged him to leave me be. When I finally felt the urge, he removed the dressings and the plug and gave me a pot over which to squat. I was now smooth except for a small tube that I had not seen before. I closed my eyes at the sight of that raw, bloody canal.

It took a while, but when I was able to produce, I screamed in pain as the hot liquid shot through my exposed tube for the first time. I thought that I might lose my senses, but as I wanted to avoid falling into my own puddle, I managed to remain upright. When I had finished, I was surprised to see Nart's eyes shining. He opened his palms to the sky and bellowed, "May God above be praised!" Never had the sight of a man at his business been so pleasing to him, he told me later. My wound had been festering, and he had been greatly afraid that I might suffer the agony of an obstructed tube, a death too ugly for words.

Pari was still waiting for my answer. "How modest you are! Most men would quail at the sight of that razor. I still remember my father's astonishment when he heard your story."

Long before I had been cut, I had gone to a tavern and watched a dancer twirl her wide purple skirt over her head while the other men dared me to grope her. She shot me a seductive smile, but after a while, her mischievous flirting began to remind me of the way a boy toys with a lizard. Finally, spotting her large, rough hands, I came to a startling realization: She was a man! My face went hot with rage as the dancer grinned and whirled, and I felt ashamed that I had been duped. But now I was just like that dancer—indeterminate, strange to all, always provoking fierce reactions because of what I had done and what I lacked.

"I was very young," I said in my defense.

"Not that young."

"I was inordinately fervent."

"And now?"

I paused to think about it. "I have learned to moderate my actions."

"You are perfectly controlled here at court. I suspect you would be ideal for secret missions."

I bowed my head to acknowledge Pari's praise with the correct amount of humility.

"What is the difference between men and women?"

I looked up, surprised once again.

"I imagine you must have a better answer to this question than any other man."

I thought for moment. "They say men want power and women want peace. You know what the truth is?"

"What?"

"Everyone wants everything."

The princess laughed. "I certainly do."

"In that case, in what ways might I be of service to you?" I knew she already employed several hundred eunuchs, ladies, maids, and errand boys.

"I need a man to gather information for me inside and outside the palace," she said. "His trustworthiness and loyalty must be impeccable, his energy high, his need for sleep and amusement very low. That man will have no desires outside of his work for me. His silence about my activities will be obligatory. For these services, I am prepared to pay a substantial salary."

She named a figure that doubled what I earned. I felt suspicious: Why was the offer so good?

"By serving me, you will be at the heart of palace politics," she added. "You must have a strong stomach to be successful. The challenges ahead will be severe, and if you can't bear them, you will be discharged. Do you understand me?"

I said I did.

"You may begin your duties tomorrow morning here at my house."

I thanked her and was dismissed. As I put on my shoes, I felt my brain prickling with possibility. After twelve years of service, my work at the palace had finally begun in earnest.

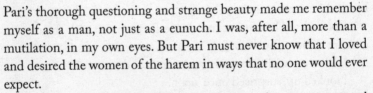

Pari's thorough questioning and strange beauty made me remember myself as a man, not just as a eunuch. I was, after all, more than a mutilation, in my own eyes. But Pari must never know that I loved and desired the women of the harem in ways that no one would ever expect.

Prior to my operation, I had been lying with a woman named Fereshteh almost every night. The first time had been on the day that my mother and my sister, Jalileh, left the city of Qazveen, traveling by donkey rather than by horse, in so much disgrace that our neighbors dared not look at them. I remember pacing the length of my boyhood home, which had been sold. One cushion remained in the room where my family used to gather for afternoon tea; I perched on it and watched the snow drown the bushes and the fountain in our garden. That night, in a tavern, I drank until my old life disappeared in a fog. My new friends recited poems and were happy to keep me company while I paid for jugs of ruby wine. I banged my fist on the wooden table and called for more to drink, and then more, and sang heartily to every tune. After midnight, I stumbled into the fresh snow and discovered Fereshteh, who was still new at her trade. Her large dark eyes were revealed by the black chador that covered her hair, and she was shivering in the cold. She took me to a room not far away and advised me not to drink. In her arms, I discovered my body for the first time, and I sank into her the way a thirsty traveler in the desert thrusts his head into a spring.

Toward dawn, we whispered our stories to each other in the dark. Fereshteh had been flung out of her home by a stepmother who claimed that she had made advances toward her only son. Her father was long dead, and there was no one to defend her. I told her that I, too, was about to be evicted from the only home I had ever known. Fereshteh comforted me as only a tormented fellow soul could do, and in the weeks ahead, I wanted nothing but to be in her arms. I spent every night with her that I could afford. Ah, that was a time of such fierce pain and pleasure I couldn't imagine ever experiencing it again.

In the days after my operation, any touch caused my entire body to ache. Pain became an extraordinary armor that repelled even the lightest physical contact so that my body could heal. I longed for the cessation of the pain, which seemed like the greatest possible gift. Once my body had healed, however, the mental torments began. In the morning, I would go to urinate expecting to handle my parts, and suddenly, my hands empty, I would feel as if I were falling. The vertigo was so great I feared I would slip into the latrines. Was I male? Female? What was I?

Then I would remember why I had done it, and I would steady myself, remove my plug, do my business, and emerge still shaken by my changed state.

I wanted Fereshteh, my only lover, to know what had happened to me. I tried to find her, but another prostitute told me she had left town. As time went by, a curious thing began to happen. My lips remembered the softness of Fereshteh's tongue; my chest longed for the butterfly-wing beat of her eyelashes; my thighs tightened at the thought of gripping her hips. The beauties of the harem started to turn my head. They could show each other all their glories, and why not? No men were around to make them feel uneasy. Secretly, I enjoyed every glimpse, but there was no corresponding rise in my middle. Frustration coursed through me. What good was desire to a gelding?

One day, while soaping myself in the baths, I became aware of a strange new impulse. I was like a man who has lost a limb but believes for a moment that he can leap up and swing his legs over a horse. As I ran the rough *kisseh* over my skin, my groin and lower back buzzed as if I had been grazed by lightning. I gasped, awash in sensations that were more diffuse but deeper than any I had ever felt. It was as if my freshly healed wound had reinvented my capacity for pleasure.

I thought of Fereshteh's deeply grooved waist, so fine in my hands, and her quick tongue. I yearned for her. Brushing the *kisseh* over my belly, I whooped with joy and growled deep in my throat. The other eunuchs, most of whom had rounded shoulders and soft thighs that made them look womanly, turned their heads in surprise. I felt like a cypress tree ravaged by fire and presumed dead, until one day, by the grace of God, new green shoots sprout from its charred heart.

On my first day in Pari's employ, I said my morning prayers and walked from my quarters in the harem to her home just inside the Ali Qapu—literally the grandest gate—shortly after dawn. A handful of trusted nobles had been granted homes inside the main palace gate, but Pari was the only woman who enjoyed this honor. Most royal women were confined to quarters deep inside the walled harem and permitted to exit only by permission from the Shah.

It was early; I would probably be the first to arrive. I said good morning to the guards, who lounged in the shade of the massive brick gate. They were at their ease until they unlocked the huge wooden doors and allowed members of the public to stream in to petition the Shah or his men at one of the administrative buildings on the palace grounds.

The princess's home was located behind high walls. I knocked, and when the door was opened by a servant, I stepped into a court-yard filled with the invigorating scent of pine. A long fountain led the way to a small but elegant building decorated with yellow and white tiles patterned with interlocking hexagons. After entering the house through a carved wooden door, I was escorted right away into Pari's *birooni*, the formal rooms in which she greeted visitors. To my surprise, her staff had already assembled. Dozens of eunuchs and errand boys stood in order of rank awaiting her command, and maids moved in and out soundlessly with trays of tea. I was struck by the taut air of discipline in the room, so different from what I had experienced when serving Mahmood's mother.

"Javaher, you are late," Pari said. "Come in and let's get to our business." She indicated the place where I should stand and frowned, her coal-black eyebrows darkening her forehead.

Pari's birooni was more austere than any of the other women's, who often competed with one another by adding lavish touches to their quarters. She sat on a cushion atop a large dark blue carpet, but rather than displaying golden songbirds or gardens of flowers, it was illustrated with mounted princes pursuing onagers, zebras, and gazelles, as well as bowmen aiming their arrows at lions. In alcoves lay neatly placed reed pens, ink, paper, and books.

A latticed wall at one end of the room permitted Pari to receive male visitors to whom she was not related. A young man in a blue velvet robe was standing on the other side of the lattice. We could see him through the lattice, but he couldn't see us.

"Majeed, I am pleased to introduce my new chief of information, Javaher Agha," Pari said, adding the title used for eunuchs. I had asked around about her vizier and learned that Majeed was young but destined for high service. He was from an old Shiraz family, which, like mine, had served the court for generations.

"Majeed is my liaison to the nobles of the court," Pari added. "Javaher, you are my liaison to the world of women, both inside and outside the palace, as well as to places where Majeed's nobility would not permit him to go without being detected."

She might have said the same thing about my own nobility, had my father not been accused of treason and killed. The old shame of it brought heat to my cheeks, and I bristled with the urge to prove myself the better servant.

"Javaher, you will observe me at work. I will deploy you later once you understand what I do."

"*Chashm, gorbon,*" I replied, the short form of "by my eyes, I would sacrifice myself for you."

For the rest of the morning, I watched Pari attend to routine business. Her first task was to check on the progress of the annual celebrations at the palace of the life of Fatemeh, beloved daughter of the Prophet. Women schooled in religion must be hired, food prepared, and rooms decorated. Then one of the Shah's eunuchs arrived to ask Pari how to process an unusual document because no one else could remember the protocol. The princess rattled off the order of the necessary signatures and named the men who must provide them, without even looking up from the document she was signing. Next, Pari read through a stack of messages and suddenly burst out laughing.

"Listen to this," she commanded us.

> *Princess, I wrote forty-eight sparkling lines about your dad*
> *You said you liked them: Are you in fact mad?*
> *If not, please send me what you pledged*
> *A rain of silver to keep me and my children fed.*
> *I humbly beg you to deliver what is overdue*
> *Then I will pen more dazzling gems for you.*

"Who could resist such a plea? Go to the head of the treasury and make sure the court poet is paid at once," she ordered Majeed.

In the afternoon, Pari held her usual public hours and saw palace women with a variety of requests: donations for the upkeep of a saint's shrine, positions at court requested for relatives, the need for more tutors. At the end of a long day, the princess agreed to see an out-of-town petitioner, even though she was tired and the woman was described to her as unfit for royal company.

The woman was shown into the room holding a sleeping baby, whose breath rasped when it exhaled. Her purple cotton robe was tired from days of journey. Her feet had been bound with dirty rags. My heart filled with pity at the sight of this friendless pair.

The woman bowed deeply and took her place on the visitor's cushion. She told Pari that her name was Rudabeh and that she had come all the way from Khui, not far from the border with the Ottomans. Her husband had divorced her and banished her from the home she had inherited from her father; he claimed it was his. She wanted it back.

"I am sorry to hear of your troubles," Pari said, "but why didn't you take your case to one of the Councils of Justice that aid citizens with disputes?"

"Revered princess, we went to the Council in my town, but the members are friends of my husband, and they said I had no claim. I had no choice but to appeal to someone here in the capital. I came to you because I heard that you are a protector of women."

Pari quizzed her on the details of her loss until she was convinced that the woman had a strong case. "Very well, then. Javaher Agha, you must escort our guest to a Council of Justice so that she may present her problem, and tell them I sent her."

"Chashm," I said. "The next meeting is in a week."

"Have you any money or any place to stay?" Pari asked.

"I have a few coins," the woman replied gravely, "and I will make do," but as she glanced down at her drowsy child, her eyes filled with fear.

"Javaher, take this mother to my ladies and ask them to shelter her and give her plenty of fresh herbs so that milk flows for her child."

"Thanks be to God for your generosity!" Rudabeh exclaimed. "If I may ever assist you, I would gladly offer my eyes to cushion the steps of your feet."

"It is my pleasure. After you return home, write to me and tell me all the news of Khui."

"I promise to be your faithful correspondent."

When I had first joined palace service, a eunuch from the Malabar coast of Hindustan asked to train me. Balamani was a charcoal-skinned fellow with a big belly and dark circles under his wise old eyes who spent his day in casual conversation with maidservants, gardeners, physicians, and even messenger boys. He had an easy laugh and an avuncular manner that made his people feel that he cared about them. That is how he learned everything about the day-to-day news of the palace: who was jealous of whom, who was in line for promotion, and who was on his way out. His informants would tell him about things like the bloody contents of a noble's chamber pot long before anyone else realized the man was dying. Balamani's currency was information, and he traded it like gold.

Balamani told me to memorize the *Tanassour*, a book that listed the proper titles used to address every type of man. I had to learn that *mirza* placed after a man's name, as in Mahmood Mirza, indicated that he was a prince of royal blood, whereas *mirza* used before a man's name was merely an honorific. When I made mistakes, Balamani sent me back to the book: "Otherwise the nobles will flay your back until it resembles a red carpet."

Once I knew how to address all the palace inhabitants, Balamani taught me the art of gathering information from them in such a clever way that I appeared to be dispensing it, as well as how to pay for it when necessary and how to use it as political capital. "You have no jewels between your legs or on your fingers," he said once, "so make sure to acquire currency in your mind."

Balamani called every bit of information a "jewel"—*javaher*—and asked me daily if I had any for him. The first time I offered a gem to Balamani, I earned my nickname. After shadowing an errand boy who served one of the Shah's ministers, I discovered that he was delivering messages to an unsavory book dealer. It turned out that the minister was trying to sell a priceless gold-illuminated manuscript he had intercepted before it reached the court treasury. When Balamani informed the Shah, the minister was dismissed, the book dealer was disciplined, and I was reborn with a new name. "Javaher" was normally used for women, but it became my badge of honor.

I loved and respected Balamani like a favorite uncle. Now that he was older, I nursed him when he had bladder complications, probably due to the removal of his male parts, which caused a susceptibility to painful infections. I also did his work when he was too sick to do it himself. As second in command to Anwar, the African eunuch in charge of the harem, he had plenty to do.

Working for Pari, I used all I had learned from Balamani to forge deeper connections with people close to the women of the royal household—maids, ladies, and eunuchs. Of special interest to the princess were those wives and consorts of the Shah who had adult sons. She wished to know their aspirations for their boys, particularly if they sought to place them on the throne.

One afternoon, I returned from an errand and chanced upon Pari and her uncle, Shamkhal Cherkes, talking quietly together. Shamkhal was an unusually big man, broad of shoulder, with large hands and forearms the width of a mace. His face was sun-browned from riding, and when he talked, thick muscles bulged in his neck. His enormous blue and white turban, fashioned of two fabrics twined together, made him appear even bigger than he was. Pari looked as fine as a vase next to him, as if she had a different maker altogether.

". . . prepared for what happens after . . ." I heard Pari saying.

Pari began naming kinsmen and Shamkhal replied either "with us" or "not with us." A few times, he said, "I don't know."

"Why not?" asked Pari each time, until finally she became exasperated and said, in a tone that brooked no argument, "We must know these things or we will fail."

"I promise to have more information the next time I see you."

His deference toward her surprised me.

A few days later, I found a way to ask Pari about which man she planned to support for the throne. I told the princess that I had been hearing rumors about how Sultanam, the Shah's first wife, had been searching for a suitable wife for her son Isma'il, even though he was imprisoned. She suspected that Isma'il's lack of male children might be the result of a curse placed by enemies, and she had been consulting herbalists about how to open the gates of his luck.

Pari drank in this news. "Good work."

"The speculation is that she intends to make him the next Shah," I added.

"So does every mother of a prince. We will have to wait and see. But we must be ready."

"For what?"

"For whatever happens, so we can rally behind whomever my father designates as heir. The nobles have shown themselves to be divided, and I want to avoid another civil war at all costs."

"How will you do that?"

"By making sure that the heir gets all the help he needs to be successfully crowned shah."

"And who is that?"

"My father hasn't announced his selection."

"Some say Haydar is the best man," I said, trying to gauge her reaction, "although he has lived all his life in the palace."

"He is untested."

"And some think Isma'il is better, because he was such a brave warrior."

Pari's eyes were sad. "He was my hero when I was young. My heart has ached for him in his exile. None of the royal family has been permitted to write to him or receive his letters, except for his mother."

"Do you think he would govern well after an absence of so many years?"

"Choosing an heir is my father's concern," Pari replied sharply. "Ours is to ensure that a strong network of supporters is in place well before it is needed. Do you understand?"

"Yes, esteemed lieutenant," I answered, "but I would have thought you might advocate for your brother, Suleyman."

Pari's mouth flattened. "I am not a sentimentalist. He is no match for the men he would have to rule."

So Pari was planning a decisive role in the succession! I suspected that a large batch of letters she had recently sent were intended to rally support, but for whom?

For me, it wasn't merely a matter of curiosity. If Pari's star fell with the Shah's death, mine would plummet.

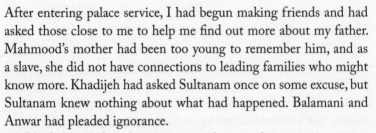

After entering palace service, I had begun making friends and had asked those close to me to help me find out more about my father. Mahmood's mother had been too young to remember him, and as a slave, she did not have connections to leading families who might know more. Khadijeh had asked Sultanam once on some excuse, but Sultanam knew nothing about what had happened. Balamani and Anwar had pleaded ignorance.

I had also tried to obtain access to the court histories to examine them for information about my father's murder. Each time, I was told that a servant of my station was not permitted to lay eyes on confidential court documents. Years passed without progress. I had yearned to rise up through the ranks so that I would have access to powerful men who possessed the information I sought.

After Pari hired me, I went to the office of the royal scribes to introduce myself as the princess's new chief of information. The scribes worked in a large room illuminated by light streaming through tall windows. The men sat upright on cushions, their wooden desks over their laps, or wrote on top of chests made of inlaid wood that contained their supplies. The room was as quiet as a grave. The reed pens the men used hardly made a sound. The scribes who wrote letters for the Shah worked side by side with court historians who documented every breath of importance in the realm.

I made the acquaintance of the head of the guild, a venerable old master named Rasheed Khan, who wore a black turban, a long white beard, and had wise eyes that looked red and tired from too much close work. He was known for the clarity and beauty of his handwriting, and had trained many of the men who now worked for him.

My new employer has a scholarly bent, I told Rasheed. Once in a while, I might need to look at the court histories, perhaps even one currently being written about Tahmasb Shah's long reign. Would that be a problem? Oh no, I was assured, any business required by the favorite daughter of the Shah would be treated with the utmost respect. All I would need was a note of permission written by Pari. Manuscripts could even be borrowed if she so wished, so long as they were not currently being worked on.

Praise be to God! The princess's name worked like a magic spell.

In the middle of the night, there was an urgent tugging at my bed-clothes, as if a jinni of ill fortune were disrupting my dreams. He was small, with large dark eyes and a crooked smile, and he would not let go. He tugged and tugged, and I batted his hand away, trying to lose myself in the blackness. But the tugging grew more insistent until I opened my eyes and, in the moonlight, perceived Massoud Ali, the nine-year-old errand boy Pari had placed in my service. His face was unwashed, and he hadn't wrapped his head in the tiny turban that he was usually so proud to wear.

"Wake up! Wake up, by God above!"

I sat upright, tensed for attack. Balamani, who was a heavy sleeper, turned over on his bedroll in the small bedchamber we shared.

"What is it?"

Massoud Ali leaned close to my ear and whispered, as if it were too terrible a thing to say out loud, "Alas, the light of the universe has been extinguished. The Shah is dead."

There was fear in his dark eyes.

"Balamani!" I called. He mumbled that I was the son of a dog and rolled over.

"Wake him gently," I told Massoud Ali.

I threw off the bedclothes, slammed my arms into a robe, and shoved my hair inside my turban.

Tahmasb Shah, who had ruled for more than fifty years, dead? He who had survived several poisoning attempts and a grave illness that lasted nearly two years? It was as if Canopus had been extinguished, leaving all of us mariners struggling to navigate in darkness.

Only a few weeks before, the Shah had granted me the boon of serving his favorite daughter. "Do not forget, no other child is dearer to my eyes," he had said, stabbing his finger at the air to emphasize his point. "You must swear to sacrifice your very life for hers if need be. Do you swear it?"

I rushed into the gardens near my quarters, which bloomed without shame in the early dawn. Birds sang in the cedar trees, and the purple and white petunias were in full flower. A wave of vertigo assailed me; everything at the palace would now change—the ministers, women, eunuchs, and slaves the new shah favored. What would happen to Pari? Would she retain her role as a favorite? And what would become of me? Who would survive?

I found Pari in a dim room illuminated by flickering oil lamps. Her eyes were red with weeping, and her face looked drawn and old. Two of her ladies, Maryam and Azar, attended to her, holding her hands and dabbing at the tears on her cheeks with a silk handkerchief.

"*Salaam aleikum,* esteemed lieutenant of my existence," I said. "My heart sheds tears of blood over your loss. If I could take away the poison of your pain, I would consume it with as much joy as if it were halva."

The princess beckoned me to approach her. "It is the worst heartbreak of my life. I accept your condolences with gratitude."

"How could this have happened so quickly?"

Pari's eyes looked like glass. "I went to his side yesterday evening as soon as I learned he had a fever," she replied in a voice thick with grief. "He told me his problems had started at the hammam. After his manservant coated his lower limbs with a depilatory, he felt a stinging pain, but ignored it until he noticed that his legs had turned bloodred."

How like the Shah to want his body to be spotless when it was time to pray.

"He leapt up from his bedroll and jumped into a pool. His manservant, who had been fetching sliced cucumbers, followed him into the water fully clothed, ripped off his turban, and used the cloth to wipe the sticky cream off my father's legs. By then, they were already badly burned."

"May God save us from harm!" I said.

Pari took a sip of her tea and cleared her throat. "Naturally, he suspected poison and instructed his chemists to examine the depilatory. His physician applied a soothing balm to his legs and told him he would recover. My father continued about his daily business, although he said his legs felt like poles of fire. By evening, he could no longer stand without agony, and he took to his bed. That is when he called for me."

She took a long breath and sighed deeply, while her ladies murmured soothing words. "When I arrived, I applied cold compresses filled with rosemary to his forehead, but his fever continued to mount. In the darkest hours of the night, it was as if his brain were boiling like a stew. Before long, he lost his ability to speak or to reason. I prayed and tried to comfort him, but his crossing into the next world was racked with anguish."

"Revered princess, no daughter could do more! May his soul be in peace."

"For this I hope and pray." Pari wiped the tears angrily from her cheeks. "If only I could just grieve!" she cried.

A look of understanding passed between us. If she had been anyone else, she would have visited her father's grave site every day for forty days and watered it with an ocean of tears. But Pari did not have the luxury of woe; she must get to work on the succession. I pitied her.

Shortly after dawn prayers, I arrived at the mourning ceremony in Sultanam's quarters, where the royal women had gathered to lament the loss of the Shah. The Shah's first wife was known by her honorific, which meant "my Sultan." Her home had an open-air sitting area on the ground floor with views of the rose gardens, and the guest rooms were furnished with pink silk carpets and embroidered pink and white velvet cushions. Today the rooms were filled with the plaintive wails of the women.

I entered a large sitting room and put out my hands to accept the sprinkles of rose water offered to me by a servant. In the center of the room, an old woman seated cross-legged on a wooden platform was reciting the Qur'an from memory. The words flowed out of her so easily that I guessed she knew the entire blessed book by heart. The ladies seated on cushions on the floor around her wore black robes, and their hair was uncharacteristically loose on their shoulders, uncombed and wild. They wore no kohl on their eyes, no armbands, no earrings. Adornment was prohibited by grief, and its absence made them look more vulnerable than in their ordinary courtly attire.

Sultanam greeted a new arrival and accepted her condolences. Upright, she seemed to consume the space of two women. Her layered robes made her appear even wider than she was, despite her tiny feet and ankles, which looked too small to support her. Her curly white hair fanned out like a pyramid from her tea-colored face and slanted eyes, and it was easy to imagine her as a proud horsewoman of the Mowsellu tribe, which she had been long ago. Her face did not bear any of the puffiness that comes from sincere weeping, nor did tears well up spontaneously in her eyes. I imagined that nothing could be more joyous to her than the possibility that her son Isma'il would be released from his confinement—and perhaps even crowned shah. But that was the kind of loyalty you would expect of a mother. Who knew if after nearly twenty years of prison, Isma'il was fit to rule?

Close at hand was Sultanam's plump maid, Khadijeh, whose face glowed like the moon. My heart sped up, but I forced myself to turn away as if she meant nothing to me.

The room was crowded with dozens of women who had been favored by the late Shah during his long life. His three other wives, Daka Cherkes, Sultan-Zadeh, and Zahra Baji, had claimed the best places close to the reciter. Next came eight or nine adult daughters of the Shah and their children—too many to count—followed by several consorts and their children, and finally, a much larger circle of women who had never shared his bed.

Pari was sitting close to her mother, Daka Cherkes. The two women had wrapped their arms around each other, and their heads were leaning together in sympathy. Daka was known for having a mild and placating personality, quite the opposite of her daughter, whom she often tried unsuccessfully to rein in. Copious tears watered Daka's cheeks, and I suspected she was concerned about what the Shah's death would mean to Pari's future.

Sultan-Zadeh, the Georgian mother of Haydar, began tearing at her fine camel-colored hair. The older women disliked her because she was one of the few who had ensnared the Shah's heart, and they had done everything they could to thwart her attempts to gain status. No wonder the tears in her green eyes looked real.

Pari whispered something in her mother's ear, arose, and disappeared down a corridor. I followed her into one of the side rooms, where women were comforting one another in smaller groups. My blood froze at the thought of the Shah lying silent and cold in his death room in the palace. Something started to loosen in my own breast, and I concentrated on quieting myself as I scanned the room. Pari was sitting with Maryam at her side. Her walled-in silence was far more awful than the shrieks and cries of sorrow from the others.

I crouched down beside her and whispered, "Lieutenant of my life, is there any service I can provide to you right now?"

"Watch them all in the main room," she replied, "and when this terrible day is through report everything you have seen."

The women in that room had not moved except to keen. But behind them, servants were whispering to one another as if bursting with news, and Balamani was talking to a slave; he had a disturbed look in his eye.

As the reciter's voice rose high and sharp, the women filled the air with terrible moans, and the space grew hot and thick with the smell of rose water and sweat.

When Balamani stopped talking to the slave, I walked toward him softly. He didn't notice, so I tugged his robe to get his attention. He jumped like a cat about to pounce, his big belly bouncing.

"It is me," I said soothingly, "your doctor."

The gray skin under his eyes looked darker than usual. He smiled slightly and said, "If only you could cure me this time."

"I can see that something new ails you," I replied.

"Ah, friend of mine, if only you knew what I know."

I felt a twinge of disappointment that he had won this skirmish. "What is it?"

"The succession."

"Who will it be, then?"

"That is just it," Balamani whispered, an edge of terror in his voice. "No one knows how to proceed."

"What does the chief of protocol say?"

"Saleem Khan? He says nothing."

"Nothing?"

He leaned closer to my ear. "There is nothing to say, because there is no will."

A loud expostulation escaped my lips, and I bent my head and pretended to be overcome by a fit of coughing. No will? Who would tame the Shah's ferocious sons, each of whom probably dreamed of being ruler, not to mention the sons of the Shah's brother Bahram? My vertigo returned for a moment.

"May God save us all! How will the heir be decided?"

"If all goes well, the nobles will agree on the new shah, and the other Safavi sons will accept him."

"And if it doesn't?"

"They will ally behind different men and throw the land into chaos."

"What do you expect?"

"The worst."

I resumed my post and watched every gesture like a hawk in search of prey. A few of the women were reading from copies of the Qur'an, but most were so involved in their grieving that they were not moving or talking much. From time to time they drank from vessels of melon *sharbat* served on large trays, or nibbled at halva to keep themselves strong. They would need to be strong.

The reciter had begun recounting stories of the blessed Prophet's family. Her voice surged high with pain as she described baby Ali-Asghar, whose throat was struck by an enemy arrow and who drowned in his own blood. Pinpricks stung my eyes. I remembered the dirt falling onto my father's body, the screams of my mother and sister, and my own anguish. Now was a respectable moment to vent my grief, for my father, for the fate of my mother and sister, for the dead Shah, for Pari, and for the future of us all. Pari's eyes caught mine, and I saw sympathy there. For a few hours, there was nothing but unity in the room as we recalled and relived the sorrows we had known on this earth.

It was late afternoon before the Shah's eldest female relation, Fatemeh Beygom, made her ceremonial appearance at the proceedings, dressed in proper court attire.

"Good women," she said to the crowd, "you have mourned with your hearts full and shed all the water in your body in the form of tears. Now it is time to halt this river of suffering and return to your private grief. To God above we give our trust, from God above we beg for protection."

The room became very quiet. The women began wiping away their tears, smoothing their hair, and gathering their things, all rather slowly, as if they were reluctant to leave the safety of shared mourning.

As the royal women began to say their goodbyes, a group gathered around Sultanam. Even the tallest among them looked like frail reeds near her broad body. One of the first to leave was a consort of the Shah's who had two young sons and could be expected to throw her weight behind one of the adult contenders. I watched Sultanam kiss her with gratitude. No doubt she would rally the support of her allies behind Isma'il.

Women were also lingering around Sultan-Zadeh, Haydar's mother, ostensibly to console her. Her face was red from the exertion of honest weeping, yet there was a spark in her eyes. The Georgian women approached her; then Gowhar, the late Shah's eldest daughter, gave Sultan-Zadeh a goodbye kiss on each cheek and whispered into her ear. Sultan-Zadeh brightened. Gowhar said a perfunctory goodbye to Sultanam, wrapped herself in her black chador, and departed.

The room was emptying rapidly. Pari paid her respects to Sultan-Zadeh, and both women uttered condolences about the rewards in heaven for a life well lived.

"Everything will be different now," Sultan-Zadeh added, her pretty mouth pursed as if she were about to plant a kiss on Pari's cheek. "May I hope for your support of my son Haydar?"

I knew Haydar as a spoiled pleasure-seeker who had never made a serious study of the business of governing. But when had that ever stopped a prince from believing he deserved the throne?

Pari drew back. "How can you ask now, when my father is so newly—?"

Sultan-Zadeh's lip curled slightly, as if she were a small starved animal baring its teeth.

"I mean no disrespect. I suppose you would understand if you had your own sons."

Pari ignored the slight. "No matter how eager you are for your son's advancement, you should not breach the established traditions," Pari replied. "There is a procedure to follow when there is no will. Do you know what it is?"

"No."

"The elders meet and discuss who is the best candidate. That is what happened when my father was selected. In times of uncertainty, procedure is all we have."

"But, Pari, let me tell you why my son—"

"Not now," said Pari, moving away from her.

Sultan-Zadeh frowned, and her pretty green eyes looked hard.

Pari crossed the large room to kiss Sultanam. The two women talked politely for a few moments, even though Sultanam had never approved of Pari because she dominated her husband's attention.

As the princess took her leave, the somber, grieving face that Sultanam had shown Pari transformed, and her strong white teeth flashed in a nakedly victorious smile. As soon as we left the building, I told Pari what I had seen.

"How they delight in the idea of squelching my power!" she said as we walked past the garden of red and pink roses. "Until today, they didn't dare be so bold. Now I expect to bear the brunt of all their aspirations. My mother will plead with me to marry and be safe, but a life of safety is not what I desire."

I was struck by how different Pari was from everyone else. A desire to protect her surged through me.

"I promise to fight to keep you secure."

"I thank you," Pari said, resting her hand for a moment on my arm.

I heard footsteps behind us and turned around to see Massoud Ali speeding past the rosebushes toward us. He was panting, but that didn't prevent him from trying to tell us something.

"What is it, my little one?"

"All the noblemen have left their mourning ceremony and are gathering for a meeting at Forty Columns Hall," he said, almost out of breath.

"About the succession?"

"Yes."

"You must go," said Pari.

"Chashm," I replied. Since the royal women could not show themselves at the men's meetings, I would be Pari's eyes and ears. I told Massoud Ali to wait for me while I walked Pari back to her house. As we entered the gate to her courtyard, she was making plans. "As soon as you return from the meeting, we must review the details for the public mourning ceremonies for my . . ."

I was shutting the heavy door behind us when her voice trailed off. Pari stopped moving and her shoulders slumped dangerously. For a terrible moment, I feared that she might drop to the ground.

"Princess," I said softly, rushing to her side, "I know all too well what oceans of sorrow drown your heart."

Her eyes filled. To my astonishment, she draped her arms on my shoulders and clung to me like a child, her head against my chest. Sobs shook her long, thin body, and hot tears soaked the front of my robe. I tried to stand as firm as the famous cypress in Abarkuh that has witnessed three thousand years of human sorrow.

When her sobbing had subsided, Pari begged me for a handkerchief. Her eyes were bloodred, her nose wet with mucus. I handed her the cotton handkerchief that hung from my sash and watched her dry her eyes and her face.

"My heart is breaking over the loss of my father," she said.

"I understand. I have shed the same bitter tears."

"I know you have. Thank you for allowing me to steady myself upon you"—here she noticed my stained robe—"and make you wet."

We were alone, so I decided to take a risk. "I am honored to be your human handkerchief. Never fear, it was like bathing in a river of diamonds."

I glanced at the gleaming mucus on my robe.

Pari managed a smile, then could not prevent a small, sad snort of laughter, after which she had to dab further at her nose. She tossed the handkerchief back to me.

"Here, you need this more than I do."

CHAPTER 2

AN ANIMAL MOOD

Jamsheed's delusions opened the gates to greed, disorder, and despair throughout the land, even in places where chaos had never existed before.

In a tiny corner of his kingdom, there lived a ruler named Mirdas who was so pious that he arose every day to pray in his garden before it was light. He was the lord of thousands of sheep and goats, and he shared their milk, cheese, and meat so that no man in his kingdom ever went hungry. His one weakness was that he was too indulgent with his only son, Zahhak. One day, Zahhak was approached by the devil, who expressed surprise at how patiently he waited for his father's throne. Since his succession was ordained, surely there could be no harm in hastening it. Why should an old man be in charge rather than someone as vigorous and fresh as he?

That night, the devil dug a deep hole on the path that Mirdas took every morning to the fire temple where he said his prayers, and covered it with leaves and branches. The next morning, when Mirdas walked forth into his garden, he fell into the hole and his spine snapped. The poor man howled and groaned, but none heard him, and finally, in great agony, he expired. So justice was supplanted by injustice, and a cycle of terror began.

Massoud Ali and I left the walled quarters of the women, which lay deep inside the palace, through a thick wooden door embedded with metal in the middle of a tall wall. We saluted Zav Agha, the old eunuch on duty at the checkpoint leading to the birooni—the outside.

"Not long until retirement?" I asked.

"Only a few months, God willing, if I survive this latest upheaval!"

He and Balamani often talked about the fierce ocean and the fresh fish of their childhood on the Malabar coast of Hindustan, before they had been cut and sold as slaves. Now, as free men, they longed to return there.

Massoud Ali and I wound our way through twisting corridors studded with armed guards until we reached the large courtyard near the Ali Qapu gate. We traversed the courtyard, passing through a second gated and guarded checkpoint that led to the treasury, library, hospital, pharmacy, and morgue. Massoud Ali's forehead was so pinched that I wanted to cheer him. I asked him if there were any games he liked to play with the other errand boys, but he shrugged. He was thin and small, and I surmised that even younger boys would be able to pummel him.

"How about backgammon?"

"I don't know how."

"I will teach you. It is the game of shrewd statesmen."

His smile flashed so briefly it was as if he hadn't learned how to use it yet.

Shortly after the intersection of the two main avenues that crossed the palace grounds, we arrived at Forty Columns Hall, the palace's most important meeting place. It was one of my favorite buildings because its large entrance portal was left open during the warmer months to a view of the fruit orchards and flower gardens.

A court poet had once written more than a hundred lines about the exquisiteness of the melons grown on the palace grounds, and with good reason.

Inside the hall, its high ceiling was arched, sectioned, and painted in pale shades of orange, turquoise, and green, overlaid with a pattern of gold flowers much like the design on a fine silk robe. Thick carpets and plush cushions covered the floors.

Massoud Ali stood against the back wall with the other errand boys; I sat beside Balamani among the palace eunuchs. Balamani and I frowned at each other; we hadn't learned anything new. Today the normally sober hall was alive with speculation about who would be the next shah. Members of the Ostajlu and Mowsellu tribes sat nearest to the platform where the late shah used to emerge and speak; this was their privilege as men of the sword who had helped the Safavi dynasty to the throne. Several Georgian and Circassian leaders who had married into the royal family claimed seats of honor, too. These groups had begun to vie for power against the more established tribes and against the most powerful men of the pen, who were in charge of keeping accounts and writing royal letters, orders, and histories. My father had been one such man, and for a moment I imagined the two of us sitting together near the top of the room, dressed in dark silk robes in honor of the Shah's passing.

Saleem Khan, the master of palace protocol, entered the room. He possessed a voice that could tame an army of men. When he called, "Come to order!" the nobles fell silent. The chief mullah of Qazveen, whose black turban and robes were a sobering sight, walked slowly to the front of the hall and said a prayer for the dead. Every head in the room was bowed, as if weighed down by the uncertainty of the future.

After the prayer, Saleem Khan announced that a member of the Safavi dynasty wished to address us. The brown velvet curtain at the back of the platform stirred, and Haydar Mirza stepped out and stood in the Shah's place. He was a slight young man with a nervous left eye that sometimes blinked too much. His fitted dark gray robe made him look even smaller than usual.

"Greetings to all the valued retainers of the Safavi court," he began in a nasal voice that was too quiet to be heard well. "I give my thanks to you for attending upon us on this terrible day. Together we mourn the passing of my father, the fulcrum of the universe, even as we must turn our attention to what lies ahead. I call on you, great ones, to help me fulfill my father's wishes for the future."

Not even the fringes on the nobles' sashes stirred as they waited to hear what he had in mind, but Haydar faltered.

"I request your indulgence for a moment," he finally said before disappearing behind the curtain. We heard the high-pitched murmuring of a woman.

"That sounds like his mother," I whispered to Balamani.

"If he can't get through a meeting without her help, how does he expect to rule?" Balamani growled. Speculation filled the room until Saleem Khan's voice boomed like a cannon, and the room quieted again.

Haydar emerged from the curtain too quickly, stumbling as if he had been pushed out. In his fist was the great golden sword of the Safavi dynasty, a beautifully crafted weapon encrusted with emeralds and rubies. The matching belt at his waist emanated rays of light when he moved.

"I hereby declare myself your new shah and demand your loyalty unto death!" Haydar shouted. "Those who serve me will be well rewarded; those who oppose me will pay the consequences." He tried to thrust the sword high into the air, but the weapon was too heavy and his arm faltered midway.

The room exploded. Men leapt to their feet—some cried out in surprise, others shouted their support.

"Squelch your chatter!" commanded Saleem Khan, and gradually, the men settled down.

Haydar's uncle on his mother's side, Khakaberi Khan, asked to be recognized and stood up to help his nephew. "By what authority do you make this claim?"

Haydar handed the sword to Saleem Khan. From deep in his robe, he produced a rolled document and held it high for all to see.

"By my father's will," he said.

There was a low, powerful roar of disbelief.

Haydar unrolled the document and read it aloud. It named him as the only lawful successor to Tahmasb Shah and urged the courtiers to show loyalty to him as his father's choice.

"I know the Shah's writing better than my own," challenged Mirza Shokhrollah, the treasury chief, whose long gray beard wagged when he spoke. "Let me see that document."

"Here it is," replied Haydar, waving the paper but refusing to relinquish it, so Shokhrollah had to approach the platform. After a few moments, he said in a surprised tone, "I would swear the writing was the Shah's."

Pari's uncle, Shamkhal Cherkes, arose to have his say. "Everyone knows there is a lady in the royal palace whose handwriting resembles his," he said, his index finger pointing heavenward for emphasis. "How can we be certain that this isn't her handiwork?"

"Whether you doubt the writing or not, everyone knows my father's seal," Haydar said, pointing to the will. "Surely you don't deny that this is it?"

"Any seal can be copied," Shamkhal replied.

"This one is authentic, I swear," said Haydar.

"In that case, let the Shah's seal be brought forth for comparison," insisted Shamkhal.

On occasion I had seen the Shah use the seal on his most important correspondence; he had worn it on a chain around his neck. Mirza Salman Jaberi, the head of the royal guilds, including the seal makers, was deputized by the treasury chief to visit the death room and make an impression of the Shah's seal on a blank page.

Meanwhile, Saleem Khan announced that refreshments would be served. An army of servants rushed in with trays of hot cardamom tea, while others carried plates of nuts, dates, and sweetmeats. In the midst of the distraction, Sultanam's chief eunuch, a broad-shouldered man with a thick neck, slipped out of the hall.

"What do you think?" I asked Balamani.

"I think Haydar is lying. If the Shah wanted him as heir, why didn't he announce his choice before he died?"

"But that would have put Haydar at risk of assassination."

Balamani snorted. "And he isn't at risk now? He is like a lamb waiting to be skinned!"

While we were drinking our tea, Mirza Salman rushed back into the room with the seal soft on a fresh sheet of paper. He presented the paper to Saleem Khan, who unrolled it.

"I believe it is one and the same as the seal on the will," he announced, and passed it around the room for all the men to see.

As the nobles were peering at the seal, Sultanam's eunuch returned to the hall, panting lightly, and whispered some information into the ear of her brother, Amir Khan Mowsellu. His eyes widened, and before the eunuch had finished, he arose to speak.

"One of the exalted mothers of the palace visited the Shah early this morning after his death," he announced. "As she was wailing over his body, she chanced to feel the seal at his throat and was surprised to feel the residue of soft wax in it. This suggests that the seal had been used recently, or possibly removed and returned."

The room erupted into shouts once again. Saleem Khan demanded quiet and ordered that the guards of the Shah's body be summoned. The first guard, who was almost as wide as he was tall, swore that the seal had not been removed during the night, and so did the others. But everyone knew that the guards could have been bribed, and the heat in the room began to intensify when there was no definitive answer about the validity of the will.

As squabbling broke out, Balamani looked on with disgust. "This is just what I feared. Each group lobbies for the man who will benefit his own people, not the man who will make the best shah."

"And who would that be?"

"The great vizier Nizam al-Mulk wrote that after death, all rulers will be led before God with their hands tied. Only those who were just will be unshackled and delivered to heaven. The rest will be pitched straight into hell, their hands lashed eternally."

"How fitting!"

I thought Mahmood would be a far better ruler than Haydar, although he was still too inexperienced to govern on his own. But I kept my opinions to myself; as Pari's servant I must support her choice.

It took some time before Saleem was able to restore order by yelling in a voice so fierce it must have been heard outside the palace's thick walls. He glared at the courtiers who would not be still, his face red with exertion and annoyance.

After everyone was quiet, Haydar spoke again. "I promise you all that my rule will shine with fairness to every tribe and to every man," he proclaimed.

As evidence, he called on his servants to assist him, and they wheeled in carts filled with treasures. He reached into a cart and began passing out gifts. Amir Khan Mowsellu received a solid silver samovar, so finely engraved it was impossible to imagine using it for something as ordinary as tea. Mirza Salman took possession of two large blue and white porcelain vases from China. Other members of the court received silk robes of honor, so valuable they would be worn only on the most formal of occasions. Gifts piled up beside each nobleman until the room resembled a bazaar.

"He is robbing the treasury before it is his!" Shamkhal Cherkes charged in a loud whisper.

But as the gifts were distributed, the mood in the room softened while each nobleman contemplated his good fortune.

"Good courtiers, I ask you again: May I have your support?" Haydar sounded more confident than before.

How dismaying that even rich men can be swayed by trinkets!

"You have mine," said Hossein Beyg, the leader of the Ostajlu. He was joined by a chorus of voices, although most of the men did not identify themselves. Everyone knew the risks of supporting the wrong side.

A messenger entered the room and spoke in secret to Saleem, who interrupted the proceedings to make an announcement: "My good men, because of the events of this day, I have been informed by the chief of the royal bodyguard that the guards stationed outside the palace gates have refused to disperse until the succession has been resolved. No one will be permitted to enter or to exit the grounds."

Haydar stepped back onto the platform and glanced around him like an onager facing a circle of hunters. His left eye began blinking so uncontrollably I had to look away. After listening to more high-pitched murmuring, he demanded, "Open the gates!"

"I don't have the authority to tell the military men what to do," Saleem replied. "It is the privilege of the Shah."

He looked surprised by the words that had just issued from his mouth. Hadn't Haydar declared himself our leader?

Balamani leaned close. "It is Thursday, which means it is the Takkalu tribe's turn to guard the Ali Qapu gate. Is Haydar's head stuffed with rice instead of brains?"

The Takkalu had had a rivalry with the Ostajlu for decades.

Haydar looked pained and said quietly, "I am the rightful shah, and in this time of darkness, I call on God's protection as his shadow on earth. This meeting is dismissed."

He stepped off the platform and left the room, escorted by guards and eunuchs. Saleem Khan called an end to the assembly, and then the nobles began clustering together to rally for or against Haydar's candidacy.

"Do you think he can succeed?" I whispered to Balamani.

He opened his palms and shrugged. "Whatever happens, they might as well lay out the skewers!" he said, looking at the angry noblemen who surrounded us. "Some of these men will choose the wrong candidate and get turned into kabob."

I grimaced at his awful prediction. Our eyes met, then flicked away. Neither of us had seen such peril in all our years of service.

I rushed back to Pari's quarters, eager to discover whether she would support Haydar's bold move. Pari entered some time later, her cheeks as flushed as a dancer after a performance, her black hair poking out of her kerchief at odd angles.

"What happened?"

"Haydar and his mother summoned me and demanded my support. When I demurred, Haydar threatened to imprison me. I bent low, kissed his feet, and pretended to recognize him as the rightful shah. Only then did he let me go."

Her eyes widened and she took a deep breath, as if she had just understood the extent of the peril she had escaped.

"Lord of orders, who will receive your support?"

"I don't know yet."

I paused to strategize. "If Haydar has many armed followers outside the palace, he may prevail."

"Go to town and bring me news."

"How will I get out with all the palace gates blocked by the Takkalu?"

"Majeed will give the head guards some money. They know I am not Haydar's ally."

I exited through one of the palace's side gates—the guard waved me through—and walked toward the main bazaar. On such a warm, sunny day, mothers should have been bargaining for goods and children chirping with pleasure about being outside. But the streets were deserted. When I arrived at the main entrance of the bazaar, its huge wooden doors were bolted shut. By God above! Never in my lifetime had the bazaar been closed on a Thursday.

I rushed to an old, abandoned minaret and climbed its slippery stairs. From the opening once used for the call to prayer, the whole city glittered in the sunlight, its mud brick homes interspersed with mosques, bazaars, and parks. The walled palace grounds dominated the city, resembling a huge garden carpet divided into orchards whose trees and flowers competed for beauty. The northern palace gate was heavily guarded. My eye was drawn to the Ali Qapu's yellow and white tiled walls at the southern entrance, where hundreds of Takkalu soldiers of the royal bodyguard, along with their allies, stood in formation, their swords, daggers, and bows and arrows at the ready.

Where were Haydar's supporters? Why had they not come out for their new shah? I went to the home of his uncle, Khakaberi Khan, but saw no activity there, then knocked on the doors of a few other supporters to no avail until I arrived at the home of Hossein Beyg Ostajlu. A large group of men armed with swords and bows were assembling in his courtyard. I saluted a fellow with a scar across his cheek that flamed red, matching the thick red baton held erect in his turban that proclaimed him as a *qizilbash* loyal to the Safavis.

"What is the delay?"

He scowled. "Who are you?"

"I serve in the harem."

"Half-man!"

He adjusted his parts to reassure himself that they were still there. Grabbing his sword, he rejoined his fellow soldiers as if I might contaminate him with my condition. I would have liked to see him facing a castrator's long, sharp knife; then we would know who was more brave.

A soldier on the street told me of a rumor that Isma'il had arrived in the city with thousands of men. Haydar's supporters had delayed storming the palace, fearing a massacre.

"But how could Isma'il get here so fast?"

He shrugged and gestured toward Hossein Beyg, who was mounting his horse. "He has decided it is a lie."

Hossein Beyg called for the Ostajlu to assemble, and they began marching toward the northern gate of the palace. Soldiers from other tribes streamed out from nearby houses until thousands claimed the street. They raised so much dust that people who had come out to look began clearing their throats and coughing. It was only a matter of time before fighting would begin between Haydar's and Isma'il's supporters, and the thought of those tough qizilbash soldiers meeting in combat made my blood turn to vinegar.

I found Pari being comforted by Maryam. Her hair had been brushed until it shone straight and black under her white silk kerchief, and she had changed into a black silk mourning robe embroidered with gold squares that made her look long and tall. The turquoise and gold earrings shaped like half-moons that gleamed around her face had been a gift from her father. She had written a few letters since I had left, which were on a silver tray awaiting delivery to the courier. Her eyes looked even more troubled than when I had left.

"At last!" she said when I was shown in. "What is the news?"

"Princess," I panted, "thousands of Haydar's soldiers are marching to the palace under the leadership of Hossein Beyg."

"May God protect us all!" said Maryam, looking frightened.

"Are there enough of them to overpower the Takkalu?" asked Pari.

"I think so."

Pari jumped up. "I must tell my uncle to stop them."

I wondered why she seemed so certain all of a sudden about what to do. "Princess, what has happened?"

"Not long before you arrived, my father's chief chemist reported that the orpiment was strong enough to strip the hair off a hide. It may have been an accident. Still, how could I ever live under Haydar's reign?"

"May God exact vengeance on evildoers!"

Pari handed me a cloth purse. "This is the key to the door from the Promenade of the Royal Stallions into the women's quarters," she said. "Tell my uncle that I grant him permission to enter and remove Haydar, so long as he is spared from harm. Return here as quickly as you can."

I stared at the purse. "But men are never permitted to enter the women's part of the palace," I protested.

"I am authorizing it."

Astonished, I put the bundle under my turban and took my leave. When I arrived at Shamkhal's home, I told his servants I had an urgent message and was shown in right away.

Shamkhal opened the purse and peered at the key. His eyes began to glitter like those of a raven who has just found a bag of treasure.

"This is our best hope," he said with glee.

"Pari wished me to tell you that Haydar should be delivered safe from harm. The esteemed princess asked for a token indicating your agreement."

I wanted proof that I had delivered this most important part of the message. Shamkhal stood up.

"Tell her this:

The man we oppose will suffer a great fall,
Yet shall remain unscathed in the care of Shamkhal.

In exchange, I insist that my niece Pari
Remain distant from the soldiers and their fury."

"Chashm," I replied. As I took my leave, I heard Shamkhal shouting for his servants and directing them to go to the homes of his supporters to raise men for Isma'il.

I started back toward the palace. Outside the Ali Qapu the Takkalu and their allies were still on guard, unopposed. I knew one of the captains, and when I told him I had been out on errands all day, I received permission to enter after being checked for weapons. When I finally arrived at Pari's house, she was waiting for me.

"May you not be tired!" she said.

I wiped the sweat off my forearms.

"What did my uncle say?"

"He promised to do your bidding," I said, reciting the lines of poetry he had improvised.

She smiled. "Good work."

"Princess," I said with agitation, "the soldiers have probably started fighting. Anything could happen."

"Make haste. Go to the birooni and find out what you can."

First, I decided to go to the harem kitchens because the cooks always knew the latest news. The large building, which usually bustled with ladies, maids, and slaves, was deserted. Flour and water had been mixed and left in large bowls. Mint had been washed but not hung to dry, and onions and garlic had been chopped and abandoned. Their sharpness stung my eyes.

I walked through the building, feeling something strange I could not name. As I passed an oven for bread, my tread made a deeper sound than elsewhere. I turned back and opened the oven. It was full of charcoal and ash, but in the far corner I spotted a patch of bright blue silk. I thought about the robes of everyone I knew until finally I remembered: It belonged to one of the Shah's physicians, who must have been shown into the harem during the Shah's final illness.

"Physician Amin Khan Halaki, your robe is showing!" I hissed. The cloth disappeared as quickly as a mouse pulls its tail into a hole.

"Who are you?"

"Javaher Agha, servant of Pari Khan Khanoom."

"Can I leave?"

"Not if you wish to remain alive."

"Then throw me some food, at least."

Grabbing some cucumbers and grapes, I thrust them in the oven and wished him luck. I proceeded to the checkpoint to the birooni and saluted Zav Agha, whose brow looked permanently creased with worry.

"Is there any news?" I asked.

"Not yet-t-t," he said, his few remaining teeth knocking together in fear. He opened the door and allowed me to pass through.

I walked swiftly to Forty Columns Hall and glanced around, but it was empty. I kept walking until I approached the northern wall of the palace, where I was alarmed by the sound of deep, dull thuds. I suspected that a group of soldiers had grabbed a cannon and were smashing it against the wooden gate, which groaned as if being tortured.

"Haydar Shah, open up and let us in!" a man yelled from outside. "We are your friends."

Ignoring the usual palace decorum, I ran through the courtyard and all the checkpoints until I was back in the harem. Just as I reached a large plane tree, the ground trembled so sharply I suspected an earthquake, but then I realized it was the pounding of horse's hooves. I halted abruptly, feeling like an ant caught between a man's thumb and forefinger.

My heart beat faster as the tall wooden door that led from the harem to the Promenade of the Royal Stallions creaked open. Soldiers streamed into the gardens, brandishing their swords while shouting Isma'il's name and trampling the red rosebushes near the walkways. The unprecedented sight of men in the women's space, which had never been violated by outsiders, shook me to my core.

Shamkhal rode toward me on a black Arabian steed and pulled on the reins.

"Where is Haydar?" he shouted.

"Probably in his mother's quarters. It is the building with the two cypress trees in front."

I pointed the way.

Shamkhal directed his men to ride toward the gate to the birooni and hold off Haydar's supporters if they tried to enter the harem. Then he spurred his horse in the direction of Sultan-Zadeh's home. One of his captains, Kholafa Rumlu, whose costly helmet inscribed with protective verses from the Qur'an gave away his high rank, spotted something in the distance and shouted, "Who are you?"

I caught a glimpse of three women in chadors, their faces hidden by *pichehs,* concealed among tall flowering bushes. The tallest among them was wearing pink silk shoes.

"Calm down; we're just going to buy bread," one of them called to him in a lilting voice. "The kitchens are empty, and our children have nothing to eat."

"Shamkhal Cherkes, come back!" Kholafa yelled. Shamkhal turned his horse around and rode with Kholafa and a few soldiers toward the women. The women clung to one another, looking like frightened gazelles trapped by a circle of hunters.

"Remove your pichehs!" bellowed Shamkhal.

A woman wrapped in a black chador protected the others by spreading out her arms and corralling them behind her, causing the one in pink shoes to stumble.

"It is not your place to demand such a thing!" the woman in the black chador replied bravely.

"If you are innocent, you have nothing to fear," replied Kholafa. He tore off the woman's chador, picheh, and the kerchief covering her head, and she screamed as her long, dark hair cascaded over her shoulders and onto her breast. It was Awva, one of the ladies in charge of the kitchens. I gasped, horrified to witness such a transgression.

Another of the women came forward, volunteering herself, and the captain uncloaked her. She, too, cried out as the men stared at her naked face and unusual red hair, feasting on the spectacle of her. I didn't recognize her.

"Who are you?" demanded Shamkhal.

"We serve the ladies of the royal court," replied Awva haughtily, refusing to identify herself any further.

She and her friend crushed the third woman between them while facing out toward the soldiers, locking their arms backward around each other's midsections to protect her. I thought about standing up to defend her, but a suspicion had entered my mind, and I decided against taking action.

"You will throw dishonor on the Safavi house if you insist on revealing her," cried Awva. "The penalty will be your lives!"

Kholafa waved his hand as if to give up. "Let them go," he said scornfully. "They are only women."

"Let her prove it then!" shouted Shamkhal, his eyes fiery.

"You have lost your senses. Do you want to get us killed?" Kholafa replied.

I heard clubs striking wood and realized that Haydar's men were challenging the barricades and the guards at the checkpoint from the birooni. By God above! We could all be killed in a matter of minutes.

The women began trying to break their way out of the circle of horses by ducking in between the restive mounts. The men closed ranks to trap them, and then Shamkhal grabbed the woman's chador and picheh and ripped them from her body.

"Spare me!" she screamed in a strangled voice. When Kholafa tore off the kerchief covering her short hair, my suspicions were confirmed: It was Haydar. He put his hands out to protect himself, and his left eye twitched as if he were in his death throes.

From behind the checkpoint, Haydar's men shouted out a chorus of comfort. "Haydar, we're here to protect you! Help is at hand!"

Haydar turned toward their voices and shouted out, "Hurry!" as he flung himself toward an opening in the circle of horses. Shamkhal and Kholafa jumped off their mounts, pushed away the ladies, and lunged for him. Haydar lost his footing and dropped to the ground with a loud thump. The pink shoes flew off his feet, and his legs sprawled as the men struggled to pin down his arms.

There was a roar in the distance as the first of Haydar's supporters breached the gate into the harem. I recognized the soldier with the thick red scar. He uttered a battle cry so fierce it curdled my blood, and he thrust his sword at me as he thundered past. I avoided being skewered only by falling facedown in the dirt.

"We have no choice. Finish him!" I heard Shamkhal say. When I looked up, he had succeeded in pinning Haydar's arms behind his back. Kholafa drew his sword and thrust it twice into Haydar's abdomen. A wet red stain sprang to life on his gray robe. As it spread across his belly, Haydar grimaced and clutched his middle. His groans were thick with blood.

Awva and the other lady began screaming in horror, folding in half at the waist and hitting their knees and temples with their hands. Their cries were more awful than anything I had ever heard.

Shamkhal's soldiers hoisted Haydar's body onto their shoulders and began marching toward the checkpoint leading to the birooni. By then more of Haydar's supporters had breached the harem, including Hossein Beyg Ostajlu. He stared at the broken body in the bloodied gray robe.

"Alas! Our shining hope has been cruelly destroyed! May you and your families be cursed until the end of their line!" he shouted, along with a string of profanities. He and his soldiers skirmished briefly with Shamkhal's men, but what use is a group of supporters without their shah? Before long, the men behind Hossein Beyg spurred their horses toward the birooni, fearful of being killed. Hossein Beyg's guard closed ranks around him, and he escaped in the confusion.

Shamkhal directed his men to leave the palace grounds through the door that led to the Promenade of the Royal Stallions and to take up guard outside the Ali Qapu. As they marched out, he tossed me the large metal key. I followed, slammed the heavy door behind them, and locked it securely.

The rosebushes nearby had been decapitated. A nightingale began to sing in one of the cedar trees, reminding me of a lament. *My red roses threw open their skirts for you, but now their petals darken the ground like tears of blood.* Dust coated my clothes, and my mouth tasted of bile.

I stumbled to Pari's house and told her and Maryam what had happened. Their faces turned pale when I described Haydar's death. "It is as if the dirt of my grave is covering my head!" the princess said. "Why didn't my uncle do my bidding?"

"It was God's will," I replied, trying to offer comfort.

Her thin body seemed as fragile as a long-necked rose-water sprinkler made of glass. Although I would have liked to comfort her, I knew Maryam would soothe away her woes better than anyone else could.

I returned to the dormitory that housed the eunuchs who served the harem. Our building, which was notable only for its modesty, now struck me as a sanctuary. Collapsing onto a wool cushion in the guest room, I shed my soiled outer robe and told a servant to bring me tea with plenty of dates. My hand seemed palsied as I lifted the vessel to my mouth.

Before long, Balamani joined me. His eyes were pink, the lids puffy.

"Do you mourn for Haydar Mirza?" I asked.

His eyes grew large with astonishment. "What do you mean?"

I couldn't help myself: I felt a surge of satisfaction that I knew the world-changing news before he did.

That evening, I was weary and in need of comfort. Some men would have turned to opium or *bang,* a vision-inducing drink made with hemp, but I didn't think either would help. I placated my stomach with bread, cheese, and fresh herbs, then went to my room and listened to Balamani's sonorous snores. Lying on my bedroll, I watched the events of the day repeat themselves before my eyes, the red stain on Haydar's gray robe growing in my vision until it filled the blackness of my room like a suppurating wound. When the moon appeared in a window in the roof, spots of blood blemished its smooth white surface. The spots grew until the moon became a bright red disk bleeding its course across the sky, and I awoke with tense limbs and ragged breath. I could not stay still. I arose, dressed, and walked on a path fringed by plane trees until I reached the entrance to the long, low building that housed Sultanam's ladies. I whispered to the eunuch on duty that I had an urgent message for Khadijeh, placing a coin in his hand as I spoke.

Khadijeh was alone, having sent her bedmate elsewhere. Her eyes were bright in the moonlight, and the ends of her long, curly hair looked tipped in silver.

"I couldn't sleep," she whispered. "I keep thinking about what happened today."

"That is why I came."

"Did you see it?"

"Everything," I replied, unable to keep the horror out of my voice. Men had been executed while I had served at court, but never with so little civility.

"You are shivering!" Khadijeh pulled back the wool blanket. "Come get warm."

I removed my turban and outer robe, and slid in beside her with the rest of my clothing on. She laid the front of her body against my back and wrapped her arms around me. I felt the roundness of her breasts through her cotton nightclothes, and my skin warmed as if I were in front of a blazing fire.

"Aw khesh!" I said gratefully, absorbing her heat. "You warm me outside and in."

In response, she kissed my neck. Her lips smelled of roses. How shocked the late Shah would have been to learn that one of his ladies held a eunuch in her arms!

"Where were you today?" I asked.

"Hiding with Sultanam, in case Haydar's men took over the palace," she said, her body stiffening.

"I am glad you are safe."

Her dark eyes were serious. "Tell me what you saw."

"Are you sure? I don't want to frighten you."

"You can't," Khadijeh replied sharply. "I stopped being afraid the day the slavers threw my mother's corpse over the side of the boat."

Khadijeh had been so transformed by her days at court it was easy to imagine she had come from a noble family. In fact, she and her younger brother had been captured from the east coast of Africa as children and bought by an agent of the Safavis. As a young girl, Khadijeh had already been a beauty, with skin the rich color of copper, and blue-black hair so curly it reminded me of hyacinth flowers. At first she had been apprenticed to the mistress in charge of tea, learning how to blend teas so that they were fragrant and to brew them for deepest flavor. Then she had asked to be transferred to the head of cuisine, with whom she had served an apprenticeship of eight years. An ordinary walnut cookie with cinnamon, cumin, and a dash of something odd but savory that she would not reveal—fennel? fenugreek?—fired my mouth with surprise every time I tasted it. Once Khadijeh mixed some fierce pepper into a bowl of saffron pudding—she had a mischievous side—and giggled at the shock on my face when I tasted the first bite. I devoured the whole bowl, my tongue burning with gratitude.

Both Khadijeh and her brother, Mohsen, had fared very well. Sultanam had taken notice of Khadijeh's cooking and had welcomed her into her service, and Mohsen had become one of the royal groomsmen.

I covered her hands with mine and told her what I had seen, sparing her the worst details.

"Why did Pari take such a big risk? If Haydar had won the day, she and her uncle would no longer draw breath."

I felt a surge of pride. "She was very brave."

"Remember, you could have been killed, too." Her eyes looked moist in the moonlight.

"It was a gamble," I admitted, "but Pari has changed the course of history. There will be no Haydar Shah."

She snorted. "Pari is like a wild horse. You had better make sure she doesn't buck you off into the jaws of a lion."

I laughed off her comment, roared like a lion, and pulled her closer. She shushed me but failed to repress a giggle. No one paid much attention to how the ladies amused themselves in the harem, since no one except the shah could take a woman's virginity or impregnate her. But Khadijeh and I were safe only as long as our alliance remained secret.

"What is going to happen now?"

"Isma'il will be summoned and crowned."

"How soon will he arrive?"

"No one knows."

She sighed. "All the sweet certainty we once had has vanished."

"Has it?" I teased. I tugged gently at the corner of her mouth with my teeth, feeling her lips bloom, soften, and part to allow my tongue in. My skin stirred as if all my pores were on alert, and I shrugged off my robe, then hers.

Let it never be said that eunuchs have no feelings of desire! Because I had been cut late, I retained more feelings for women than eunuchs who had lost their parts as children. To be sure, it is not the same as when I was uncut, because it is not dictated by the mercurial rise and fall of an unpredictable instrument. Instead it is a feeling of exquisite attentiveness unclouded by personal urgency. I search for Khadijeh's most sensitive parts, putting angles and corners to use that no man would think of employing, from elbows to toes. I squeeze my nose into dark, steamy places where she would never have expected such a visit. I nibble and slurp and suck. If a part of Khadijeh is in need of touch—the skin over her collarbones, or the bottoms of her feet—I find it, the way a master caresses the sensitive strings of a *tar* to engender the sweetest sounds. The one part I do not touch is Khadijeh's virginity, but there is no need for a man of skill to do that.

That night, I played Khadijeh with all the fingers of my hands. Holding her from behind, I roamed all over her body with my lips and breath, from sunny desert to wet oasis. I watched her cheeks bloom and heard her breaths come faster and faster until she could not control herself. For my labors, I was rewarded with small animal grunts, high-pitched groans, and then finally, wild, uncontrollable cries as her limbs stiffened and jerked in all five directions.

After she had rested, she lifted her body on top of mine, and I felt her delicate ribs against my chest. Her skin glowed dark and rich, like tamarind in the moonlight. The earthy scent at her breasts was of ambergris, making me feel as inflamed as a tomcat stalking its mate. I put my hands at her waist, traveling to the parts that flared into globes, both high above and down below. She toyed with my lips, the gateway to paradise. Her tongue traveled down my neck and stopped where she pleased, flicking lightly, teasingly. Putting my hand to the back of her head, I bid her drink more fully, but she pinned my wrist to the floor: She would proceed at her own pace.

Her tongue entered my ear, left its moistness, continued its journey. She traveled down to the flat place between my legs with her tongue and delicately teased the exposed edges of my tube. By God above! No uncut man can imagine what it feels like to have an internal organ stroked, to be caressed in a place never intended to see light. No such man will ever know the sensitivity of those tissues or how fiercely mine responded to her lips, like the leaves of a plant unfurling in response to heat. She lingered there until I came alive, but she would not stay. Her breath came to my lips again and she made her visit to each place that cried out for her. Yet now I could not stand her teasing. I rolled on top of her and opened my legs over her lips, astride her. Her tongue flicked out like an animal's. She held on to the backs of my thighs while I twisted with pleasure. When I had experienced all I could stand, she stopped, and I sighed with the satisfaction of a man who has been cared for through and through.

I grabbed a blanket and pulled it over me, not so much for warmth but because I didn't want Khadijeh to see my groin exposed by the dawn. Sometimes when I was with her, I would dream that I still had all my parts, before waking up to the startling sight of my flattened pubis.

On my cheek, I felt Khadijeh's warm breath, and my bones became heavy with sleep. I allowed myself to doze for an hour in the comfort of her arms. How contented I would be if I could stay with her all night! I had been her secret companion for more than two years, but had never been able to wake beside her.

While it was still dark, I awoke and dressed so that we would not be discovered. Khadijeh was sleeping soundly, her cheek resting in her hand. I pulled the bedcovers around her and whispered, "Good night, and may God bring us together again soon." Then I tore myself away.

The hammam for eunuchs was separate from that of men who might be disturbed by the sight of our flush pubic areas and our exposed tubes. It had small brick alcoves for washing and a large central pool with turquoise tile for bathing. The pool was surmounted by a dome whose windows let in sunlight and starlight. The hammam was deserted at that early hour, and I suspected that my arrival might have displaced a few jinn. After what had happened the day before, they would be wise to be more afraid of humans than we of them.

To make the necessary Grand Ablution after sexual contact, I said the name of God and then washed my hands, face, arms, ears, feet, legs, and private parts, gargled and cleaned my head. My chin and cheeks felt rough, so I asked the bath attendant to give me a shave. Because I had been cut so late in life, my facial hair still grew, although more slowly than before.

As I soaked in the hottest tub, I felt as if I were trying to cleanse myself of the gruesome scene I had witnessed. The hot water normally leached away all my worries, but not today. I would not feel safe until a new shah was in place, and yet, only a prince among men would do. I longed for a visionary, like Akbar the Great of the Mughals, who reenergized his huge bureaucracy, or Suleyman the Lawgiver, the statesman, conqueror, poet, and patron of the arts who steered the Ottomans to world-dominating splendor. Hope stirred in my heart at the thought of such a boon, yet how rare it was!

After dressing, I made haste to attend on Pari at her house. She had donned her darkest mourning robes and was in her writing room applying her seal to a letter. Beside her lay an open book penned in exquisite calligraphy with illustrated pages. It was the *Shahnameh*.

"Good morning, lieutenant of my life," I said. "How is your health?"

"Surprising," she replied. "I still walk and breathe on this earth, unlike my poor father and his ill-starred son. I can hardly grasp that there are now two royal corpses in the palace, one of a son who may have killed his father, and one of a father whose erstwhile allies have killed his son. I have turned to Ferdowsi for guidance, but nowhere in the *Shahnameh* do I recall a like situation that could advise or console me in my grief."

"Princess, I remember that in the middle of the poem, Ferdowsi laments the death of his only son. Do you recall how he interjects himself into the story to announce his grief?"

"I do. That is the keenest statement of mourning that a man of such personal restraint could make—yet no consolation is offered."

"Perhaps none is possible."

She sighed. "None is possible."

"I am hopeful that this will be your final sorrow."

She looked so youthful and vulnerable that I was reminded of her brother Mahmood when he was small, and I felt a pang. I missed him.

Her smile was pained. "I would be grateful if that were true. God willing, Isma'il will take the throne, but at what cost? Never would my father have approved of one of his sons being hunted down and murdered like a rabbit. Even Isma'il, who our father felt betrayed him, was not dispatched like a piece of meat. It is a disgraceful insult, one that makes my shattered heart feel more shattered still."

"Princess, you did everything you could. It was God's will."

She paused for a moment. "Your service to me has been a consolation. I wish to thank you for all you did yesterday."

She handed me a cloth bag, which I opened to discover a stack of finely embroidered blue silk handkerchiefs. They showed a noblewoman reclining on a carpet under a walnut tree, her attention focused on a book. My heart soared: For the first time, Pari had entrusted me with one of her personal possessions. From now on, I would carry one of her handkerchiefs inside my robe in case she needed it.

"Thank you, Princess. Your confidence in me fills me with joy."

"I heard you avoided an attempt on your life by one of Haydar's men. I didn't expect you to be so brave."

I bowed my head, thinking about how ruthlessly the eunuch Bagoas led the ancient empire of Iran, crushing even mighty Egypt.

"I am going to need someone of your mettle in the days ahead. Until Isma'il arrives, nothing is certain. I have written to him this morning and advised him to come quickly so that the nobles whose aims have been disappointed don't rebel. Take this letter to my chief courier and tell him to deliver it at once."

In her public reception rooms, Pari positioned herself behind the lattice. The hall was crowded with people, from lowly errand boys with messages from their masters to noblemen like her vizier Majeed, who was the first admitted. He spoke in a breathless, high-pitched voice, as if he had not been able to calm himself since the events of the day before.

"Esteemed princess, the court is in chaos. Many nobles who supported Haydar have fled in fear of their lives. The ones who have remained don't know to whom to report. The cooks have abandoned their kitchens."

Pari's eyebrows shot up in surprise. "Go to Anwar and tell him to meet with the head cook. Their first responsibility is to restore the service of the kitchens immediately."

"Yes, esteemed princess," Majeed replied, "but Anwar won't know from whom to take his orders, now that the Shah is dead."

"Tell him his future depends on taking them from me."

Majeed's brow furrowed and his lips contorted before he blurted out, "And where is he to get the money?"

"From the royal treasury, of course."

"The chief treasurer is nowhere to be found, and the officials whose seals are needed are gone."

"I will find those people and demand their help," Pari said. "In the meantime, tell Anwar I will pay for it out of my own purse."

"But much silver will be necessary!"

"My good vizier, perhaps you don't realize that I have inherited my legal share of my father's fortune."

Majeed looked as perplexed as a man whose horse has just bolted away from him, never to return. "But only your exalted father was allowed to—"

"Don't delay. You will need to be persuasive."

"What am I to say?"

"It is an order from Safavi royalty. Now go."

Pari's voice was so crisp that Majeed's entire body stiffened in response, like that of a captain receiving his orders to lead a charge. Then he bowed his head in submission. Pari looked as implacable as a general, and I stared at her, astounded. May God be praised! She had just seized the reins of state!

I returned to fetch the next man in her waiting room and noticed that the crowd was growing. The questions and demands were relentless. Would she say the funeral prayers for her father herself? Where should Haydar's body be interred? How would she protect the noblemen who had not taken sides in the dispute? What about the wives of the men who had died in the skirmish, what would become of them and their children? Would she advocate for the son of a close friend of her father for a high government posting under the new shah? One after the other, men begged for favors.

By the late afternoon, Pari's eyes were weary. "Who is next?" she asked me with a sigh.

"Mirza Salman Jaberi, head of the royal guilds." He had just arrived, but as he was one of the fourteen officials closest to the late Shah, I escorted him immediately to the visitors' side of the lattice, and then I returned to Pari's side. He was a short, thin man who made the very air around him feel crisp with purpose.

"And what do *you* want?" Pari snapped. "Surely the business of the guilds can wait."

He didn't seem perturbed. "Indeed it can. The guilds are fine."

"Well, then, what is it?"

"Nothing, esteemed princess. As a devoted servant of your late father, I came to ask if I might offer assistance to you."

Pari raised her eyebrows in disbelief. "You have no requests?"

"None. I merely wish to serve you."

Pari whispered, "He is the only one who is man enough to offer some help!" When she noticed my affronted expression, she apologized.

"Where do I start?" she said to Mirza Salman. "Everything is in disarray. Where is everyone?"

"Hiding. Waiting. Worrying."

"The nobles must return to their posts to keep the government functioning until Isma'il arrives. I wish to call a meeting to give them their orders."

"But only the shah or the grand vizier can call a meeting. No one else outranks them."

"There is no such man. What do you suggest?"

Tahmasb Shah had gotten so tired of grand viziers that he hadn't bothered to appoint a new one.

"I will say that a high-ranking member of the Safavi house has ordered the meeting, but not who. The nobles will think it is a prince. Have your uncle preside for you so that everything is proper."

The fact that the same Farsi word was used for "he" and "she" would help our cause.

"It is good advice."

"By the way, I have a tip for your ears only."

"Yes?"

"Whatever you plan to achieve at the meeting, don't rely on the chief of the treasury. I know him well. He will bow only to the authority of the new shah."

"What makes him so confident that my brother will retain his services?"

Mirza Salman chuckled. "True. Some people see their wishes as their destiny."

"Do you?"

He hesitated for the first time. "No. I see my actions as my destiny, in accordance with the will of God."

"Well said. We will need men like you. Call the meeting then for tomorrow morning at my house."

"Chashm."

After Mirza Salman was escorted out, Pari said, "What a surprise! How well do you know him?"

"Not well," I replied. He had been part of the second innermost ring of men who served the Shah. Those people kept a tight lip and rarely socialized with their inferiors.

"I remember Mirza Salman carried out an unpleasant task for

your late father by disciplining a cabal of gold sellers who tried to cheat the court. His guilds have been as clean as a bathhouse since. He would be an excellent ally, I think, and an equally fierce enemy."

"We will watch him then and discover how true he is."

"What is our chief goal at tomorrow's meeting?"

Pari's hand trembled a little as she smoothed a lock of hair away from her face. "Preventing a coup."

Deh! I had not heard any rumors.

"Whom do you suspect?"

"The Georgians and the Ostajlu might decide they are better off supporting another prince."

"I will redouble my efforts at gathering intelligence."

But first, Pari asked me to take a message to her uncle Shamkhal requesting that he preside over the meeting the next day.

"Princess, I thought you were angry at him about the death of Haydar."

She sighed. "I am, but I need him."

In the history of the Safavis, no woman had ever taken charge of the men so directly. We left nothing to chance. I helped the princess select the cloth that would separate her from the nobles, since such an exalted woman would never show herself to a group of men to whom she was not related. We settled on a bolt of thick blue velvet patterned with scenes from the hunt, most notably a repeating motif of a mounted prince thrusting his sword through the belly of a lion.

Pari concealed herself behind the draped cloth while I stood in different corners of the room to listen for how well she could be heard. Her voice was melodious: very low for a woman, but with an agreeable timbre, and it didn't take much practice before she could easily be heard at the far corners of the room.

"One thing, princess. Your father spoke slowly. If you do the same, you will make the men pause and listen just as he did."

"Very well. Have I forgotten anything?"

"Since you won't be able to see the expressions on the men's faces, I will report anything notable to you."

"You will be my eyes, as you are around the palace." She smiled, and I felt as if the sun were warming my skin.

The next morning after dawn prayers, I went to my post at Pari's house. As soon as it became light, I was gratified to see both men of the sword and men of the pen arriving. They filed into her public rooms and arranged themselves on cushions according to rank, forming a semicircle around the curtained area. The air seemed heavy and portentous, as before a storm.

Shamkhal Cherkes's wide shoulders and enormous white turban made him look like a giant when he mounted the platform. He welcomed the men and bade them listen well to the words of his niece, favorite daughter of the late Shah. Majeed stood near Pari's curtain, ready to convey any private messages she might wish to send. I chose a position on the side of the room where I could see everyone. As I stared at the battle-hardened men, the enormity of our task seized me. The late Shah had barely managed to keep them under control. The Ostajlu and the Takkalu had fought a bitter civil war, and there were countless feuds and grudges between other groups that had to be navigated. We must find a way to tame the men at all costs.

Pari's voice was clear and strong. "Nobles, you honor the memory of my blessed father—may God's judgment upon him be light—by your presence here. You are the shining stars of our age, recognized by my father as such during his lifetime. But don't forget that a heinous act has recently occurred: a near takeover of the palace by those who wished to install their candidate on the throne."

Several men looked as if they wished to flee. Others, like Mirza Shokhrollah, the chief of the treasury, smirked.

"Despite these horrors, our responsibility at this moment is to ensure the security of the state. Every man must perform his job, but not every man has stayed at his post. Where has everyone been?" Her voice was loud and strong as she issued the challenge.

No one replied.

"The palace can't run itself. All of you are needed until a new shah is in place. I want to hear from you now," she continued. "Despite what happened a few days ago, I am going to ask you—all of you—to support Isma'il as shah. Well?"

Amir Khan Mowsellu stood up to speak first. "You have our full support," he replied in a booming voice.

Since his sister Sultanam was Isma'il's mother, it was no surprise that Amir and his allies heeded her call. But some of the other men did not join in, and they began whispering and conveying their disapproval with a flick of their hands, precisely the kind of discord we had feared.

Mirza Salman arose to speak. "You have my pledge of loyalty as well," he replied, "and perhaps I can help others by posing a question. Noble daughter of the Safavis, sometimes men are misguided in their choices. How can you expect them to support Isma'il if they fear for their lives because they threw themselves behind the wrong man?"

"That is right!" came a chorus of voices.

"It is true that men are sometimes ill-advised," Pari replied. "Since the situation was confusing, I don't wish to punish those who made the wrong decision if their intentions were to act for the good of the state. Therefore, if you are all willing to pledge your loyalty to Isma'il, I will promise to advocate on behalf of those who supported Haydar and to help break the rod of royal displeasure."

"What guarantee do we have that he will listen to you?" asked Sadr al-din Khan, an Ostajlu leader who had dared to show his face.

"I have been in communication with him."

"But did he offer amnesty? Show us the letter!"

"I don't have an offer of amnesty. I will ask for one."

Some of the men paused to think about that, knowing how powerful Pari's advocacy could be. But Sadr al-din Khan was not satisfied.

"That is not good enough," he replied.

Pari was silent behind the curtain. I suspected she didn't know what more to promise to assuage him and avoid a revolt. Both Majeed and Shamkhal looked at a loss. My heart seemed to flip-flop like a fish on dry land. I had never had an official role in a meeting of such importance, and I did not know what to do.

Pari's cousin Ibrahim Mirza stood up to speak. He had been

Tahmasb Shah's favorite nephew and had even been permitted to run his own bookmaking workshop long after Tahmasb had lost interest. He had the ancient Iranian mien—thick black curls, smooth wheat-colored skin, rosy cheeks, and shapely lips, but his good looks could not hide that he had supported Haydar.

"Now wait a minute," Ibrahim said in a loud voice. "Amnesty is only the concern of people who were on the wrong side. But it is hardly the most pressing issue, is it? Almost no one has laid eyes on the prince for twenty years. How do we know he is not blind, sick, or a crazed fool?"

"That is heresy. He was a hero to all of Iran when he was young!" shouted Amir Khan Mowsellu.

"Maybe so, but what about now? A just leader is the only thing we should care about when the future of our country is at stake!" Ibrahim replied.

From the conflicted looks on the men's faces, I understood that not everyone agreed. Most nobles wished to advance the interests of their own people. As a "double-veined" child, with intertwined Tajik and Turkic strands, I wanted a shah who wouldn't be swayed by petty jockeying for power.

"Isma'il will be such a leader!" declared Amir Khan Mowsellu, but his words met deadly quiet.

"Who knows?" asked Sadr al-din Khan. "The prince isn't even here. Why doesn't he arrive and claim his throne?"

"He will enter the city any moment now," argued Kholafa Rumlu.

"It is easy for you to say—you who can expect a fat reward!" complained Sadr al-din Khan.

Kholafa had been the mastermind who spread rumors that Isma'il and his troops had arrived, thereby dooming the Ostajlu. He smiled at Sadr al-din Khan. "That is because I used my head."

"Some would argue that you were merely blessed with luck."

The two men jumped to their feet and began hurling insults at one another. Some of the Takkalu began poking fun at Sadr al-din Khan, delighted by the disgrace of their longtime Ostajlu rivals.

"Choke yourselves!" commanded Shamkhal, but no one was listening.

I slipped behind the curtain to check on Pari. Her face was shiny, and her cheeks looked hot.

"Change strategy," I advised. "Tell them you need help getting the palace in order. That is something they can all agree with."

In the hall, Shamkhal had to threaten to call for the guards before the nobles quieted down again.

"My good men, I require your assistance," Pari told them. "We have urgent problems—broken gates and poisoned arrows on the palace grounds, instability in Qazveen, and a closed bazaar. Won't you help a royal woman when she needs you?"

"All of that will require funds," said Mirza Shokhrollah.

"You may proceed with a report from the treasury."

His large, soft jowls wobbled as he claimed that he could not provide what she needed. The princess pressed him for reasons. He launched into a list of obfuscations until she lost patience.

"Do not forget who I am," she commanded in a cold voice. "Until just a few days ago, I had my father's ear. Do not think for a moment that I won't protect the interests of the dynasty as fiercely as he did—with or without your help. All of you must return to your posts. Tomorrow morning, we will begin with reports from each department, including the treasury. It is your job to ensure that the next shah doesn't meet chaos and confusion upon his arrival. I should not wish to report that you were absent when you were needed most."

Shamkhal cut off further discussion. "Heed the words of the foremost daughter of the Safavis! You are dismissed."

Shamkhal showed the men out, including Majeed, so that Pari could emerge. I lifted the curtain, and she came out wiping her face with a cloth. She looked as wilted as day-old basil.

"I didn't accomplish what I had hoped. How unruly they are! I will send an urgent message to Isma'il and tell him how delicate the situation is."

"God willing, he will come soon," I replied, hearing the alarm in my own voice.

"I hope so. I feel as if I am holding on to his throne with a thin silk thread."

Shamkhal returned and approached his niece. "You did well, my child," he said, but his hooded eyes did not look happy.

That afternoon, as Pari and I began working, the princess's mother came to see her unannounced. She walked into the room so quietly that neither Pari nor I heard her until she greeted her daughter, and we looked up from a document to find her standing there.

"Mother, be welcome," said Pari. "How is your health?"

"I endure."

Pari raised her eyebrows. "May I offer you some tea? Sweetmeats? A cushion for your hip?" Her tone was considerate, but I sensed her impatience.

Her mother declined refreshments and sat down stiffly near Pari, a proximity that made it difficult to see any common traits. Daka Cherkes Khanoom was a woman of about fifty who didn't appear to have had the strength to pass on anything of herself to her daughter. She was small-boned, with fair skin and pale brown eyes.

"Daughter of mine, star of my universe, I think you know why I have come."

Pari's smile was strained as if she were bracing for what was ahead. Daka stared into her daughter's eyes, and to my surprise, the princess looked away. I had seen Pari tolerate much in the last few weeks, but never had I seen her look so uncomfortable.

"You have refused me the pleasure for years, but the time has come for you to think about marriage."

I was alarmed by the thought. If the princess married, I would be under the command of her husband, not her. What if he were a boring old drudge? Pari made my mind feel as alive as a buzzing nest of bees.

"Can't you see that I must manage the affairs of the palace?"

"My dear child, how long do you think that will last?"

"Only God knows."

"You have always prided yourself on your reason. Isma'il will arrive and take the throne, and then what will you do?"

"I will advise him."

Her mother's gaze was pitying. "You haven't spent as much time with Sultanam as I have," she said. "Lately, she has been in an uncommonly good mood. Once when she did not think I was near, I heard her singing, 'farewell, ill-favored fairy!' meaning you. If any woman will advise her son, it will be her."

Pari's mouth turned down in displeasure. "She doesn't know what I know, and neither does her son. If a man is to be appointed a subgovernor, which four officials must affix their seals to the document and in what order? All she can do is whisper her likes and dislikes in his ear. He will soon tire of that."

"It doesn't matter. She will poison his mind against you."

"Mother, you overestimate her."

"She wishes to bury you. I beg you to let me find you a new protector in the person of a husband."

Her mother took Pari's hand, her eyes shining with hope. "We will look for a handsome man whose face will be like the sun to you every morning. Someone as strong and as fierce as a lion to hold you in his arms."

Pari withdrew her hand abruptly as if the very idea made her wish never to be touched again.

"Mother, who could that be? Who can match the purity of my blood but a son of my father?"

"None, but what about a son of his brother?"

"Ibrahim, Badi, Hossein—they all have first wives. I will not be married as a second wife."

Daka grabbed her cushion as if to brace herself against her daughter's arguments. "Pari, you know that someone could be found if you wished it."

"What, some noble who is posted to the provinces? I would be bored."

"But, daughter of mine, don't you wish for children?" Her mother looked desperate. "What about grandchildren for me? I grow old. I can't wait forever."

"Suleyman and his wife will provide them for you, I am certain."

"Pari, where is your womanly feeling? I tell you, there is nothing more satisfying than holding your own child in your arms. You don't know it yet, but I pray that you will soon."

"I have told you many times that I am content as I am. I take after my aunt Maheen Banu."

"Not exactly. You have not predeceased your protector, and therefore, you must be cautious."

Maheen Banu had served as one of Tahmasb Shah's most sagacious advisors all her life. People at court couldn't stop talking about how she had argued for providing military assistance to the Mughal emperor Homayoun when he needed it. In gratitude, he had ceded the entire province of Qandahar to Iran.

Pari didn't reply. Her mother adjusted the scarf over her hair, the lines at her lips deepening with determination.

"I mean no disrespect, but your father was very selfish. He kept your aunt as a bride for the Mahdi, in case the Hidden Imam should return from occultation to bring justice back to Iran during her lifetime—"

"—and he kept a horse saddled at all times, I know, Mother, I know, so that they could depart whenever they wished."

"But you he kept for himself," her mother added in an accusatory tone. "I can't forgive him for putting his love for you over what was best for you."

"Mother!" said Pari. "What he did was best for me, too."

"It is true that no woman had his ear like you did, but that is why so many are now eager to see your demise."

Pari's generous lips curved into a frown. "People love to dwell on the pain of others; they love to stick their fingers in it and suck on it as if it were honey. But I won't allow them to feed at my hive. I didn't leave my father's side, for the simple reason that I preferred his company to that of any other man."

"You can't assume you will retain your old position."

"You must let me see what fate brings me," said Pari, her voice rising in exasperation.

Daka looked as if she would not give up. "Pari, I didn't want to say this, but I am frightened. Let me keep you safe. You know I would sacrifice myself for you!"

She tore the silk scarf off her head, revealing thin, graying hair. She bent her head forward, yanked out a few hairs from her mousy pink scalp, and laid them in front of her daughter.

"As your mother, I demand that you heed my counsel!"

She grabbed another few strands and prepared to yank them out. It was awful to witness.

"Ah, ah, Mother, stop!" Pari cried, grabbing her hand and pulling it away from her head.

Daka let her wrist go limp. "My child, this time I won't be dissuaded. All I ask is that you consider a list of candidates. If none pleases, you may say so. But if you are in trouble, a rapid marriage could save you. I won't leave this cushion until you give your assent."

From outside we heard the call to prayer. The day was passing.

"Pari, you must not be so stubborn. Times have changed, and you must change, too."

"On the contrary, Mother. Other women are moonlike, waxing and waning. Not me."

"Please, my child. I beg you. As the woman who gave you your first milk, I have rights that transcend your own will."

Pari sighed heavily; her mother had made the one argument that no child could deny. "All right then, if you must, but do not make this quest public."

"Why not?"

"Because it is my last choice."

"My child, how strange you are!" her mother said in vexation. "What kind of woman wouldn't wish to be married?"

Pari looked away. "You would not understand—it is not in your blood."

"Voy, voy!" said her mother. "I have never pretended to royal blood like yours. But perhaps your blood is what makes you such an oddity compared to other women."

"Perhaps," Pari replied, in a tone as final as a door being slammed. "Mother, I wish I could sit with you all day, but now you must give me leave to do my work."

"It is granted," Daka replied, standing up stiffly. "But do not forget—protecting you is my right. You must keep that in your heart, even when you dislike how I choose to do it."

"I will, Mother." Pari softened. "I remain your devoted daughter."

"I know."

Daka marched out of the room with the pride of a wounded old soldier who has finally won a long-running battle.

Pari shook her head as if to clear it and sighed. "Hope flares in her heart again!"

"Princess, will you never marry?" I asked, hoping she would say no.

"Only God knows," she replied vaguely. "The truth is that I don't think about it much, but it gives my mother something to do. Now let's attend to our planning before the hour grows too late."

That evening, I received a letter from my sister, Jalileh, who was now fourteen. I tore it open, eager to hear her news. Jalileh was living with my mother's second cousin in a tiny town on the hot, humid coastline of southern Iran. She wrote to me every few months, which allowed me to monitor the progress of her life and her studies. Supervising her education from afar had been difficult, but I had insisted that my cousin find the best tutor available, and now, despite my cousin's complaints, I sent money to the woman directly.

Jalileh wrote that the weather on the Gulf had become hot and moist, making it difficult to keep her mind fresh, but all that had changed when she began studying the poetry of Gorgani.

> *His words are so beautiful they make me want to jump up and dance. When he suggests that we seize our fondest desires before our clay crumbles, I wish to become his disciple! But then my tutor reminds me that I must learn to be as steadfast as the sun, and I quell my racing heart and obey.*
>
> *Dear brother, does my writing please you? Might some employ-*

ment be found for me close to you? I am almost grown, as our mother's cousin keeps reminding me, and I am impatient to be useful.

If only I could do something! Jalileh now wrote a better hand than many of the ladies at court. I longed to ask Pari to employ her, but as she had just hired me, it was too early to request such a great boon. I would not break Jalileh's heart—and my own—by promising her anything until I was sure. The memory of the last time I had seen her still lay heavily on me, her little body twisted around on the receding donkey, her arms stretched out to me, her face so streaked with tears it looked as if it had melted. Nor could I forget my mother's parting words: "Restore our honor. Not for me, but for your sister."

I wrote Jalileh right away, praising the beauty of her handwriting, and I asked her to be patient.

Before nightfall, I took a walk around the center of Qazveen. The pigeons in the square near the bazaar flapped their wings forlornly, hungry for their usual crumbs. The large wooden gates were still closed, and no peddlers lined the streets. I proceeded to a nearby tavern where I knew the bazaaris liked to go, and introduced myself to a few of the men as a merchant from Tabriz. The men's faces were drawn with worry, and conversation was slow until I bought and shared a few jugs of wine, as well as tea for the strictly pious.

"Let's hope we don't die of starvation," I said, trying to open the floodgates of the conversation.

"What is worse—starving to death or being assassinated in the streets?" asked an old fellow with shrewd eyes. Shouts of laughter filled the room as the men joked about the worst way to die.

"You are right, brother," I said, as if I knew what he was talking about. "Can I pour you a little more?"

It didn't take long for me to learn that the bazaar was still closed because of a string of murders. The rumor was that the Takkalu had been assassinating Ostajlu to get revenge for all the years they had been favored by Tahmasb Shah, and then others began taking the liberty to settle scores with people they envied or despised.

"Someone needs to tell those donkeys at the palace to do something," the old man grumbled.

At the next day's meeting, after being briefed by me, Majeed, and Pari, Anwar sounded alarms about the closed bazaar. The palace was not receiving its usual deliveries, the kitchens were merely limping along, produce was rotting in the fields, and soon trade would be affected. "The heartbeat of the country is slowing to a halt," he concluded.

The men listened carefully because Anwar, who prayed without fail three times per day, was known for both piety and honesty. The late Shah had honored him by putting him in charge of harem operations and of efforts to fund mosques, wells, and pilgrimage sites.

"The merchants refuse to open because ordinary citizens are being slaughtered," Pari added from behind the curtain. She could not challenge the Takkalu openly without inciting a civil war.

Her uncle stood up. "I think we should send soldiers to arrest the evildoers and have them put to death. That will set an example that others will wish to avoid."

"Isn't that an extreme measure?" Pari asked. I remembered what had happened to Haydar and worried about Shamkhal's thirst for blood.

"Not if we give the citizens fair warning first," he replied.

The chief of the late Shah's private army, Khalil Khan Afshar, who had been named Pari's guardian when she was a baby, interjected his opinion. "We should deputize a group of soldiers to ride through the city and announce that anyone found to be plotting or executing violence will be punished," he said. "We will spread the word far and wide."

"Do that," said Pari, "and remind them that judgment over another man is the province only of the shah and his Councils of Justice. My brother will prosecute the known murderers once he has been crowned."

"If he is crowned," said Sadr al-din Khan Ostajlu from the back of the room. "He has to arrive first, doesn't he?"

"He is on his way," insisted Pari.

"Esteemed princess, we will deploy the soldiers tomorrow," said Khalil Khan. "Is there anything else you wish us to do?"

"There is," she replied. "All the Takkalu should ride to my brother's side and pay their respects as soon as possible."

I almost laughed out loud: Pari was learning quickly. If the Takkalu left, the Ostajlu would feel less besieged and would be less likely to revolt.

"The other men should return to their posts and report to me on the progress they make every day."

"Chashm."

"I don't see why we should follow these orders," argued Mirza Shokhrollah. "You are not the shah."

"Do you doubt the purity of my blood?" Pari asked sharply.

"Not your blood," he replied. "We honor you for your ties to the Safavi dynasty."

"In the absence of a crowned shah, I will do my duty by ruling this palace and everyone in it, including you."

Mirza Shokhrollah did not reply, but made a face to indicate that he did not take her seriously, and he began reciting a poem.

> Since women don't have any brains, sense, or faith
> Following them drags you down to a primitive state.
> Women are good for nothing but making sons
> Ignore them; seek truth from the light of brighter ones.

Mirza Shokhrollah looked around as if expecting support, but there was an uncomfortable silence. No doubt some of the men in the room agreed with the sentiments, but it was insulting, possibly even treasonous, to degrade a royal princess of Pari's stature. I would have liked to stuff his long gray beard into his mouth.

"You had better watch your wayfaring tongue," Shamkhal said, puffing himself up like a snake about to strike. Next to him, Majeed looked like a mouse in search of a hole. How intimidated he seemed by his elders! If I had his job, I would be moving from man to man to rally support for Pari.

I went behind the curtain to check on the princess. "That poet was hardly the greatest thinker on the topic of women," Pari retorted in a loud, strong voice. She paused for a minute, closing her eyes, and I felt as if I could actually see lines of poetry being composed on her pearly forehead. In the commanding voice that she used to recite, she countered with her own verse:

> *A fine silk robe can do well to hide*
> *The pompous ass who is hidden inside*
> *To know the truth that only God knows*
> *Look beyond the fineness of clothes.*
> *Seek much further to what is below the skin*
> *Shatter the barriers, discover what is within.*
> *By glitter and glamour don't be deceived*
> *Truth lies beyond what the eyes have perceived.*
> *Ask "What is just? What is true? What is real?"*
> *Only pigs devour garbage without a squeal.*

Mirza Salman guffawed, and the rest of the men followed. Storm clouds gathered over Mirza Shokhrollah's brow.

Mirza Salman stood up to speak.

"Princess, I will be glad to assist the chief of the treasury in producing the report. My men are available."

I dashed out in time to see Mirza Shokhrollah glaring at him. "That won't be necessary."

"I am at your service," said Mirza Salman with a mocking smile.

"No, thanks," the treasury chief said again. "I don't need your help."

"In that case, how soon can we expect the report?" Pari said from behind the curtain, a note of triumph in her voice.

Mirza Shokhrollah hesitated. "I don't know."

"Really? Everyone knows how smoothly Mirza Salman's guilds run and how thorough his reports are. Surely yours can be, too, now that you have his assistance."

Mirza Shokhrollah glared at Mirza Salman, who met his gaze without flinching. If anything, his slim body became even more erect.

"I will see what I can do." Mizra Shokhrollah scowled as if Pari were a night soil collector who had presumed to give him orders.

Shamkhal stood up and said quickly, "You heard the favorite daughter of the late, lamented Shah. You are hereby dismissed."

The men filed out in separate groups of supporters of Isma'il and Haydar, their disunity evident. I hoped Isma'il would hurry. It was only a matter of time before the nobles decided to go their own way, as they had when Tahmasb was a child ruler. That was my worst fear: that the men would factionalize, give support to other candidates, and boost one of them to the throne. Then Pari's power would dwindle, and all my hopes would turn to ash again.

When I finally had a moment to myself, I went to the building that housed the royal scribes and asked to speak to Rasheed Khan.

"He is away today," said his assistant. Abteen Agha was a eunuch with chubby cheeks and a high, womanly voice.

"I need to have a look at the *History of Tahmasb Shah's Glorious Reign*," I replied. "The princess has asked me to do some research for her."

It was a fib, but a harmless one.

"Where is your authorization letter?"

"She sent it a few days ago."

Abteen Agha went off to check the status of the letter.

When I had asked Pari for the letter, I had wanted to confide in her about my father, but hadn't dared. I feared that revealing my quest would make her suspect that my loyalties were divided. Instead I told her that her letter would make it easier for me to unearth information for her.

Abteen returned soon with a sour look.

"What exactly do you want to examine? The manuscript is thousands of pages long, reflecting the Shah's nearly eternal reign. I am not going to bring out all the pages for you."

I would have to sweeten him up with a gift. For now, I simply said, "I need to read about the principal officers who served Tahmasb Shah."

"All right then. Come back another day, and I will have the pages for you."

"Tomorrow?" I must have sounded overly eager.

"Do you have worms?"

Abteen was one of those functionaries who like to make everyone wait so that they understand how important they are. But as discretion was more important to me than hurry, I told him I would be back the next day.

The following afternoon, I returned with a fine brass bowl engraved with silver flowers and felicitous inscriptions. Abteen accepted the gift without fanfare and went to get the pages. He placed them in front of me on a low table inlaid with bits of mother-of-pearl and ebony.

"Mind you don't bend or soil the pages," he said.

"I have been around good paper before."

"All right, then."

The paper had been dyed with something like onionskin so that it was a pleasing ivory color and easy to read. All the pages consisted of short biographies. First there was a long list of the men of God who had served the Shah as religious leaders, followed by nobles descended from the Prophet. Then came lists of governors, viziers, and men of the pen, eunuchs in charge of the royal household, astrologers, doctors, calligraphers, artists, poets, and musicians.

Some of the men had found great fortune and been rewarded with land or governorships, but others had taken a fall. One man had been accused of being part of a blasphemous religious sect and executed. Another had fallen in love with a manservant that the Shah was quite fond of and so was killed. Still another had stolen money and had been sent away in disgrace. As I read through the story of the men's afflictions, my heart began to bleed with sympathy. So many had gone the way of my father!

Eventually, I came upon the long list of accountants, scribes, and historians. My hands grew warm as I perused the list. I didn't know if my father would merit an entry. Often, the historians ended their lists by writing, "None of the others are important enough to mention," or words to that effect.

But then my heart seemed to stop in my chest:

Mohammad Amir Shirazi: Born in Qazveen, he served the Shah for twenty years, becoming one of his chief accountants. Many colleagues praised the accuracy of his accounts and his swift dispatch of court business. He seemed destined to rise up through the ranks of the men of the pen, until one day he was accused of crimes against the Shah and executed. Later, doubts were raised about the truth of the accusations. In his world-illumining mercy, the Shah did not execute his accuser, but it is also possible that his decision was influenced by the fact that the man had powerful allies whom the Shah didn't wish to offend. Only God knows all things with certainty.

Why, oh why, had the historian not mentioned the courtier's name? What rank was he that the Shah hadn't punished him?

I decided to take a risk and ask Abteen. After I beckoned to him, he approached with an exasperated sigh.

"See this entry?"

He peered at it and then looked up. I have never seen a man read so fast. "What about it?"

"What is the name of the courtier?"

"How should I know?"

"Aren't you a historian, for God's sake?"

"If it is not written down, it means we don't know. Who has time to run around verifying details about minor officials? Nobody is going to give a damn about this Mohammad Amir in the future."

I stood up abruptly, bumping into the table and upsetting the manuscript page, which floated to the floor.

"I give a damn!"

The historian stooped to pick up the page, then tripped on his long robe as he stood up. "You have bent it, you donkey! I told you to be careful."

"As careful as you are with your facts?"

He cursed me and I walked out, surprised to see that my fingers were lightly stained, as if I had dipped them in my father's blood.

Isma'il wrote to Pari that he had received her letter and would depart from Qahqaheh shortly to resume his rightful role in the capital. When he had first heard of his father's and Haydar's deaths, he had barred the gates to the prison, certain that it was a trick, and waited until a crowd of trusted noblemen had appeared outside the gates. After they had confirmed the news, he allowed them to be opened again. He wrote that he looked forward to seeing his sister after an absence of so many years, and he thanked Pari for her service on his behalf. He signed the letter, "your loving brother."

Pari was elated by his kind salutation. "He sounds just like the lion-man I remember!" she said, her eyes moistening with relief.

But that was all we heard from Isma'il for days, until Sultanam told us that he had decided to stay on at Qahqaheh to allow nobles to visit him. When still he failed to arrive, we discovered that he had voyaged to Ardabil, the home of his ancestors, to visit the shrine there, and lingered for longer than expected, sending no word as to when he would appear.

Pari had no choice but to take full charge of administering the palace. Because of her orders, the kitchens were reopened and the denizens of the palace filled their bellies gratefully. The hospital on the palace grounds resumed operation, the sick received consolation from men of religion, and the dead were properly buried. The Takkalu left town to visit Isma'il, and the murders in the city ceased.

Even though the palace began to function again, we were not calm, because the palace was teeming with rumors. Haydar's mother, Sultan-Zadeh, infuriated by the murder of her only child, had been making efforts through her allies to find a worthy opponent to Isma'il, if for no other reason than to thwart Sultanam's ambitions. And a group of nobles was weighing the possibility of rallying behind Mustafa Mirza, the late shah's fifth son, in a bid for the throne.

When I passed people in the gardens they averted their eyes, not knowing who would be their next master or whether any confidence would result in future betrayal. One morning, I surprised Anwar at the baths before it was light. He leapt out of the water, ebony knees bent and muscular arms raised to fend off an attack, and uttered a battle cry so fierce it curdled my blood. When he realized it was only me, he dropped back into the water, displacing a good deal of it.

"Only an idiot would sneak up on me like that," he growled.

When I reported the rumors to Pari, her face darkened with distress. "Why doesn't Isma'il hurry! I have written to him again about the need to claim his place, yet still he gallivants around the country. What makes him so restive?"

"Lieutenant of my life, you must vanquish the rumors," I said. "Once they gather, men will suspect that no one is in charge and throw their support behind another."

Pari sighed. "It would be unthinkable to lose the throne now, just when it is within our grasp."

"Then we must convince the nobles that they have no choice."

At the next meeting, Pari swore to the men that her brother was on his way to Qazveen with an army of twenty thousand soldiers. "'Sister of my heart,'" she read out loud from a letter we had composed together the day before, "'I grant you my authority to govern as you see fit until I return to take the throne. Do not brook any opposition from those who would try to derail my ascension, which has been ordained by God.'"

She paused a moment for effect. "If you don't wish to believe me, you can explain yourself to our new shah and see what he makes of your disobedience."

Her voice vibrated with authority, just as a great orator's stirs his listeners to accept the justice of his arguments. I could feel its power surge through my heart, making me eager to fight for whatever she demanded. And it was not just me. I heard Ibrahim Mirza say to

Mirza Shokhrollah in a low voice, "She has it—the royal *farr*. Do not cross her."

Shamkhal and Majeed exchanged a glance of excitement and Majeed leapt up, his face glowing with triumph, to repeat what Ibrahim had said to another noble, and then he sped to the other side of the room to make sure the words traveled from man to man. I could not contain myself: I repeated Ibrahim's words to the amirs nearest me. Their faces softened as they stared at the curtain and imagined the glory behind it.

"Mirza Shokhrollah, I need to hear from you."

"It is understood," Mirza Shokhrollah replied in a subdued tone.

"Good. I expect the full report on the treasury tomorrow even if it takes you all night to prepare it. As for the rest of you, soon you will see with your own eyes that Isma'il's candidacy is assured. So now I ask you, do you promise to make this country whole again by supporting Isma'il? I want to hear an answer from every man."

Isma'il's supporters responded right away: "Al-lah! Al-lah! Al-lah!" they chanted, sounding like loyal soldiers marching in step. Even the Ostajlu added their voices to our forceful affirmations.

By then, I had gone behind the curtain where Pari sat, and when she heard the men shout out, she jumped to her feet triumphantly as if she had just mobilized an army. Shamkhal arose and declared an end to the meeting. Mirza Salman and Majeed began conferring together, looking as surprised as if an untested polo player had scored a decisive goal. I, too, was awestruck: Pari had the royal farr, a radiance so irresistible that the men responded like sunflowers following the sun.

A few days later, Pari received a letter from Isma'il giving her authority to govern the palace as she saw fit in his absence. He thanked her for her efforts and told her he could not wait to see her with his own eyes, "a woman of true Safavi blood, a sister-in-arms, and a fierce protector of our family and our crown." A reward awaited her upon his return, which he was eager to bestow.

Pari read me the letter, her eyes bright with hope.

CHAPTER 3

MAN OF JUSTICE

After Zahhak became king, the devil installed himself as his cook and proceeded to teach him a taste for blood. On the first day he made roasted partridges, on the next lamb kabob, and on the third he stewed veal with wine. Zahhak was astonished and pleased, for man had never eaten meat before, and he plunged his tongue gladly into blood and bone. When Zahhak asked what he desired as a reward for his excellent cooking, the devil replied, "Just one favor, oh lord of the universe—I wish to kiss the royal shoulders."

Zahhak thought it was a small boon, given all the devil had done. He offered his shoulders gladly and allowed the devil to plant his black lips on each one.

The next morning, Zahhak awoke to the sound of slithering near his head. He pulled the bedcover away from his body and gasped out loud at the sight of a serpent growing out of each shoulder. In horror, Zahhak grabbed a knife and slashed through one, then the other, but as soon as the decapitated snakes had wriggled in their death agony, new snakes grew out of his shoulders. They hissed and attacked each other in front of his face, sparring until he felt he might go mad.

When the devil sauntered in that afternoon, Zahhak begged for a cure. "My friend, the only way to get any peace," the devil told him, "is to pacify them with food. The diet is simple: men's brains."

Zahhak ordered his nobles to deliver two young men the next morning. The men were murdered, their skulls cracked open, and their brains scooped out to feed the snakes. Then their mutilated bodies were returned to their families for burial. The next morning the same calamity occurred, and the next. Every day, the brightest and most promising young men were torn away from their families and sacrificed to the throne. Little by little, the best minds in the country were destroyed, and evil gave birth to more evil.

Early that summer, Isma'il finally arrived on the outskirts of Qazveen. After setting up camp in fine embroidered tents softened with silk carpets, he and his men waited for his astrologers to inform him of the most auspicious moment to enter the capital. He had spent years studying astrology while in confinement and wouldn't even leave his tent unless the readings were favorable. Pari was pleased that he showed such prudence, but secretly I hoped the stars would hurry.

By then, Pari had accomplished much. The killings had stopped in the city, and merchants reopened the bazaar. The palace had been repaired enough so that evidence of the invasion was faint. The noblemen were hard at work at their posts. Pari continued holding morning meetings with them, and now they submitted to her authority with no question. Mirza Shokhrollah had produced the treasury report and released the necessary funds so that business could proceed in earnest. Much remained to be done, but Pari had made sure that Isma'il wouldn't inherit chaos.

The princess sent me to her brother's camp with a letter of welcome and the gift of a fine astrolabe engraved with silver. I rode to the camp on one of the royal horses on a hot morning, hoping for a glimpse of the shah-to-be so that I could report on how he looked and perhaps take a kind word back to Pari. The camp was huge, and there were so many men delivering gifts that it was late by the time the astrolabe was recorded, and I had to ride back empty-handed.

Fifteen days later, the astrologers finally determined that the stars were auspicious and Isma'il set his arrival into Qazveen for the following morning. We had a lot to do. I reported to Pari's house after the midday meal to help plan for his arrival and was surprised to be escorted to one of the private rooms near her bedchamber.

I expected something resembling Pari's austere public meeting chambers, but this one had peach-colored carpets, thick velvet cushions, and an entire wall painted with a mural of the legendary Shireen bathing in a river, her high breasts like pomegranates. Shireen lounged in the water so voluptuously that I felt as if she were offering her white-skinned thighs to me, and I turned away in confusion.

I heard Pari's loud, frank laughter, a sound so rare that it seemed unfamiliar. She cried out, "Come in, Javaher! I need your help on a vital matter of statecraft."

She and Maryam sat together on one cushion, while Pari's industrious lady, Azar Khatoon, was rummaging in a trunk.

Azar drew a bright red robe out of the trunk and held it up for us to see, her pretty face transfixed by pleasure.

"That is one of my favorites," Pari said, taking the thick silk into her hands.

Woven into the fabric was a portrait of a young nobleman in a blossoming garden, a falcon perched on his fist. The feathers in the falcon's wing mimicked the folds in the young man's turban, conveying the profound oneness of the man and bird. Any human would be lucky to be loved as much.

"It is fit for a shah!" Maryam said.

"Yes, but too bright for the first meeting with my brother," Pari replied. "I am still in mourning."

Azar pulled out another garment, this one with a repeated pattern of bright orange poppies and a delicate young doe. Gold-wrapped thread made the garment glow as if infused with sunlight.

"Bah, bah, that one is lovely," Maryam said, her honey-colored eyes sparkling. Maryam was one of dozens of pretty village girls who had been brought to court to serve Tahmasb Shah, but who ended up becoming companions to the royal women if he showed no interest in bedding them. Her family had probably gotten a little money or a goat in exchange.

Pari took the robe from Azar and laid it against Maryam's body, spreading out the wide sleeves so that they covered her arms. Her golden hair flowed over the robe as if there were no separation between the two.

"The little doe with the pretty face reminds me of you," Pari said teasingly. "You may take that one."

Maryam's eyes widened with disbelief. Her everyday attire was lovely, but nothing could match the fineness of the robes made for the princess. She wrapped her arms protectively around the robe and stroked one of its sleeves with the tip of her fingers. "It is softer than skin!" she said, and Pari smiled.

"I need a robe in a much darker color," Pari told Azar, who plunged her hands obediently into the trunk, though her mouth looked bitter. After some time, she pulled out a brown silk taffeta robe, whose surface seemed to shimmer. Pari caressed the robe with satisfaction.

"Touch this one," she said to Maryam, who leaned forward to feel it.

"Who wove it?" she asked.

"The head of the taffeta weavers' guild, the master Borzoo."

Even the Venetians declared his silks to be finer than any produced in their own city. I held the robe gently. It was light enough to fold up into a package the size of my hands, yet as sumptuous to behold as velvet. A delicate pattern of gold brocade peonies seemed to tremble on its surface as if in a light breeze. White roses paraded on its pale orange borders, which were edged with stripes of brown, orange, and blue.

Maryam urged her to try it on, and Azar slipped the robe over Pari's outstretched arms. It fit tightly at her bodice and tapered to meet her narrow waist, then flared out pleasingly over her legs. The delicate brown made her black hair look darker than usual, while her cheeks blazed with color.

"You are magisterial," said Maryam.

I stared at Pari and had the strange feeling that I was looking at the late Shah. "You are the very image of your father," I blurted out. To some women, that would not have been a compliment, but Pari's smile was immediate.

"Now I need help choosing the garments to go with it. Maryam, you have the best eye for this."

Maryam bent over another trunk and assembled a pale blue

tunic, beige trousers with bands of flowered embroidery at the ankles, a silk sash with bands of orange, beige, and gold, and a chain of dark rubies and pearls for Pari to wear on her forehead. Meanwhile, Pari directed Azar to put away the other garments, which she folded and stored away as tenderly as if they were precious gems. Then Pari called for tea and sweetmeats and for her box of earrings. Massoud Ali brought in a brass platter with small chickpea cookies shaped like clovers and round walnut cookies that made me think longingly of Khadijeh.

Maryam spooned a surprising amount of sugar into her tea. Only a member of the court could be profligate with something so costly.

"Your brother will be pleased to see you in such finery," she said.

"I hope he will recognize me. I was a child of eight when he was sent away."

Pari watched Maryam peruse her earrings, her eyes lighting with pleasure when she came upon an especially beautiful pair. Maryam looked up to find us staring at her, and a smile played at her lips.

"What do you remember of him?"

The princess put down her steaming glass of tea. "He was always in good spirits, his big laugh booming from one end of the courtyard to the other. My heart would leap at the thought of seeing him."

"How often did he visit?"

"Often," said Pari, her voice soft. "He gave me my first lessons in archery. He would even stand behind me and help me draw the bow. He could have allowed the archery masters to teach me, but he knew I adored him. After he left on campaign, I practiced every day. I liked to imagine myself riding on a horse beside him, shooting arrows and striking targets."

She looked thoughtful for a moment. "I wanted to be just like him."

"Why was he sent away?" Maryam asked. She bit into a thick date and took a sip of her tea.

Pari called a eunuch to carry away the trunks of clothing and told Azar to follow him. Only when they were gone did she begin to speak. With troubled eyes, she explained that she had been too young to understand what had happened. Although everyone agreed Isma'il had bravely beat back the Ottomans in the north, accounts differed as to why he raised his own army without his father's permission. Some contended the purpose was to try to vanquish the Ottomans forever; others accused him of intending to overthrow their father. Before then, Tahmasb Shah had barely been able to squelch coups organized by his mother and by his brother Alqas, and dissent had become intolerable to him.

"Yet it is also possible that my father was envious. It wouldn't be the first time a man has wished to shine as brightly as his warrior son."

"What a tragedy to think of a family separated for so long," said Maryam.

"It was a dagger through our hearts."

Maryam took her hand. "When Isma'il sees you in that gazelle-colored robe, he will be pleased by the way you reflect the beauty of your family."

Pari's eyes brightened. "People always told us we looked more alike than any of my father's children."

"I trust he will welcome your good counsel," said Maryam.

"It will be difficult for him if he doesn't. My father's courtiers have alliances and arguments that span generations. All Isma'il knew before his imprisonment was how to command Turkic warriors, not how to manage Tajik administrators, Jewish tradesmen, Armenian exporters, Zoroastrian priests, Arab mullahs, diplomats from the Christian lands, emissaries from the Ottoman and the Indian courts, and all the other supplicants we see on a daily basis. He needs me."

"Isma'il will be lucky to have such a powerful ally," Maryam said.

"Not just an ally."

Maryam looked at her, puzzled. "What more could you be?"

Pari made as if pulling back the string of a bow; then she released her hand as if shooting the arrow.

"I want to be his closest counselor, just as my aunt was for my father."

"Has he agreed to this?"

Pari looked away. "Why wouldn't he? The same royal blood runs through our veins."

"Esteemed princess," I said, "I think we should plan what you will say to the new shah to obtain his favor."

"Obtain his favor? I am the reason he will be crowned!"

"True, but I don't think we can be too careful."

"There is no doubt he will shower her with love," interjected Maryam, her warm eyes beaming so much admiration at Pari that I was discomfited to witness it.

Maryam turned back to her task of perusing Pari's jewelry. After a moment, she said, "I think I have found just the right pair. Try these."

She showed Pari a pair of gold earrings shaped like moons with dangling pearls and rubies.

"Come here and put them on me."

Maryam leaned over Pari and gently inserted the end of each earring into her pierced ears.

"Bah, bah! How lovely you look."

Pari looked up into her eyes, which were only a handsbreadth away, and Maryam's cheeks bloomed like a pink rose. Then Pari reached for her chin and held it, her eyes filling with an animal gleam. Maryam's lips parted. The moment lengthened until I became uncomfortable and pretended to a fit of coughing. Finally, Pari turned around and dismissed me.

"Tell my servants not to disturb us," she said as I left, her eyes fixed on Maryam's.

No wonder she cared so little about marriage! Why would she wish to ally herself to a man who could take away all her pleasures? The hunger I had witnessed in Pari's eyes reminded me unnervingly of myself before I had been cut. With Fereshteh, I had been like a lion sinking its teeth into the flank of an onager, my appetite ferocious. How different I was now.

I felt glad Pari had found someone to love, and even gladder that she trusted me enough to show how she felt. The women of the court who didn't marry, either by chance or by choice, must either find love quietly among themselves or remain loveless and thwarted forever. When Maryam brushed Pari's hair or drew a line of kohl on her eyes, the affection that poured through her fingers was as visible as sparks. The palace women scrubbed each other's backs, drew henna designs on each other's bodies, helped each other through the screaming pain of birth, washed each other's dead, and held each other's hands in moments of joy and grief. I envied them sometimes. They lived in such a deep state of feeling for each other, whether love or hate, that it surrounded them like the weather.

As I left Pari's rooms, my eyes rested on Shireen's painted thighs and I thought with a pang about Khadijeh. She had ripened to bursting. She was likely to marry one day, as I could not offer her the things an uncut man could provide. But that did not mean I had been able to prevent myself from loving her.

The next morning, Isma'il rode into Qazveen on a fine Arabian mare whose saddle and bridle were studded with jewels, followed by a large retinue on foot, including soldiers in battle armor and dozens of young men dressed in velvet bearing hawks on their fists. The streets of the city were lined with citizens who had come out to witness his arrival. They had decorated every corner of the city with flowers and laid out an avenue of brightly colored carpets to welcome him. Citizens dressed in their best robes stood on the carpets and chanted blessings as he passed, and musicians placed at every corner of the city filled the air with sweet sounds to honor his arrival.

Isma'il's men left him at the home of Kholafa Rumlu. Kholafa would expect significant rewards for assisting in the killing of Haydar, no doubt. The first one was that Isma'il would honor him by staying at his house. Isma'il would remain there until his astrologers decided the right moment had arrived for his entry into the palace itself, at which point more auguries would be taken and the coronation would be scheduled.

As soon as he had settled into Kholafa's house, Isma'il started receiving visitors. One of the first to be called was a small group of royal women including the princess. She asked me to accompany her, and when I arrived early in the morning to take her to Kholafa's home, I drew in a breath at the sight of her in the rich brown robe, the ruby jewelry gleaming on her forehead. Maryam, who was an expert in the seven types of makeup that made a woman's wardrobe complete, had scrubbed her skin until it shone, painted artful lines of black kohl on her eyelids, reddened her lips and cheekbones with madder, and anointed her with a perfumed oil that smelled like myrrh and lilacs.

"You are even more beautiful than a princess painted by the master Behzad!"

"Thank you," Pari said. "At last I will meet my dear brother again, and rediscover one of the loves of my youth! I thought this day might never come." Her eyes sparkled with joy.

Pari covered herself in her chador and entered a domed palanquin draped with orange velvet. Her lower-ranking eunuchs bore her through the gate to Kholafa's house at the northern end of the city, while I walked alongside them. It was a hot day, but our walk was canopied by the leaves of the large walnut trees that had been planted in abundance in this part of the city. Was there ever a better tree? The stately, gnarled trunks exploded into generous fields of green above us.

As we passed the large gated homes along the street, citizens made way, stopping to stare at Pari's retinue.

"What rich velvet!" sighed a woman wrapped in a tattered robe.

I too felt envious of Pari, but for a different reason. How my heart would be pounding with excitement if I were about to meet my own sibling, Jalileh, after an absence of so many years. Would she look like my mother? Like me? Would she be understanding when I revealed I had become a eunuch? I had not told my mother before she died, nor had I wished to convey the news to Jalileh by letter. Would her eyes grow tender when I told her the truth, or—

I tripped on a stone, and the captain behind me barked that I had better pay my respects to royalty by paying closer attention to the road.

When we arrived at Kholafa's house, we used the knocker for women, a large brass circle, and were greeted first by his wife, who led us to a room in the *andarooni*—the area restricted to ladies and intimates of the family. It had finely knotted blue wool and silk carpets on the floors, embroidered cushions, large silver vases full of fresh flowers, trays heaped with grapes, peaches, pistachios, and sweetmeats, and fruit sharbats in large flagons.

Pari greeted the women who were already present, the late Shah's four wives Sultanam and Sultan-Zadeh, Pari's mother, Daka Cherkes, and Zahra Baji, along with their ladies and attendants. Sultanam's eyes and wrinkled cheeks glowed with motherly pride. Khadijeh sat near her to attend to her, her eyebrows as lush as brown velvet. I thought about the *donbalan*—sheep's balls—I had eaten the day before and felt the heat rise at my groin. Despite the sobriety of the occasion, I imagined what we would do together the next time I saw her.

Everyone looked her best in her mourning clothes except for Sultan-Zadeh, whose poorly tied headscarf and red eyes testified to her grief over the death of her son. She kept her head bent as if trying to be invisible.

Before long, Isma'il entered the room accompanied by a small retinue of fierce-looking eunuchs. The ladies rose and began ululating and shouting out praises to God. Isma'il stood there in a gray silk robe and accepted the tribute, and when he seated himself on a handsome embroidered pillow that had been placed for him on the best carpet in the room, the ladies sat down again on their cushions. Along with other servants, I stood at attention at the back of the room.

He was a medium-sized man with small eyes and a thin beard threaded with gray. He appeared confident and regal, quite unlike the boy Haydar posturing in front of the elders with his sword. Isma'il claimed the best seat in the room like a man who believed he was finally getting what he deserved.

But he hadn't aged well. He appeared to be a man in his fifties rather than thirty-eight. The bones in his body seemed too fluid, as if held in a sack of animal gelatin rather than muscle. Looking closely at his face, I detected an unhealthy sallowness as if he were rotting from within. No one would ever mistake this slack-bodied man for the fierce warrior he had once been.

"Welcome, womenfolk," he began. "This morning, I had a private audience with my mother to express my gratitude to her. All the years I was away, she never relinquished hope that I would return. She is the shepherd of my conduct—of my life as a man, of my wives-to-be, and of my future. Mother, all praise is yours for my life and for the crown that I will soon wear upon my head!"

I couldn't help but think that the praise for the crown should be Pari's, but perhaps he was simply being exuberant.

Sultanam could not contain herself. "*Insh'Allah!* My thanks go to God for watching over my son. To show my deepest gratitude for your safe return, I hereby pledge to build a mosque and a seminary in Qazveen."

There was a low gasp, for we all knew the costs of hiring architects, engineers, and tile makers, and the labor of a building crew for several years. But all the late Shah's wives and children had recently been informed by the treasury of the fortunes they had inherited after his death, which for the most favored, like Pari, included the revenue from entire towns.

"Your piety is an example to all women," he replied.

Isma'il greeted his father's wives, each in order of seniority, including Sultan-Zadeh, until finally his attention came to Pari.

"Sister of mine, the last time I saw you, you were a little girl," he said. "How things have changed. Throughout my journey, I have been flooded with reports of your doings at the palace. Your reputation is larger than you could ever guess."

Pari bent her head to accept his tribute. I waited expectantly for him to shower her with words of praise, as he had his mother.

"Tell me—do you find me much altered?"

Pari lifted her head in surprise. She didn't seem to know what to say.

"I wish to know the truth."

A mist veiled her eyes for a moment.

"I see before me the brother who was kind enough to teach me when I was just a child, though he was already a great warrior," she said gently.

"Teach you what?"

"The art of the bow."

"And just look at me now!" he said with a ghastly laugh. Judging from his thin arms, he didn't have enough strength to pull back a bowstring.

"It would be my fondest wish for us to shoot together again soon," said Pari softly. "I am at your service."

"And I suppose you will teach *me* this time," he replied. Although his tone was playful, the skin on my neck tightened.

"I shall forever be your pupil," she replied. "I will never forget how you trained me to hold my bow and showed me to keep the target foremost in my mind. Find its soft fleshy weakness, you said, and strike where you cannot fail. I took those lessons to heart. After you left I practiced often, and when you didn't return, I asked for you. One of our father's generals took pity on me and told me your locations while you were on campaign. I requested a map of the region, which was drawn for me by a royal cartographer, and marked your progress on it with bits of turquoise."

She stopped there, no doubt wishing to avoid reminding him of his humiliating incarceration.

"And then what happened?"

"One day the map disappeared, and so did your name," she replied. "I am very grateful God has sent you back to us again."

"It must be like seeing a man from the dead," he said. His yellow countenance made it difficult to disagree.

"I see a noble shah with cheeks as red as pomegranates," Pari protested.

He waved his hand to forestall any more talk he could not believe. "Speaking of which, I visited our father's grave early this morning."

Pari tensed. Her father was still buried in a temporary grave at a nearby shrine, pending Isma'il's decision about where to inter him permanently. The other ladies began wailing, as they must do when the late Shah's name was raised. Tears sprang to Pari's eyes, while Isma'il's remained dry.

The moment was so awkward that I was glad I could justify loosening the silk handkerchief that I carried at my waist for Pari and offering it to her. She wiped her eyes and said, "Now we shall weep together, brother of mine."

He laughed again, a ghoulish sound. "My tears are all dry," he said.

His manners were very poor.

"Your suffering has been great. My biggest wish is to devote myself to you, dear brother," Pari said quickly, to change the subject. "I promise to be useful."

"Yes, I imagine you will, having spent so many years basking in the light of our father. What a waste!"

Pari drew back on her cushion. "I am very grateful to have benefited from his wisdom."

"Oh, dear sister, don't take offense. I only mean that his knowledge could have been put to better use by a child who could be shah."

Pari looked bewildered.

"No matter," he said. "That hasn't been my fate, yet look what grand surprises God has brought me. I have selected a caravanserai in Ardabil as a gift to express my thanks for your service."

"Thank you for your generosity," said Pari.

It was a rich gift, since its rents would be a regular source of income, yet I was certain she would rather have had a humbler one given with true gratitude.

"You are welcome."

"Brother of mine," said Pari, "perhaps you will wish to hear about palace business. There are pressing matters to discuss."

"All in good time." He shifted on his cushion. "There is only one thing I want to know right now. How did the nobles behave?"

"With confusion."

"Did they treat our family with respect?"

"Yes, for the most part."

"Who didn't?"

"I should hate to identify anyone. The situation baffled them."

"But I insist on knowing."

"Perhaps you have already heard that a few nobles refused to heed me. When I read to them from your letter, however, they fell into line."

"Who? You must not hold anything back from me."

"Well, it was mainly Mirza Shokhrollah, the chief of the treasury, and his supporters."

"I see. I will take that into account."

"Thank you."

"Brother, may I tell you now about court business?" Pari was overeager, but it was impossible to know how soon he would allow her to see him again. Isma'il's eyes scanned the area around him as if he needed something.

"What is it, my son?" asked Sultanam.

"Nothing," he replied. "I must go."

He arose abruptly, signaling that the meeting was over. All the ladies stood up, surprised.

"I thank you all for your attendance. Now I leave you to feast, while I attend to a matter of some urgency."

He hadn't even graced the women with his presence during a meal. They looked at each other, perplexed, except for Sultan-Zadeh, who seemed relieved. Pari's mother and Zahra Baji filled the awkward silence by offering their congratulations to Sultanam.

I took the damp handkerchief from Pari.

"What is wrong with him?" she asked in a low tone.

"I fear he has forgotten himself," I whispered. "He wouldn't be in power if it weren't for you."

"Yes, whether he admits it or not."

"Perhaps he requires time to settle in. It must be difficult to be a prisoner one day and a shah the next."

"It was like speaking with a hermit who has forsaken proper manners," she said, her face drained of color.

Servants entered with tablecloths and the beginnings of a feast of roasted meats and stews, but Pari told me she had no appetite and didn't wish to stay. As she said her farewells, pleading a womanly ache, Khadijeh smoothed both ends of the kerchief that covered her hair and caught my eye. I adjusted my sash, our signal that I would visit her later in the evening, and she looked over her right shoulder to give her assent.

When it was so late that the moon had risen and all that could be heard was the howling of jackals, I arose from my bed to go see

Khadijeh. The moon was obscured by a cloud, and I had to count the steps to where the path branched to the one I followed to her quarters. When I arrived, the eunuch on duty was asleep on the ground, his head against the door, his jaw open, his weapon slack in his hand. All the better for my purposes, since it saved me a coin. I stepped over him into the building and walked down the corridor softly until I came to Khadijeh's door, which I pushed open. Despite the late hour, she was dressed and seated in a dark corner of the room. I sat beside her and took her small brown hand in my own.

"How I needed to see you!" she said. "Was it easy to get past the guard?"

"He is as fast asleep as if he were dead."

Khadijeh smiled. "I put a sleeping potion in a jug of wine and offered it to him," she admitted.

"Why?"

"Because he must not know you are here. No one must know," she added vehemently, and then flung her arms around me and buried her head in my neck. I felt a tear on her cheek.

"Khadijeh—soul of mine—what ails you?" I asked, perplexed.

Her body trembled against mine. "I am to belong to another."

My throat closed for a moment. I held her tightly and stroked her hair, inhaling the rose oil she used on her temples.

"Alas! I hoped it wouldn't be so soon."

She pressed herself against me, and I felt the roundness of her breast and thought about how she would soon be pressing against someone else.

"Ah, my beloved. How I will miss you!"

"And I you," she said, tears springing to her cheeks.

"Who is your intended—a warrior from the provinces?"

"Better than that."

"A nobleman here at court?"

"Wrong again."

"What could be better than that?"

"You won't believe it. It is the new shah himself."

"Deh!" I stared at her in surprise.

"It is the truth."

"How wondrous is your fate. When you were ill on the slavers' boat, when you and your brother were burned raw by the sun and scorned by men, you probably never imagined yourself as a queen!"

"Never," she said, "except in my dreams. It is, of course, a temporary marriage."

The Shah would save his four permanent marriages for women of good families with whom he wished to make alliances.

"No matter! One day you will be a royal mother, with your own quarters and your own servants. If you have a son who lives and prospers, you could become as powerful as Sultanam."

I was babbling to avoid facing the terrible truth: that the one sweetness I had in the world was about to be taken away and given to a man who had done nothing to earn it.

"I would be grateful to have my own household rather than serving at the whim of others."

"How did this come to pass?"

"Ever since Isma'il was released from prison, Sultanam has been talking about finding him a wife. In his letters, he has fretted that he has only been able to sire one daughter. Sultanam thinks someone has laid the evil eye upon him, and she is determined to remove the curse. He will marry a few noblewomen to cement his political alliances, but I am the first woman he will take into his bed. Sultanam has consulted auguries and believes I will bear him sons. She has ordered me to wear charms and report on our activities—busybody that she is!"

"She won't have such influence over the noblewomen he marries, who will have their own mothers to advise them," I said. "And she will be happy to give you to her son, because she knows firsthand the loveliness of your character."

"I have done my best, even when I didn't wish to be a servant."

"This is your just reward." I felt my throat tighten again with sorrow.

"Insh'Allah. Javaher, you are kind. You always have been."

"My beloved, your absence will leave a hole in my heart. I—"

My voice stopped dead in my throat, my grief so consuming that I could not continue. Khadijeh pressed her face against mine, and the tear that slid down her cheek coursed over my own. We clung to one another as if it were possible to remain joined forever.

Khadijeh reached for my sash and pulled it open. The sheep's balls I had eaten seemed to stir in my blood, and I put my hands on her collarbones and lifted the clothes off her body. I removed my robe, tunic, trousers, and turban, and pushed her gently back into the cushions. I started with small bites on her buttocks, teasing the soft, generous flesh. I traveled to her ears and plundered them with kisses, then teased her lips with my tongue. I skipped, for the moment, the parts of her that were crying out for me, and visited the soles of her feet. I sucked and nibbled, and I began to hear Khadijeh's breath rise until it sounded almost as if she might lose herself right then. I journeyed back across her calves and thighs to return to her breasts, so round and firm, and kissed the rubies that surmounted them. She rolled gently from side to side, thrusting first one breast at me, then the other.

When I was sated, I traveled farther down, kneeled in front of her, lifted her legs onto my shoulders, and began drinking at her trough. I started with teasing, flicking movements, and then as she became crazed, I became very slow, licking her with my full flat tongue, pressing my nose into her stream-filled cave, and finally, when her eyes looked as glassy as if she had consumed a strong cup of bang, I reached out to her nipples and stroked them with great gentleness. She became as wet and fertile as an oasis, and I felt as if I were drinking the milk and honey of paradise. Then I let my tongue become fleet, surprising her, and before long, Khadijeh's legs began trembling and jerking so hard, I was almost thrown. Her eyes rolled back in her head, and her hands clutched at the cushions. I held her gently until she was through.

She remained motionless for a while, and all I could hear was her soft breathing. Then she rolled her body against mine and held me.

"Your place will be empty," she said.

A profound sadness washed over me as I imagined how many women I would meet, only to have to say goodbye to them when they found someone to marry. Most women crave children, and that was the one thing I could not provide. Yet I was still a man, wasn't I?

When she had rested, Khadijeh attended to me. In her embrace, caught up by the scent of frankincense in her hair and the things her mouth could do, I was able to forget for a moment what I was about to lose.

It was close to dawn—far too close—when we were finally done. I rushed to put on my trousers as well as the rest of my clothes. Then I arose and said my tender goodbyes, touching her hyacinth curls as I took my leave.

"When will you return?" she asked.

"Never."

"Never?" Her eyes looked hurt. Being promised to the shah had not stopped Khadijeh from risking everything to see me. I was grateful that she still cared.

"It is too dangerous, especially for you. We can't risk any suspicion now that you have been claimed."

I leaned over her and laid my palms tenderly against the sides of her neck, feeling her heart's pulse in my fingers.

"I will always think of you," I said, "and will hope for your happiness."

"And I yours!" she replied, but I caught a trace of pity in her tone.

The eunuch on duty was still asleep, even though the birds had already started singing. When I was a good distance away and concealed by trees, I threw a handful of stones in his direction to wake him up. He would be punished if discovered snoring when he was supposed to be protecting the ladies—including the slave soon to be favored by the shah. But I had thrown the stones much harder than I intended, and they struck his calf and foot. He uttered a loud curse and leapt up to regain his post. I sped away. A sharp gust of wind rushed through the gardens, concealing the sound of my steps and moaning as it stripped the trees of their leaves.

Back in my room, I fell asleep for another hour. I dreamed that my penis was so erect that it hurt like a wound. All I wanted was to plunge myself into a woman to relieve the ache. Dark-eyed Fereshteh appeared like a savior in my dreams, seeking out my penis with her soft hands, making it even larger and more racked by pain. Tormented, I crawled on top of her and slid in. Just at the moment when I was about to find release, Fereshteh's eyes filled with disappointment.

"What *are* you?" she asked accusingly. My penis shrank.

I woke up, sweating all over. Seeking out my parts with my hands, I encountered a sickening void and wrapped my arms around my chest to keep from groaning out loud.

The next day was Friday. Pari sent Massoud Ali to me with a message that I was at leisure until the following morning, when she planned to hold the usual daily meeting with the nobles. Thus liberated for the first time in weeks, I went to the Friday mosque outside the palace to say my prayers. The mosque was located at the end of the Promenade of the Royal Stallions and had been founded during the reign of Harun al-Rashid. Its turquoise dome was lightened by white swirls of tile that made it look as if it were whirling into the heavens.

Later that day, I took Massoud Ali to town with Balamani and a few of the other eunuchs, and we bought fresh skewers of lamb kabob in the bazaar. We walked to a stream not far from the palace and cooked the lamb over a hot fire, and then we ate the charred meat with bread and drank tea with dates.

As the stars began to come out, all of us took turns telling stories, and Massoud Ali asked if he could tell one to me.

"My youthful Ferdowsi, please go ahead!"

Massoud Ali tucked a curl into his turban, which he had just learned to wrap correctly, and whispered a story in my ear until his eyes grew heavy and he wished to be cuddled as if he were a small child. I took him back to the palace so he could get a good night's sleep, while the rest of the eunuchs went to a tavern, where they could eat opium until they felt completely at home with themselves.

By the time I rejoined them, the tavern was full of men talking and laughing. Balamani had stretched out on a cushion and was sharing a jug of spirits with Mateen Agha, another eunuch.

"Did you tuck him in?" Balamani asked.

"First I had to wipe away his tears."

He sat up abruptly. "What is the matter?"

"He told me a long story about a boy enslaved by a jinni. The jinni kills his father, marries off his mother, and makes the boy do his dirty work."

Balamani looked puzzled.

"Massoud Ali's mother remarried when he was six and abandoned him at court. The jinni is the only way he can explain it."

"Poor creature! What kind of mother would do that?"

Balamani passed the jug of spirits to Mateen, who refilled both of their cups.

"As soon as I retire," Balamani added, "I am going to marry a widow with a couple of boys just like Massoud Ali. Praise be to God, I will have a family of my own."

"Get out of here, papa!" scoffed Mateen. "What is going to stop your widow from craving a tent pole?"

Balamani laughed uncomfortably; he had never experienced sexual desire. "I suppose Javaher can tell me how to . . ."

His words trailed off abruptly when he looked at me. I drank some bang, and then I drank a lot more. There came a happy moment when it didn't matter so much that Khadijeh was no longer mine, and the other eunuchs began to rib me for singing alone and in such a broken voice.

Pari continued holding her daily meetings with the nobles, but some of the regulars began to drop away. Shamkhal sent us a message that he was too ill to attend meetings. Shokhrollah's absence was unexplained until Mirza Salman brought us the surprising news that he had been appointed grand vizier. Pari and I were shocked that her brother had chosen him even though she had reported on his poor conduct.

At about the same time, Pari received a letter from Rudabeh, the woman who had come to her for help in reclaiming her home. Rudabeh had returned to Khui and was waiting for the local Council of Justice to revisit her case. She wrote that there was talk of rebellion in her province of Azerbaijan in favor of the Ottomans and that attempts were being made to recruit citizens to join the effort. "I pray every day for our safety—but please send help!" she wrote in handwriting that looked shaky with fear.

Pari sent Majeed to the new grand vizier to ask for funds to put down the rebellion in Azerbaijan. When he was unable to get an answer, despite repeated efforts, Pari decided to visit Isma'il herself and bring the problem to his attention. Tahmasb Shah's peace treaty with the Ottomans had endured for more than twenty years, and Pari was fearful that the treaty might collapse.

I advised her to bring her brother an offering, since he hadn't shown her favor on our first visit.

"An offering? So many gifts are pouring into the royal treasury that the official record keepers can't even keep up with them in their ledgers."

"I know," I said. "Instead of a gift, why not write your brother a poem celebrating his great deeds as a warrior? That way, you will soften his heart and make him receptive to your demands."

Pari thought for a moment and then said, "You are right. I need a better weapon than reason."

She called for pen, ink, and a writing table, sat down on a cushion, and began composing in Farsi. From time to time she lifted her head and asked me to fetch her books, such as court histories that recounted the details of the battles in which Isma'il took part. Once she had her theme, I helped her develop resonant rhymes.

In half a day, Pari was able to write a long poem that celebrated Isma'il's prowess as a young warrior and anticipated the brightness of his reign. When she had finished composing, she called for paper made of linen and hemp. It was so fine that I was moved to give silent thanks to the Chinese eunuch Cai Lun, the first man to make real paper.

I read Pari's poem out loud to her, while she wrote the words slowly in her most elegant handwriting. The next day, I accompanied her to Kholafa's house. She was greeted by his wife, shown with respect into the andarooni, and offered many refreshments, but we waited a long time before being granted a visit. An awkward silence settled on the room, during which Pari flicked at the fringes on her sash. It was a humiliating experience for a princess who only months before had been able to command the Shah's attention whenever she asked for it.

Finally, Isma'il deigned to see his sister. He still looked sallow, as he had the first time. He and his mother sat so closely together it was as if they were reconnected by an umbilical cord.

"Brother of mine, thank you for agreeing to see me," Pari began. "I have come to offer you a small gift, although I fear it is unworthy."

Pari proffered the poem, which was encased in a strong leather binding to keep it flat. Isma'il beckoned to indicate that he would receive it, and one of his servants came forward with a silver tray and brought the poem to him. He opened the binding and began reading, and I waited breathlessly until a few moments later, when a smile broke over his face.

"Here, Mother," he said. "I beg you to read this aloud, so that you can enjoy it, too."

Sultanam began reading, and Isma'il leaned back to enjoy Pari's fluid lines. In them he emerged as a young warrior astride a horse, filled with loyalty to his country, drawing his bowstring and striking his target with ease. His mother's voice increased its excitement as the poem leapt forward, and I, too, felt as if I could see him on the battlefield, his sword flashing in the sun, his future as bright as his heart.

"Bah, bah, it is beautiful!" he exclaimed when she was done. "Who wrote it? I should like to meet the man and reward him."

"I did," replied Pari in a modest tone.

"Indeed? Then you are very talented. Did you know that I, too, compose poetry?"

"I hadn't heard."

"As I suspected, there is much you don't know about me. I write under the pen name Adeli."

The name he had chosen meant "man of justice."

"Justice will indeed be yours," Pari replied.

"I should like to hear your other poems."

"Thank you. Perhaps you would also like to hear some of the poetry I commissioned about our father."

"Yes, we must plan an evening together very soon. We can recite to each other."

"I would be honored," Pari said.

Isma'il called for more refreshments, during which time I suggested to Pari in a low voice that we should go. But she pressed ahead, even before the sharbat arrived.

"Brother of mine, may I tell you about a matter of state?"

His eyes became suddenly wary, his tone cold. "What is it?"

She changed course and said, "I only meant . . . I wondered if I could assist you with the governorships that need filling. I could suggest some good men."

"Everyone wants to suggest his own men," he replied. "The problem is, whom can I trust?"

"I can advise you," Pari said confidently.

"There are vipers everywhere," he replied, his eyes darkening. "Again and again I have escaped their venom through the grace of God."

The princess looked puzzled.

"Do you know why it took me so long to come to Qazveen? I foiled several assassination plots by changing my plans on a moment's notice. It is a wonder I arrived safely."

"Thanks be to God for His beneficent protection," Sultanam said, her protective gaze on her son.

"And now that I am here, I see that the palace is divided into those who supported me and those who didn't. I haven't stayed alive for twenty years in confinement only to be assassinated upon my return by traitors!"

"Of course not. May God keep you safe," Pari replied.

"Yet my enemies are everywhere," he continued. "I won't feel secure until my coronation, when every man and woman makes a vow before God to obey me and is reminded that the punishment for disobedience is death."

"Your heart will be much easier," said his mother.

The astrologers had recently determined that all the stars were aligned perfectly, and the coronation had been scheduled for the following week.

"But even then I will have to be vigilant, because men's hearts are blacker than dirt. My greatest wish would be to have the contents of every man's mind revealed to me like the pages of a book so that no thought of treachery could ever escape my eye. Then, and only then, would I feel safe."

The princess and I exchanged a troubled look.

"It will be some time before I know who has my interests foremost in mind," he added, his eyes resting on his mother.

"Brother of mine, I offer my services whenever you need them. As you know, the nobles have been meeting with me every morning so that the business of the palace can proceed."

I was glad Pari had mentioned the meetings. Now Isma'il couldn't claim that she was doing something behind his back, and could tell her what he thought about her actions. I awaited his answer anxiously.

"Yes, I know about the nobles who come to you," he replied. "Time will show me who is loyal."

It was an odd answer, neither positive nor negative, and I wondered if he included his sister in his concerns about loyalty.

"I wouldn't recommend a man to you if I was uncertain about him," Pari said. "There is one man whom I question, however: Mirza Shokhrollah."

"I remember your concerns," replied Isma'il, "but his confusion over whether he should serve a woman was understandable."

"I am royalty," said Pari. "There is no confusion there."

"True. Still, I need men like Mirza Shokhrollah. He understands court finances better than almost anyone."

Pari was unable to prevent a frown from flitting across her face.

"My son," interjected Sultanam, "it is time for your afternoon rest. Little by little, you must regain your strength."

"Just one moment—my business is vital," Pari replied.

"Yes, Mother," said Isma'il, ignoring the princess. "How grateful I am to have someone who looks after my well-being. I will go now and have my nap."

Sleep, when there was so much to do?

"Thank you for the poem. We will speak again soon." He arose and took his leave, his mother following closely behind.

As we walked back to the palace, Pari's eyes seemed to be looking inward. When I asked her if I could do anything for her, she replied sadly, "All the time I imagined my brother coming home, I never suspected it would feel like I was talking with a stranger. I only hope that time will turn him back into a brother."

"Esteemed princess, I think he is afraid of you. He is all dark instinct and confusion, while you are like the sun of reason."

"And that means I shall have to prove to him day by day that my intentions are loyal."

"That is wise."

We strategized about the best ways for her to show her loyalty, but before we could implement any of our ideas, Isma'il announced that he would not see anyone but his closest advisors until after the coronation. When Pari received the news, the hurt in her eyes was deep. How could Isma'il cut off his own sister, the person who had done so much to bring him to the throne? Was someone close to him sullying her name?

Early the next morning, I went to Shamkhal's house with a small bag of silver in my hand. When a servant opened the door, I asked to see one of his eunuchs, whom I knew from when he had served at the palace as a messenger boy. As I kissed him on both cheeks, I slipped the bag of silver into his sleeve and asked him whether his master had been ill. He said he hadn't. When I pressed him for details, he whispered that Shamkhal had been invited to keep company with Isma'il every day.

I returned to Pari's and told her I had something to reveal to her, but that the very thought made me choke. Fortunately, she did not require the lengthy protestations of regret that were usually necessary in such a circumstance.

"Out with it."

"Is it possible your uncle has found favor with Isma'il?"

"Of course not. He would have told me."

I assumed a concerned look, as if worried about his health. "But we haven't seen him for days. Do you think he is still ill?"

"He must be."

"Perhaps, then, he would welcome a visit from you."

Pari's eyes sought mine. "What exactly do you know? Speak!"

"Isma'il has invited him to make daily visits."

"Him, not me? How have you learned this?"

"I paid someone to find out."

"With whose money?"

"My own."

"When did I grant you permission to do that?"

"You didn't."

Her brows knitted together, and I feared a storm. "Are you implying that my uncle is betraying me?"

"Surely not, esteemed princess. I simply thought you would wish to know his movements."

I had to be diplomatic.

"How dare you? If my uncle finds out you were spying on him, you will be pounded into pudding."

"My duty is to protect you, no matter what."

"That is what all servants say to earn their keep," Pari scoffed.

It wasn't uncommon for palace servants to put themselves at risk to earn their master's trust, but my own reasons went deeper. Lately I had begun to develop tender feelings for Pari. Her vulnerability brought out all my protective urges, almost as if she were the sister I had never been able to watch grow up. Seeing her struggle with what fate had allotted her made me think about Jalileh and how much I wished I had been able to soften the blows she had endured. Something in my face must have spoken out loud, because the storms on Pari's forehead cleared.

"I won't judge your actions until I investigate this matter further. You prove your loyalty to me every day."

I let out my breath. I hoped she would begin to think about how she could appear to serve Isma'il rather than demanding things from him.

"Esteemed princess, the nightingale finds it easy to be loyal to a rose," I said. "Your task is much thornier than mine."

CHAPTER 4

THE ROSE IS HEARTLESS

During Zahhak's reign, a noble child named Fereydoon was born. The destiny of this child was so powerful that his birth penetrated and disturbed the sleep of the king. Zahhak dreamed that Fereydoon would become a brave warrior and unseat him from his throne. He awoke in terror, so disturbed that he ordered a manhunt for the child.

When Fereydoon's mother, Faranak, heard about the king's edict, she agonized about how to protect him. Where could she conceal him in a place no one would look? One day she passed a resplendent cow whose coat of hair shone with thousands of colors. She approached the cowherd and asked if he would allow his glorious animal, Pormayeh, to nurse her only child. He agreed, and Faranak entrusted him with her son. Pormayeh nourished Fereydoon every day on her sweet milk until he grew into a strong little boy. Still, Faranak sensed that he was not safe. After he was weaned, she secreted him away to India, where she found a sage who promised to teach him all he knew.

Zahhak was not far behind. Having learned that a cow had nurtured Fereydoon, he had his men inspect all the cows in the land until they located Pormayeh, whose coat still shone with thousands of colors, and he butchered her with his own hands. After the deed was done, peasants must have gathered round and stared at the dead cow, aghast that a life-giving animal should be so wantonly slaughtered. What a terrible waste, they must have cried, tears streaming and bellies rumbling. What kind of king would destroy a nurturer of men?

The coronation was scheduled for the hottest month of the year, so most of the festivities would take place in the Promenade of the Royal Stallions for the public and under pavilions within the palace for the courtiers. Preparations at the palace had started from the moment that Isma'il had been welcomed at Kholafa's house. All the chambers had been aired, scrubbed, and perfumed with frankincense from Yemen. Roses were cut and placed throughout the palace in large vases. A grand feast was under way; all of the cooks in the court's private kitchens had been hard at work. The trays of sweetmeats alone would probably feed all the citizens of Qazveen.

On the morning of the coronation, the palace was astir well before it was light. Balamani and I went to the baths with the other eunuchs. We donned our best robes and turbans and proceeded to the large courtyard closest to the Ali Qapu. All of the servants of the shah—the royal family, the men of the pen, sword, and religion, the eunuchs, the messenger boys, and the male slaves—were assembling there in order of rank. I took my place among the eunuchs, well behind Anwar, whose position in charge of the royal household made him one of the most exalted servants, but far ahead of those who served ladies of lower status than Pari.

Before long, we heard the pounding of horses' hooves and the powerful blast of the royal drums. Thousands of us stood up to greet Isma'il. The palace gates were opened, and we saw the crowds of citizens lining the Promenade of the Royal Stallions to welcome the new shah. Isma'il charged in on an Arabian mare, whose skin was so dappled it looked wrapped in snow-white lace. Its saddle was covered with a crimson velvet cloth worked with silver. Great shouts of welcome rose up from among us: "Thanks be to God!" "The star of the universe has arrived!" "We would sacrifice ourselves for you!"

Isma'il was followed by a large retinue on foot, including soldiers dressed in battle armor. As he rode through a channel that had been cleared for him, all of us fell to the ground and placed our foreheads against the courtyard's stones, which vibrated in response to the horses' hooves. Saleem Khan commanded all of us to stand, and we arose as a single body to salute our new leader. Isma'il wore a green velvet robe, sober yet very fine, bound by a white silk sash threaded with gray, and a turban of the same white silk with a gold aigrette surmounted by an emerald the size of my eye. Around his waist, a jeweled belt held a curved damascened sword. The jewels threw off brilliant sparkles in the morning sun, so bright that they looked as if they might annihilate any man they struck.

The Shah proceeded through the palace to Forty Columns Hall, and all of us followed. The crowd was so large that many of us had to assemble in the gardens outside the hall. The long fountain was lined with courtiers, and all of the open-air pavilions were thronged. Only royalty and the highest-ranking nobles fit inside the hall.

When every man was in his proper place, Isma'il mounted a jewel-encrusted throne. Then Saleem Khan recited his lineage, starting with the mystic Safi al-din, who gave the Safavi dynasty its first inspiration, followed by the great deeds of his grandfather Isma'il, who declared Shi'ism the official religion of Iran; his father Tahmasb's long reign; and his own valor on the battlefield. A crown the length of a man's arm was offered to Isma'il on an engraved silver tray. The crown was decorated with small pearls and beads of pure gold, and at its peak gleamed a ruby the size of my fist surrounded by diamonds. Isma'il removed his white turban, revealing wisps of thin black hair. He lifted the crown and placed it firmly upon his balding head. No one could crown an adult shah except for himself, since no one overmastered him but God.

Saleem Khan spoke to the assembly. "I call upon all of you to take the oath of loyalty to Isma'il II, our new shah. Today you swear to follow his commands, to protect him at all costs, and to offer your lives for his. Remember, your oath is a legal contract; the penalty for breaking it is death."

Our voices raised such a thunder that I am certain it was heard in heaven. At last, after months of waiting, we had a new leader!

The orderly palace I remembered under the late shah would finally return, and peace and prosperity would be our everyday fare.

Isma'il's favorite companion, Hassan Beyg Halvachi Oghli, knelt down to pull off the Shah's dusty riding boots and replaced them with pristine gray silk slippers. Hassan Beyg had voluntarily endured five years of confinement with Isma'il at Qahqaheh, earning his master's trust. Anwar described him as a trained monkey; now that monkey would sleep under bedcovers embroidered with gold.

Saleem Khan called Sultanam's eldest son, Mohammad Khodabandeh, to approach the Shah. Mohammad walked toward him slowly because of his poor vision, led by his handsome eldest son, sixteen-year-old Sultan Hassan Mirza. As the elder brother, Mohammad might have wished to compete for the throne, but his near blindness made him ineligible. I had heard that he had no such desires and not enough force inside him to master other men. Rather than governing, he preferred to spend his time listening to poetry. He bent low, reaching out his hands tentatively in search of his brother's feet. When he finally found them, he kissed their insoles and congratulated his brother with dignity.

Next came the late Shah's sons born of other wives, consorts, or slaves: among them was the feckless Suleyman Mirza, Pari's brother, whose clay had not received the blessings that had gone to her. He lumbered to the throne. Mahmood, by contrast, although still young, strode confidently toward the Shah, his bearing erect from his lessons in swordsmanship and horse riding. I felt a surge of pride. He kissed the Shah's feet in a good-natured but not servile fashion.

After all of Isma'il's brothers had come forward and kissed his feet, they were followed by their uncle Bahram's sons and then their children. All the highest-ranking members of the clergy, dressed in their black robes, came forward next; the Shah would be their spiritual guide. Then followed the Mowsellu nobles of Sultanam's family, their red batons fiercely erect in their turbans even as they bent down for the kiss. Other qizilbash were honored, too: the Rumlu, the Shamlu, the Qajar, and the Afshar, followed by the Georgians, the Kurds, and the Circassians. As Shamkhal bent to perform the kiss, Isma'il flattered him with a smile.

Then salutations were read by ambassadors from Murad III of the Ottomans, Akbar the Great of the Mughals, Zhu Yijun of the Ming, and Abdullah Khan of the Uzbeks, the most exalted and powerful rulers on earth, as well as a few from those who ruled the Christian kingdoms to the west, Philip II of Spain and Elizabeth I of England, who were currently sparring with one another over faith. Each of the great empires had sent delegations with hundreds of emissaries and dozens of animals laden with precious gifts. The richest offerings were presented for all to see, including a beautiful copy of the Qur'an by the finest calligraphers of the Ottoman court, huge blue porcelain vases from the Chinese emperor, and ewers made of gold from the Uzbeks. A hush fell on the crowd when a mahout sent with the Mughal delegation paraded an elephant before us. I had never seen such a creature before, nor such costly trappings. The animal wore a jeweled cap on its intelligent brow, and its tusks were wrapped in sheets of gold.

When the ceremony was almost finished, I slipped away, walked through the checkpoints, and entered the harem. The women had sworn their oath to Isma'il earlier in the day, and now they were taking turns watching the ceremony from screened areas on the top floor of Isma'il's new residence. He had spared no expense in appointing the building. The large guest room where the women had gathered was filled with the sweet aroma of jasmine and the soothing burbling of a fountain that wafted up from the floor below, which was open to the air. I slipped off my shoes; the carpets were made of such thick silk that they seemed to caress the soles of my feet. A wall decorated with battle shields caught my eye. One was made of lacquered black leather with a central medallion of gold, pale turquoise, and pearls; another boasted open silver metalwork with a spray of emeralds, like drops of dew caught in a spiderweb.

The ladies had attired themselves in robes the felicitous colors of a sunrise and laid chains of gems against their foreheads or under their chins. How beautiful they were, from the golden-haired women of the Caucasus to those from the south whose curls glistened as black as naphtha! They kept their eyes on the coronation scene below, and the room buzzed with excitement when the elephant moved into view.

"Look at his jewelry."

"If you had half as much, you would be rich!"

The elephant let loose a steaming pile of dung, and shouts of laughter erupted throughout the room. It had been months since anyone had felt free to celebrate, and the excitement seemed almost hysterical.

Although Pari had told me she would be there, she had already left. I pretended that she had instructed me to wait for her, so that I could watch the other women.

Sultanam sat near Khadijeh, her new daughter-in-law, and held her hand on her day of motherly triumph. Sultanam seemed to have expanded in width so that everyone in the room appeared insubstantial beside her. Khadijeh, who was seated on a cushion at her right, looked as ripe as a peach. I couldn't deny that her marriage agreed with her. When she saw me, her lips curved into a tender smile.

I had never before seen Khayr al-Nisa Beygom, Mohammad Khodabandeh's wife, who lived with him in Shiraz. She had small, stern features except for her mouth, which was so large that it seemed to overpower her whole face. As she watched the ceremony, she kept adjusting her legs on her cushion as if she couldn't get comfortable.

"How my head aches!" she complained, her voice loud and high-pitched.

Sultanam offered her rose water, herbs, and cool compresses, but Khayr al-Nisa rejected all of them.

"Look!" said Khadijeh. "He is arising to take his leave." Through the latticed windows, I saw Isma'il mount his horse and canter in our direction, while all the men bowed low.

Sultanam leaned toward Khadijeh like a conspirator. "So now it is official. After nearly forty years of waiting, the bird of hope has stirred in the ashes of my heart and taken flight! How sweet the beat of its wings! How my heart soars!"

Khayr al-Nisa's lips turned down, but she kept her eyes carefully averted from Sultanam's. If not for her husband's blindness, she would have been queen of all Iran.

Sultanam didn't seem to care how she felt. She put a hand lightly against Khadijeh's flat belly. "Is it too much to ask that I should also be grandmother to the next shah? May God forgive me for entertaining this hope on a day when my other hopes have been realized—but may he also look kindly on my desire."

Khayr al-Nisa's torso twitched as if she had been struck. At that moment, a maid offered her saffron rice pudding on a silver tray. She reached out her hand as if to accept, but then, with an almost imperceptible flick of the wrist, she sent several bowls flying to the floor. They landed with a great crash on the carpet, the embroidered pillows, and on her, the sticky pudding clinging in great white clumps.

"Forgive me!" wailed the maid, her face twisted with fear. Khayr al-Nisa glared at her. Servants rushed to clean the spill.

"Ah, ah! How clumsy you are. I must go change."

"Yes, I suppose you must." Sultanam dismissed Khayr al-Nisa from the room with a condescending look.

"What a spoiled child!" she said to Khadijeh after Khayr al-Nisa had left. "It is lucky for the rest of us that she is not queen."

Two grand celebrations were planned for that evening in the birooni and andarooni. Pari was obliged to join a celebration for the women organized by Sultanam, and she sent me to attend the festivities at Forty Columns Hall. My stomach rumbled in anticipation of the rich dishes that would be served, giving us our first taste of the new Shah's generosity. But even more than that, I hoped that Mahmood Mirza would be there. Ever since he had left, I had had to train my heart. I told myself I had no claim over the boy, other than as his teacher. Yet you cannot spend eight years with a child without feeling as if he were a member of your own family. Mahmood was just two years older than Jalileh, and I knew him better than my own sister. I missed him and wanted to find out if his new life suited him.

Forty Columns Hall glittered in the night. Servants had decorated it with so many hanging lamps that its arches and painted ceiling glowed, and the hall was flooded with golden beams. Bouquets of freshly cut flowers bloomed in the corners of the room and spilled their perfume into the air. The doors opened onto the large garden, illuminated on this night with torches so that all of nature seemed part of the celebration. Heaping platters of fruit and nuts hinted at the lavishness of the meal to come. Balamani found me so that we could feast together, and we took a seat on one of the cloths that had been laid out in the garden under a sky thick with stars.

When Isma'il entered Forty Columns Hall that evening, everyone stood up. He was wearing a saffron-colored robe, the color of gaiety itself, and had put a jaunty blue feather in his turban, despite the recent death of his father.

"I have prepared a special indulgence tonight," Isma'il told us. He sat down on a jewel-encrusted portable throne, and all of us sat with him. Then he raised his hand, and a servant ran out of the room to do his bidding. After a moment, from a nearby room, the high, sweet sounds of a three-stringed *kamancheh* filled the air. I turned to Balamani, surprised. In my twelve years at court, I had never heard festive music in the palace. After Tahmasb Shah had become devout, years before my arrival, he had fired the court musicians and dancers. The court had become a sober place, one that favored learning, effort, and religious devotion.

The musicians entered the room and sat down on cushions placed near the Shah. The orchestra consisted of the *kamancheh*, a reed flute, a six-stringed *tar*, and a *daf* drum with metal rings that gave percussion such a rich sound.

All of a sudden, a voice emerged from the other room that seemed to be pouring directly from the singer's heart. I sat riveted, held still by wonder. A voice! Singing! It filled the palace with its deep longing, bypassing all objections, cutting straight to the soul. The singer entered the room, his arms open wide to the Shah, and sang lines of poetry about the heart's search for the gates of spirit and how he would gladly sacrifice himself for a glimpse of light under the gate.

When the song ended, the group of musicians changed its tune. The *daf* marked out the beat clear and strong, and then the lively, sweet sounds of the *kamancheh* took over. The vocalist began singing about the joys of love everlasting. I felt my feet begin to move, and I could see from the flutters in Balamani's robe that the rhythm had moved him, too. I didn't think it possible to dance at the palace, but my body strained against my robe like a lion against his cage. Around me, a surge rippled through the men's bodies, and they began to move faintly, with longing.

The Shah tilted his head as if he was listening deeply. I watched his bare foot begin to tap in time to the music, softly and then more emphatically until it was pounding against the carpet. Suddenly he sprang up and thrust his hands in the air. He began stamping to the beat, and with his arms held high, he formed powerful rosettes by twirling his hands. That was all he needed to do before two small boys ran to join him, unconstrained by the majesty of the royal person. The children swayed to the music, their faces transfixed with pleasure.

Some of the nobles jumped up and lifted their arms, circling their hands in time with the beat. At last I need resist no longer! I leapt up and pulled Balamani with me, stamped my feet as if to destroy the floor, raised my arms, and snapped my fingers to crack the air with noise. Balamani's kind old eyes shone as he paraded his big belly, and I could imagine him as an impish young man, full of life. We eunuchs looked different from women when we danced, more like proud cypress trees than swaying rosebushes, but with our arms lifted high in the air, our hearts were wide open.

"Not only music, but dance, too! The late Shah would have his head for this!" Balamani whispered as he stamped by me, his face beaming with glee.

"But what harm?" I replied. "Only the impious can't listen to music for fear of what it will make them do."

"The late Shah would have had your balls, too!"

I laughed as lustily as if I still owned such treasures.

The tune ended and we sat down for a rest, as did others. Everyone looked as if they could not believe what had actually happened, and a touch of embarrassment coursed through the room.

When the musicians took a break, all the men returned to their places, out of breath, and wiped their foreheads with silk handkerchiefs. Isma'il dropped to his cushion and grabbed a confection from his wooden box, which always accompanied him, and swallowed it without chewing. I searched for Mahmood Mirza, but it was crowded and I didn't see him.

Late in the night, a grand feast was served, and we ate richly from silver platters laden with roasted meats, vegetable stews, rice brightened with saffron, fresh greens, and sheep's yogurt, as well as platters of dates and halva, pastries, and flagons of drinks. Then we all arose and danced again. The merriment only increased as the evening progressed and dancing girls emerged and entertained the men. For the first time since Isma'il II had been crowned in Qazveen, pleasure invaded every spirit and hope took root in every heart.

Before I thought it possible, I heard the first call to prayer, signaling the approach of dawn. It seemed as if I had just closed my eyes when Massoud Ali tugged at my bedclothes and told me that a visitor had asked for me. I arose, heart racing. We entered one of the palace buildings near the Ali Qapu that was used to greet visitors. A young man who had his back to me was observing a mural on the wall. When he turned, I saw it was Mahmood Mirza.

"Esteemed prince!" I exclaimed. "Your visit brings joy to this eunuch's heart. What may I do to increase your comfort? Massoud Ali, bring tea and sweetmeats for our honored guest!"

The boy scuttled out of the room.

"I came to town for the coronation," replied the prince, "and I am about to ride home, but first I thought I would stop in and see my ostaad."

"Blessings upon you, my child! Your heart is made of diamonds to remember your old teacher. How you gladden me with your joyful presence."

Mahmood sat on a cushion, begging me to join him and be comfortable. I asked for his news with as much excitement as if I had been his older brother.

"How are things in Shirvan?"

"It is a minor posting, but I like it. Several of my father's trusted servants advise me about how to govern. I love the open plains and the animals so thick they travel in caravans. There are more animals than people in the province, which suits me well."

His eyes gleamed as he leaned forward, warming to his subject. "You know, the province is teeming with wild horses. Sometimes I am able to catch one of them, and lately I have been experimenting with interbreeding them with our mares. I never knew how much I would enjoy living outside the confines of the palace. There it is just me, my men, the animals, and the sky above. It is a fine life!"

He opened his arms enthusiastically as if embracing the wild spaces that he loved so well. I understood for the first time how constrained he must have felt by life in the palace, and I was glad he had broken free of it.

"My good prince, you have always had a loving touch with animals. Your skill with horses even as a boy astonished everyone. Thank God above you have found your calling! But I am sure you are destined for even greater things."

"Greater things?" he said, a question in his voice. "To me, God is great, and so are the gifts He gave to man. Those are all I need. I was never good at books. You did your best with me, though, and I am grateful for how hard you worked to shape this poor vessel into a better form."

He smiled a big, boyish smile, and my heart lurched.

"A rose could not be cultivated unless it contained the heart of a rose."

He accepted my compliment and reached into a saddlebag. "I brought something for you."

Mahmood handed me a parcel, which I unwrapped slowly. It was a copy of the *Shahnameh* written in an exquisite hand, its margins decorated with gold leaf. Although I had studied the book and had memorized parts of it, I had never been able to afford my own copy to read whenever I wished.

"This is a small gift for all the years you worked with me," he said. "After I left, I came to realize how much you had done. Without your determined training, I never would have been qualified to be a governor. You instilled an appreciation of learning in me, despite myself, and for this I shall love and respect you always."

I could no longer speak. I knew it was presumptuous of me, but he was the closest I would ever come to having a son. I loved him.

"My esteemed prince!" I finally said, straining to keep my tears at bay, "how you fill your old master's heart with joy. I am proud of you. May your way be blessed, may God put sweet fortune into your path, and may your burdens always be light."

"Insh'Allah," Mahmood replied, his eyes dancing. He stood up, and I noticed that he was dressed for riding.

"I have a long journey ahead of me, and I must go," he said. "I will call on you the next time I come to Qazveen."

He said his farewells and promised to return soon.

Massoud Ali came in to ask if I needed anything. He appeared to be in an uncommonly good mood.

"What makes you so happy, my little radish?"

"I have never seen you smile before!"

After sending Massoud Ali to bed, I decided to report to Pari's quarters for duty since I was already awake. In one of her antechambers I found two old women waiting for the princess, unsupervised. How negligent all of Pari's servants had become during the festivities! One of the women had a wrinkled face, with lines radiating away from her eyes and mouth, and her back was hunched. The other's hair and eyebrows were frosted with gray. Both wore humble cotton robes, but there was an air of insolence about them.

"Who are you?" I challenged.

"We wish to see the princess," said the hunched one in a gravelly voice. "Only she can redeem us."

"We need money, a place to stay, something to eat, and her blessings. A little jewelry would be nice, too," added her gray-haired companion.

Both women burst out laughing, and I realized I had been duped. The one with the gray locks was Pari.

"Princess, what a transformation!"

"It is all Maryam's doing. She made the clothing and painted our faces and hair. Then we went to a gypsy encampment and watched the women dance. How pretty their voices are, how bright their robes!"

A gypsy encampment? If Isma'il discovered they had slipped away, he would have their heads. But how had they gotten out of the palace? All the doors from the harem were heavily guarded.

"Next, I will make you a gypsy outfit with beads and coins," Maryam promised, a wicked gleam in her eyes.

"If I like it, perhaps I will dance for you," Pari teased back.

"Were you recognized?" I asked, thinking ahead to the need for an alibi.

"Not at all!" Pari was overcome with delight. "We even got close enough to look at the gypsies' wares, and we bargained hard for a few necklaces."

"If we hadn't, they would have known something was wrong," Maryam added.

"What a different life those gypsy women live; they are like birds compared to us," Pari said.

Their cheeks were bright with color. I had never seen them so carefree and happy.

"Did the palace guards look the other way?" I asked incredulously, still trying to discover how they had escaped. Women were not allowed to leave the harem except under carefully defined circumstances. They could accompany the shah wherever he wished to take them—to one of his other palaces, on a hunting trip, or to a picnic. With permission and with escorts, older women could travel to visit the households of their sons. Other cases were decided as the need arose.

"Ah, Javaher! You can't expect me to reveal all of my secrets," Pari replied with a toss of her snowy hair.

The expression on my face sent Maryam into fresh fits of laughter.

The coronation celebration was a masterstroke on the part of the Shah. He had finally thrown us a crumb of joy, and we gobbled it up as if it were a whole meal. It was followed by three days of leisure, during which Sultanam invited her son and all the women of the harem to a picnic in the countryside. The women immediately began preparing and packing luxurious foods and games, excited by the rare outing. The whole household was busy until Friday morning, when we set out right after morning prayers. I left the palace with a group of eunuchs armed with daggers and swords as part of the advance party; we rode for about an hour until we arrived at the palace's favorite picnicking spot near a river, and eunuch guards were posted around a huge perimeter so that no men would accidentally wander into the women's sphere.

It was a clear, hot day, the hawks zooming overhead as if racing with the clouds, the mountains bluish in the morning light. The day before, servants had staked large tents to provide shade and laid down mats and cushions. Archery targets had been set up, and games like chess and backgammon, as well as balls for the children, were placed a safe distance away. Fires had been laid for barbecuing meat and boiling rice, and an oven dug in the earth to bake bread.

A cloud of dust announced the arrival of those royal women who were adept at riding. The army of Arabian horses, so beautiful in dappled shades of white, tan, and brown, bore hundreds of chador-wrapped women on embroidered saddles with red, yellow, and silver fringes. Some rode sidesaddle, but Pari rode like a man, leading the pack with the grace of a soldier.

Older women and children followed not long after in carved

wooden palanquins that had left the palace earlier in the day. Isma'il
had ridden separately, with his own guard, and when he approached
the site, he sent his guards far away. Then the ladies shed their head
and face coverings, revealing bright short-sleeved robes, padded
trousers, and low boots.

We breakfasted on tea, cheese, nuts, fruit, and puffy bread fresh
out of the oven. Pari and her mother jumped up and began strolling
arm in arm near the river, talking animatedly. Other women followed, their girls in tow; the herbalists among them collected plants.
Boys kicked off their shoes and dared each other to get wet in the
river; others played with balls or wrestled. Massoud Ali observed
them, his shoulders sagging. I called him over to the games area and
taught him the rudiments of backgammon. He picked it up quickly,
and when I praised him, I was rewarded with a shy smile. I found
another novice player for him to test himself against and watched
their young foreheads pucker with concentration as the game deep-
ened.

Khadijeh and Isma'il had mounted their Arabian mares; they
spurred their horses and disappeared into the distance in a mock race.
All the unmarried women followed them with their eyes, watching
Isma'il's horse overtake hers. When they returned, Khadijeh's cheeks
were glowing like the moon, and for a bitter moment, I hoped she
would not take pleasure in his male parts.

Before lunch, Isma'il invited Pari to shoot with him, and we all
gathered around the archery range. Women spoke together so excitedly that Balamani and Anwar had to march to opposite ends of
the field and demand silence. Finally, all was ready, and Pari stepped
onto the range. I was eager to see how well she could shoot. Her
brown cotton robe draped gracefully over her long, lean body as she
threaded an arrow between her fingers, placed its nock against the
bowstring, drew it back to her cheek, and fired. The arrow obediently
struck a target, and her ladies ululated so loudly that the air seemed
to vibrate with their high-pitched cheer. One voice was higher and
louder than the others: Maryam's.

Pari waved her hand to indicate that no further ululation would
be necessary. Then she began firing one arrow after the other at tar-

gets placed near and far. The arrows thwacked into the middle of the targets with so much regularity that they mimicked the beat of a drum, and a thin veil of sweat shimmered on her forehead.

Pari stood aside to relinquish the targets to Isma'il. The bowmen cleared her arrows from the targets and stepped away. Isma'il reached out tentatively for his bow. He pulled back the bowstring with great effort, his arm trembling, and shot a few arrows, which missed their mark. Sweating profusely, he tried a few more. I shifted anxiously from foot to foot until, finally, one of his arrows struck the edge of a target. The ladies ululated so loudly, led by Sultanam, that the birds flying overhead veered away from us.

Isma'il ceded the range to Pari. Instead of politely pleading fatigue, she turned her attention to an empty target and struck it with arrows marking north, south, east, and west. Her ladies couldn't help themselves; they ululated again, their tongues moving faster than the eye could see, but I was beginning to feel uncomfortable.

Pari placed another arrow against the bowstring and concentrated so hard and for so long that the whole crowd seemed to hold its breath. Not a single silk sash fluttered while we waited to see what the princess would do. Finally, when the suspense was almost too great to bear, she loosed the arrow. It flew straight and true, striking the middle of the target to mark Mecca, the center of all things. All of us gaped in amazement at her prowess.

Isma'il's lips drew down at the corners. "Let's hear your voices for my talented sister," he choked out.

Pari beamed with pride. Isma'il approached his mother and conferred with her for a moment.

"My mother says it is time to eat," he announced and walked away without firing another shot. Balamani gave me a knowing look.

Servants began bringing out platters of barbecued meat. Balamani and I walked toward a blanket near the water and sat down.

"Pari is the better marksman," I said. "Why should she conceal it?"

"The greatest skill, for those close to the Shah, is making him look good."

"You believe he is quite so fragile?"

"He is a man, isn't he?" He crooked his index finger obscenely, and I snorted with laughter.

Massoud Ali came running to us, his eyes shining with excitement. "I won a game! I won!" he said with a grin that seemed as huge as his face. "I beat Ardalan."

"Of course you did, my little radish," I replied. *"Mash'Allah!"*

Out of the corner of my eye, I could see the errand boy scowling in our direction. Ardalan was known for getting into scraps. I fixed a stare on him until he looked away.

Anwar and a few of the other eunuchs joined us for the meal. A platter of lamb kabob arrived, its juices soaking the bread underneath it. We waited for Anwar to begin. Wrapping a piece of lamb in lavash, he began telling a story about how his father, who had been a chief in Sudan, had decided a dispute over a sheep. In the end, all the parties felt that they had gotten the better deal.

"Now that is good diplomacy!" he concluded, and we all laughed.

"I wish I remembered my father better," Balamani said wistfully. "I was younger than Massoud Ali when I was brought here."

Several of the other eunuchs murmured that they had also arrived as children.

Massoud Ali looked puzzled. "Your parents brought you to court?"

"No, my child. My father was very ill, and I spent my time at the seashore trying to fish or find a little work. One day, a dhow sailed in, and a sailor asked me if I wanted to train as a captain's boy. I got my family's blessing and joined the crew, surprised to find eight or nine boys already on board. Before we arrived at the next port, the sailors strapped us down and chopped off our parts. One of the boys, Vijayan, got an infection and died. He was my only friend on board."

Balamani brushed at his eyes. "A few weeks later, we arrived at a port. After we were fully healed, an agent of the court bought us and brought us here."

Massoud Ali stared at Balamani, his eyes round, as if he couldn't believe that the robust man in shining silk robes whose orders were law had once been a child slave.

"What about you?" Massoud Ali asked me innocently. An odd

hush fell on the group. Some of the other eunuchs looked away or fidgeted.

"I remember my father well; he was a courtier before he was killed," I blurted out, hoping someone could help. "I am still trying to find out what happened."

Massoud Ali's brow became so furrowed that I wished I hadn't said anything.

"God willing, you shall," replied Anwar.

In the distance, I spotted an old, ripped ball used by horsemen in their games of *chogan*. I got up and kicked it around until all the stuffing had leaked out of it, and then it was time to pack up and go home.

After Isma'il was crowned, many people who had previously fallen out of favor with his father felt safe returning to Qazveen and attempting to win royal grace. One of them, a former court astrologer named Looloo, wrote to me unexpectedly to say that he had known my father and wished to see me.

Late one afternoon, I walked toward Looloo's home in the southern part of the city. My path took me through the Ali Qapu gate and past the large, beautiful homes that lined the Promenade of the Royal Stallions, most of which were owned by nobles and their kin. Nearby lay the town's main bazaar and just beyond it, a river full of cold mountain water that pierced the heart of the city. Families picnicked on its banks, their children dashing around with glee, and smoke from charcoal fires danced above them.

I took the long way through town just for the pleasure of it, passing the part of the bazaar where animals were sold. Sometimes there were rare animals like cheetahs for sale or strange creatures from as far away as Hindustan or China. The healthy odor of sheep and goats filled the air. The bazaar was crowded with men examining the animals' mouths and flanks and bargaining for the best creatures.

The sound of young boys' jeers made me stop. Surrounded by the youths was a small goat with its head bowed. A single eye dominated the center of its forehead. Its nostrils were missing, and for lack of another way to breathe, it drew rasping breaths through its mouth.

One of the boys poked the goat with a stick. Another pelted it with a stone. The animal backed away, though it had nowhere to escape, and its frightened eye darted around in fear. Rage coursed through me.

"Scatter, you brats! Leave the goat alone or I will whip every one of you until you bleed."

I grabbed the ringleader and pulled the stick out of his hands. When I lifted it above my head, the pack scattered, leaving the boy alone. Fear blurred his eyes.

"Now you are just as scared as the goat. Have some mercy, illiterate!"

"Let me go," he whimpered. I released him and sent him on his way with a poke in the back.

The sight of the Friday mosque's turquoise dome restored my spirits, its swirling white lines seeming to carry all of mankind's hopes heavenward. Past the mosque lay the flat stones in the town's cemetery. I hurried my pace, my heart heavy. My father was buried there. It had been a long time since I had visited his grave. I knew I should pay my respects more often, but every time I thought about it, my stomach burned at the idea of going to him empty-handed. I wanted to visit only when I could rejoice that justice had been served, and when I could whisper to the soul of my mother, who was buried in the south, that I had heeded her cry for revenge.

Beyond the cemetery lay a cluster of small homes where people of modest means lived. The neighborhood, though not wealthy, was tidy and well kept. Looloo's home looked as if it had only three or four rooms. How had a court astrologer come to this? Such men were usually well rewarded.

I found Looloo in his birooni with his two sons, who were about my age. The paint on his walls was old but very clean, as were the wool carpets on the ground. The men were sitting on simple cushions and drinking glasses of tea, their legs sprawled out in front of them. I thought with regret of how I had never been able to share such simple pleasures as a grown man with my father.

"Welcome, my friend!" said Looloo. A black cap covered his head, and the lines at his eyes looked like the rays of the sun. His white beard and mustache were closely cropped and bright against his walnut-colored skin. "Your presence adds joy to our festivities. Please join us for tea."

The astrologer was in the middle of describing how he had once accompanied Tahmasb Shah on a fishing expedition to a river full of small, tasty trout. He had lost his balance and fallen in, getting soaked from his beard down. When he emerged wet and confused, the Shah burst into laughter, and the astrologer, though embarrassed, joined in with his whole heart.

"My sons, be sure to take any dunking with a sense of humor, even a big one," he concluded.

When they had finished their tea, his sons left, and Looloo turned his attention to me.

"Thank you for visiting. I was released from service by Tahmasb Shah shortly after you joined the court. I have returned to see if I can find employment with the new Shah, and I hoped you could help. Also, I wanted to see how you were getting along after all these years."

"I apologize, but I don't recall your name. Did you know my father well?"

"Just as a passing acquaintance. How sad for you that his life was cut short when you were so young."

"It was," I replied. "For many years I have been trying to find out exactly what happened to him. Do you know anything about his murder?"

Looloo tugged at his black cap. "Yes, but I must caution you that I always seem to be telling people things they don't wish to hear. The reason I was banned from Tahmasb Shah's court was because of an astrological reading that outraged him."

"I wish to hear everything. I have always wanted to clear my father's name."

His eyes darkened. "I can't help with that."

I was taken aback. "Why not?"

"Every man wishes to think his father innocent," he said.

"Mine actually was."

"How would you feel if you learned yours wasn't?"

"I wouldn't believe it."

"My friend, let me tell you what I remember. Your father was a good man, may God be praised. But the reason he was killed is that he was discovered diverting money from the treasury."

"That is preposterous! We had plenty of money. My father wasn't a common thief."

"No, he wasn't," Looloo agreed. "He didn't take money for his own personal gain, but to fund a rebellion."

"My father was a loyalist to his core! He would never have done such a thing."

"Sometimes being a loyalist means rebelling," he replied. "It is one of the paradoxes of serving the court. I wouldn't be at all surprised if he had decided to rebel for your sake, with the idea of bequeathing you the results of his labors."

"I have faced such malicious slander about my father ever since I was a young man," I said, in an angrier voice than I intended. "I am sick of it!"

The astrologer's eyes were compassionate. "Yes, I can see that."

"Who made these allegations against him?" I said, feeling the angry perspiration gathering at the back of my neck.

"I think it was another accountant."

"But why?"

"Most likely he would have found a discrepancy in the accounts and reported it, or if he was eager, he might have taken justice in his own hands by murdering your father and explaining himself to the Shah later."

Something in Looloo's sincere demeanor made me feel I should listen. As I tried to speak, my voice closed in on itself and grew tight. "Your words bruise me. I have been trying to return the luster to my family name. How can I do that, especially in my own heart, if my father wasn't loyal?"

"Some men would consider your father moral for trying to change a situation he felt was wrong. It takes great bravery to do that."

Could it be true? Could I love my father for being a rebel?

"You and your mother were probably the dearest things to him in the world. He must have felt very strongly to risk so much."

"But do you think he had good cause? What are the just reasons a shah can be removed?"

"If you are the shah, there are none," Looloo replied with a laugh. "But from the point of view of citizens, the reasons can include incapacitating illness, imbecility, inability to sire an heir, or madness."

"What about evil behavior?"

"That, too," the astrologer said. "The question is how much evil is too much. That is when some men, like your father, take the law into their own hands. Had he been successful, everyone would now praise his name."

My father would have become one of the closest allies of the new shah, and as his son, I would have been catapulted to high position. I might well have married one of the shah's daughters. That much was true, but the rest of his story didn't make sense.

"If the Shah thought my father was guilty, why would he allow me into his service?"

"For two reasons. First, you astonished him by becoming a eunuch in order to serve him. How many men would do that?"

He paused and stared at me curiously. I stayed mute, not wishing to explain myself yet again.

"Then, before he met you, he asked me to prepare your astrological chart. Did you know that?"

"No."

"I discovered something I have never forgotten. The conjunction of planets present at your birth indicated that your destiny and the dynasty's are interwoven like warp to weft."

"Is that such a big surprise? I work for them."

Looloo laughed. "You don't understand. The chart is the reason you were taken into service."

"Why?"

"Your stars foretold that you would help spur the rise of the greatest Safavi leader ever."

"Me?"

"Yes."

"How?"

Looloo chuckled, his eyes crinkling at the corners. "The stars are never quite that specific. I suggested that the Shah stay attuned to details that might emerge in his dreams, which gave him excellent guidance all his life. But that is about all I know, because I was banished not long after."

"What crime did you commit?"

"The Shah asked me to make charts for all his sons to determine who would be the greatest leader. He didn't like the results."

"What were they?"

"Not one of them was destined to be great, and I refused to pretend otherwise."

"Is that why he didn't name an heir before he died?"

"Possibly. It may also explain why he was so eager to hire you and keep you in his service."

"What a surprise!" I said, thrown into a whirl of confusing thoughts. "But there is something else that bothers me about my father's story. The official court history says that the Shah decided not to punish his murderer because he was so highly placed, but doesn't name him. Do you know who he was?"

"No, but I suspect that once the Shah had been apprised of the murder, he would have talked the matter over with one or two of his closest advisors. After deciding not to punish the murderer, they would have all kept his name quiet for the same reason the Shah decided not to punish him to begin with."

"Why wouldn't his name appear in the court histories?"

"Did you ask the historians?"

"One of them claimed he didn't know."

"There is another possibility: What if the man is powerful and still alive?"

I thought for a moment. "They would omit his name?"

"Why should they risk his wrath?"

"By God above! You may be right. Thank you."

"You are welcome. Please return to take tea with me and my sons at any time. We would enjoy your company."

"I will. And I will be sure to recommend your services to the palace."

"I am deeply grateful. As you can see, I could use the work." He gestured around him at the threadbare carpets and humble furniture. I thought about the court astrologers I had known, who spent much of their time observing the stars in the countryside at night. They rode out of town on the finest Arabians I had ever seen, sparing no expense on trappings or tents or tools. How costly it was to fall out of favor!

Balamani was already asleep when I returned to our quarters. I lay on my bedroll and thought about my father, remembering how he would come home every day in time for afternoon tea, spin stories about the court, and make my heart thrill at the idea of being part of it. But now that I was grown, I realized that my father had chosen to show me only the brightly shining silver of the court, not its old, tarnished samovars.

But had my father really been a rebel? The more I investigated, the more the truth seemed to recede from my grasp.

I resolved to look again at the *History of Tahmasb Shah's Glorious Reign*, taking notes on all the accountants who had served the Shah during my father's time, as well as all those leaders who had been the Shah's closest confidants. I didn't dare approach them outright, but I would try to piece together the picture by collecting all the tiny shards of information I could find.

The next day, I awoke early and discovered that Balamani was already gone.

As I was dressing, Massoud Ali came in with a letter for me. His sleeve fell away, revealing large purple and yellow bruises.

"What happened?"

He shrugged and looked down. It took quite a bit of prompting to get him to admit that Ardalan, the errand boy, had pummeled him after being bested again at backgammon. I made a mental note to reprimand him, and I told Massoud Ali that I would send him to a tutor for lessons on combat.

"But right now," I added, "I want to tell you the most important story you will ever hear. It is a long one, so I will tell it to you in parts. At the end of it, you will know how to stand up to bullies like Ardalan."

Massoud Ali's fingers went to a bruise as if to soothe it.

I sat down on my bedroll, even though I had much to do. "Once, long ago," I began, "there was a ruler named Zahhak whose evil knew no bounds. The way Ferdowsi tells it, all the world's problems started when he decided to usurp his father, who had been a just leader. One day, with some help from the devil, he . . ."

Massoud Ali hung on every word, his eyes wide. When I got to the part about how Zahhak had destroyed Pormayeh, he jumped up angrily as if he wished to save the cow. I promised that I would help him learn how to defend those who needed his help.

It was late, so I sent Massoud Ali off on his duties and rushed to the hammam. Many other eunuchs had already gathered there to clean themselves before Friday prayers, and the sound of their voices echoed throughout the room. Balamani was in the largest tub, pouring bowls of warm water over his bald, charcoal-colored head.

"Aw khesh," he said in satisfaction as the water coursed over his broad, smooth body.

After greeting him, I soaped myself, rinsed with buckets of water, and slid into the tub, where he was scrubbing a callus on his thumb. Before I had time to adjust to the heat of the water or to tell him what I had learned the night before, he asked, "How is your health?"

"God be praised," I said. "And yours?"

"From your cheeriness, I can tell that you haven't heard the news."

When I shrugged and admitted defeat, his black eyes twinkled merrily. In the business of gathering information, Balamani was still the master, I the student. Since it was impossible to know when trifling details would become valuable, he collected them all. If you pick up a few shards of colored tile, he explained when I had first joined the palace, you have nothing, but gather enough shards and you can piece together a mosaic.

Balamani poured another jug of water over his head, then wiped his face. "Hossein Beyg Ostajlu was captured yesterday trying to leave the city. After hearing about that, I decided to go to the home of one of the Ostajlu nobles to quiz his eunuchs about the tribe's status at court. Not far from the palace gates, I noticed a number of fine tents had been torn down, stomped on, and soiled. A man was rummaging under one of the tents trying to collect abandoned items. He told me that a few days ago, the Shah sent a message to the Ostajlu in the form of an arrow. It had been lodged in one of the palace's plane trees during their invasion, and its arrival at the Ostajlu camp chastised them for entering the palace grounds and attacking royalty.

"On the morning of the coronation, the Ostajlu pitched their tents and sent a written reply. 'We recognize we are in disgrace,' the message said. 'We can't take another breath on this earth without pleading for forgiveness. We beg you to tell us our punishment so that we may one day fill our lungs with the sweet air of royal grace.'"

"What was the Shah's response?"

Balamani raised his eyebrows. "He sent a group of soldiers to tear down the tents, and looters walked away with silver platters, embroidered pillows, silk robes, and even carpets."

"What a humiliation! Have the Ostajlu been welcomed back?"

Balamani grimaced as he scrubbed at the tender flesh below his callus. "We will see," he said. "They have been ordered to present themselves today."

"On a Friday?" I asked, incredulous. The late Shah had never conducted business on the holy day.

Balamani stopped scrubbing. "The meeting is at Forty Columns Hall. Shall we observe it together?"

"Of course," I replied.

By the time we arrived, the hall was already packed with men sitting cross-legged knee to knee. The heat from the bodies made the room seem suffocating, and the acrid smell of sweat hung in the air.

I couldn't help but look at all of them with a new eye. If Looloo's guess was right and my father's murderer was alive, could he be here? I stared at men with long gray beards and creased foreheads as well as those in the prime of youth with thick black mustaches and smooth, sun-browned skin. Might I be looking at him?

Near the portable throne that marked the Shah's place sat most of the qizilbash leaders, as well as the Circassians including Pari's uncle Shamkhal, who looked uncommonly ruddy and well. Mirza Shokhrollah sat closest to where Isma'il would emerge. The leaders of the Ostajlu, the Georgians, and the Kurds sat clumped together in disgrace behind all the others for having supported Haydar. Hossein Beyg Ostajlu looked as frightened as if it were the last day of his life.

Balamani and I claimed a cushion at the back of the chamber. Saleem Khan called the meeting to order in a more sober tone than usual. The Shah entered and sat in front of a mural that showed his grandfather mounted on a horse, thrusting his spear at a warrior who had tried to resist the establishment of his rule. The Shah was wearing a pale blue robe and olive green trousers, colors so complementary to those in the painting that it was as if he had stepped right out of the battle scene. His mouth was set in an angry grimace, and the pillows under his eyes made me suspect that he had not slept enough the night before.

"You may plead your case," he said to Sadr al-din Khan.

"Oh glorious light of the age," said he, "we the Ostajlu gave our lives with enthusiasm during the wars fought by your father and grandfather, supporting their reign in every way. We support yours, too. At some junctures, though, your servants take the wrong path. We are guilty of having rallied behind the wrong man, but please understand that it came from a desire to keep the Safavi throne intact. We beg your forgiveness and wish to perform any punishment you require to be reinstituted into your good graces."

"You say this now," he replied, "but this is not the tune you were singing a few weeks ago. Hossein Beyg, stand up."

Hossein Beyg got to his feet and faced the Shah. I remembered how fierce he had looked when he led the men into battle, but now he appeared small inside his robe and trousers.

"By all accounts, you were the leader of the soldiers who stormed the palace. Is that true?"

"Yes, defender of our faith, it is true."

"How dare you support my opponent?"

"O merciful Shah, I am not the only one. There were many who did not understand that your star was ascendant. If you arrest me, you might as well arrest most of your court."

"That is true," replied the Shah, "but you were the one who led the invasion and desecrated the sanctity of the women's quarters. How can you expect such a violation to be forgiven?"

"O light of the universe," said Hossein Beyg, with the ferocity of a man who knows he is fighting for his life, "it was a time of lawlessness and uncertainty. We acted with the intention of protecting the royal grounds, and we were not the only ones who did so. A large group of—"

"Choke yourself!" said the Shah. "A man can find no end of excuses for his actions on earth. Why should I believe that you would become loyal?"

"Clemency makes a man loyal," Hossein Beyg replied in a quiet tone. "Kindness is answered with greater kindness."

"Your words are empty; they don't convince me," said the Shah. "Why shouldn't I execute you? You are a conniver and a plotter."

Hossein Beyg bowed his head respectfully, speaking to the ground near the Shah. "Your own father was faced with insubordination many times. He showed mercy by imprisoning his enemies— even members of his own family whom he suspected of rebellion."

Others would have fallen to their knees, cringing and begging. His bravery filled me with admiration.

"Don't dare to compare yourself to me!" replied the Shah. "Nothing you have said mitigates what you have done. If you had been successful, I wouldn't be here, and I see no reason to trust you. I therefore order your execution, to be carried out tomorrow morning."

He gestured to the guards. "Remove him from my gaze."

The guards grabbed Hossein Beyg and dragged him toward the rear door. He turned back to the assembly and stared directly into

the eyes of the Shah in violation of every rule of respect and protocol. I was astonished to see a man daring to behave as if he were the
Shah's equal. The faces of the men around me were transfixed with
horror.

"May God punish you for this first of your sins!" Hossein Beyg
shouted, his words falling on the room like a curse. "May you fear
for your life every day you are Shah. May your children be murdered
without mercy, just as you have condemned me. Men of the court,
take heed! You will be next if you don't root out this viper in your
midst."

The guards pummeled him so hard in the face and chest that he
fell to the floor with a thud. They forced him to his feet and pushed
him out of the room, but the expression on his face remained stoic
and dignified.

I was appalled. Hossein Beyg had pled his case well before a
man who had been a prisoner himself only a few months before. I
thought the Shah should have treated him with more mercy.

After his removal, the room was so silent that you could hear the
flapping of birds' wings outside. Rather than being the gentlest of
sounds, it was like listening to a beating.

"Sadr al-din Khan, your men are the cause of this disorder," added
Isma'il Shah. "There is nothing you can say to redeem yourself for
what you have done. However, I am indeed merciful, and therefore
I order you merely to be imprisoned along with your accomplices."

He named five men, two of whom were governors, and the
guards lifted each man to his feet and pushed him toward the door.

I thought about the terrible warren of palace prison cells, which
stank of mold and grief. They were always bitterly cold, even on the
hottest days of summer.

The Shah scowled as they were led away, and twisted restlessly
on his cushion. "Those of you who remain in this room, look around
you. Do you notice anyone missing from your ranks?"

I checked the room, annoyed that I had not thought to do so
earlier. Balamani had a knowing look in his eyes.

"Kholafa Rumlu," he whispered.

Balamani could look around a room and see more than any other man. He could recite every noble family's lineages and their proper titles until day turned into night.

"Perhaps you have noticed the absence of Kholafa, which you may find surprising since he was one of my greatest backers. The news about him will freeze your blood."

No one had been a greater devotee!

"Not long ago, I offered Kholafa a new post in our government, which required him to give up his existing position. He refused to relinquish his title. Then I suggested that he be put in charge of the royal zoo."

I suppressed a horrified laugh. Overseeing the zoo was an insult to a man of Kholafa's rank.

"Kholafa refused to respond to my royal command. For his pride and disobedience, he too will pay the price of his life."

I heard a low expostulation from Balamani. My heart felt as if it had stopped beating.

"As you ponder the fate of Kholafa and Hossein Beyg, don't forget that your fate could be the same. Tell them, Saleem Khan."

"God is great, and the Shah is his deputy here on earth. The punishment for disobedience is death," said Saleem Khan.

We replied in unison, "We pledge submission to the light of the universe."

But the Shah hadn't finished yet.

"And another thing, while I am on the subject of violations of the royal person and palace. It has come to my attention that a number of courtiers have continued to call upon those who are most dear to our honor. I am certain you would agree that there is nothing as important as honor—nothing. Visiting them is absolutely forbidden."

If he had objected, why hadn't he said so earlier? No doubt he had been afraid of Pari's power.

None of the courtiers dared to say a word; they bowed their heads, hoping Isma'il would not demand accountability from them. I stared at Shamkhal but could detect no surprise in his expression, nor did he utter a single word in support of his niece.

Mirza Salman asked permission to speak, which I thought brave under the circumstances.

"O commander of all that is pure, in your absence, many of us were concerned about the security and safety of the palace. We thought that no one could guide us better than a close descendant of your revered father. We sincerely hope that we haven't erred."

Isma'il looked pleased by this pretty speech. "In such a situation, when the palace is in chaos and no Safavi prince is present to make decisions, you did well to listen to a member of the family," he replied. "But everything is different now. I am here to lead you, and therefore no such ministrations are required—or allowed. Do you understand?"

"Perfectly," replied Mirza Salman.

The Shah signaled to Saleem Khan that the meeting was over, and that was that. In Tahmasb Shah's time, the discipline of malefactors would have been mitigated with rewards to those who had provided good service, or something else that would have relieved the sorrow we felt over the death and imprisonment of men we all knew. How different things had become.

When the Shah arose, we stood at attention as he walked to the door, followed by the pillars of state and by the guards. After he left, the courtiers who had survived the ordeal began speaking together in quiet but fervent tones. Some wiped their brows, while others muttered prayers of thanks that they had not been taken. I heard Ibrahim Mirza speaking too loudly to one of his friends.

"I would say this is cause for celebration," he said in an ironic tone, "that is, for those of us who are still breathing. Why not join me for refreshments at my home? I've commissioned a new book, and I would like to show you some of the illustrations."

The prince was beloved among artists and calligraphers for spending so much of his fortune on books. He must have been trembling on his cushion over his support of Haydar, though he was making light of it now. Why, I wondered, had the Shah spared him?

His friend didn't have the heart to celebrate. "Maybe later," he said. "Right now, I am going to the mosque to give thanks to God."

Balamani turned to me and said, "It could have been worse."

"How?"

"Isma'il had to show the stone in his fist. If he hadn't punished his enemies, the moment the meeting ended, groups of courtiers would have started plotting to bring him down. Now they will think twice about the consequences."

"But why Kholafa? Isn't it excessive to kill your ally because he didn't care for his new posting?"

"*Vagh-vagh*," said Balamani, imitating an angry dog. "All that was just an excuse. Kholafa was responsible for making him shah. No ruler wishes to be so obligated to a mere man."

His words were like a dagger in my heart. I suspected that a shah like Isma'il would wish to be obligated to a woman even less.

When I entered Pari's quarters, she was seated with a pen in her hand and a letter on her lap, which she set aside.

"You look as if you have seen a jinni," she said. "What happened?"

"The Shah has shown his wrath by ordering the executions of Kholafa and Hossein Beyg," I replied in a rush, "and has imprisoned Sadr al-din Khan and other supporters of Haydar."

"Voy!" Pari replied. "That is much too harsh!"

"Esteemed princess, he has also demanded that the courtiers refrain from attending meetings with the royal women."

"For what reason?"

"He said it was an insult to the honor of the Safavis."

"Of course he would," Pari replied angrily. "It is the easiest thing to say because no courtier can protest such an accusation. What he can't say is that his sister is better at governing than he is. I can't remain silent when those men are about to be executed, especially Kholafa. I will go plead with him immediately."

Pari picked up her pen and wrote a letter to Sultanam demanding Isma'il's ear. It said, in part:

> Now that you are queen mother of Iran because of my key
> I beg your help in unlocking your son's clemency.
> Throw open the doors to his generosity
> And remember: One day, you might need aid from me.

Sultanam replied with a message telling her to come to her quarters in the late afternoon, when she had tea with her son. When we arrived, we were shown into a small guest room with fine carpets. Sultanam and Isma'il sat very close to one another, drinking tea spiced with cardamom and eating sugar crystals brightened with saffron. With her broad frame and wedge of curly white hair, Sultanam looked twice as big as Isma'il, who was still thin despite the richness of the palace diet. Pari saluted Isma'il as the lord of the universe, thanked him for inviting her into his presence, and inquired after his health. The formalities done, Isma'il did not delay.

"I know why you are here," he said. "The answer is no—no more morning meetings."

This shah, I thought, did not understand the first thing about diplomacy.

"Light of the universe, that is not my purpose," Pari said. "I come to you with great humility to ask a favor."

"What is it?"

"I have heard of your decision to execute Kholafa Rumlu and Hossein Beyg. As your sister and as a member of the royal family with years of experience at court, I beg you to show them mercy."

"Hossein is a traitor, and Kholafa is an ungrateful wretch. They don't deserve mercy."

"Perhaps not, but the question is how the noblemen will view their executions," Pari said. "If you kill Kholafa, they will wonder why a man of wisdom and high standing, who did everything to bring you to power, has been sacrificed. Being fearful of the same fate will make them dangerous. If you kill Hossein Beyg, they will understand why, but show clemency and they will see you as merciful."

"Why do you care? What are these men to you?"

"They are nothing to me, but it is a matter of justice. Kholafa was your biggest ally. I think we owe him thanks for his support."

"And Hossein Beyg?"

"The loyalty of the Ostajlu is worth a great deal."

"Even though he was a traitor?"

"He wasn't a traitor; he simply didn't select the winning side."

Isma'il turned to Sultanam. "Mother, what do you think?"

Pari looked at her expectantly; she had often been successful in begging Tahmasb Shah for clemency and had no doubt saved Isma'il himself.

"I think your sister is right about Kholafa," Sultanam said. "Why destroy a brilliant strategist?"

"To demonstrate that no disobedience will be tolerated is valuable."

"But it wasn't disobedience; it was merely disagreement," Pari interjected.

"What is the difference?"

Was the Shah incapable of seeing the distinction?

Pari looked bewildered. "Surely you will permit your subjects to disagree at times?"

"Of course," he said. "I am listening to you right now, aren't I? But Hossein Beyg is a lost cause. By opposing my accession, he will always be a rallying point for the dissatisfied. As for Kholafa, his execution sets an important example to the others about the behavior I expect. By dying, he will serve me better than by living."

"But, brother of mine—"

"I have made my decision."

"I beg you to reconsider. When our father was alive, his brother rebelled against him several times, but it wasn't until Alqas joined forces with the Ottoman army that he had him captured and executed. Surely your noblemen deserve mercy."

"I am not Tahmasb," Isma'il said, "and I intend to be quite a different shah than he was."

Pari looked exasperated. "But if not for his clemency, you yourself would not be alive!"

Isma'il's face flushed with anger. "I am alive because it was God's will that I should become shah."

No one could disagree with that.

"Kholafa isn't the only person at court who needs to be disciplined," he continued. "Some wish to usurp my power, but they won't succeed."

Pari remained calm at the insinuation. "I offer my opinion with the sole goal of strengthening your rule, brother of mine."

Isma'il snorted. "Next time, you should wait to ask if I desire your opinion."

Pari drew back, offended, and turned to Sultanam for reinforcement.

"You must heed the words of my son," Sultanam said quietly.

"But you are depriving a man of his life, the only worthwhile thing he has! Surely you would expect an argument."

"On the contrary, I expect to be thanked for listening," he said.

Isma'il put a roasted pumpkin seed in his mouth and cracked it open. I hoped Pari would say something conciliatory, but she frowned, as if a bad smell had invaded the room.

Isma'il spat out the shell. "There is nothing left to discuss. You may go."

Pari arose stiffly and walked out of the room without thanking him for seeing her. I asked permission to be dismissed and followed behind, cringing at the disrespect she had shown.

"I should have fought harder," she said as we walked through the gardens. The roses looked wilted in the heat.

"What good would that do?"

"Perhaps none, but I owe it to Kholafa. He deserves to live."

"May God have mercy on his soul tomorrow," I replied. "Yet I think it is most important now to earn back Isma'il's trust."

"He doesn't desire honesty."

"Isn't it vital to convince him that you are his ally?"

"Not if it means compromising what is right," she said angrily.

The men would be executed in the morning. I felt sorry for their wives and families, for I knew how their faces would twist with agony when they received the bodies wrapped in bloody white sheets. Their children would suffer, too: I remembered Jalileh's screams of distress even though she was too young to understand what had happened. And yet, rather than advance the cause of the condemned, Pari had managed to hurt her own standing with Isma'il.

Pari was watching me closely. "What is it, Javaher? If your brow could make storm clouds, it would be pouring."

I took a deep breath. "Princess, you know the old saying: The rose is heartless, yet the nightingale sings to it all night long."

"Why should I sing to a stem of thorns?" she scoffed.

"Because you want to win."

Her face darkened. "Shit-eater!"

I was offended and slowed my gait so that she would know it.

Pari waited for me to catch up. "Javaher, I know your advice comes from the bottom of your heart, but you cannot understand the fury that seizes me in his mule-like presence."

"Princess, don't you fear for your life? Look how casually he destroys his allies."

Pari threw back her head and laughed. "The blood of the Safavi lions roars in my veins!"

A few evenings later, Pari summoned me to her house to fetch her most private correspondence and deliver it to a special courier. I arrived at the same time as Majeed, whom I escorted behind the lattice. His cheeks looked yellow with fear. In a shaky voice, he told us that when he had gone home that evening, he had been prevented from entering his own door by a group of soldiers, who told him that all his possessions had been confiscated by order of the Shah.

"Esteemed princess, have I offended you in any way?"

"No, my good servant."

"Then why—?"

I scrutinized Majeed carefully. A man who wishes to succeed at court can't collapse when the earth trembles, because when it shakes, pitches, and rolls, he will break into seven hundred and seventy-seven pieces. A bubble of hope opened up in my heart, for Majeed seemed to be crumbling.

"Do you think you can still be effective as my vizier? Be truthful. Whatever your answer, I shall treat you fairly."

"I am afraid that showing my face at court would seem like an aggravation. Perhaps another man would do better . . ." His voice trailed off, as if he hated himself for admitting it, and his young face looked as soft as rice pudding.

"Very well, then. Stay out of sight, and I will contact you to serve me when the court is safe."

"As you wish."

Pari made him pledge to spread the story that she herself had requested the expropriated house. Then she released him from her service with a generous sack of silver for his expenses and the promise to resettle him in a new home. I showed him out and joined Pari on her side of the lattice.

"How I miss my father!" she said, her voice thick with feeling. The princess bowed her head for a moment to compose herself, and the room was silent except for the sound of the wind outside. Then she said, in a tone of wonder, "How did you survive your grief all those years ago?"

I had to think for a moment; no one had ever asked me that question before.

"Princess, I wish I could give you an answer coated in honey. The best I can do is to suggest that you bask in the memories of his love, the sweetest balm for your heart."

She sighed. "I shall."

"Why do you think Majeed's house was taken?"

I was certain it had to do with her behavior toward the Shah, but knowing the specific reason was essential.

"I sent him back to Mirza Shokhrollah to ask for an army to protect our northwestern border. The grand vizier must have spoken out against me," she said, but looked uncertain.

"Is it possible that the Shah objected to your plea for clemency?"

"If so, his response is cruel," she said. "Every citizen has the right to the Shah's ear."

Pari batted at her temple to brush a strand of hair away from her face, but there wasn't one. She sought neatness in times of distress. Something in her gesture made me wonder if she was telling the truth about everything.

"Can you think of any other reason for this punishment?"

"No. On the occasions that I disappointed my father, he told me why and allowed me to make amends. He didn't punish my vizier. What a sinister way to make a point."

"Esteemed princess, how shall we break the scepter of royal displeasure?"

"I don't know."

I decided I would risk making a visit to Khadijeh, who might be able to tell me what was in Isma'il's heart. "I will see what I can find out about this, discreetly, of course."

"Good," she said. "Before you go, I wish you to think upon something. Now that Majeed has been released temporarily, I would like you to become my acting vizier. The position will pay more and will require becoming my liaison to the noblemen of the Shah's court."

Panah bar Khoda! I was rocked by surprise to learn that Pari believed in me enough to make me her most trusted officer. I would have expected to serve for many years before receiving such an offer. A current of emotion rushed up and down my spine, and it took a moment before I could trust my voice.

"Thank you, esteemed princess. What a great honor! May I think about it until tomorrow?"

"Give me your answer in the morning. But please remember, Javaher, how much I have come to rely on you."

She said this so sweetly that I felt ready to lay down my life for her.

Khadijeh had moved into one of the buildings that the late Shah had used to house his favorite ladies. I told the eunuch on duty that I wished to see her on a matter of business for Pari Khan Khanoom, and he announced me and allowed me to pass.

Khadijeh received me dressed in a robe of orange silk, which was brightened by her clove-colored skin. Seeing her, so unlike the other courtiers draped in dark colors, was like happening upon a field of poppies. Gold bracelets made music at her wrists. She smiled at me, but because her ladies were present, maintained her formality. I told her I needed to see her on a delicate matter about a woman in distress. Khadijeh waved her chief lady, Nasreen Khatoon, to a distant corner of the room, where she could observe but not overhear. The planes of Nasreen's face were sharp and beautiful, but I only had eyes for Khadijeh.

"With all respect to your new status, you are even more glorious than ever to my eyes," I said quietly. "Your new post agrees with you."

Her smile was bright. "I am happy to be my own mistress."

"I am sure many are asking for your favor," I said, feeling a squeeze at my heart, "but I am here about a troubling matter."

"What is it?"

In a quiet voice, I told Khadijeh about Majeed's house and asked if she had heard anything from Isma'il that would help explain the ferocity of his anger.

Khadijeh looked as if she were searching for an answer. "I don't know him very well yet," she admitted. "He summons me at night and delights in my company, but doesn't say much."

"And you delight in his?" I could not help asking.

"It is not the same as with you," she said gently.

I was glad to hear that, but brought myself back to my duty. "Has he said anything at all about Pari?"

"You won't wish to hear it."

"I must hear it."

"He called her a pretend shah."

"On what grounds?"

"I can't remember. It was a passing comment."

I thought about it. "She has been leading the amirs in meetings, so I suppose in that way she resembles a shah."

"Shahs are men," she pointed out.

"So true," I said, "but she has the royal farr."

"He does, too," she said, "and he demands more deference than you might expect. I think his years as a prisoner have made him feel entitled to it. When he speaks to me about the cruel destruction of his youth by his father, the pain in his heart flares on his face like a flame. The princess should never appear to cross him."

"It will test her severely," I said.

"That is too bad. He is the Shah, and she has sworn obedience to him like everyone else."

"Has anything happened lately that he might hold against her?"

"I heard of one thing," Khadijeh said in a whisper. "Someone sent a group of soldiers to combat a rebellion in Khui. The Shah is very angry that it was done without his knowledge."

Ya, Ali!

"Was it Pari?"

"He didn't say."

I thought back to my last meeting with Pari; her answers now struck me as intentionally vague. My head grew hot with anger. Was I not to be informed of a clandestine military action of such a magnitude? Was my life to be put at risk without my consent? I might as well be one of Pari's tea boys.

As I struggled to master my feelings, I was certain I felt Nasreen Khatoon's eyes on me, but when I glanced up she was standing against the far wall of the room looking at the carpet in front of her.

"By the way," I said to Khadijeh in a lighter tone, "the color of your robe suits you very well."

"I keep a sober robe handy in case I need to throw it over my clothes when someone important comes to visit." She giggled at her own audacity.

"Your spirit refreshes my soul. Are you happy?"

"I have everything a woman could want," she said, gesturing around her. I noted the soft, new carpets on the floors, the matching velvet cushions, and a rich assortment of blue and white porcelain dishes arranged in alcoves. "And the best part is I have more time than ever to cook. Try this."

She handed me a plate of *paludeh,* the long thin rice noodles enlivened by sugar, cinnamon, rose water, and one strange spice I couldn't name, which shocked my tongue into uncommon joy.

I ate it in a rush of fierce hunger, licking my lips. This taste of Khadijeh's delights made me keenly aware of what I had been missing in past weeks. I dared not look at her for a moment.

"Little did he know what a treasure would come to him when he married you."

She smiled. "There is another thing that makes me happy, and that binds you and me together. The Shah has appointed my brother, Mohsen, as the master of cavalry to Mahmood Mirza. He loves his new posting."

"Congratulations. What does he say of the prince?"

"Mohsen said that the two of them get along like family."

"That gladdens me!"

"And you, how are you faring?" She didn't attempt to conceal the tenderness in her voice, which flayed my heart. My skin longed to feel the heat of hers, my nostrils cried out for the scent of her rose oil after it had mingled with her flesh, and my thumbs itched for the feel of her—

"Javaher?"

I clasped my hands in front of me to keep them still. "The princess asked me to be her acting vizier."

She looked awed. "What a big honor, and so soon!"

"But if the Shah dislikes her, it could prove to be a difficult job—and dangerous."

"I promise to let you know what I hear."

"Thank you."

"I imagine your new position will allow you to help your sister more than before."

"It will, but my chief desire is to bring her to the capital. I still don't have the funds necessary to care for her here or to provide her with a generous dowry."

"May God rain silver on your head!"

The memory of Jalileh's long lashes, made starry by tears the last time I saw her, pierced my heart. "I don't even know her anymore. All these years, I have not been able to visit her."

"How could you, when you have been sending all your extra money for her upkeep? I am certain you are the light of her eyes."

"I hope so."

Khadijeh noticed Nasreen Khatoon looking at us. "I think you had better take your leave."

"May I come again?"

"Yes. Be sure to come accompanied by court business," she replied, and called her ladies to rejoin her.

"Nasreen Khatoon, prepare a robe with some tunics and trousers for charity," she commanded. "You will deliver them to Javaher Agha when they are ready."

For Nasreen's ears, I said formally, "The princess will be pleased to know that you have pledged clothing to a woman who has lost her home. I will report to you how Rudabeh fares."

"It is my pleasure," Khadijeh replied.

With longing, I remembered the sweetness of her thighs under my tongue. The rip in my heart, which had just begun to heal, tore afresh and bled. It could not be helped: In the harem, there was no avoiding a former love and no escaping the relentlessness of desire. Khadijeh, who knew me so well, pretended to be busy with the paludeh so that I could preserve my dignity and take my leave.

Pari was drinking tea when I greeted her with a grim face.

"Javaher, do you bring me ill news?"

"Yes. I have thought carefully about your offer to make me your acting vizier. I am sorry, but I can't accept."

Pari looked shocked at my bluntness. No one but a fool would reject such a promotion.

"Are you joking?"

"No."

"What is it, money?"

"No."

"Are you frightened?"

"No."

"Well, then?"

I looked around as if I hated for the truth to be squeezed out of me and hesitated until I had her full attention.

"Princess, the game of this court is as intricate as the pattern on the carpet you are sitting on. A vizier and his commander must work together with as much unity as a husband and wife; otherwise they can lose everything."

"True. And so?"

"The best marriages, in my observation, are based on trust."

"Javaher, are you proposing to me?" she asked jokingly.

"In a manner of speaking."

I paused for effect and watched her eyes grow serious.

"Well?"

"My proposal—such as it is—goes further than the usual half-hearted alliances, as when a husband requires his wife to tell him everything while he enjoys living a secret life. Do you know what I mean?"

"Of course. Which of us is the husband?"

"You are."

She laughed. "That suits me better than the other way around."

"I know."

"So I shall wear the turban, spend the silver, and make the decisions."

"Yes."

"And what shall you do?"

"I shall provide excellent counsel and prevent you from making mistakes that could kill us both."

Pari looked uncomfortable. "Such as?"

"I have it on good authority that Isma'il has intercepted money sent to support soldiers on our northwestern border and is choking with rage."

"Oh," she said, and her face went white. She brushed at her kerchief, looking for absent strands of hair.

"Why didn't you tell me?"

"Javaher," she said passionately, "you know as well as I do that there are spies all over the palace. I have to be very careful about whom I trust."

"I know," I said. "That is why, in asking for your trust, I offer to lay down my life for you if necessary. But if you can't trust me, I would rather be in charge of your handkerchiefs than pretend to be your chief strategist."

I waited, firm in my resolve.

"Is there anything else?"

"Do I have permission to speak honestly?"

"Yes."

"To win over the Shah, you must cage your feelings."

"But he does nothing!" she cried, her cheeks blazing. "How can I stand by and watch the ruination of my father's hard work? How can I let the people who live around Khui rise up in rebellion—I, who know so much better than he what to do!"

"But, Princess, our job must be to persuade the Shah to do what is right."

"I don't wish to! I want to rule on my own," she blurted out, and then looked as if she had accidentally released an angry jinni from a bottle.

At long last, she had admitted it! In my bones I had sensed the ferocity of her ambition. It was like a mountain, looming over everything and impeding all progress. Now we could finally discuss what she craved and what was possible.

"Even your father didn't allow such liberties," I replied. "To rule at all, you must have a willing partner. At the moment, you face a shah who has thwarted and punished you."

Pari jumped up, her dark robe fanning out around her as if it wished to escape her fury. "Are you suggesting I have done something wrong? How dare you?"

I stood my ground. "I am the son of a noble," I said quietly, "and I trust that I have served you well so far. I respect your royal blood with every drop of my own, but, Princess, if I see you on a path to destruction, I will say so. Never shall I be like a cringing dog that evinces affection only in order to obtain scraps, even if you release me from your service—never! For I would rather tell you the truth at my own expense than betray you with false kindnesses. So I promised your father, and so I shall do always."

The blood pounded in my temples as I turned my gaze on her.

"You are the one who dips so freely in the ocean of smooth words," she replied angrily. "What do you suggest?"

"As your vizier, I would do my best to calm the waves," I said, "but it won't be possible if you keep taunting the Shah."

She sat down again, smoothing her robe around her. "I am willing to keep you better informed of my plans," she conceded, "but I won't promise to accede always to your advice."

I could see from her stormy brow that I had pushed her as far as was possible. "Agreed."

"Now are you willing to become my acting vizier?"

"It is the greatest honor of my life to accept," I replied. My heart soared like that of a soldier prepared to die for his commander. "I pledge to always encircle the emerald of your trust with the gold of my loyalty."

"That is better than any marriage vow I have ever heard!" she said, a hint of flirtation in her tone. "But I presume it is a metaphorical one."

"Of course."

"In that case, I accept."

The princess's eyes, which looked a little moist, sought mine. I felt as if we had made a pact binding us together forever.

Pari called Azar Khatoon and told her to fetch something. She returned with a package wrapped in silk and presented it to me. Inside I found a dagger in a black leather scabbard. Its fearsome steel blade bore protective words from the Qur'an worked in gold by a master metallist.

"May it keep you from harm," Pari said, in a voice more tender than she had ever used with me before. Then and there I fastened the scabbard to my sash.

"I will wear it always."

The next day, we discovered that Isma'il had quietly married two women. One of them was an Ostajlu, which demonstrated that he had forgiven the whole tribe and welcomed its nobles, except those that he had executed or imprisoned, back into his closest circles. The other was a big surprise: Shamkhal Cherkes's daughter Koudenet Cherkes, who had been raised away from court.

Pari was furious. She summoned her uncle, and he came after

dark, like a thief. Pari told me to sit in a nook outside one of her private rooms and observe the meeting secretly, so that I could remember his exact words and discern whether he was telling the truth. I suspected she wished to tongue-lash her uncle, but would spare him the humiliation of doing so in front of a servant.

When Shamkhal entered the small room, he consumed so much of its space that his muscular arms and chest seemed to press against the walls.

"Salaam, daughter of my sister!" he said in a booming voice as he lowered himself onto the cushion across from hers. "I am glad to see you looking as bright as the dawn itself. What is the emergency?"

"Is your health better, dear Uncle?" Pari replied sweetly.

"Better?"

"You were sick, remember?"

He paused for a moment. "Ah, of course! I am healthy now."

"That is good to hear. I assumed I didn't see you for so long because you were ill. And now I hear that your daughter has become one of the Shah's new wives! What an honor."

Shamkhal was watching her closely. "It is."

"I understand that the Shah has invited you to visit him every day, as well."

"Who told you that?"

Pari smiled with the certainty of her information.

"In short, the Shah has seen fit to favor you, while he has decided to punish me. Why is that? Don't we share the same blood?"

"We do."

"Well, then?"

"It is fate, I suppose."

"Uncle," Pari said, her tone sharp, "a shah does not marry the daughter of a man, thereby tying his bloodline to that of royalty for all time, unless that man has provided a great service to him or has promised to do so."

There was a long silence. Shamkhal looked terribly hot next to his glacial niece. In the small room I could see every bead of sweat that formed where his turban met his brow.

"Someone has damaged me in the eyes of the Shah. Having

noticed your recent success, I can't help but wonder if it has been responsible for my problems."

Shamkhal burst out laughing. "Of course not. You have managed to create your problems all by yourself."

"Such as?"

"Haven't you learned that this shah won't permit haughty behavior? You may be correct about the rebellion, but you have behaved like a fool."

Pari looked stung, and I was secretly glad. Her uncle was able to talk to her in a way that I could not.

"How do you expect to win him over now?"

"I don't know," she said bitterly. "Right now, I want you to answer my question: What have you done for Isma'il?"

"I took care of Haydar, remember?"

"Others helped vanquish him but were diminished anyway."

"I do whatever he asks."

Pari leaned her slender body toward his. "Have you spoken of me to him?"

"No."

"Why not?"

"Too dangerous."

"All this time, you have been thinking only of your own success!"

"Of course not," Shamkhal said, adjusting his legs underneath his robes. "Don't forget that I represent thousands of Circassians. If I am honored at court, all our people will benefit. We can't ignore that."

Pari gave him a knowing look. "And you yourself will become very rich."

"That, too. Remember, the Circassians have only been a force at court for thirty years. We still don't get the gifts of land and gold that the shah bequeaths to the qizilbash. The Circassians need a man like me to lobby for them."

He had a point, but the scorn in Pari's eyes was impossible to miss. "Don't you understand the Shah's strategy? He has offered you an alliance in order to curtail my power."

"True."

"I thought you were my ally."

"I am your ally forever," Shamkhal replied earnestly. "You are the child of my favorite sister, and there is no woman like you in all of Iran. But your desire to rule is not the only thing that matters."

Pari drew back, sensitive to the insinuation that she sought power for her own sake. "Haven't you noticed that nothing is getting done at court?"

"Of course. Isma'il doesn't know how to govern. He issues an order and then rescinds it. He has no idea whom to trust. His rule is a disaster so far."

"Then how do you expect to help?"

"I know you could do a better job and I will advocate for you when the Shah learns to trust me, but no advocacy will work unless you change your ways. Isma'il doesn't feel he owes you anything. He is suspicious of your power. If you don't bow down before him, you will never get anywhere."

"But he is incompetent!"

"Don't you understand? Your business now is rehabilitating yourself." His tone was kind but patronizing, as if he were addressing a child. How the power between them had shifted!

Pari was silent for a long time. Desperation entered her eyes. Even though her uncle was right, it disturbed me to see her suffer. I had to stifle an urge to interrupt their meeting.

"Uncle, my father honored you after I advocated for you. Now you must help me as I helped you."

"I will," he said, "but not right away. Our shah doesn't feel secure. That is why I visit him every day and do whatever he asks of me. That is why I have even offered him my best Circassian soldiers as his personal guards."

"Why didn't you defend me at the meeting?" Pari's back was pressed against her cushion as if she were trying to draw support from it.

"Because he is like unexploded gunpowder: One must not set him off."

Shamkhal reached for one of her hands and held it between his old bearlike paws.

"I will help you as soon as I can," he said. "Trust me."

That is what everyone said to Pari, yet who, in fact, could she trust?

"Daughter of my sister, I took a risk by coming to see you today. Isma'il would object if he knew, even though we are kin. For this reason, I am not going to visit again unless absolutely necessary. It is silly to fuel his anger right now."

Pari looked crestfallen; her long, thin frame seemed fragile compared to his robust one. "So you, too, are abandoning me?"

"Not abandoning you," he said. "Waiting quietly until we have a chance to pounce."

"Insh'Allah," she said softly, but when she sought the comfort of his gaze, his eyes flicked away.

After we discussed Shamkhal's advice, Pari finally admitted to the need to repair her relationship with Isma'il Shah. Together we drafted a letter to him begging forgiveness for any transgression and requesting a meeting to show her contrition. It was a fine document, filled with flowery language and deep submission. As Pari wrote it out in her excellent hand, she grimaced now and again. But it had its intended effect: The Shah summoned us to a meeting a few days later.

I put on the "head-to-toe" that Pari had sent to me right after I had accepted my new appointment. Although such garments always accompanied a big promotion, they were finer than I had expected. The dark blue silk robe was patterned with small pale blue irises on golden stems. The robe was brightened by a pale gold shirt, a blue and gold sash, and a golden turban striped pink, black, and blue. Dark leather shoes printed with gold arabesques completed the outfit. The fineness of the head-to-toe shouted out my new rank.

"As your new acting vizier," I said, enjoying the sound of the words, "I must remind you that the greatest humility will be required to move Isma'il's heart in your favor."

"I know, I know," she said impatiently.

We walked through the gardens and entered an elegant court-yard with a long rectangular pool of water flanked by caged parrots, which filled the air with their chattering. We stood by the pool until a eunuch arrived and showed us into a more secluded waiting room. After a while, we were summoned into Isma'il's private sanctum, the room where I imagined he met with Khadijeh and feasted on her beauty before taking her to his bedchamber to perform his nightly work. I tore my eyes away from the carved wooden door that led into his private quarters and tried not to think of how the servants outside would listen to the symphony of their grunts and cries. The bitterness of my feelings twisted in my belly and made me wonder whether I could ever love another woman. How could I let myself, knowing that she would one day push me aside?

When Pari and I were ushered into the room, I bowed with my hand on my heart. Sultanam was just leaving, but when the princess introduced me as her acting vizier, she congratulated me and greeted me as "the shining light of Pari's sword of wisdom." I thought of my father. How I hoped he was looking down on his son with pride!

The ceiling and the walls of the room were decorated with tiny mirrors arranged in patterns. Light came through a window in the roof and was reflected a hundred times into each shard of mirror, so that the room seemed to shimmer. Looking more closely, I saw a spot of darkness in the mirrors and realized it was the Shah's eye, shattered into prisms of darkness that were reflected a thousand times around us, as if he were watching our every pore.

The Shah lay reclined against silken cushions, his legs sprawled out in front of him, his jewel-studded turban flung to the side. With his balding head exposed, he looked like an ordinary man, as subject as anyone to the cruelties of nature. On a silver tray in front of him, tea steamed in glasses, accompanied by a six-sided inlaid ivory box.

"Come sit down," he said, his tone gentler than it had been dur-ing our last meeting.

The princess did so, while I hugged the wall at the back of the room to be close in case she needed anything.

"Light of the universe, I am here to do your bidding as your loyal sister," she said, her voice soft, her gaze averted.

He offered her a glass of tea, which she accepted, and took one himself. Opening the box in front of him, he removed a confection and placed it in his mouth but didn't offer one to Pari.

"I hope you are sincere in that desire," he replied. "I haven't seen evidence of it so far."

Pari stiffened but made an effort to be polite. "My brother, perhaps you haven't heard the details of what I have done on your behalf. It was I who gave my uncle the key to the harem so that he could lead his men onto the grounds and defeat those who supported Haydar."

"I have heard," he replied, "but of course, it was the will of God that I should come to power."

"And I was His instrument," she said, her voice low and soft. "I did what I could to assist you, and all I have wished for since then is to be your ally."

"My ally?" he replied. "You can't be my ally if you insist on going your own way. Your actions have proved to me that you are willful."

"What actions?"

"Funding an army."

My legs tensed in alarm. Pari didn't deny the charge, which would have been dangerous. Her cheeks bloomed with color, but her voice remained quiet.

"Do you think I can stand by and watch the disintegration of the momentous treaty our father fought for? What kind of daughter of the Safavis would I be?"

Isma'il looked away. "I have seen to that problem by appointing a new subgovernor of Azerbaijan, who will be responsible for investigating the problems in Khui."

"Who is it?"

"You will wait until I announce it to everyone at once."

He sat up on his cushion, his back straight and angry, as if responding to her unspoken charge. I suspected the Shah had not selected anyone, and Pari looked as if she thought the same.

"What about naming Ali Khan Shamlu? He is loyal," she pressed.

"Pari, you know as well as I do that we can't have two governments. Not even our father, who loved you so much, would have
permitted you that."

Pari sat up until she and Isma'il appeared to be of equal height.

"I don't want two governments," she said. "I only wish to ensure
our success in governing. Brother of mine, you were young once, and
I think you felt as I do. When you were sent away to the fortress at
Qahqaheh, it was because of your great zeal. Your mother told me
that you wanted to score such a decisive victory against the Ottomans that they would leave us alone for generations. You took it
upon yourself to raise an army for the good of your country, though
some called it a rebellion."

"That is true."

"With zeal similar to your own, I instructed Ali Khan Shamlu to
enforce the Treaty of Amasiyeh, and I spent my own money with the
sole purpose of protecting our land. Isn't it almost the same as what
you did? Don't we share the same royal blood?"

She opened her palms to the ceiling to emphasize her point, and
it was as if she were offering her open heart at the same time.

"The same blood—but not the same purpose. It was stupid of
our father to sign that treaty when I could have led us to victory."

"But that's all in the past now!" Pari protested. "Brother, I beg
you to let me help you," she added in a pleading tone that made me
hope for the best. "I advised our father for years, and I could be as
useful to you as I was to him."

"You didn't move a muscle without his approval," he replied. "Yet
you have tried to move a fighting force without my say. I am a military man, while you have never even seen a battlefield. The fact that
you dare to employ such grandiose tactics can be explained by only
one thing: pride."

He tapped two fingers against his box of confections to emphasize his last few words.

"Pride? But this is what I have trained for all my life," Pari protested. "I didn't learn by my father's side for so many years for nothing."

"I differ from our father on this point," Isma'il replied. "He didn't
wish you to marry and leave him."

"Nor did I wish to marry."

"I suspect you didn't know who you were getting when I became shah," he said. "If you had wanted to rule through someone, you should have thrown yourself behind Haydar."

"Haydar didn't have the makings of a shah," Pari said. "But if for some reason he and his soldiers had won, my support for you would have meant my death at his hands. You have shown courage on the battlefield, and I have tried to show my mettle here at the palace. I thought—I hoped—you would be pleased by my fealty."

The edges of Pari's silk robe trembled.

"Your fealty?" His laugh sounded as ghastly as the howl of jackals at night. "Whatever do you mean? You once said that as a child you loved me, but where is the truth in that?"

Pari stared at him, perplexed. "You doubt the love that I bore you as a little girl? Surely you must have felt how I wanted to burst with joy when you spent time with me."

"And I loved you as if you were my own daughter," he said, and the truth of his feelings clouded his eyes. "I would have done anything for you."

"And I for you," Pari replied.

He laughed again. "If only I could believe that were true."

"What makes you doubt it?"

"If you loved me so much, what did you do to release me from prison when you had our father's ear?"

"Release you from prison? I was a child of eight when you were taken away!"

"You weren't a child forever. You could have urged our father to set me free. Did you ever speak in my favor?"

"You don't understand. Our father turned yellow at the very mention of your name, sometimes even at the mention of another man with the same name as yours. I remember that when one of the nobles referred to his own father as a donkey, the Shah reached over and struck him in the face. The man was lucky to escape with his life. Another time, he asked his children to recite poetry to him, and I began reciting a tale from the *Shahnameh* about how two of the sons of the legendary king Fereydoon had rebelled against him and tried to destroy him, although he had given them most of his kingdom. Our father began to look very ill, and without warning, he vomited in front of everyone. I didn't understand why until I was older and realized that what he saw as your rebellion tormented him every day. Even your mother couldn't change his mind, although she begged him so often that he refused to see her or visit her bed. How could I, as a child, hope to calm such wrath?"

"Did you ever try?" he repeated, his small black eyes fierce.

Pari remained silent.

"That is what I thought," he said. "And why would you? By the time you were fourteen, you had his ear to yourself. If you had succeeded in bringing me home, I would have usurped your place. I was the golden son, beloved by all, and the warrior who had led the country to victory. How could you have competed with that? You would have married Badi al-Zaman and lived in some far-flung province for the rest of your life."

"That was never in my plans," she replied. "It never occurred to me that I could gain some advantage through your disgrace."

"And yet you did," he replied. "You were my father's companion while I wasted my youth. For this reason I am just now trying to beget sons as an old man, and I have shriveled in body and in mind. It is a wonder I didn't become a madman, locked away as I was! But what happened to me is ugly enough."

His eyes burned with anger as if he thought Pari was responsible for everything he had endured. For the first time, I understood the extent to which the fortress at Qahqaheh had imprisoned Isma'il's soul, darkened his heart, and blackened his vision. It was chilling to see his feelings so nakedly displayed.

"I was not the shah to make such decisions about your fate," Pari replied staunchly. "Our father sent away his own mother and punished his own brother when they rebelled. On the heels of that, how could I convince him of your innocence?"

Isma'il snorted. "Sultanam told me you did everything you could to shut her out. You pushed all the royal women away and took the place that belonged to me."

"I could never hope to be you, brother of mine," she said.

Isma'il bucked impatiently against his cushion, and the tiny mirrors in the room reflected his movement a thousand times before becoming calm again.

"Then why did you try?"

Pari's face was flushed, and yet I saw goose bumps on her arms. Her chin jutted forth defiantly.

"The minute it was possible to do so, I delivered the palace to you."

Isma'il sat up against his cushion, and now somehow he seemed the taller of the two.

"You are as aggressive as a man. Not long after I arrived at court, Mirza Shokhrollah told me how you pushed the men to declare you had the royal farr. What could be more insulting to a new shah? How dare you assert such a thing? But now the royal farr has passed to me. You are no longer the Shah's favorite, and you may not make policy decisions on your own. If you do, I will consider it an act of disobedience. Is that understood?"

The cords at Pari's neck tightened and she looked as if she were choking. She bent her head and remained silent long enough for him to know that her reply was given under protest.

"Chashm, gorbon," she said, her voice thick with anger.

Now that it was clear that Isma'il thought Pari had usurped him from the time she was a child, I surmised that he had interpreted all of her subsequent actions as part of the same grab for power. As her new vizier, I must intervene.

"Light of the universe, may I have permission to speak?"

The Shah looked as if he would welcome any diversion. "You may."

"We are so awed by the royal radiance that we cannot always say what is foremost in our hearts," I said, speaking for myself and Pari. "If there have been errors in the past, we are deeply regretful, and we seek only to right them in the royal eyes."

"It is fitting that you are awestruck by my presence."

"How can we serve in a way that would please the light of the universe? That is the reason we live and breathe. We will do anything"—I looked at the princess for confirmation—"that would satisfy the shadow of God on earth."

Isma'il glanced at Pari. She clenched her jaw, bowed her head, and humbled herself as far as she could.

"Brother of mine, I swear that is my fondest wish," she said.

"How can I know that you will work for me, not just for yourself?"

"I would like to prove myself to you—to be your confidante—to use all I have learned to advance your interests."

Pari was on the right track at last. Kiss his feet! I commanded her in my head.

"There is so much I can do," Pari continued, and I became ill at ease again. Why couldn't she stop there?

"I can advise you on the best governors to rule, recount the deeds of all the khans who served our father when you were away, or provide you with suggestions for wives—and that is just the beginning."

He looked skeptical again, his desire to believe her fading as quickly as it had bloomed.

"I have plenty of men to advise me," he said.

"Then what can I do?"

He was at a loss, but then he rallied. "If you like, I will arrange a marriage for you to help fill your days. Small children are very demanding of their mothers."

Pari shivered as if ill with a fever, and I was reminded of a maple denuded of all its leaves by an autumn wind.

"How very gracious," she replied coldly, "but I prefer to remain alone and devoted to the memory of our father."

"It is up to you," he said indifferently.

Yet again, I was maddened by his lack of statecraft. After you kick a faithful dog, even if it has misbehaved, you would be well advised to throw it a bone. Otherwise, don't be surprised if it sinks its fangs into your throat. But it was Pari's task to try to tame him, since she had the most to lose, and instead she had merely managed to make him growl.

As we left, Pari looked as if the fire that raged inside her might consume all who were near her. Her cheeks and her normally pearly forehead were red, and a wave of heat emanated from her body. I didn't dare to touch her even by accident for fear she might loose her rage upon me.

When we were in the gardens far from malicious gossips, Pari's words tumbled out on top of one another. "How dare he claim the royal farr! It remains with whoever deserves it most," she said between gritted teeth. "We will see who that is."

"We already know it is you."

Pari sighed. "I have been given all the tools of a ruler—except the blind, blunt instrument that seems to matter—but none of the opportunities. When I read through history, my desires don't strike me as so exceptional. Genghis Khan placed his daughters on the throne in every corner of his empire, where they ruled in his name. Our qizilbash ancestors allowed women more freedom because they lived a nomadic life. Those traditions are being buried, alas, and our women with them."

"It is the same in many places," I replied. "Yet the ruler of England has been a woman for the last twenty years because her father didn't produce a male heir."

"That is not quite true," said Pari. "King Henry had a son or two, but they weren't born of the one wife he was allowed to marry at any given time. What a foolish practice to deny his children their patrimony."

"It is very limiting," I agreed.

"But what a boon for Elizabeth. Here we are awash in male heirs; the dozens of women my father bedded made sure of that. My only chance is as an advisor to one of his grown sons or as a regent, which would suit me best."

"You would be an excellent ruler," I replied, "but I must admit I had to learn this by serving you. Esteemed princess, I used to think my father superior to my mother. After I began serving the royal women, I learned they could surpass men in intelligence and strategizing."

"How well you understand! Sometimes I feel like the one solitary creature of my kind, malcontent with the way the world is made and my place in it. Yet what am I but what those around me have created?"

Her black eyes became as transparent as pools, and I felt as if I could see straight into the dark loneliness of her soul, which reminded me of my own.

"Lieutenant of my life," I replied softly, "I empathize with your troubles with all my heart."

She put her hand on my arm. "I know you do," she replied. "How curious it is that you were sent to me: I would never have expected to feel such kinship with a eunuch."

The tender bud in my heart bloomed, its petals unfurling so quickly that my chest ached.

"Remember when I asked you, months ago, about how you got cut? I know you suffered a great deal. Selfishly, though, I am glad it was your fate, because otherwise I would never have come to know you as I do. What a precious jewel you are! How brightly you shine!"

It was a sign of her great generosity that she lavished such compliments on me right after her lowest moment with the Shah. Feelings that I had never allowed to show prickled my eyes. Rather than being criticized or derided for what I didn't have, I felt appreciated, for the first time, for all I knew and could do. An understanding passed between us that seemed as bottomless as a well.

With great delicacy, Pari suggested that perhaps I wished to return to my quarters and refresh myself with afternoon tea.

CHAPTER 5

TEARS OF BLOOD

One of Zahhak's subjects was a blacksmith named Kaveh, who worked hard at the forge every day to support his family of eighteen sons. Kaveh was a blessed man until Zahhak began requiring each household to deliver a tribute of young men to feed the hungry snakes on his shoulders. Kaveh's bounty of sons made him unluckier than most. He watched his sons get taken away one by one, and each time, their heads were smashed and their brains delivered to the serpents. The blood boiled within Kaveh, but what could he do? No one dared refuse an order from the king.

At the palace, Zahhak's peace was still being disturbed by his nightmare about Fereydoon and by intimations that his own rule had been unjust. One day, he decided to create a record of his reign that would clear his name for all time. He ordered his scribes to write a proclamation describing him as a paragon of justice in every respect. Then he commanded the nobles of his court to sign the statement. Once again, no one dared refuse an order from the king.

As the days grew darker, colder, and shorter, a new order was created at the harem. Sultanam, who had the Shah's ear, was at the top, with the Shah's new wives jockeying for power below her. Pari, who was now firmly associated with her dead father and the past, had been neutered. No longer her father's advisor or the protector of the dynasty, she was relegated to the role that out-of-favor women played, doomed to struggle to find relevance in any way she could. In this, she was like many courtiers who strove to ingratiate themselves to the court after dishonor. But if Isma'il reigned for a long time, it would be a long wait.

When someone fell out of favor with a shah, it was common to enlist allies to help with rehabilitation. The allies would report on the offending party's feelings of contrition and would request clemency, or suggest a way to placate the shah. They would look for moments when he might be likely to soften, such as times of good fortune or religious celebrations that incited feelings of charity. Such petitions could carry on for months or years and might require enduring punishment. But I was hopeful. The Ostajlu were now the Shah's best friends again. It could be done, and it could be done in a matter of months, as my own case had shown.

"Princess, be patient," I told Pari. "I myself once endured the same cold winter. The best thing we can do now is to enlist your allies' help in creating a thaw."

I said this in part to try to console myself. With Pari so out of favor, my new role as her acting vizier didn't provide the access I had expected, but rather obscurity and irrelevance.

During that time, Pari spent long hours in correspondence, writing to kinswomen and courtiers all over the realm to keep apprised of goings-on and to petition those who could help her. After she asked for assistance from her half sister Gowhar, who was married to Ibrahim Mirza, Gowhar revealed that despite Ibrahim's support for Haydar, he had been invited to visit the Shah daily and had been selected as the Guardian of the Shah's Most Precious Seal. She promised to talk to Ibrahim and let Pari know if there were any opportunities to soften the Shah's heart. Gowhar was delightfully irreverent; once when she visited Pari, she sang a song Ibrahim had composed that referred to Shamkhal as the Ingratiator, Mirza Shokhrollah as the Naysayer, and the Shah as the Vacillator. Pari laughed so hard, she told me, she was at pains not to spit out a slice of quince.

The princess and I agreed that Mirza Shokhrollah's position as grand vizier was a great obstacle. In addition to the fact that he had criticized her in the Shah's presence, he was neither efficient nor clever. Isma'il needed a smart deputy who could compensate for his own weaknesses. Pari began doing what the royal women have always done: working quietly to discredit an official she disliked and replace him with her own man.

We decided it was wise to continue to cultivate Mirza Salman. Pari asked me to visit him and take his measure, but before I could, he sent a message asking to see the princess, even though the Shah had expressly forbidden the nobles from visiting her.

From behind the lattice, Mirza Salman told us that he had been reconfirmed as Guardian of the Royal Guilds. We both felt that he deserved much better. He also reported that the business of the court was at a standstill—many governors had not been appointed, the Councils of Justice were barely functioning, and the rebellion in Khui had been ignored. For about an hour, the three of us strategized about whom to contact and what exactly they could do to throw doubt on Mirza Shokhrollah's effectiveness.

"Ah, Princess! I miss your glorious efficiency," said Mirza Salman as he prepared to take his leave.

"Thank you," she replied. "I have dreams of reshaping the court so that it is neither the strict and pious regime of my father nor the lackadaisical playground Isma'il prefers, but rather one that re-creates the glorious age that produced so many great poets and thinkers: Hafez and Rumi, Avicenna and Khayyam—such an age requires prosperity, peace, and tolerance. Yet it is possible, I swear."

"It will rival the promise of paradise!" Mirza Salman said, his eyes shining.

"It is worth dying for," I added.

***

Pari's quarters had always been filled with people, but after she fell out of favor, they were eerily quiet. I was able to spend more time at her side, helping her compose letters and discussing strategies for her rehabilitation. Sometimes, on cold days, we created a *korsi* by throwing blankets over a table and heating up the space underneath it with a charcoal brazier. Then we thrust our legs under the blankets—*awkh joon!*—and recited poetry to one another, including our own compositions. Pari shared her heart with me more than before, telling me of the great sorrows of her young life—the loss of a beloved mare, the death of her favorite aunt, Maheen Banu, but most of all, about her passionate desire to steer Iran into a period of greatness. I began to feel, when we were alone, that we were not just princess and servant—we were *hamrah*, companions on the same road.

One day, Pari confessed her fear that Isma'il would try to claim Maryam, her dearest treasure, as a way of punishing her further. Her eyes grew soft when she spoke of Maryam, which emboldened me to ask about her.

"How did she first find favor with you, Princess?"

"Her father offered her to the court because he had eight daughters and no dowry money. I was fifteen then, and I urged my father to take her in. After five years of training as a hairdresser, Maryam entered my service. Before I knew it, she had bewitched me."

"And you, her."

A handsome blush appeared on Pari's cheeks.

"I have made her wealthy, but she tells me she finds all the riches in the world by my side." She glowed with satisfaction as she said this, and I thought about how often she must have faced sycophants who pretended to love her. I was glad that she was not blind, like so many other courtiers, to honest feeling.

"And what has become of her sisters?"

Pari looked at me curiously. "God be praised, she has provided six of them with excellent dowries."

"Princess, I confess there is someone I wish to help in the same way," I blurted out. My heart was full as I confided in her about Jalileh and showed her one of my sister's letters, which I kept in an inside pocket of my robe. Pari glanced at it and was sufficiently impressed to read out loud the part where Jalileh revealed her ecstatic feelings about Gorgani's poetry.

"What a thoughtful child! Surely no one is more important to you in the world."

"Except for you, lieutenant of my life."

She ignored the flattery, which pleased me. "And how strange that you, too, have had to live far away from a beloved sibling."

"It is a dagger through my heart. My fondest wish would be to bring Jalileh to serve in the harem, if you think there might ever be an appropriate position."

I waited with trepidation, knowing I was asking for a great privilege.

Pari's eyes were sympathetic. "I will try to grant your request, but not yet. It will not be wise until I am returned to favor."

My heart soared with new hope, and I wrote to my mother's cousin right away to tell her the news. I worried that my letter was premature, but I was so eager to brighten Jalileh's long exile that I sent it anyway. Then I redoubled my efforts to help restore Pari's reputation.

On the longest night of the year, the royal women usually stayed up very late together, telling stories, eating soup, feasting on pomegranate seeds and sweets, and celebrating the coming return of the light. After everyone went to sleep, I used to creep into Khadijeh's warm bed. Even though I could no longer do that, the arrival of the shortest day of the year made me long for her.

After my bath, I dressed in a fur-lined hat and robe to fight the cold. In the palace gardens, my breath steamed white around my face, and everyone I passed was veiled in the same way. I thrust my hands into my sleeves to keep warm. The trees in the palace gardens were stark and lined with snow, the flowers long gone, the bushes pruned back. The snow had been cleared from the palace walkways but the ground was frozen, and before long, I could feel the cold pushing its way through my leather boots.

On my way to Khadijeh's, I passed a woman who reminded me of Fereshteh, my erstwhile lover. She had the huge dark eyes and rosebud mouth that I had so admired in Fereshteh when I was young. I was seized with nostalgia for our time together and wondered what had become of her.

It had been a revelation to show Fereshteh all my parts and to explore, with the enthusiasm of a nomad conquering new mountain passes, every corner of her body. It was she who first explained to me the mysteries of women's cycles. With no shame, she showed me her blood. With no shame, she reached for my *keer*. The sex words she used reddened my sheltered ears, then stiffened me like a tent pole. I had never known another woman as frank as she. I still hoped to see her again one day and tell her of my strange fate.

I entered Khadijeh's building, saluting the eunuch on duty. The thick walls of the building defeated the worst of the cold, and the rooms were heated by charcoal braziers. Even so, I kept my outer robe wrapped around me and quickly drank the cardamom tea I was offered when I stepped inside.

The spice made my blood circulate faster, and my heart thudded in my chest. After some time, a seamstress came out of Khadijeh's rooms, holding in her arms several new silk robes that had been pinned to indicate changes. I was shown in, and Khadijeh greeted me formally. She wore a violet robe that made her skin look like dark satin. Her high-cheekboned lady, Nasreen Khatoon, gave me an appraising glance.

"Your arrival brings happiness, Javaher Agha," Khadijeh said.

"Thank you," I replied. "I wished to tell you about the fate of Rudabeh, the woman for whom I requested help the last time I visited you. She has written to my commander from Khui to inform her that her case has finally been settled there."

"That is excellent news," Khadijeh said.

I rubbed my hands together and shivered as if I were still cold. Khadijeh turned to her lady and said, "See to it that our guest is served hot coffee."

"Chashm."

Nasreen rose to do her bidding, leaving us alone except for a eunuch who sat out of earshot near the door. Coffee was new to the court, and only the favored had access to it. It would have to be boiled fresh, unlike tea, which always simmered at the ready in a samovar. That would give us more time.

When we were finally alone, Khadijeh's whole body relaxed. I thought of her tamarind skin and how it once seemed to warm like honey under my hands.

"How are you? You look as lovely as the moon."

"I am well," she replied in a soft voice, "but not as well as I was."

"The new wives?"

"Not just that," she replied. "It is that I see him less now that he has new women, and my chances to bear his child decrease."

"You have hardly begun!"

"Yes, but the more distracted he is, the less he will visit, and the less likely are my hopes."

I couldn't argue with that logic, but I said, "With you so moon-like? You have no competition."

"Ah, but I do," she replied. "You won't believe what has already happened—and why I am so fearful."

She rubbed her nose with a gesture so endearing I wanted to wrap my arms around her.

"Khadijeh, soul of mine, what is it?" The endearment escaped my lips.

"She is pregnant!"

"Who?"

"Mahasti, a slave that he has taken, like me, in a temporary marriage. She is one of those straw-haired women from the Caucasus whose pale beauty is so prized."

"She is already with child?"

Fresh agony filled her dark eyes.

"How do you know?"

"My ladies talk with her maids. She has been sick every morning, but at the midday meal she eats like a starved dog. She has an obviously thickening belly and complains of sore breasts at the hammam, and her servant has been boasting so loudly it will be a wonder if she doesn't call down the evil eye on the child."

"That is very reckless of her."

"But why isn't it me? I have been with him the longest."

"Remember, when other women are heavy with child, he will turn to you at night. You will have him to yourself again!"

My heart dripped tears of blood as I comforted her, and I tried to pretend that I meant what I said. I was rewarded when a wan smile flashed on her face.

"I hadn't thought of that," she said.

"Khadijeh, who wouldn't want you?"

She smiled again, even more sadly.

"Has he said anything to you about the pregnancy?"

"Not a word, but he talks endlessly about how he longs for an heir, like all men."

I tried to keep my face neutral, but hearing this from Khadijeh was like a dagger in my heart. I wondered for a second what the child of our loins would look like, and a curly-headed boy with a mischievous laugh danced in my head, tormenting me.

"Please forgive me," she said quickly.

"It is nothing." It would do no good to discuss this with her, and I must make haste before her lady returned.

"And that is not the only news. An astrologer told him the child will be a boy."

"You must make a charm for yourself—you are good at that."

"I face Mecca every day and pour water on my head. I make tonics to aid fertility, including one with ground rhinoceros horn. Still, pray for me. If you happen to go to a shrine, be sure to whisper my suit to the saint."

It cost every fiber of goodness that I had within me to say, "I promise." She looked so hopeful I was happy to have lightened her mood.

"Before your lady returns, I must ask you—has he said anything lately about the princess?"

"He hasn't mentioned her name," she replied, "but he is always frightened that someone will try to usurp him. Whenever he disrobes at night, he takes off his sword and dagger and lays them within arm's distance of the bedroll so he can find them in the dark."

"I can't blame him."

Khadijeh leaned closer and whispered, "Once, in the middle of the night, I arose to get a drink of water, and when I returned, he threw himself on top of me and reached for his dagger, shouting 'assassin!' The guards rushed in, but by then he had felt my breasts against his chest and understood his mistake. His eyes looked as unpredictable as a wild dog's, and he chided me for misleading him. I was so frightened that after he fell asleep, I pressed my body close to his so that he wouldn't forget I was there, and I didn't close my eyes for the rest of the night." She shivered.

Isma'il remained so troubled about his own safety that he had come close to murdering my beloved Khadijeh! I had to shove my hands into my sleeves to quell my urge to throttle him.

"Poor creature!" I said. "If anything ever happened to you, I would—"

Khadijeh hushed me gently with her eyes.

"It is all so strange," I added. "The treasury functionaries count and recount every piece of silver for fear of being one coin short. The formerly gleeful bandits are so wary of him that they have stopped robbing travelers. Not even the qizilbash chiefs dare to rebel."

"Every day Isma'il was in prison, he expected to be assassinated. That hasn't changed. I think he fears his own kin the most."

"But he doesn't fear you. Otherwise he wouldn't leave his dagger within reach."

Nasreen walked in a moment later with coffee on a silver tray. I thanked her, adding that I would enjoy chasing the cold from my blood, and I drank the coffee in a few gulps.

"May your hands never ache!" I said. The coffee Khadijeh served was the best. I ate a rice flour and pistachio pastry, which I recognized immediately as Khadijeh's own from the way it tickled my tongue, and then I pretended that we were still speaking about Rudabeh.

"To finish my story, she has just regained possession of her house. She is so overjoyed that she sent you a gift."

I unrolled a piece of embroidery displaying poppies and roses. It was stitched on pale cotton in an extremely fine hand, so fine you could not distinguish the individual stitches.

Khadijeh touched the cloth. "What skilled fingers! Please convey my thanks to Rudabeh, and tell your commander I am always happy to help a woman in distress."

"I will do so." With that, I protested that I had already consumed too much of her time and said my farewells.

I was stricken with concern for Khadijeh. What if the Shah had attacked her before coming to his senses? His mind was even more disturbed than I had realized, and his nighttime fears were the proof.

When I entered Mirza Salman's waiting room for the first time as Pari's vizier, I felt as if I had arrived at the pinnacle of my career. Mirza Salman's salon was filled with qizilbash nobles and other men of high stature. Men went in and out of his rooms at a regular pace, an efficiency that pleased me. Because of my new status, I was shown in quickly.

Mirza Salman worked in a small, elegant room with arched openings in the walls, attended by two scribes who sat on either side of him with wooden desks on their laps. One of them was finishing a document, while the other sat poised for current business. Mirza Salman congratulated me on being appointed Pari's vizier, and I thanked him for seeing me. I told him that Pari wished for him to know the sad news that her cousin Ibrahim's brother, Hossein, had died unexpectedly in Qandahar, leaving the province without a governor. The Shah had honored Ibrahim and Gowhar by visiting them to express his sympathy, but had forbidden them from wearing black.

Mirza Salman frowned. "And so?"

"Hossein was running Qandahar as if it were his own. There were concerns he might rebel by making an alliance with the Uzbeks."

"So now that Hossein is dead," he said, "the Shah has no reason to be kind to Ibrahim?"

Mirza Salman had a quick brain.

"That is what the princess fears. She has written to Ibrahim and Gowhar to tell them she thinks they should leave town, especially since they supported Haydar. She wants to know if you can help them."

"I will try."

"Meanwhile, Pari has asked her uncle to advocate on your behalf. He remains in good standing with the Shah and will look for opportunities to suggest that you be promoted."

"Thank you."

"It is always my pleasure to serve."

Mirza Salman scrutinized me for a moment. I sensed that he wished to take my measure now that I was Pari's vizier.

"You say that as if you really mean it."

"I do."

"Your personal sacrifice is still mentioned at court as a paragon. What an uncommonly large gift you gave to the throne!"

"Larger than you could possibly imagine," I joked.

Mirza Salman laughed but couldn't conceal a slight shudder. He eyed me the way one regards an unpredictable sharp-toothed animal, with a mixture of curiosity and horror.

"With balls as big as that, perhaps you should have been a soldier."

"I like this job better."

"I have always dreamed of being a military man," he said, and I noticed that he had decorated one of his walls with old standards used in battle. "But administrators like me are thought to be too soft."

I made the obligatory sounds of protest.

"Now that your star is ascending, I will keep my eye on you," he added.

"Thank you," I said, wondering if I could goad him into revealing some information. "I always wished to fulfill my father's dreams for me, especially after what happened to him."

"I remember your father," Mirza Salman replied. "A good man, true to the throne. I imagine he was pulled off his course by smaller minds."

I felt perspiration under my arms. My heart began to race and questions flooded through me, but I concealed my feelings.

"I suppose you are right," I said agreeably. "Do you know who pulled him off course?"

"No."

"Naturally, I have always wanted to know more about the circumstances of his death. We were never told."

I tried not to appear overly eager.

"Did you check the court histories?"

I thought quickly about how to get him to talk. "There is only a brief mention of the accountant who killed him," I lied. "No doubt you recall who it was. I have always heard that your memory far surpasses that of ordinary men."

Mirza Salman looked pleased and thought for a moment. "He had one of those common names . . . Isfahani? Kermani? Wait a minute . . . Ah, yes! Kofrani, that is it. If I am not mistaken, his first name was Kamiyar."

Finally, a name! I played along. "What a memory you have! How did you hear about his involvement?"

"Palace rumor, I suppose. It has been so long, I don't remember the source."

"Has he retired?"

Mirza Salman was watching me closely. "Alas, he went to meet God a few years after leaving palace service."

I had been congratulating myself on luring Mirza Salman into my trap, but now I realized he was far too careful to make a slip: He wouldn't have uttered the man's name if he had been alive.

"May he meet his just reward."

"Would you wish to revenge yourself upon him, if he were living?" he asked. "He was an excellent man. I wouldn't be surprised if he thought he was protecting the Shah."

I had to decide in an instant if it would be better for him to think me fierce or flaccid. For Pari's protection, I decided on the former.

"I would cut him."

Mirza Salman was no innocent, but he stared at me as if I were a crazed dog who might attack for no reason.

"But if he killed my father mistakenly, perhaps I would just lop off his male parts and call it even," I joked.

Mirza Salman laughed uneasily.

"Do you know why he was never punished?"

"No." His eyes flicked away, and I had a feeling he knew more than he was saying.

I thanked him and left, abuzz with the name that he had planted in my mind. Kamiyar Kofrani. The murderer of my father. The name was ugly, and the man must have been, too. But worst of all, he was dead, and Mirza Salman had confirmed my father's guilt. Now I could neither argue his innocence nor revenge myself on his killer. After all these years, I had finally collected a missing piece of colored clay from the mosaic of my own past, but I was too late to do anything about it.

That night, I waited impatiently for Balamani to finish his work so that I could tell him what I had learned. I longed for the sweet relief of confiding in a friend, and I hoped he would be able to shed more light on what had happened. But he did not arrive at the usual time.

The hours went by, the moon rose, and still Balamani did not appear. I began reading the *Shahnameh* that Mahmood had given me, and its felicitous rhymes helped keep me awake for a long time before I succumbed to sleep, the book on my chest. When finally Balamani entered our chamber, it was daylight. He removed his outer robe and sat on his bedroll, his face drawn with fatigue.

"What happened?"

"One of the Shah's women was pregnant, but she lost the baby a few hours ago. She is sick with grief."

"Mahasti?"

"No, another slave. She was losing a lot of blood. We sent for a physician and a woman schooled in religion to console her."

"That is terrible news."

"Then I had to go to the Shah's quarters and wait until he arose to tell him what happened. He took his time."

Balamani looked more melancholy than I would have expected. "What is troubling you so?"

He threw himself back on his bedroll. "While the lady was suffering, I was flooded with memories of my mother's death. I was only about four years old. A group of women came to our house and shut me out of her room; I remember their awful wails. No one ever told me what happened, but now I suspect that my mother died in childbirth. Today I had the eerie feeling that I was one of the attendants at her deathbed. I feel sometimes as if all the moments of my life existed simultaneously—as if I am living in the past and present at the same time."

"May God keep the souls of your family in His gentle embrace."

He sighed. "You are lucky to have a sister. In memory of my lost sibling, I shall give double my usual amount to the orphans of Qazveen. And now, tell me your news. Why are you awake so early?"

I sat up. "Balamani, I have finally learned the name of my father's killer. It was Kamiyar Kofrani!" I blurted out.

"You mean the accountant? How do you know?" He didn't sound as surprised as I thought he would be.

"Mirza Salman told me."

"Are you sure he is the right man?"

"Do you think Mirza Salman would lie?"

"Any man can lie."

I thought his answer very strange. "What about this Kofrani—was he a good servant?"

"Yes. One of the best."

I did not like the sound of that.

"And his children?"

"He had three boys. One of them is dead, but I am fairly certain the other two serve the government in Shiraz, and have wives and children."

"Which I will never have. I hope they all burn in hell." I stared at him suspiciously. "How do you come by so much information about them?"

"Javaher, you know that I know almost every family who has served at court for the last fifty years."

I lifted the blanket off my bedroll with so much force that it flew onto the floor.

Balamani shrugged off the rest of his clothes and got into his bed. "My friend, I can understand why you are angry. But since the man is dead, what can you do?"

I glared at him from my bedroll. "That is good advice—unless your father has been murdered, in which case something must be done."

"Remember that I lost my father all the same. Or rather, he lost me to a slaver. But I haven't been spending my time trying to track down the merchant who chopped off my eight-year-old penis and sold me to court."

"Wasn't it wrong?"

He snorted. "If it wasn't, Muslims would castrate their own boys instead of buying gelded Hindus and Christians."

"Aren't you angry?"

"It is not that simple. If I hadn't lost my *keer*, I would never have feasted on kabob, lived in a palace, or worn silk. My family was as poor as dirt."

"Balamani, stop equivocating."

Compassion softened his eyes. "My young friend, it is not just your father's murderer you have to forgive."

"Who is it then?"

"Yourself."

"For what?"

"For what you did."

Rage surged through me. "All this time, I thought you wanted to help me!"

"Of course I do," he replied, but for the first time I could remember, he sounded as if he didn't really mean it. I maintained an angry silence. Balamani rolled over and began snoring before I could think of what to say next.

A group of Sufis met on Thursdays to whirl their way closer to God. From time to time, I attended their *sama* to imbibe the peacefulness of the ceremony. After hearing the news about my father, I decided to avoid the usual Thursday-evening leisure activities, which I had no stomach for, and go to the *sama*. I sent a message to Pari that I was ill and left the palace through a side gate.

The Sufis gathered in a large building with windows high in the walls and roof, so that the room was dappled as if in the shade of a walnut tree. When I arrived late in the afternoon, the ceremony had already begun. The anguished notes of the flute called out the desire of the reed for reunion with its maker, throwing me deeper into memories of my father.

I took a place on a cushion and watched the Sufis whirl. They wore long white tunics belted at the waist, white trousers, and tall tan hats, while their spiritual leaders performed music to help guide their journey. The aspirants used one leg as a pivot, turning their bodies around it with surprising speed. To keep their balance and channel divine energy, they lifted one arm to the sky, palm up, and directed the other to the earth, palm down. They whirled for a long time, turning as gracefully as a leaf twirling on an autumn breeze. Their inward-focused eyes made it look as if they had briefly left the earth, and their white tunics billowed around them so that they resembled the pure white roses in the royal gardens.

I weighed the burdens on my heart. My father, whose soul cried for justice. My mother, who had died without the satisfaction of seeing her family's honor restored. My sister, who had been deprived of the ordinary happiness of growing up with loving parents and siblings. I thought of the parts of my body that were missing and of the sons I would never have. Had I made the right choice, if I could not avenge my father? Had my sacrifice been for nothing? As I watched the Sufis whirl, I wished I could spin with them and purge my heart of all its suffering.

Eventually, the music slowed and the men began turning more slowly until they gradually came to a halt. They paused to collect themselves, then drifted to a group of cushions to sit and refresh themselves with tea and sweetmeats. They looked peaceful and happy. I envied their stillness. In the press of my daily service to Pari, it was easy to forget that such communion between the self and the divine was a gift always at hand.

An older man with a face as lined and as bumpy as a walnut shell sat down beside me. I greeted him and asked about his health.

"Don't worry about me," he said. "The world is ending, alas! And it is all because of a sheep."

"Indeed? Now how is that?"

"The sheep has become ill," he replied. "It fell down with limbs so straight and stiff it could no longer right itself."

"Your riddles are too deep for this humble seeker. How does that presage the end of the world?"

"There are no riddles at all, my child! Not for those who know the truth."

I pretended to be distracted by a tray of tea carried by a boy.

"We are in disgrace," the old man insisted, his wrinkles deepening with concern. "All of us."

"May I offer you some tea?"

I stood up to signal the boy.

"I don't need tea. I need a remedy."

I agreed with him silently about that. "Is there anything I can help you with?"

"The Ostajlu," he blurted out, which surprised me into sitting down again.

"What about them?"

"A Sufi sold them a sick sheep," he said, "and now they are angry."

It sounded simple enough. "Why not have a specialist examine it, with restitution to follow if required?"

"It is too late," he replied. "Men have drawn their daggers and each other's blood."

I sighed. "If it was only a squabble, put your trust in God, arbiter of all things."

"God was on our side," he whispered, leaning toward me as if I were a conspirator. "Our men beat back the Ostajlu, who have not forgiven us."

"Your men must be fierce," I said, to encourage him to talk.

"They are fierce, but few. Now they are in hiding, fearing for their lives. The world is ending, alas!"

He uttered an unearthly groan after he said this, but the men around us paid no attention. I persevered.

"Why is the world ending?"

"They wish to destroy us!" he said, his voice rising, and it sounded as if he might start raving. "Who can hope to resist the combined efforts of all the qizilbash?"

"All the qizilbash? Isn't the argument just with the Ostajlu?"

"It is, but all the men of the sword have been sent against us."

"They have? By whom?"

The boy arrived with the tea. The man placed a date in his mouth and took a swallow of tea. I stared at him, wondering if what he said could be true.

"By the one and only," he replied, obviously too frightened to name Isma'il Shah.

"But why would he send them against the Sufis?"

As the man paused to drink more tea, I remembered that the Sufis had regarded Kholafa as their spiritual leader.

"They fear our power," he replied.

"May God keep all your members safe from harm."

"Insh'Allah."

I drained my tea, thanked the man for sharing his company, and left quickly. Why would the Shah feel it necessary to use the pretext of a quarrel over a sick sheep to punish the Sufis? He could punish anyone he wished. And if the Shah wanted the Ostajlu to take revenge on the Sufis to prove their loyalty to him, why would he bother to send all the qizilbash? I had to figure out how these strange, misshapen shards might coalesce into a picture of perfect clarity.

I rushed back to the palace and told Pari what I had learned from the Sufis, enjoying how her eyes drank in the information. But then she frowned.

"I thought you were ill."

"I was," I said quickly. "I went to the *sama* for its healing powers."

Pari looked skeptical. "For your own protection, you had better make sure to tell me what you are doing."

"I will."

Before we were able to discuss my conduct or the meaning of what I had heard, her mother arrived with her ladies. I paid my respects and then awaited orders near the door.

The princess greeted her mother and called for refreshments, but she fidgeted so much on her cushion that her discomfort was obvious.

"My child, I come bearing news. Remember I said I would return to you with a list of qualified suitors?"

"I do, but I am busy today," Pari replied, her long forehead crinkling. "I face several crises more pressing than finding a husband."

"Hear me out," said her mother, wincing as she placed her hip on a cushion. "I received a letter this morning from a kinswoman in Sistan, whom I had written to ask about the marital status of your cousin Badi al-Zaman."

Pari sighed, and I echoed her impatience silently.

"Don't worry that I will suggest him as a possibility," said her mother. "Badi al-Zaman is dead. He was found in bed with a dagger in his heart."

Pari's eyes clouded, making her look as if she could no longer see. "May God be merciful!"

"It is not just him," her mother added. "He had an infant son only a year old who was found strangled in his bedchamber."

We were all shocked into silence. Azar Khatoon's shoulders rounded as if she had received a blow. I could feel my face crumpling in disbelief like the faces around me.

"What a horror," breathed Pari. "What could be more fragile, more beloved, and more precious than a baby boy? What more sickening than the murder of a child brought into the world with great suffering by his mother? It is unimaginable."

"May God shelter his tiny soul," whispered Daka Cherkes.

"We must not lose our ability to reason now that we need it the most," Pari said. "The child's death assures us that this was a political murder designed to destroy Badi al-Zaman's entire line. Who is responsible?"

"The letter didn't say. However, it is clear that the people of the region are disgusted with the rule of the qizilbash, and they intend to set up their own ruler."

"So we have another rebellion on our hands!"

"I am afraid so."

Pari's eyes locked with my own; I knew at once what she feared. "Has anyone had news of the other princes in the last few days?"

"I haven't," Daka said.

"Javaher, go check on Ibrahim and Gowhar immediately."

I rushed out of the palace and down the Promenade of the Royal Stallions to Ibrahim and Gowhar's house. I hoped that my errand would find them safe. If so, I would be honored by the opportunity to glimpse their famous library, which housed thousands of books, including a priceless manuscript of Jami's poems ten years in the making.

I was not even permitted to enter their courtyard. Armed soldiers halted me and told me that Ibrahim was under house arrest. Breathless, I returned to Pari's quarters, only to be greeted by the sound of great wails. Pari's mother clung to her, tears flowing. Pari held her gently, trying to soothe her.

"What happened?" I asked Massoud Ali, whose eyes were dark with horror.

"Pari's brother Suleyman is dead," he whispered.

I rocked back on my heels in shock.

"Pari's half brothers, Imamqoli Mirza and Ahmad Mirza, have also been found slain in their chambers."

They were only twelve or thirteen years old. I dropped to a cushion, my mind clearing all of a sudden as all the tiny bits of colored clay formed themselves into a mosaic. With the qizilbash busy chasing the Sufis, no one remained to protect the princes and Isma'il was free to order the remaining nobles to execute whomever he wished. I was grateful that Mahmood lived in a remote province in the heart of the Caucasus, but the news filled me with terror, and I resolved to warn him right away.

"Why does God visit so much sorrow upon me?" Daka exclaimed through her tears. "First my husband, now my only son. I will never bear another. Was any woman more bereft?"

"Or any daughter?" Pari replied. "How much death must one witness?"

"My child, you who are still young have already endured so much!" Daka brushed her fingers under Pari's dry eyes, searching for water. "Why don't you mourn?"

"Black clouds are pouring rain on my heart," Pari replied. "The weather inside me is as bleak as any you have ever seen. But I won't allow myself to break at a time when I may be able to help princes who are still alive."

"You poor child!" Her mother collapsed into sobs.

"Mother, I must abide."

Pari's eyes searched mine, begging for the balm of good news. "What have you learned?"

My stomach lurched with a desire to make her feel better. "The Shah's guard has been posted at Ibrahim's, but I believe he is still alive."

"Come, Javaher, we must see if someone will help us defend him."

"Yes, and the other princes," I said quickly, "like Mahmood." I choked saying his name.

Pari called for her wraps, and I followed her out the big wooden door, while her mother was helped by her ladies to her own quarters.

"I blame myself for not thinking fast enough," Pari said to me. "I saw some soldiers assembling in the Promenade of the Royal Stallions yesterday. When you told me about the Sufis, I should have fig-ured it out. Which of the Shah's nobles would know the full extent of his plans?"

"Perhaps no one. I suspect he would have called in his men one by one when ordering the executions."

"We shall go see Sultanam. I am hopeful that her mother's heart knows more."

As we walked through the gardens, a hard freezing rain fell, lash-ing us with its sting. The princess's face looked as if it was covered with tears. She wiped at her red eyes, and only then did I understand that she had not been able to prevent the escape of rivers of grief.

When we entered Sultanam's quarters, Pari asked her eunuch to show us in to see the great lady. He replied that he would ask if she was available.

"It is an emergency," Pari said. "We won't leave until we see her."

"As you wish."

Before long, we were summoned. Kicking off her wet shoes out-side Sultanam's door, Pari entered the room. I arranged the gold-embossed black slippers neatly and placed my boots beside hers.

Sultanam was seated on a cushion dressed in a black mourn-ing robe. Her eyes were bloodshot, and her magnificent curly white hair was loose and wild around her shoulders. Pari greeted Sultanam respectfully as the "first wife of my revered father." After Sultanam welcomed her, Pari dropped to her cushion and began speaking in a quiet, serious voice.

"Know that I will humble myself in any way to gain your help," she said. "Five princes are dead, including my brother, another is under house arrest, and the fate of the others is unclear. Does your son intend to destroy the entire dynasty?"

Sultanam's eyes filled with water and her mouth bowed in defeat.

"I wish I knew what was in his heart," she replied. "This after-noon, after I heard about the princes, I went to see him. I threw myself on my knees, tore at my hair, and begged him to spare my son Mohammad Khodabandeh and his five children. Isma'il declared that rebellion is everywhere and that I must leave it to him to root out evildoers."

The two women exchanged a sympathetic look.

"I am deeply sorry for your loss," Sultanam added.

"And I for yours."

"Are all the princes at risk?"

"Not all," she said. "After I swore that I would die from grief, Isma'il promised to spare Mohammad and his children, as long as they stay away from Qazveen. Still, I have sent a courier to Mohammad and to his eldest son, Sultan Hassan Mirza, to tell them to regard any strangers as potential murderers."

"But Mohammad doesn't even qualify for the throne," said Pari. "Why would Isma'il condemn a man who is already blind?"

Sultanam sighed. "Perhaps you don't realize how children change," she said. "They start life attached to your body, but grow into foreigners."

No one said anything. What was there to say when even the Shah's own mother didn't have an explanation for his behavior?

"Revered lady," I said, "may I ask if the sisters of the Shah are also at risk of his wrath?"

Sultanam looked at Pari. "I don't believe he would hurt a woman," she said. "After all, even the brightest of them may not take the throne."

"Never mind about that," said Pari, careless as always about her own safety. "What about the other princes?"

"I don't know," said Sultanam with an air of helplessness.

"But Ibrahim is under house arrest. He is one of the flowers of our dynasty, as you know. I ask you, with great humility, can you plead with your son to save him?"

"No."

"Why not?"

"I have already extracted a concession from my son. The rest is in God's hands."

Pari looked as if she thought Sultanam had not understood her words. "Do you understand that my other brothers and cousins are at risk of being executed?"

"I will pray for their safety."

"That is not enough."

Sultanam remained seated and composed. "I have done what I can."

Pari looked as if a vein had snapped inside her head and poured blood into the skin of her face.

"I need more help than that. You are queen of all women, charged with protecting the health of the dynasty."

"This Shah's hand is stronger than his mother's."

"A queen mother must do more than protect her own interests," Pari insisted. "Think what my father would say if he knew that you were abandoning his other children to the grave!"

Sultanam was stung. "Those are fine words coming from a woman who promotes only herself."

"Forget about me. Stand up and do your duty!"

"You seem to think a woman can do anything, but she can't. Don't forget, you are a woman, too. Despite all your maneuvering, a woman will never take the throne."

"Who cares what swings between my legs?" Pari's voice rose, her body stiff with rage. She stood abruptly, walked out the door, and grabbed her black slippers. "At least I would have been a good shah rather than a murderer."

"You are neither a prince nor a mother, so what use are you? You should have chosen an appropriate role rather than aspire to one you could never own."

Pari stumbled as if she had been struck. She turned toward the room and threw a shoe at Sultanam's head so quickly that the lady didn't have time to shield herself. My breath stopped as the black leather slipper flew toward Sultanam and slid over the part in her hair, then slapped against the wall, leaving a wet mark.

Pari had already disappeared down the corridor, leaving me to face Sultanam's wrath.

"A thousand apologies for my princess," I said quickly. "The enormity of her grief has disordered her mind. Please forgive her."

Sultanam's cheeks were red with anger. "She has never learned to control herself. She will lose her head if she keeps up this way."

"I beg forgiveness," I replied, mortified. "May I remove the offending shoe from your presence?"

Sultanam made a dismissive gesture with her hand. I retrieved the shoe and asked if I might follow the princess. When permission was granted, I fled Sultanam's chambers. Pari had put a shoe on her right foot and was walking home through the wet gardens with the other foot bare. The ground was frozen in some spots, and her foot was already tinted blue, but she seemed impervious to the cold. I handed her the shoe, and she slipped it on as if nothing had happened.

"What did she say?"

"That you have no manners."

"Better to be ill-mannered than a coward."

Pari was right: Sultanam had a duty to protect all her husband's children and grandchildren, not just those who had sprung from her loins.

"We must send word to the qizilbash leaders, if we can find any in town, and ask if they will advocate for Ibrahim," Pari said. "We should also send speedy couriers to the princes who are still alive, and to their guardians, to tell them what has happened and urge them to go into hiding. We will save them if we can."

At her house, the princess flew into action.

"Azar Khatoon!" she yelled fiercely, and her chief lady sped into the room. Her lively step made her just the type of person that Pari liked to employ.

"Bring me paper, fresh ink, two reed pens, another wooden desk, and hot coffee, in that order," she said. "Run!"

The lady disappeared with alacrity, and we could hear her calm but firm orders to the other servants.

"Princess," I said, "we must word the letters carefully in case they fall into hostile hands. Let us write about the princes as if our goal is to inform the recipients that those who fall out of the Shah's favor inevitably come to evil ends. In this way, we won't appear to be opposed to his will in case the letters are intercepted."

"Very clever," she replied. "Both of us will write letters at the same time, and I will sign them. We must reach as many members of my family as we can."

Azar brought in a silver tray with coffee, which we drank to give us fortitude. I balanced a desk on my lap, smoothed out a sheet of paper, and dipped my reed pen in ink, wiping it to avoid smudges. I penned the first letter as quickly as I could and passed it to Pari for her signature; then I penned the next one. In the middle of the night, I put the first few letters to her half brothers in a cloth bag, took them to her most trusted courier, and told him to dispatch his men immediately.

All through that long night we wrote letters to her family members, pausing only to eat a sweetmeat or drain another cup of coffee. Azar kept the oil lamps brightly lit and melted wax so that Pari could press her seal into it as soon as each letter was dry. When our forearms became tired from writing, her lady massaged them with vigor. As she kneaded my arms, I relaxed into my cushion and stared at the pretty beauty mark near her lip. I was achingly tired, and lonely. I wondered if Azar Khatoon would take me into her bed, but her indifference announced to me that she had no need.

We heard the first call to prayer while sealing the final letters. I wrote a quick additional note to Mahmood, although Pari had already written to him, urging him to take care of himself in every respect, and I signed it, "your loving tutor."

Pari's eyes had deep hollows under them, and I was certain they mirrored my own.

"I pray that we will save your family," I said. Eight of her brothers and male cousins were still alive, as far as we knew.

"Insh'Allah," she replied, and then she looked at me with new compassion in her eyes. "Now I know something of the heart-tearing sorrow that you endured when you were a young man. Death is always ugly, but to lose a family member to murder is horrifying. Alas, my broken heart!"

"Princess, I am so sorry," I replied softly. "Please know that I understand that no consolation is possible."

I put the letters in a bag and made another trip to her chief courier, silently praying they would be delivered in time.

A few hours later, Pari told me to go to Ibrahim's house to check on him again. It was a cold morning, and the streets were icy as I walked down the great avenue, whose trees were now all bare. I hoped that having made his point, Isma'il Shah would show Ibrahim mercy. Perhaps this time, I would be admitted to his house and catch a glimpse of him that I could take back to Pari as a treasure.

When I arrived, I was relieved to see that the Circassian guards were gone. I knocked using the round knocker for women, and one of Gowhar's ladies opened the door. She told me that I could find her mistress in the courtyard.

"I cannot accompany you," she added brusquely. "I must attend to my own work."

I suspected her rudeness had to do with the fact that the household had been turned upside down by the guards. I proceeded down a corridor and passed a large room whose shelves were so bare they looked blue in the early morning light. No doubt this had been the famous library, but where were the books? My heart clenched at the sight of loose manuscript pages on the floor, some bearing the imprint of men's boots.

As I approached the courtyard, I smelled a fire, which was strange for this snowy time of year. Outside, a great bonfire roared to the heavens, tended by an elderly man. Gowhar sat on the frozen ground near the fire as if she were a common servant, her back rounded under her dark robe, her sober face reflecting the leaping flames.

"Salaam aleikum. I bring greetings from Pari Khan Khanoom," I said. Gowhar continued staring into the flames, silent as the grave. A wave of discomfort overtook me.

"My lieutenant asks after your well-being and wishes to know if there is anything she can offer to help you."

Gowhar closed her eyes and two large tears slid down her cheeks. "Pari was right. We should have left."

She collapsed into sobs so piteous I am certain they would have broken even Isma'il's heart.

"They killed him this morning," she added, "and didn't even have the grace to kill me with him."

No words, no expressions could suffice in such a case. I was speechless.

The manservant poked at the fire, which ejected bits of burned paper into the sky. I suspected Gowhar had tried to destroy incriminating papers, but then I noticed several charred poetry manuscripts, their pages browned and curled.

"Agha!" I cried out in alarm to the manservant. "Some books are being burned by accident!"

He looked away. Gowhar threw back her head and laughed, making a terrible sound.

"Not by accident."

I stared at her.

"Isma'il will not have them!" Gowhar cried. She opened her palms and gestured to the air around her. "They're safe at last."

"You mean—you mean—" I could not put the question into words. "Where are they?"

"I burned them."

"All of them?"

"All except for those," she said, gesturing toward the charred remains in the fire.

Thousands of books—the work of countless scribes, gilders, and illuminators—converted into smoke in one morning! The loss was too large to fathom.

Gowhar's triumph faded when she saw my expression. Her sobs racked her body with so much force that she gasped and choked. I rushed to Pari's house and fetched several eunuchs and a lady physician. They brought a sleeping potion to Gowhar, who drank it and said, "I pray I may never wake again."

In the midst of all of these calamities, Mirza Salman summoned me to his office to tell me that Shamkhal Cherkes had been named

Guardian of the Shah's Most Precious Seal, taking Ibrahim's place. Ibrahim's grave had not even been dug when the announcement was made. How quickly a favorite had been destroyed, and how quickly all traces of him were already being rubbed away!

Pari resolved to visit her uncle to ask him to help save the remaining princes. As guardian of the seal, he now held one of the highest positions in the land.

"We can no longer think of ourselves, nor worry about proprieties," Pari said sternly. I didn't realize what she meant until she reached into a nearby trunk and handed me some women's clothing: a black chador and a picheh for covering the face.

"As soon as we leave the palace, you must remove your turban and cloak yourself in these."

"Leave the palace?"

"We are going in secret to see Shamkhal at his home. That will protect him from having to acknowledge our visit."

"That is forbidden!"

"Javaher, we have no choice."

If we were caught, I would be punished for allowing her to leave. I was risking my livelihood and possibly even my life. But Pari spoke the truth: What good would our lives be if Isma'il killed all his brothers and, possibly, his sisters?

"Princess, how do you expect to get out?"

"Follow me."

We walked through the harem gardens so quickly that the air around Pari seemed to move out of her way. I followed her to a remote corner of the grounds, which were surrounded by smooth walls too high for anyone to climb. To my surprise, she disappeared into thick hedges. Beyond them lay an old pavilion that might have once been used for outdoor picnics, but was now crumbling and surrounded by weeds. Pari stepped into a room inside the pavilion, whose flooring consisted of green and yellow glazed tiles, some of which were chipped. Bending down in the middle of the floor, Pari pushed aside a large, heavy tile, panting with effort. A wide opening led down into a passageway.

"*Ajab!*" I said. So that was how she and Maryam had managed to visit the gypsies. Nothing about the princess could be predicted.

We walked down an incline into the dank passageway, and I pulled the tile into place above us. We continued in the dark until we reached a tall wooden door, which Pari unlocked with a key the size of my hand.

"I don't have a lamp," she said, "but I know the way without fail. Hold the end of my kerchief so you don't get lost."

Pari locked the door behind us. The tunnel was as cold and silent as the grave.

"You must never speak of this," she said.

"I promise," I replied, delighted that she trusted me enough to reveal her secret exit.

We walked for a long time before arriving at a second door. Pari unlocked it and we entered another passageway, stepped up on a landing, and kept shuffling in the dirt until we emerged into another crumbling building in a copse of trees in one of the rarely used parks near the Promenade of the Royal Stallions.

I wrapped myself in the picheh and the chador, holding the black cloth under my chin. It was possible to see through the loose weave of the face veil, but I felt blinded. As we traversed the park, I tried to mimic Pari's graceful gait.

"You walk like a man," she complained. "Take tiny steps, not wide strides. Move like the shadow of a cloud."

I pressed my legs together and minced my steps, the way I saw women do.

We walked briskly down a side street to the neighborhood where Shamkhal lived. Men leered at us and uttered coarse suggestions that made me feel strangely dirty. Was this what it was like to be a woman, always on display? I missed my usual comfortable anonymity.

Pari announced us to Shamkhal's servants as his sisters, refusing to remove her face covering before being shown into her uncle's presence.

Shamkhal was drinking his afternoon tea. He looked at the shapes in front of him with surprise, until Pari began speaking and it seemed that he recognized her voice. Then he told his servants to leave and stay away until he called for them. As soon as the door closed behind him, Pari lifted her picheh, and I threw off my wraps altogether.

"By God above!" Shamkhal said, his normally florid face whitening. "How did you get permission to leave the palace?" He rushed to the door to make sure that it was bolted tight, but even with the door firmly closed, his eyes darted around.

"Has someone smacked you in the head? Imagine how you would be punished if Isma'il found out."

"I had to come."

"What risks you take!"

Pari sat down while I stood at the back of the room. "I am here because of the princes who have been killed," she said in a strangled voice.

"I am deeply sorry."

"I didn't come for condolences. I came to ask when the men of the Safavi court are going to halt this slaughter."

Shamkhal stepped back. "How can we do anything? The murders are by direct order of your brother, the light of the universe."

"Uncle, please omit the palace formalities. The Shah has destroyed half of the dynasty. Are the nobles going to do anything about it?"

"What can we do?"

"Disordered shahs can justifiably be removed."

"But this one isn't insane, sick, or blind. We don't have a valid reason."

"Isn't injustice a reason?"

"There is no injustice when it comes from the Shah!"

"That is palace garbage," Pari said. "Don't the nobles care about what is happening?"

"Of course they care. No one is happy about this state of affairs."

"Have you asked the qizilbash nobles to help?"

"No, because they have been sent to kill the Sufis."

"Why? They don't deserve it."

"I know."

"Are the nobles men or not?"

His shoulders stiffened. "Isma'il's spies are everywhere. No one can breathe without him hearing the sound."

"By God above! I am an unarmed woman begging for help, and no one will do the right thing?"

"What is the right thing?"

"When a leader at other courts has been found to be of unsound mind, their nobles ask his eldest female relatives for permission to unseat him. If permission is given, they remove him. I suppose their men are braver than ours."

He looked as uncomfortable as if she had held a hot poker near his eyes. "I wish I could help."

"Aren't you and the other men afraid that he won't stop at killing his own flesh and blood?"

"Of course. Every man is hoping that by showing fealty, he will remain unscathed. Any sign of disloyalty is so rapidly punished that we don't even dare to think disloyal thoughts."

"My father was right to imprison him," she said. "I wish I had taken heed. He understood things about Isma'il that none of us knew."

"True."

"Can you at least protect Sultanam's grandchildren?"

"Not if the Shah wishes them dead."

"Shamkhal! What has become of you?"

"I survive as well as I can. That is all a man can do under these circumstances."

"It is an ugly way to live."

His broad face seemed to swell with anger. "You think so? It is much less ugly than other possibilities."

"Meaning what?"

"Meaning at least I advise Isma'il on a daily basis, arguing for clemency and mercy. I attempt to influence his decisions by pointing out examples of goodness. What do you do?"

"He hasn't given me a chance to do anything."

"My point exactly. You treated him with disdain. You defied his orders. You didn't take the time to become a trusted servant. As a result, you have had no influence at all."

Pari's face flushed dark. "I deserved better."

"Why?"

"Because of all I know. Because of who my father was. Because I am better at governing than he is."

"All of that is true, but it doesn't help us now. I begged you to bow before him and show your humility. But you wouldn't make compromises, so you have been rendered impotent."

"At least I am not a coward. I stand tall for what I believe."

"Those are very fine words," he said. "They will probably sound even better when you turn them into poetry. But what good are words? Now when you are needed the most, you can't even get an appointment to see your own brother."

"I'm glad that I don't bow my head before his ridiculous orders, like you do. How many men will you stand by and see murdered?"

"As many as is necessary, while I influence him as much as I can and adjust when I can't."

"What if you awake to find his men hovering above you with a cord in their hands to strangle you?"

"I will have done my duty as well as I could."

Pari was so exasperated she hit both sides of her head with her hands. "It is like trying to get a rat to stop feeding at the latrines!"

"You are the shit-eater!" Shamkhal bellowed, his voice so loud I felt it in my teeth. "What if you try to remove him and awake to see those same men waiting for you?"

"At least I will die knowing I have done what I could to oppose him."

Pari stood up abruptly and wrapped the chador over her body.

"Daughter of my sister, wait a minute. Everyone would be grateful if you were able to tame him."

"How can I do that now?" she replied. "All of you men were happy to allow him to shut me out of palace affairs. How quick you were to do so!"

"It was a direct order."

"But if you had argued against it, I might have retained some influence. Maybe I am impotent, but you helped Isma'il put me in that position. Now how is anyone to stop him?"

Despite his big black beard and broad shoulders, Shamkhal looked helpless for a moment.

"I don't know. We will have to wait until the qizilbash come back from chasing the Sufis to see if they will help."

"But their absence is making it possible for the princes to be exterminated!"

Shamkhal opened his palms to heaven as if to say the matter was in God's hands.

Pari's lips turned down with disgust as she flipped the picheh over her face. "And they say that women are cowards!" she exclaimed as she clutched her chador under her chin and strode toward the door. Her uncle didn't plead with her to stay. Clumsily, I covered my face and body.

Outside, the princess could not contain herself.

"Oh great God above," she prayed as we walked down the street, "look kindly on your child, I beg you. Advise me on the correct course of action, for I am lost. These times are as dark as times have ever been. Gazzali has written that without justice there is nothing—no loyalty, no citizenry, no prosperity, and finally, no country. We are at risk of losing everything. Oh Lord, show your servant a ray of light in her darkest moment!"

I echoed her prayer as we entered the park, descended into the passageway, and walked quickly in the cold. I felt relieved not to be on the street, where there was a possibility of being discovered. We emerged into the crumbling pavilion without incident, flung off our wraps, and walked back to her home through the harem gardens. In her rooms, the princess sat down, looking shaken. Her own uncle! It was the worst blow of all.

"Who can we turn to now? Mirza Salman?"

Her smile was ragged and defeated. "He is a man of the pen of second rank. The qizilbash won't listen to him."

Pari's eyes looked unveiled for the first time in months. What I saw reminded me of the despair of a prisoner being led to execution.

Her hands lay palm up in her lap, small, tender things, the henna designs now faded. She looked down at them for a moment.

"I am frightened," she whispered.

I was thunderstruck by the rawness of her admission. Deep in my heart, it stirred a desire to sacrifice myself for her. I had fight enough for three men, and I vowed to do all I could to keep her safe from harm.

CHAPTER 6

THE CALL TO BATTLE

Kaveh received word that his eighteenth and last son had been called to present himself to Zahhak and his snakes. Upon hearing the news, he abandoned his forge and marched to the palace, the thick muscles of his forearms clenching with rage. So great was his anger that he rushed past the guards and interrupted Zahhak while he was holding court.

"Illustrious King," he roared, his eyes flashing like the sparks from his forge, "you rule over seven realms and a treasury bursting with gold. Why must you rob me of my only wealth? If you are as just as you claim, you will leave my last son alone rather than perpetrating such evil."

Zahhak tasted metal on his tongue. How could he defend his own actions? He longed to make himself look clean in the eyes of the world.

"I will release your son," he replied, issuing the order. "Now you must sign this proclamation attesting to the justice of my reign. Is that easy enough?"

When Kaveh read the proclamation and saw the names of all the nobles there, his cheeks turned purple, his eyes bulged, and the muscles in his neck throbbed.

"What a pack of cowards you all are!" he shouted at the nobles. "How can you put your names to such lies and still call yourselves men?"

With a great roar, he ripped the document to bits and stomped on it, while the nobles gaped at him as if he were a mad dog. Then he stormed out of the palace in a rage. At the town's central square, he tore off his blacksmith's apron and raised it high in the air on the point of a spear so that people could see it far and wide. They flooded in from everywhere and rallied around his cause.

"Justice!" they cried. "Justice!"

The ladies' section of the palace was as quiet as a graveyard, and the faces of most of its inhabitants were drawn with sorrow. Fear permeated every room like a dense, stagnant fog. Was it over? Who would be next?

My mother's cousin wrote to ask when Jalileh could be sent to Qazveen, and I was suffused with relief that Pari had told me to wait. Never would I put Jalileh, who was unschooled in the intricacies of palace politics, at so much risk. I wrote back and explained as best as I could, without any details, that the situation was unsafe.

After all the mourning ceremonies for the dead princes were completed, Pari summoned me to her home. Azar Khatoon showed me into her most private chamber, where Pari met intimates like Maryam and her mother. It was the one with the mural of the nude Shireen, fine peach-colored silk rugs, and matching cushions. Pari was reading a copy of the *Shahnameh*, one that I had never seen before. The book was open to a page of ornate calligraphy illustrated by a gilded painting, rich with jeweled colors.

"Salaam aleikum," she said when I came in. "I am happy to see you. I never thought I would feel gratitude at the mere fact that someone I cherish is still living and breathing."

"Thank you, kind princess." My heart flowered under the warmth of her words.

"What sorrows we have endured together! If I had known they would be so great, I wouldn't have burdened you with becoming my vizier."

"Princess, it has been the greatest honor of my life to serve you. I would have done so no matter what," I replied, and that was the truth.

"I am glad to hear that," she said. "I hope you still desire to be in my employ."

"With all my heart."

"I expect that you don't say so lightly. The tasks ahead are very grave."

I waited.

Pari looked thoughtful. "It is strange how many portents are around us, if only we care to see them. I have been rereading the story in the *Shahnameh* about how Zahhak demanded that the skulls of young men be cracked like walnuts so that his snakes could feed on their brains. It was no more than a story to me until recently, but now I see it afresh. Haven't we experienced the very same disaster? Our leader has destroyed some of the brightest stars of his court, from young meteorites educated in the princely arts ever since they were small, to bright blazing suns like Ibrahim who are born only once in a generation. Our leader has become the very image of Zahhak."

Everything in me had been trained to be loyal to the Shah. I couldn't help but look around to see if anyone was listening.

"Until now, he has spared Mohammad Khodabandeh and his children, but it is still possible he will send someone to destroy them. If he and his family are murdered—and may God prevent it—who will be left to lead the dynasty?"

"What about Mahmood Mirza? What about Isma'il's unborn child?"

"I don't know who will survive. My responsibility in this matter is to defend all the princes who might lead the dynasty in the future. I must do everything I can to protect them."

"That won't be easy."

"As things stand, it is impossible. I can no more prevent Isma'il from sending out assassins than I can tell the sun when to rise. There are those who believe they can control the orbits of the planets, but I am not one of them."

The gravity of her tone and the privacy of our meeting made me acutely sensitive to whatever was coming next.

"In times of confusion, I turn to the *Shahnameh* because my father held it so dear. I have been reading it for Ferdowsi's guidance about the righteous ways to handle a disordered shah. He is very cautious on this point. After all, he was hoping for remuneration from the Ghaznavi sultan and couldn't be seen as opposing his reign, even indirectly."

I had continued reading my own copy of the *Shahnameh* almost every night, holding it with affection because it had been a gift from Mahmood.

"But look what happens to the voracious Zahhak: Kaveh sparks a rebellion. So even Ferdowsi, who is usually so careful not to offend the institution of royalty, is willing to suggest that a truly evil shah must be resisted."

Pari was drawing a noose of logic around my neck, and I didn't wish to be captured in a knot that couldn't be untied. My face must have shown my feelings, because her voice softened.

"Sometimes, one person must make a sacrifice for the good of all others," she added. "Kaveh was such a man. What an inspiration he is to all who suffer from tyranny! I can't sit by any longer while a fire consumes the house of our future. Too often, I have acted in the hope of some gain for myself. Now I must act for others, regardless of my fate."

She said this with so much delicacy and such understanding of her own flaws that I was touched at the core of my heart.

"May God always protect you! You are the brightest star among women."

"Thank you, Javaher. But tell me: Do you feel as strongly as I do that our leader is disordered?"

"Yes, of course. Your revered father would never have killed his own kin with no reason."

"I know the sacrifice you made to serve him was dear. Now I am going to request that you make an even greater one, but I won't demand it from you. It must be freely given."

A feeling of dread suffused me. "What are you asking for?"

"Your loyalty."

"That is always yours. What else?"

"Your assistance."

"With what?"

Pari lowered her voice. "He must be removed."

My heart began pounding like the drums that march men to war. How could I agree to what she was asking of me? For a man to raise his hand against his leader, for a sister to strike at her own brother—that was cause for death if discovered, and for eternal damnation if God deemed it unjust.

The princess wanted to rip the proclamation. Yet we couldn't do it the way Kaveh had done, because our shah was not a character in a poem; he would simply have us put to death if we openly protested his rule.

Pari was scrutinizing my face. "Javaher, will you help me bring justice to this land?"

"In the name of God above!" I thundered. "I have delivered everything but my last breath to this dynasty, including the possibility of raising my own sons. Now must I turn traitor in order to serve this same line? What kind of servant would I be? What truth would ever seem solid?"

"Your questions are fair," said Pari, "but I suggest that you would be serving the cause of justice. That can be the only reason for agreeing to such a request. You have my permission to assist me only if you believe the cause is righteous."

If she had said anything else—if she had mentioned personal gain or glory, I would have refused her. But she was reaching for the only part of me that was tender to her request. Isma'il had become the very image of Zahhak; there was no denying it. Would we remain silent and allow him to destroy us at his whim? Or would we become as brave as Kaveh?

"What do you intend for him?"

"The fate he brought to others."

"Even your father, may his soul be at rest, let Isma'il live," I argued.

"My father had the authority to imprison him and render him powerless. We do not. I have recently asked Sultanam if she would allow the qizilbash chiefs to remove him on the basis of insanity, but she said no. There is only one way to rid ourselves of this scourge, just as there was only one way to unseat Zahhak."

"This defies all I have been taught ever since I was a youth! How can you ask this of me?"

"How can I not, when it is the only just thing to do? He will kill us all if we leave him be."

"All my life, I have striven to be loyal to the throne. After my father was murdered, I wished to set an impeccable example."

"You have done so."

"Thank you. But now I must throw away my morals and rebel?"

"Sometimes it is the only choice."

"I can't answer yet; I must think."

"I understand," she said, "and I honor your need for reflection. Return to me as soon as you have made a decision."

As I took my leave, I glanced back and was struck by the pretty picture she made. Sitting on a cushion in a purple robe embroidered with sparrows, surrounded by a delicate manuscript illustration of courtly women and men in a garden, with elegant peach silk rugs beneath her, she exuded feminine grace and learning. The lushness of her surroundings, the fineness of her robe, her curved, regal forehead, all made her look rare and delicate. Yet buried within her tall, thin frame was something harder than I had ever seen in her father, something harder still than what lay in the qizilbash warriors whose turbans held the erect red batons that made them look like giants. She had come to a conclusion so awful it would incite many a warrior to flee, but she didn't flinch from it.

Pari's request made me restless, and so did not knowing about the fate of Mahmood. I still had had no letter from him and no news. I hoped Khadijeh might be able to enlighten me about the Shah's state of mind and whether his murderous rampage was finished. I went to her quarters and asked to see her, explaining that I brought news from the princess. There was no need to explain further, since by then the palace was buzzing with visits from one lady to another to comfort those in mourning.

When I arrived and was shown in, I was surprised to see Khadijeh dressed all in black, her hair covered by a black silk scarf, which made her tamarind skin look pale.

"My condolences," I said, as I took my seat on a cushion across from her.

"Thank you. And mine to you."

I wasn't related to anyone who had died, but had dressed soberly to reflect the state of the palace.

"I have come to speak with you about a private matter on behalf of my lieutenant," I said. Khadijeh turned to Nasreen and told her to bring me hot coffee.

The minute she had left, Khadijeh said, "You look as if you have seen the dead."

"I feel as if I have," I replied. "Six princes have been killed, and Gowhar is behaving like a madwoman. She is so sick with grief I am not certain she will find the strength to live. It is terrible to see."

"May God shower us with mercy!" Khadijeh replied, a tear sliding onto her cheek.

I couldn't help myself. I leapt up from my cushion and claimed her hand, wishing I could take her in my arms and feel the warmth of our bodies entwined.

"Has he said anything about when the killing will stop? I fear for Mahmood!"

Khadijeh looked so startled that I regretted saying anything. She stared at the door, and I quickly withdrew my hand and regained my position on the other side of the room.

"Poor Javaher. You have reason to fear," she said softly, her eyes wells of grief.

"I know, I know," I replied. "Why are you so sad?"

"I too have suffered a terrible loss."

"But you are not related to any of the royal princes, except by marriage."

"That is true," she replied. "They are not whom I mourn. I learned this morning that my brother, Mohsen, is dead."

"My dear Khadijeh! What happened?"

She wrapped her arms around her body. "He died trying to protect someone else, which was very like him. Mohsen always watched over me and defended me when we were young."

Her eyes overflowed with tears, which she left glistening on her cheeks. "When I lost my parents, I thought I had lost all a woman could lose. But the fresh grief that fills my heart will never depart, no matter how long I live."

"How I wish I could hold you in my arms and comfort you!"

"Hush!" she whispered and looked as if she were listening for something. All of a sudden Nasreen Khatoon came in bearing the coffee, arriving so soundlessly that I wondered if she had been trying to catch a few words of our conversation. I changed the subject quickly.

"The esteemed princess would like to know if you have any special medicine that would help Gowhar vanquish the worst part of her grief."

"I do," Khadijeh said. "In recent days, I have had many requests for the mixture, and have been taking it myself. Nasreen Khatoon, please prepare another serving of the herbs I showed you and bring it here for our guest."

The lady laid down the tray and left again to do her bidding. Now I understood why Khadijeh seemed so composed. Her medicines were potent enough to take away all pains.

"Javaher—" Khadijeh said, but I interrupted her.

"How can we stop him?"

Her mouth turned down in disgust. "I only hope he doesn't call for me. How can I lie under him, knowing what has happened to my brother?"

I was puzzled. "What does Mohsen's death have to do with the Shah?"

Khadijeh sighed. "Javaher, it pains me that you must know the truth. My brother died defending Mahmood."

I felt as if an iron hand were squeezing my heart. "May he always be safe!" I said, but my words sounded angry.

She looked at me with such compassion that my rage embarrassed me. "If you don't want to know what has happened, I won't tell you."

I had no choice but to ask her.

"Mohsen was with Mahmood at a hunting camp. The Shah's men found them by following the smoke of their fire and attacked them. A friend of my brother's who was with them escaped with his life. He wrote that Mahmood was strangled, and Mohsen was killed with a dagger. Their bodies were taken back to Mahmood's home to be prepared for burial. A few hours later, Mahmood moaned and woke up. His neck was badly bruised, but he wasn't dead."

The rage drained out of me, and I breathed in the sweet air of life, just as Mahmood must be doing. It was the first time in days that the air seemed to flow easily down my throat and into my lungs.

"I am sorry, I didn't mean to get so angry," I said. "I couldn't bear the thought of losing him."

I think I even smiled, until I realized that Khadijeh's lovely face was twisted with grief.

"I wish I didn't have to tell you the rest of the story," she continued. "The assassins asked their leader what they should do about Mahmood, and he ordered that they extinguish his life. This time, they were successful."

I leapt to my feet and kicked the tray of coffee as hard as if I were trying to score a goal. The glasses broke against the tray with a crash, and the coffee threw drops all over a blue silk rug owned by the Shah.

"He was like family!" I shouted.

"I know," she murmured softly.

"We are being led by a dog! I spit on his face, I curse his eyes! May his star fall from the sky! May he burn in hell!"

Khadijeh twisted her body around in fright to see if someone had heard. I didn't care, even if my treasonous words meant my death. I strode out of the room, deaf to Khadijeh's pleas to take some of her medicine for myself. At that moment, I hated everyone in the world. Walking furiously into a secluded part of the gardens, I hurled my body against a cedar tree again and again, watching its branches quiver each time I thudded against it. Unhinged leaves drifted through the air, and broken twigs struck my shoulders. I pounded the tree as if I were thrashing the Shah to death. Then I did my duty by telling Pari the news.

While I was in the deepest throes of mourning, I reached for my *Shahnameh*, the only thing I had left of Mahmood, and opened it at random. Tears welled in my eyes and I could not make out the words. As I shut the book and placed it beside my bed, some lines written by Sa'adi sprang to mind:

> *O tyrant, who oppressest thy subjects,*
> *How long wilt thou persevere in this?*
> *Of what use is authority to you?*
> *To die is better for thee than to oppress men.*

God demanded that his leaders rule with justice, but what if they did not? Must we simply endure tyranny? Must we allow children to be murdered? Must we fear to draw a breath?

No! No! a voice inside me cried. If I didn't do anything about Isma'il, others would surely die. But if I tried to put a stop to him, would God condemn me to hell for my actions? I couldn't know. All I could do was try to make things better for those who were still alive. So I went to Pari and swore to help her achieve her mission, and we agreed to work together even if it meant the loss of our own lives.

But how to hunt such well-concealed prey? Everything was designed to foil us. The palace itself with its high walls, the scattered, guarded buildings within its grounds secluded by trees, the labyrinthine courtyards and passages—all were built to disguise the specific locations of those within. Isma'il surrounded himself with an army of servants whose lives and livelihoods depended on protecting him. He had secreted himself even further by withdrawing from most public appearances, and it was impossible to ask about his whereabouts because any query was bound to provoke suspicion.

We would have to be more clever than a shah who was both power-ful and frightened, more clever than all the walls and obstacles and guards that were purposely in place to protect him. We would have to defeat a system that was designed to thwart us.

We decided to gather more information about Isma'il's minut-est habits, which meant getting closer to those people who knew him best. Pari said she would call on his Circassian wife, Koudenet, to see what she could learn, as well as Mahasti, his pregnant slave. Sultanam could not be expected to help us, but I told Pari I would become friendly with the ladies who knew Sultanam and might learn of his movements. I wrestled with whether I should reveal to her that one of my sources was very close indeed to the Shah, but I decided not to mention Khadijeh, out of a desire to protect her.

Most interesting was the Shah's closest friend, Hassan Beyg Halvachi Oghli, who had such special status that even though he was a man, he was permitted to stay with the Shah in his private quarters. Pari gave me a nearly impossible task: to try to watch him, discover with whom he was friendly, and see if those people could tell me anything to make him vulnerable. She also instructed her other servants to report to her everything they heard around the palace, no matter how trivial.

Late one afternoon, when I returned to my room, I was surprised to find Balamani lying on his bedroll. His skin looked dusty gray, like an elephant's, and his forehead was creased with pain.

"Oh jewel of the heavens! Where have you been?"

"At my usual evil deeds. What ails you?"

Balamani pointed at his foot, which he had stretched out away from everything else. His toes looked swollen.

"I can't stand on it," he replied. "My big toe feels like it is being burned by a flame."

Balamani used to be as vigorous as an ox. It pained me to see him laid low.

"Do you want some medicine?"

"I am using a salve, but it does no good."

"Well," I said, "since your body has proved it could withstand the removal of a much bigger joint, it will no doubt heal your foot."

Balamani laughed, but his laugh had a woeful sound. "It is ridiculous to be felled by a toe."

"Ah," I said, "but a man like you will never be felled so long as he can think. As it happens, I need your intelligence."

"For what purpose, good or ill?" Balamani's dark eyes sparkled with mischief and for a moment he looked as if he had forgotten his malady.

"Ill, of course," I said. "After all, who could not feel ill over what has occurred?"

"Indeed; these are the darkest days I have ever lived."

"Tell me: Were the murders necessary?"

"The Shah's tactics are as subtle as a butcher's knife—but then again, look at how effective a butcher's knife is at doing its job. There is almost no one left who could challenge him for the throne."

A cold draft of air entered the room; Balamani grimaced when it reached his toe.

"Not to mention the vanity of it," he added.

"Vanity?"

"If the Shah has a son, he will face few rivals when he grows up."

"But what if the killings never stop?"

Balamani adjusted his heavy body against the pillows and repositioned his leg far from any obstacle.

"Javaher, be careful. The Shah has spared his sisters, but there is no telling if he will continue to believe that they won't harm him. As Pari's vizier, you could be in grave danger as well."

I decided to take a risk. I leaned close to him and whispered, "Why should a viper be permitted to rule?"

Balamani laughed out loud. "He is the shadow of God on earth, remember?"

"Do you believe this one walks in the shadow of God?"

"Do any of them?"

Panah bar Khoda! I had never heard him speak this way before.

"Men must have their fictions," he added. "If the Shah is not God's shadow, what reason is there for the elders to obey him? Which man's word would be taken as final unless it were somehow tied to God's?"

"That is not how it is supposed to be," I argued. "We offer our loyalty in return for justice, remember?"

"Of course," he replied. "But when there is no justice, who suffers?"

"Right now, many people," I said through gritted teeth.

Balamani's eyes grew tender. "I was very sorry to hear about Mahmood."

"Thank you."

My eyes moistened as if a spring had just been loosed behind them. Knowing that Balamani was one of the few souls in the world to whom I could show my true feelings, I bent my head and let flow my sorrow.

"May God give you strength in your suffering," he said gently. "Remember what I told you long ago? Never, ever love any of the royals."

I wiped my face with one of Pari's handkerchiefs and composed myself. "Mahmood is part of the reason I came to talk with you. I have a mission, and I need help."

"What is it?"

"Is there any way to prompt Hassan to beg the Shah to be merciful and stop the killings?"

"Hard to say," Balamani replied. "He spends day and night with the Shah, so no one can get close to him. That is his job."

"I need to find out more about him."

Balamani looked at me as if reading the thoughts imprinted on my soul. "You, the tender young *agha* whose tongue seemed as absent as his *keer*, are now involved in palace intrigue?"

"I won't speak of intrigue," I said, "only of wishing to capture Hassan's ear."

"Still attached to his head, I hope."

"Of course."

"Yet something smells ill."

"Your foot?"

Balamani snorted. "What information do you need?"

"How to reach him," I insisted, although what I really wanted was Balamani's help with our plans.

He paused. "Not even Hassan is going to succeed in convincing the Shah to be just."

"You may be right," I replied. "But shouldn't we try?"

"No."

"Why not?"

"*We* aren't going to do anything. I am old now. I don't wish to be like that eunuch who lost his life just days before his time came to retire and swim in the waters of Bengal."

"But, Balamani, there is a madman in our midst. We could all be cut down."

"No."

"I will be your eyes and ears—and your feet," I said. "You will direct me and I will carry out this business."

"Too dangerous."

"But I can't do it without you," I insisted. "How can you obstruct what you know to be right?"

Balamani was watching me closely. "Ah, my friend, you still don't know."

"What?"

"What you are."

"What am I?"

"You are *me*."

I was taken aback.

"Yes," he said, "I have taught you all I know, and now I pass my place to you." He leaned over and slapped my chest. I felt a surge there, which heated me to the top of my head.

"Balamani—"

"You have earned it. What you don't know yet, you will learn. It is time for you to be master."

"But, Balamani—" I said, feeling like a disciple whose master has abandoned him too soon. It was a strangely lonely yet buoyant sensation, like being released on the wind and flying high above the earth, as free as a cloud.

"Everything I am, I owe to you," I said in a voice I didn't trust.

"God sent you to me," Balamani replied humbly. "He said, 'Take this proud, shattered child and make him whole.'"

"That was asking a great deal, wasn't it?"

His smile was pained, like that of a parent helping his child through a devastating illness.

"Indeed. But don't imagine that your quest is complete. What have you discovered lately about your father?"

The sudden look of enthusiasm in his eyes surprised me. It was as if he were goading me to prove my skills.

"I haven't had time to pursue it. Solving an old murder doesn't seem as important right now as preventing a new one."

"God be with you, my dear friend," he replied, and I had the impression that I had just passed an important test. "Now get to work!"

The next time I visited Khadijeh, I used the pretext of requesting more medicine for Gowhar. When Nasreen Khatoon left the room to prepare it, I asked Khadijeh to contrive to meet me as if by accident in the gardens that evening, following the last call to prayer. After Nasreen returned with the medicine, I took my leave promptly and delivered it to Pari, but I didn't tell her where it came from.

Later that evening, I strolled through the dark among the tall walnut trees deep in the harem gardens until I found Khadijeh, who had hidden herself behind a huge tree. She had covered her face and wrapped a black scarf around her hair and body so that she could not be easily recognized. I feigned surprise when I saw her, and she replied, "Be quick. I mustn't tarry."

I stood near her under the tree and imagined, for only a moment, lying down and taking my pleasure with her there.

"Khadijeh, I need your advice," I whispered. "Are the killings done?"

She shuddered. "I don't know. He called me to him a few nights ago, and I pretended delight although I am sickened by him. To get him to talk, I told him I was glad he was destroying his enemies, and he replied, 'I plan to root them out one by one.'"

"Did he say anything about your brother?"

"He didn't even know he had been killed!" she replied. "When I told him, he expressed regret, but suggested that since Mohsen sacrificed his life for him, he would find his reward in heaven."

My throat burned from bile. "How unnatural!"

"I think his twenty years of confinement have shattered his reason."

"There are some who feel that he must go." I was testing her to see how she would respond to this unholy idea.

"Vohhh!" she said, and then she clapped her hand over her mouth out of fear that we might be heard.

She was silent for such a long time that I feared, for a moment, that she did not agree. Then, in a low voice, she confessed, "I must admit that I pray for it daily."

"How can it be done?"

"Do you mean—permanently?"

Her eyes searched mine to confirm what I meant, and then her teeth shone in the darkness like those of an animal on the prowl.

"It won't be easy. He removes his dagger when he sleeps, but I don't know which of his women would have the stomach to stab him, especially since the perpetrator of such a deed would immediately be killed. Poisoning would be more difficult to trace, but everything he eats or drinks is sampled first by the royal taster. Even my own pastries must be tested before the Shah touches them."

"Does he drink water in the middle of the night?"

"Sometimes, but he won't touch a flask—water or wine—unless its contents have been tested and sealed."

"Does he ever open a vessel and drink from it after time has elapsed?"

She paused. "It is possible he would do that in a moment of inattention—after much wine and much love," she conceded.

"What can you tell me of his other habits?"

"Very little," she said. "He doesn't announce his plans to me. But I know of one thing he can't live without."

"What is it?"

"Not long ago, I noticed that he often became irritable without provocation. A box of sweets he always kept nearby seemed to calm him. Once, when I thought he was asleep, I lifted the lid and peered in to see what kind of magical confections had tempted him away from mine. He woke up, discovered what I was doing, and became angry until I explained that I wanted to make him my own recipe of date pastries with cardamom to rival what was in the box. He smiled at me then, because he thought I hadn't seen what was there. It was opium."

May God be praised!

"How often does he eat it?"

"Every few hours, except when he is sleeping," she replied. "He receives a sealed box and keeps it with him at all times."

"So he can't live without it?"

"That is how he endured the long years of his confinement."

"Who prepares the contents of the box?"

"I don't know. It would be best to look for a situation in which he forgoes caution."

"Will you let me know if such a situation suggests itself to you?"

"I will."

An owl hooted, a bad omen, and Khadijeh shivered in the cold night air.

"I must go."

She disappeared into the garden without another word, and I remained under the walnut tree for a long time so that no one would suspect the two of us had been together.

The moon hung full and lovely in the sky. I permitted myself to think for just a moment of what might happen if the Shah were gone. Would Khadijeh be mine again? Would I be able to take her into my arms and lie with her until the sun rose? The thought of possessing her again filled my heart with joy, but that emotion was quickly succeeded by dread. Would we survive this terrible time? If there was one life I wished to shield from harm, it was hers.

When I returned to my quarters to ponder what to do next, Massoud Ali was waiting with another letter from my mother's cousin. I had come to dislike her letters. The only time I heard from her is when she wrote to demand something. I felt powerless to care for Jalileh the way I wished to, and I must pacify every demand for fear that Jalileh would be made to suffer. I broke the seal.

> *Greetings and may the blessings of God be upon you. As you know, your sister Jalileh is fifteen now and nearly pickled. Since you haven't managed to bring her to Qazveen, it is time for us to find a good husband for her and allow her to become the treasure of another family. We have endeavored to fulfill your mother's dying wish by caring for her, and although she is a lovely child, we regret that we cannot do so for the rest of her life. Can you send a generous dowry for her? We will find a good man to take responsibility for her. Please let us know if this accords with your wishes.*

The threat was clear: They were tired of caring for her. They were probably already looking for a husband. I hastily penned a reply, insisting that no marriage should be contracted without my permission and promising to bring Jalileh to Qazveen as soon as I could. I wrote that since the palace was teeming with problems, they must be patient, for I would not expose Jalileh to danger. I promised them a generous reward for all their help once Jalileh was returned to my care, but I did not send money, to avoid facilitating a marriage. I hoped my response would placate them until I figured out what to do.

Balamani had gotten much better. His toe wasn't hurting anymore, and his appetite had returned. We decided to have lunch together during the workweek, a rare treat that our duties usually prevented. We met in the guest room of our building and started our meal with hot bread, sheep's cheese, and mint, along with yogurt mixed with diced cucumber. As we began eating, the noon call to prayer resonated throughout the palace.

"Have you heard the latest rumors about Isma'il's faith?" Balamani asked.

"No."

"People say he is a secret Sunni."

"A Sunni!" I exclaimed, so surprised that I withheld a morsel of bread from my mouth.

"The clerics are angry," Balamani said, "but they can't do much about it, since their spiritual leader is the Shah."

"What a reversal for a dynasty founded on Shi'ism! The qizilbash whose grandfathers fought for the dynasty must be outraged."

"To be sure. And that is not the only reason. Lately, Isma'il has been arguing that we should start a war with the Ottomans."

"Why?"

"He wishes to regain territory lost by his father."

"But that is preposterous," I said. "Why disturb a long-lasting peace with one of the world's most powerful empires? Pari will be furious on both counts."

Balamani wrapped some greens and sheep's cheese in lavash. "I didn't say these things were logical."

"In that case," I said, "why don't those fiery, well-armed qizilbash khans take charge of the situation?"

A servant from the harem kitchens brought in dishes of stewed lamb and rice with lentils and cinnamon. I wrapped some rice and lamb in a piece of bread and ate it.

After the servant left, Balamani said, "It would mean death for many of them. You know the risks."

"So you are telling me that all those warriors, whose balls are so big that they dangle near the ground and whose penises are as thick as tent poles, are cowards?"

We laughed so hard that the walls shook.

"Balamani, I ask you again: How can I learn more about Hassan Beyg?"

"Easily," Balamani said, his dark eyes twinkling. "Not long ago, Anwar sent me to deliver a document to the Shah. Did I ever tell you I was directed to leave it at Hassan's home inside the Ali Qapu gate?"

"Don't tease me," I replied. "I know the name of every family that has a home inside the Ali Qapu. His is not one of them."

Balamani smiled, triumph gleaming in his eyes. "It is well disguised," he replied. "From the outside, it looks like an old administrative building. Go stand in the courtyard facing the Ali Qapu and look toward the city for the minaret of the Friday mosque. Walk directly toward the minaret, and when you get to the palace wall, count three doors to your right. You will see a battered old wooden door that looks as if it might lead to a servant's quarters. In fact, the door opens onto a huge garden with a house in back of it. There are always guards inside the old wooden door, so don't do anything foolish."

I laughed in admiration. He was still the master, after all.

It was easy to locate the old wooden door, but I could hardly stand there and watch it without arousing suspicion. Up on Pari's roof I found a spot with a partial view of the house's interior courtyard. Since the ladies of Pari's household used the roof to hang laundry and to dry fruits and herbs in the hot sun, I was able to conceal myself beneath a chador. Sitting on a small cushion and an old rug, I shelled peapods or picked the debris out of rice, just in case anyone observed me from below. Azar Khatoon came and went with herbs and fruit and occasionally stopped to tease me about the poor quality of my work.

"Look here!" she said, sifting through my rice and uncovering a few tiny stones. "A child could do better."

I had to agree. Mostly I kept my gaze fixed on the activities at Hassan's door. Tradesmen arrived laden with goods, which were accepted in the courtyard by servants, but no one of high rank ever went in or out. My vigil lasted for five days with no results, and I decided to stay on the roof all night as well. For three nights nothing happened. Then one night when I had dozed off, I was startled awake by the sound of a door slamming shut. The moon was bright, and I could make out the shapes of several men in the courtyard. Hassan was wearing a simple white cotton tunic and cotton trousers rather than his usual silk finery. A tight-fitting black cap covered his head. Except for his handsome face, which was unlined from sun or work, he could have been an ordinary fellow of modest means, like a merchant who owned a small shop in the bazaar. It was odd for someone so close to the Shah to be so casually dressed. The person with him had darker skin, and it was difficult to see his features clearly. His robe was brown and nondescript, and he had wrapped a cloth around the lower part of his face. Yet there was something familiar about the way he moved, a slouching gait that made me suspect it was the Shah in disguise. A few men that I recognized as bodyguards accompanied them.

The men walked toward the back of the house's gardens and all of a sudden disappeared from view. On a hunch, I threw off the chador, ran downstairs, and exited the palace through a side gate with the help of a friendly guard. I arrived just in time to catch sight of the men disappearing into one of the alleyways in the direction of the bazaar. By God above! Hassan's house must also have a secret exit that led to the Promenade of the Royal Stallions.

I assumed the men were going to a tavern or some other pleasure house, but I didn't dare follow them for fear of being discovered. I decided to enlist Massoud Ali, who would be less recognizable than me and could pretend to be out on an errand. We kept vigil together on the roof for several nights, during which his refusal to succumb to sleep and his desire to perform his job as well as a grown man made my heart swell with pride. We spent the long hours telling each other stories and playing backgammon, and I taught him a few new game strategies to try out on the other errand boys.

One night, when we were both restless, he began to demonstrate the techniques he had been learning in combat class to block hand strikes. Still clad in my disguising chador, I raised my arm as if to hit him, and he practiced batting it away and landing his own strike. Although he wasn't strong, he was very fast. At one point he scored a strike on my chest that I had failed to see coming.

We were so engrossed that I didn't notice when men appeared in Hassan's courtyard, but Massoud Ali alerted me to their movements in the dark. Stealthily the men moved toward the secret exit. Massoud Ali jumped up and raced after them, armed with a plausible excuse. I watched him until I could see him no more, a twinge of fear in my heart.

Several hours later I went to see Pari, who was wearing fine ivory cotton pajamas and a long yellow silk robe. She was sitting on a cushion, and Maryam was brushing out her long black hair, which reached her waist. Maryam must have recently applied henna to Pari's hair, because it glistened in the lamplight like a black grape bursting with juice.

"I am very sorry to disturb you, esteemed princess," I said, "but I have information for your ears only."

Maryam didn't pause her brushing. Pari said to her, "Soul of mine, you must leave for your own protection," and only then did Maryam arise and quit the room, her face sour.

I imagined she would return to brush Pari's long black hair, and then they would disrobe and hold each other in the dark. I tried to keep my mind away from the thought of the strong, wiry body of the one and the plump, peach-like curves of her fair-haired friend. I missed Khadijeh more and more. Aside from the pleasures of exploring her body, I yearned for the ordinary expressions of affection I used to enjoy, her back curved into my chest or mine against hers, the heat rising in the space between our bodies.

"What is it?" Pari asked impatiently.

"My nighttime vigil has taught me that the Shah leaves in disguise to pursue his pleasures in the bazaar," I said. "Massoud Ali has discovered that he buys halva from the same sweets vendor every time he goes out."

We discussed the merits of replacing the vendor with a man of our own, but decided it would provoke too much suspicion. Then we talked about the possibility of modifying the Shah's opium before it was formed into balls. That, too, seemed fraught with peril.

"Have the Shah's women been forthcoming about his other habits?" I asked.

"Not really. Mahasti talks about nothing but the baby in her belly. Koudenet is only fifteen, but she is not stupid. I whisper that I am trying to redeem myself in her husband's eyes and insist that if she came to know me, she would agree my cause is just. She looks as if she wonders when I will strike with my snake's venom."

Maryam entered the room uninvited. "It is time for bed," she announced. She flung back the velvet bedcover on the bedroll, revealing embroidered silk pillows, and stared at me.

"The princess is tired," she said pointedly.

Pari leaned back into a cushion and closed her eyes. "Good night, Javaher. Tomorrow morning we will talk more."

Maryam began brushing Pari's hair with the ivory brush as if they were already alone. A small sigh of pleasure escaped the princess's lips. I left them to one another and returned to my empty bed.

The goading look in Balamani's eyes when I had mentioned my father made me wish to prove my skills by solving the puzzle of his death, despite what I had said. There was a gap in the information I had gleaned from Looloo, Balamani, and from Mirza Salman that bothered me. Why would the Shah choose to protect an accountant who had killed one of his men? I was haunted by the mystery and felt humbled that I, the vaunted information gatherer, could not get to the bottom of it.

I went to the office of the scribes and requested the *History of Tahmasb Shah's Glorious Reign*. Abteen Agha, the sunken-chested eunuch, hadn't looked impressed with the fine gift I brought on my last visit, so I had taken pains to inquire about his taste in sweets. This time I brought white nougat studded with pistachios from his favorite sweets vendor. He raised his eyebrows at me as he whisked away the gift. "More business for your princess?" he asked sarcastically as he delivered the documents. I ignored him.

I found the entry for Kamiyar Kofrani easily enough and read through it. He was born in Shiraz and had been an accountant until he retired. He had married a woman who was unnamed and had four sons. Presumably two of them had died, since Balamani knew of only two living sons. He had assisted the late shah with some financial reforms that allowed the ledgers to be read and understood more easily, making it possible to uncover fraud. He had retired and died a few years later in Qazveen.

There was no mention of my father's murder, which was odd, and no reason to think that high status or family connections had prevented the Shah from punishing him for it.

Something was bothering me, something just beyond my grasp. Mirza Salman and the histories averred that the killer was dead, but Looloo's suggestion that he might be living had taken root in my thoughts. Unable to make sense of this contradiction, I returned to the entry about my father.

> **Mohammad Amir Shirazi:** Born in Qazveen, he served the Shah for twenty years, becoming one of his chief accountants. Many colleagues praised the accuracy of his accounts and his swift dispatch of court business. He seemed destined to rise up through the ranks of the men of the pen, until one day he was accused of crimes against the Shah and executed. Later, doubts were raised about the truth of the accusations. In his world-illumining mercy, the Shah did not execute his accuser, but it is also possible that his decision was influenced by the fact that the man had powerful allies whom the Shah didn't wish to offend. Only God knows all things with certainty.

I scrutinized the words, but the mosaic didn't form a clear picture; a critical piece of tile was missing. I stared at the words again, which seemed to reveal and conceal the truth at the same time. It seemed to be right there—the pieces going in and out of focus, until suddenly, I shouted out loud.

Abteen Agha's rounded shoulders spasmed, and he glared at me. "What is your problem? You could make a scribe ruin an entire page by hollering like that."

"I—finally found the answer to a question."

"Next time, keep the good news to yourself."

I looked down and reread one fragment of a sentence: *the Shah did not execute his accuser* . . .

What if the paragraph referred to two different men? The murderer was Kamiyar Kofrani. The accuser was a man with powerful allies who was probably still alive. The way the paragraph had been written suggested that someone, perhaps a scribe in the accuser's pay, had purposely obscured the truth. If so, I realized with growing excitement, I could pursue the man after all.

The next morning, I had just begun strategizing with Pari when we heard a series of long, anguished cries, followed by the sound of running. I jumped up and ran to the door, my hand on my dagger. Azar Khatoon came rushing in, out of breath.

"What is the trouble?"

"Sultanam. She is in a woeful state."

"Show her in right away," Pari said.

The moans became louder and Sultanam burst into the room, her leather slippers still on her feet. She stepped onto Pari's best silk carpets as if she didn't know they were there. Her kerchief had fallen off the crown of her head, and her white hair was a nest of snakes around her face. Her cheeks were streaked with tears, her mouth as wobbly as a suppurating wound.

"Eldest mother of the palace, what ails you?" Pari said, rising to her feet, as it was her duty to be solicitous. "How can I ease your suffering?"

"My heart has been torn out of my chest and eaten by a wolf," cried Sultanam. "Help me! By God above, help me!"

She fell to the floor on all fours like an animal and beat her fists against the hard ground. The princess tried to coax Sultanam to a cushion, but she shook Pari's hand off her arm as if the very touch burned her.

"Has someone hurt you, revered mother? Let me know who it is. I will render justice."

"Yes, you must render justice!" Sultanam cried, raising herself to a seated position. "I am sick with grief. I have lost the light of my eyes!"

"Who has been harmed?"

"It is my grandson, Sultan Hassan Mirza. I wish I could have died in his place."

My eyes met Pari's in alarm. Sultan Hassan was the eldest child of Mohammad Khodabandeh by his first wife.

"What happened to him?"

Sultanam wailed so loudly I felt the sound of her grief in my teeth. "He has been strangled in Tehran by Isma'il's men!"

"What a calamity!" Pari said. "I thought Isma'il had promised you that he would keep Mohammad Khodabandeh and all his children safe."

Sultanam's anguished wail made it clear that he had changed his mind. "Isma'il heard that some of the qizilbash were planning to support Sultan Hassan Mirza in a bid for the throne," she replied, "but I know that the boy had gone to Tehran simply because he wanted to request a better position at court. Now Isma'il has put Mohammad Khodabandeh and all his other sons under house arrest in Shiraz and Herat. I am terrified he will kill them all."

I tightened my hand on my dagger.

"May God keep them safe!" Pari replied. "Mother of so many Safavi generations, let me offer medicine to help relieve your pain."

"I don't want medicine," Sultanam raged. "I want justice!" She threw her arms high in the air and let her hands fall from above and strike her head and chest, battering herself.

"What would you like me to do?"

Sultanam stared at Pari with red-rimmed eyes. "I am here to tell you, in no uncertain terms, that my son must be deposed for the good of the state."

I could hardly believe my ears.

"Revered elder, are you certain? You said otherwise the last time I saw you."

"That is because no mother can conceive of deposing her own son, until she discovers that her son is a monster. Pari, you must take charge."

"How? The nobles won't help."

"Then you must find other means."

"What has changed your mind so completely? Isma'il has already killed far and wide!"

It was as if the princess were speaking the same thoughts that were forming in my mind.

"If Isma'il kills Mohammad and all his children, the dynasty will be finished. I must relinquish him to safeguard the future of my country."

Pari's face shone with awe. "How brave you have become!"

Sultanam's face looked like bread that has fallen flat. "This is also for myself. I do—not—wish to lose the rest of my family and be alone for the remainder of my days."

"Of course not. God willing, you will live to see many more generations."

I hoped Sultanam could help us catch our prey.

"Esteemed mother," I said, "your son, the lord of the universe, is very well defended. Surely it is impossible to remove him!"

"You must try to extract information from someone who knows Hassan Beyg."

"Such as who?" I asked.

"A prostitute named Shireen."

"How do you know such a woman?" Pari asked.

"She came to see me a few months ago after she had begun serving members of the court. After unveiling herself, she showed me the black bruises under her eyes and the welts on her legs. 'I pay my taxes like any honest prostitute,' she told me, 'and I beg you to protect me from customers who behave like madmen.'

"The culprit was the son of a khan. I directed my vizier to reprimand him, as well as to tell his father that his son would be beaten exactly as he had beaten her if it ever happened again. Shireen was so grateful for my protection that she has been feeding me information on her clients ever since. Hassan Beyg is one of them."

I almost laughed out loud at the thought of the Shah's favorite escaping into the arms of a prostitute.

"Can you get any information from Hassan for us?" Pari asked.

"No. Even the mother of a monster can do only so much. Go to Shireen and tell her I sent you."

"Where does Shireen live?" I asked, my feet as impatient to march as a soldier's.

"Near the Sa'eed water reservoir."

"Where the rich merchants live?"

"Yes; she is very beautiful."

The most beautiful prostitutes had to pay a higher tax than other women who sold themselves, but they also earned the most money.

Pari's eyes filled with admiration. "Your courage is an example to all women. I will never forget your words today, yet I know your heart bursts with sorrow over your grandchild. May I visit later today and weep with you over your losses?"

Sultanam stood up tall and broad, consuming the space of two women.

"Don't waste time grieving with me," she replied. "Just do what I command before more of my kin are executed. Hurry!"

"Chashm, gorbon."

Sultanam returned to her quarters, leaving Pari and me dumbfounded over what we had just witnessed.

"What a wonder," Pari said, her eyes liquid with sympathy. "Can you imagine bearing a child, only to have to destroy it?"

"I don't think I could do it. Could you?"

"My job is to mother my country, not bear children. Yours is the same."

Our eyes locked in understanding. How different we were from ordinary men and women! No children would issue from our loins, but we would endure the birth pangs of a better Iran. That mission, so much more grand and strange than any I had originally imagined for myself, made me buoyant with hope.

Pari gave me an engraved silver ewer to give to the prostitute as a gift, implying the promise of greater future rewards. After wrapping it in silk, I rushed toward the homes clustered around the bazaar, using the Sa'eed water reservoir as my landmark. It was one of dozens of underground reservoirs in the city that stored water directed from the mountains through gently sloping underground tunnels.

The mud-brick houses surrounding the reservoir were pleasant and well-kept. When I saw a group of children playing in the street, I asked for directions to Shireen's house. A boy led me there through winding alleys, as if he had done this many times before. When we arrived, he gestured to the house with an embarrassed look. I thanked him with a small coin.

I stepped through Shireen's wooden door into a tiny but neat courtyard with well-kept apricot trees. The brick walls of her house were covered with serene blue and yellow tiles, and I smelled musk at the doorway. I told her servant I had been sent by a member of the royal family and gave him the ewer. After being shown into Shireen's waiting room, I was served a vessel of tea flavored with rose water, along with a plate of thick dates and honeyed pastries. Birds sang merrily from somewhere in the house.

Just when I had finished my tea, a servant arrived to tell me that Shireen would see me. I arose and entered a smaller private room deep in her birooni. It was painted with a mural showing a man and a woman reclining in a garden. The woman's back rested against the front of the man's body, and his hands explored the secret passageways inside her robe, whose folds parted teasingly at her breast and knees. In the next scene, the one I began imagining in my mind, her robe would be halfway shed, revealing pomegranate breasts. Shireen's clients would be eager for her services after being so aroused.

When Shireen arrived at the door, still giving instructions to a servant, I inhaled an unforgettable perfume that combined smoke, frankincense, and rose. Her back was to me, and under her long dark hair, her cherry red robe brocaded with golden songbirds shimmered.

When she turned, I was startled by what I saw. Her dark eyes were huge, like deep wells below thick, velvety eyebrows. Her nose and mouth looked tiny by comparison. No one could ever forget such a face.

"Fereshteh!" I exclaimed. "Is it you, or do I dream?"

Her lovely eyes searched mine. Then she replied, in sober but sweet tones, "It is me. But when my servants come in, please call me Shireen. I don't use my real name anymore."

"May God above be praised!" I said. "I didn't think I would ever find you, especially after I heard you had gone to Mashhad."

"I decided to go all of a sudden," she replied, but she did not say why. "I was sorry when I learned what you had done to yourself. Payam, is it true?"

The sound of my old name brought perspiration to my brow. She was the only woman from my past who knew all about me; the only one who had seen my adult male parts. Many times I had dreamed of telling her, remembering her tenderness.

"Yes."

"Thank God you survived." Her face didn't show any of the disgust or horror I feared, nor did she turn her gaze away. I took a breath.

"When did you return to Qazveen?"

"About a year ago," she said. "I had done so well in Mashhad that I was able to make the pilgrimage to Mecca. While I was there, I vowed that as soon as I had earned enough money, I would relinquish my means of earning my living. I asked one of my clients in Mashhad to recommend me to members of the court."

"So I can call you Hajjieh Fereshteh," I said. "May God be thanked that you have made the hajj!"

"It has changed me through and through," she said. "God is merciful, and He has poured His grace on me. I am still an outcast of course—my sisters refuse to see me or accept my gifts—but I had to do what was necessary at the time."

"It was the same for me."

"Really? Why did you do it?"

Her gentle curiosity filled me with an urge to tell her everything. I began recounting my youthful despair, my dreams, and my progress since I had seen her last. As I spoke, something large and tight seemed to loosen in my breast.

"Back then, I thought it was my only choice. Now that I am older, I wonder if something deep within me wanted to sacrifice myself for my father, just as he had given his life for us."

I had never expressed that feeling before, not even to myself. How good it felt to admit the truth after so many years!

Fereshteh's gaze was affectionate. "I am not surprised. You were so young and so passionate about everything! The way you ate, the way you made love—it was as if your heart were newly born. I confess I thought of you often."

I had not expected her to say that, and her words warmed me through and through.

"And I, you," I replied, my mind alive with memories of how we had devoured each other in the dark. Her skin had been almost translucent, like fine paper, against the blackness of her hair. After our lovemaking, she had curled my body around hers like a snail snuggling in its shell.

"How has being a eunuch changed you?"

I stopped to think for a moment. "No one knows the ways of both men and women as well as I do—except perhaps you."

She smiled.

"But that's not all. Had I been a nobleman serving at the court as planned, I would have shunned many of those I have come to love."

"Is there someone you love?"

"An African slave has become my friend," I replied, trying to keep my heart still. "If I had remained a nobleman of rank, I doubt I would have spent so much time with her."

"I am glad to hear you have found love despite your changed state."

I looked at her. She was the same Fereshteh, but grown more beautiful. True, there were small lines at her mouth, but she was a ripe woman now, and her graciousness enveloped me like a sweet-smelling cloud.

"What about you? Would it have been better to remain at your stepmother's house?"

She smiled sadly. "I would have been married to the first man who asked, no matter what I thought about it. I doubt I would have been happy."

"Are you happy now?"

"More or less."

"Have you found love?"

"No," she replied. "What man wishes to make a prostitute his wife? But I have other boons, like my daughter, whom I love with all my heart."

The hope that filled me was so great I was afraid to speak. What if, by the grace of God, Fereshteh had left Mashhad because she was pregnant with my child? A little girl with Jalileh's pretty dark eyes sprang to life in my mind. Silently, I prayed to God, offering any sacrifice He desired.

"How old is she?"

"Six."

I sighed; she was far too young to be my child.

"What a lovely age."

A servant poked his head in the door and announced the arrival of another visitor.

"My friend, I wish I could stay with you longer, but for my daughter's sake, I must attend to business. Perhaps you will come another time."

"I will," I said, "but let me tell you why I am here. Sultanam has sent me. You have probably heard about the problems at the palace."

"I hear about them all the time. I have already received a message from her asking me to help you—but she called you Javaher."

"That is my palace name. Tell me, what do you know of Hassan Beyg?"

A knowing smile played at her lips. "Hassan Beyg is comely, but not bold. He trembles with fear that he will be killed when the Shah tires of him."

"Does he wish for another situation?"

"No, he is a loyalist. But he loves women, too."

I thought about how impossible it was to know a man's true face without knowing about every place he showed it.

"What does he say about the Shah?"

She paused for a moment. "Very little. If he is in a rambunctious mood, Hassan always mentions one thing—but it is quite impolite."

"What is that?"

"The Shah bloats like a pig, but nothing comes out."

I guffawed. This was the frank, funny Fereshteh I remembered from so long ago.

"Do you suppose that could make a man ill-tempered enough to kill?"

She laughed. "No doubt."

"How does the Shah treat his condition?"

Fereshteh stared at me, alert to danger. I would not have wished her to behave otherwise. No one is more dangerous than a reckless informant.

"Why do you want to know?"

"Sultanam has asked me to find out everything I can about her son. You may check with her if you don't believe me."

"I will."

"Can you ask Hassan about the Shah?"

"Perhaps." Her eyes told me she would think about it.

"I would be grateful for any help, Fereshteh. You are as celestial as your name, yet you are an earthy angel, too."

"And your eyes are still kind, but your mouth has become shrewd. May God be praised! Despite what you have endured, you have changed for the better."

No wonder Hassan Beyg visited so often! Fereshteh had a way of making a man feel embraced without even touching him. As I left, I remembered how velvety her skin had once felt under my fingertips, and how the huge wells of her eyes had always seemed to reflect my own sorrows. Her eyes, like mine, were much more guarded now.

A few days later, I received a brief coded letter from Fereshteh, which must have been penned by a scribe, since when I knew her years ago, she couldn't read or write. It said,

Remember the problem I mentioned to you? A friend says that the remedy is specially prepared digestives. Can you help me obtain some for my mother? God willing, they will greatly ease her suffering.

When I told the princess, she looked excited by the news for the first time since we had made our pact.

"I understand now. Do you?"

"I imagine the digestives loosen his bowels."

"There is more to it than that. Opium can turn a man's innards into sludge. If he is truly an addict, he is probably constipated for days at a time."

Pari's face suddenly lit up. "I have just remembered a peculiar poem by Sa'adi:

> *"The capital of man's life is his abdomen.*
> *If it be gradually emptied there is no fear*
> *But if it be so closed as not to open*
> *The heart may well despair of life;*
> *And if it be open so that it cannot be closed,*
> *Go and wash your hands of this world's life."*

"How frank! I have never heard anything quite like it," I said.

"Sa'adi didn't hesitate to write about any topic, even the bowels."

"What a gassy imagination."

She laughed. "How can we infiltrate the Shah's digestives?"

The apothecary in the second courtyard of the palace provided all the medicines used by the palace's inhabitants. Eunuchs delivered the medicines into the women's and the Shah's quarters.

"Good question. I am certain that his medicines undergo special security."

"I will pretend I am having a stomach problem and order some digestives to see what they look like. In the meantime, try to find out who brings them to him."

Late the next afternoon, I went to see Khadijeh again. I bought pastries in the bazaar and went to her quarters, claiming they were a gift from Pari. It was a rather poor excuse, but I couldn't help myself.

I was shown in to see Khadijeh in the kitchen she sometimes used within her quarters. She was wearing a purple cotton robe and lemon-colored trousers, and had wound her long hair at the back of her head. An ivory kerchief held the rest of it away from her eyes, but a few curls escaped at the back of her neck. Her dark lips looked plump enough to eat. Nasreen Khatoon was peeling a knobby quince, slicing off the thin skin with an expert touch. A pot full of quince boiled bright orange on a flame behind her, and ground nutmeg and cardamom lay ready in mortars, along with sliced lemon, rose water, and sugar.

"Good afternoon," I said to Khadijeh, who stood at the stove stirring the pot. "I bring you a gift of pastries from my lieutenant, with thanks for your help on that charitable matter we discussed earlier."

Nasreen Khatoon's eyebrows shot up.

"It is always my pleasure to help," Khadijeh replied. "Nasreen Khatoon, please bring coffee for my guest."

"May I make it here?"

"No. Get it from the main kitchen. It will be quicker."

Nasreen Khatoon's lips twitched as she left.

"How are you faring?" I asked her tenderly.

She sighed. "When the Shah touches me, my belly contracts with loathing."

I wanted to save her from him with all my heart. "One possibility has come to light."

"What is it?"

"Digestives."

Khadijeh put down the quince she had begun to peel. "Good idea. He ate some the last time he visited."

"Really? What do they look like?"

"They are about the size of a grape, and they seem to be made from herbs and honey."

"Who brought them?"

"He asked a servant to fetch them."

"Then how does he know the medicine is safe?"

"The box was closed with a seal."

"Whose seal?"

"Hassan's."

I wasn't surprised. A shah's closest companion would typically take care of the things he needed to have at hand—medicines, handkerchiefs, and the like.

"How does the medicine get to Hassan?"

"I don't know. Most likely a messenger brings it to him from the apothecary, and he tastes it before adding his seal."

"Can you obtain one of the digestives for me?"

"I can try."

The jam was boiling delicately. She stirred it, tasted it, and added more sugar and rose water. The floral scent saturated the air, reminding me of the first time we had kissed. When Mahmood's mother was ill with the stomach ailment that eventually killed her, I used to go to Khadijeh to request soft foods she could digest, like rice pudding. One day, after we had begun flirting, Khadijeh offered me a serving of baklava redolent of rose water and bade me eat it from her fingers. I licked them, and then—

"Javaher, please don't."

My hands shook with frustration. "Does he still speak of plots? Does he arise in the night and grab his dagger?"

"Not anymore. But that doesn't mean he won't strike again."

I wished we had struck at him first.

"What about the jam?" she said, staring into the bubbling pot. "Do you think I could put a dose of something into it?"

I was horrified. "Where would you get such a dose?"

"I know people."

"Don't even ponder such a thing!" I said, angry at myself for having planted the idea in her mind. "His taster will try it, and then you will be sacrificed. No matter what happens, you can't do that—for my sake."

She sighed. "I wish I could help you more."

"You are helping me more than you know. Just seeing you here makes me happy. Keep yourself safe for the sake of your future children."

Khadijeh smiled sadly. "Insh'Allah."

She lifted a spoon of the jam out of the pot and blew on it. When it had cooled, she offered it to me. I sucked the jam onto my tongue and held it there, feeling its sweetness flood my mouth. My eyes met hers, and I remembered the sweet taste of her tongue.

"Incomparable," I said. "I had better go before I violate all protocol and lay you down right here."

She looked away, and a pang in my heart prompted me to ask her a question. "Khadijeh—do you think, if you were ever free again, you and I would—"

She put down her stirrer and pressed her lips tightly together. She looked at the floor.

"I want children," she said softly, "and besides . . ."

She made a gesture of helplessness by opening her hands to the sky. I stared at her and guessed what she meant. She preferred a fully equipped man, now that she knew what it was like to have one.

She smiled even more sadly. "I am sorry."

"You are in my heart always," I said, feeling another rip in that tender place.

"Javaher—" she said, and I saw pity clouding her eyes. That was something I couldn't endure.

"I must go."

I left the kitchen just as Nasreen Khatoon returned with the coffee. I thanked her and told her I had pressing business for Pari. She looked surprised by my abrupt departure.

I should have reported to the princess for duty, but I didn't have the heart for the business of the palace. I sent a message that I was ill, returned to my quarters, and lay awake most of the night, watching the sky change from indigo to ash. At dawn, a weak, useless sun failed to brighten the dim sky.

Khadijeh sent me an octagonal wooden box inlaid with tiny pieces of gilded ivory that formed a pattern of golden stars against a shimmering white background. The box had been sealed with Hassan's red wax seal. I lifted the lid, revealing a single digestive nestled in its own compartment.

The digestive was a lemon-yellow ball about the size of the end of my thumb. The large size indicated to me that it was intended for chewing, not swallowing. It was missing a corner and bore a bite mark. I imagined Khadijeh complaining to the Shah of a stomach-ache in order to obtain one; then she would have had to eat some of it. I hid the medicine in a fold of my robe.

That afternoon, Pari summoned me to show me the digestives she had received from the apothecary. They had been sent in a plain wooden box that bore the apothecary's seal. Pari lifted the lid, and I probed one with my finger. It was sticky.

"My messenger told the apothecary that I needed a digestive as good as what he makes for the Shah. He swore to my messenger this morning that he used exactly the same recipe."

I wondered about the veracity of that. "What do they taste like?"

"Mint. Do you want one?"

"No, thank you."

"Take them now and have them re-created by an expert who will not betray us."

"Just a minute," I said, thinking it wise to be cautious. "I have obtained one as well. Let us compare them."

"From whom?"

"An impeccable source."

I unwrapped the digestive I had received. It was larger than the others, despite its missing part, and a brighter saffron. Although it smelled of mint, the fragrance of cinnamon was much stronger.

"Look at that! Are you certain it is from the Shah's private stash?"

"I am certain. I have the box as well. It is much finer than the one you received."

"Who gave it to you?"

"I think it is better not to say, for everyone's protection."

"I need a hint."

"Very well, then. It is one of his women."

"Someone you trust?"

"With my life."

"Javaher, you are worth your weight in gold."

If we had copied the apothecary's digestives, we would have been found out right away. Khadijeh had already saved us.

"What excuse have you used for visiting her?"

"I have requested charity for Rudabeh and the other women who petition you for favors."

"All right, then. Can you have the digestive re-created by someone who can't betray us?"

"I will try."

It wasn't an easy task. I needed a person skilled enough to know how to make poisons, but compromised enough to prevent betrayal.

I couldn't use anyone with the slightest connection to the Shah, so I began to think about the men who had opposed him or who had suffered a grievance. The large family related to Kholafa was a possibility, but I couldn't find any medical men or apothecaries among his kin. I didn't wish to seek some unknown person in one of the alleyways of the bazaar who might decide to betray me in exchange for money. Finally, I remembered Amin Khan Halaki, the physician whose bright blue robe I had spotted when he was hiding in the harem—unsupervised—after Haydar had tried to take the throne. I knew he had escaped because I had seen him a few weeks later in the bazaar.

The Halaki family owned a home near the river. The servant who opened his door didn't wish to let me in when he discerned from the fineness of my attire that I was from the court. He tried to claim that his master wasn't home, but I pushed open the door, stepped inside, and told him he had better rouse the physician. Cowed, the servant disappeared to do my bidding, returned quickly, and showed me into his master's public rooms with florid apologies.

Amin Khan had thick gray eyebrows that obscured his eyes. He wore a dark gray robe that added to the impression that he was trying to disappear. His jaw clenched at the sight of me.

"So it is you."

"You sound as if you were expecting me."

"Of course. I knew you would want a favor in return." His voice bled sarcasm.

"I do."

"Well, come in. I was in the middle of making something. Follow me."

We entered a large room that held the tools of his profession. The alcoves were stuffed with clay jars filled with herbs, as well as medical texts such as Avicenna's immortal treatises and a smattering of books by the ancient Greeks. The room smelled of hundreds of herbs, including a pile of something dark and green whose bitter aroma filled the air. I sneezed a few times as we continued into a courtyard, where a metal pot filled with a bright yellow liquid bubbled on top of a fierce charcoal fire. Another pot contained pale roots that were steeping. Amin Khan stirred the yellow liquid.

"What are you making?"

"My work is confidential," he replied in a tone just short of snapping.

"That is good to hear," I replied, "since that is exactly what I require."

"State your business."

"I trust you can help me," I said. "I know you will keep your promise of confidentiality, given where I last found you. No doubt you have heard that Isma'il doesn't take kindly to those he suspects of evil deeds."

"I cared for his father. Was that an evil deed?"

"No, except for the small matter of the orpiment being poisoned."

"I know nothing about that," he replied, his face closing as if he were withdrawing behind the thicket of his eyebrows.

"You would have to persuade him. I am sure you don't wish to have to do so, especially given all the people he has killed."

Amin Khan dropped the metal stirrer into the pot and uttered a curse as he fished it out.

"What do you want?" He kept an eye on the pot while talking.

"I have a personal matter to resolve," I said, "and I need some poison to settle the matter to my heart's content."

"Who is your prey?"

"The murderer of my father."

"Is he a nobleman?"

"No."

He laughed. "Don't worry, I don't believe a word of what you have said so far. What kind of poison do you need?"

"Something quick and tasteless."

"That is what everyone wants. Do you need a powder, a cream, or a liquid?"

"What do you advise?"

He looked exasperated. "It depends how you are planning to use it."

I reached into my robe and drew out the digestive I had stored there. "I need eight servings that look and taste exactly like this."

He smelled the digestive and took a small bite, chewing it thoroughly. "Wormwood, cinnamon, peppermint oil, turmeric, honey, and a touch of ground rubies. Duplicating this will cost you plenty."

"Ground rubies? How can you tell?"

Amin Khan smiled. "How much money do you have?"

I put a bag of silver that Pari had given me on the table. Amin Khan's eyebrows shot skyward.

"Your life savings? The prey must be quite important."

"I am paying for an impeccable dose—and for your silence."

Amin Khan didn't reply. He grabbed the pot of steeping roots and poured it through a sieve into the yellow liquid. The liquid jumped to the lip, bubbling fiercely. As it settled, it became white and opaque.

"When you need your order, send me a messenger requesting your stomach medicine. I will send a boy back to you who will tell you where to go in the bazaar to pick it up. I don't allow my messengers to go into the palace with such dangerous materials."

"All right."

"Once you have it in your possession, never let it out of your sight. You can guess why."

"Yes," I replied. I never thought I would be pursuing such black arts, and I was surprised to discover that his work both repelled and fascinated me. A capacity for destruction seemed to lie within me. I thought about my father and wondered if he had experienced a similar feeling.

"Who taught you how to make such things?"

Amin Khan's bushy eyebrows lowered in self-defense. "If you are hired to be the shah's physician, you must know how to make everything," he answered.

I peered at the liquid in the pot. It was cooling and reducing in size. Small islands of white powder formed on its surface. I had never seen such alchemy before.

"What is in the pot? It looks wicked."

He smiled. "It is. In a few hours, it will turn into a fine face powder. Ladies ensnare men with it as easily as if they were the devil himself."

Pari was getting thinner and thinner: Her drawn face made her cheeks look even more sculpted than usual, and her robes seemed to hang off her body. I knew she was worried about her brother Mohammad Khodabandeh's safety and that of his four children, in the absence of any guarantee from Isma'il Shah. Whenever a messenger rushed into her quarters, her eyes widened with alarm.

I offered to visit Mirza Salman and ask if he had any information about Isma'il's plans. So far, Mirza Salman had been my best source of information about my father. I grabbed at any excuse to see him again.

Mirza Salman's waiting room was crowded, but I was shown in quickly.

"The princess fears for the safety of Mohammad Khodabandeh's family," I told him. "She wonders if you think the killings are done."

Mirza Salman frowned. "Isma'il must be careful not to offend Sultanam. People will become angry if they think he has wronged her excessively. Recently, though, he made some comments that were very disheartening."

"What were they?"

"He said that everyone thought his grandfather was close to God. They were so convinced his royal farr could protect them that they would fight without armor. Today, no one believes Isma'il is anything but a man. He blames that on his father. Who can believe in his omnipotence after he was imprisoned for nearly twenty years?"

"True."

"That is why he feels he has to show his power through brute force."

"I see. Do you think Mohammad and his children are at risk?"

"Yes."

"May God protect them. How about the princess?"

"He hasn't said anything about her."

"Will the nobles try to stop him?"

"No, because only about half are against him."

"I see. And what is your strategy?"

"To survive."

"I suppose that is better than the alternative."

He laughed, but once again, I sensed that he was ill at ease with me. I decided to try to take advantage of his discomfort.

"Speaking of the alternative, may I ask you another question about my father?"

"Certainly."

"What do you remember of him?"

"Your father was an excellent raconteur who was welcome at every party he attended. But like many people who are good at talking, he didn't know when to stop."

"Do you know how his plot was uncovered?"

"From what I heard, he imbibed too much one night and couldn't keep quiet. It didn't take long for the story to find the ears of someone willing to betray him."

"That doesn't surprise me. He loved to talk."

A eunuch entered and told Mirza Salman that Mirza Shokhrollah needed to see him. I would have to hurry.

"There is just one other thing. The court history says that Tah-masb Shah didn't punish Kamiyar Kofrani because he had such important allies. Do you know who they were?"

Mirza Salman's eyes looked guarded, and I had the distinct impression that something was amiss.

"No. You have reached the limits of my knowledge on this sub-ject."

The more I investigated my father's murder, the more the truth seemed to slip from my grasp. I remained silent, which I often found was a good way to encourage people to keep talking.

"The lesson in all of this is that a man must never be sloppy at court," he added. "Look at Isma'il Shah. What discipline he has! His security is impeccable. He hasn't made a single mistake yet."

Mirza Salman was ever the slippery courtier.

"Is that what matters most?"

"Perhaps not, but it has certainly forestalled any attempts on his life."

The princess wasted no time before asking Gowhar if she knew any-one who might be able to help us deliver the digestives once we were ready. Gowhar mentioned a eunuch named Fareed Agha who had worked for her for several years before coming to serve at the palace. After Ibrahim was killed, he had visited her to pay his condolences and hinted about how unhappy he was regarding affairs at the pal-ace. Gowhar summoned him and told him that if he would be will-ing to perform a special mission for her, it would make him rich, and he agreed to hear the terms of it.

We made our plans, and then I sent Massoud Ali to Fareed Agha to tell him to meet me underneath one of the big walnut trees in the harem gardens at midnight the following day. At the appointed hour, I wrapped myself in dark cotton clothes and waited at the base of the tree, where it was as black as naphtha.

When Fareed appeared, I recognized him slightly, not because of his looks but because of his scent. The acrid smell of urine wafted around him due to some leak that must have resulted from the way he was cut. Such unfortunate eunuchs were usually put in lowly messenger jobs so that they didn't bother anyone by lingering too long. He would welcome Pari's money.

When he saw me, he looked surprised. "Is this mission for your princess?"

"Don't ask questions. My orders are to lead you to the person who has summoned you."

Fareed followed me to the back of the harem gardens and through the hedges, which had grown thicker since my first visit with Pari. The night was flooded with moonlight. We would have to hurry to avoid being seen. I stepped into the old pavilion and looked around. It was empty. I told him to wait a moment for me, and then I went into the room with the green and yellow tiles and lifted the old tile so Pari could appear. She emerged wrapped in a black chador, which concealed her head and body. She had also placed a picheh in front of her eyes so she could see but not be seen.

I called out for Fareed Agha, who entered behind me. He looked startled when he laid eyes on her. In her black clothing she was like a spirit hovering in the darkness.

"What is it, a jinni?" he asked, as if making a joke, but I could see he was awed.

"Come here," Pari commanded, and he approached a little closer, but not too close.

"Who are you?" he asked.

"I won't tell you who I am, only that I have a splendid gift for you. Behold!" she said.

She opened a bag and spilled silver in front of him on the floor. The coins struck the tiled surface like music. Even in the dark of night, they gleamed, and his eyes became round with desire as he calculated what the money would mean.

"So you are a jinni after all!"

"Not so. I am a taskmaster."

"What do you require?"

"Something very simple. I won't tell you what it is unless you agree to be employed."

"What is its purpose?" he asked.

"Ending the killings at the palace."

There was a long silence.

"So this is a dirty business."

"It is an essential business, one that requires a trustworthy man like yourself."

"Why me?"

"I thought you might be a man of justice."

"A man of justice? I have never seen myself that way."

"Most of us haven't until we are called on to do something of great importance."

He looked uncomfortable. "I am just an ordinary servant."

"That is exactly what we need. I understand that you served Gowhar and Ibrahim honorably for many years."

"True. I feel very sorry for her now."

"As do I. What do you do at the palace?"

"I make deliveries."

"Of what?"

"Food, mostly."

"Do you like working here?"

He was silent for a moment. "I used to."

"What has changed?"

"The palace has become a place of fear," he said. "One day a man is raised high; the next day his head is displayed on a stake outside the Tehran Gate. There is no logic to it."

"That is the problem we wish to address," said Pari.

"If your cause is pure justice, why do you pay?"

"In consideration of the great risk to you. We would do it ourselves, but we can't go where you can."

He took a deep breath. "Whom do you wish to extinguish?"

"I will tell you what you need to know if you accept my commission. If not, our conversation is finished. What is your decision?"

"It depends how you will protect me."

"After you perform the deed we require, you will receive these coins and will be escorted outside, where a horse will await you. You will depart for a distant city and will live as a rich man from then on."

"I would rather stay in Qazveen."

"You can't. It is not safe for any of us."

"How do I know you won't turn on me? Or blame me for what you yourself have tried to do?"

"I will give you my word."

"And why should I take your word?"

"Royal blood flows through my veins. Isn't that good enough?"

"Not if you can't prove it."

"What would satisfy you?"

"Only one thing: I need to see you."

"And how do I know you won't betray me?"

"I give you my word."

Pari laughed. "That is not good enough."

"That is what I want," he said. "Show me your face to prove who you are, and I will do what you ask."

"Don't do it," I whispered to Pari. If he could name her, and he betrayed us or was caught, people would believe his story was true.

Heedless of her own safety, Pari lifted her picheh and revealed her face. Her dark eyes were just visible in the moonlight that filtered into the pavilion. A drop of turquoise set in gold gleamed at the center of her forehead. The silver threads in her robe glowed as if she were a ghostly apparition. She was fearless—and in that moment my heart swelled to bursting.

"When you perform what I command, know that you do so by order of a princess who has the good of her dynasty foremost in mind."

He was speechless at the sight of her.

"Our time is at an end," I said. "Will you help us or not?"

He eyed the money on the floor one last time as if making calculations. I could imagine what he must be thinking: He would never have to work again, and he would live a life of ease. I envied him.

"What must I do?"

"When we summon you, you will come here alone to pick up a box. You will deliver the box to a location outside the harem and return here. Then you will receive your money and be escorted outside of the palace. Is that simple enough?"

"It is simple enough to kill a man."

"True."

There was a long silence. There was no turning back now.

"When the time is right, I will summon you," I said.

"Not so fast. I want half the money now, and half when I return from delivering it."

"No," I said. "Half when you pick up the box, and half when you return."

"Done."

"May God be with you," he said, and I watched him disappear into the dark. I returned the coins to the cloth bag. When he was far enough so that he would not hear or see anything, I gently lifted the tile, descended into the passageway, and left the bag of money there. Beside it, I placed the Shah's inlaid ivory box, which had been concealed in my room. We were almost ready.

⁂

When I awoke a few days later to the sound of music, I thought I was dreaming. It seemed as if an orchestra were exploding with joy. How long had it been since I heard such notes of happiness at the palace? I sat up to ask Balamani the reason, but he had already left for the day. Massoud Ali knocked and entered my quarters dressed in a new blue robe. A curl of unruly black hair had escaped from his turban, as if the forerunner of the exciting news.

"The whole palace is rejoicing. The Shah has an heir!"

"My little radish, are you sure you don't have some bad news for me?" I teased. "Where are the dark clouds that always ring your youthful head?"

I collapsed on my bedroll, pleased that I didn't have to rush out to attend to a problem.

"You will see nothing but blue skies today," he said. "Unless you want me to look harder for rain clouds!"

I swatted the air and told him he was a *shaytoon*—devil—which made him laugh.

"What is the child's name?"

"Shoja al-din Mohammad. The light of the universe has rewarded the messenger with a silk robe of honor. There will be a grand celebration, and all the townspeople will be invited to feast and celebrate the Shah's good fortune in the Promenade of the Royal Stallions."

He paused, his black eyes dancing. "Can we play a game of backgammon to celebrate? I bet I can beat you now."

I laughed. "Certainly. But first, how is Mahasti?"

"She is healthy and has already received visits from some of her kinswomen."

Even though Mahasti was a slave, she would be sure to claim better rooms and more servants, and perhaps she would even receive her freedom or an offer of permanent marriage from the Shah. I could only imagine how Khadijeh and the other wives felt now that she had succeeded in giving him his first son.

"Does Pari know?" I asked.

"She has just gone to visit Mahasti."

"Quick, set up the board while I get ready."

We played a game, and for the first time, I had to pay close attention to every move. Massoud Ali made his plays with skill and zeal, and although he did not win, the sparkle in his eyes revealed how much he relished the closeness of the battle.

"Mash'Allah!" I said, and rewarded him with a big chunk of halva. While he ate it, I told him another installment of the story of Zahhak and Kaveh. When he heard the part about how Kaveh had confronted the tyrant, stomped on his proclamation, and raised his leather banner in the air, his eyes widened with disbelief.

"How brave!"

"Especially because Kaveh didn't even brandish a weapon—just the strength of his own character and the truth of his own words."

"Vohh!"

"But a man who takes such a stand has to believe in it with his whole heart and soul. That is the only way that his enemy will be overcome."

"With his whole heart and soul," Massoud Ali repeated softly.

It was getting late. I sent Massoud Ali on his errands and went to Pari to find out about her visit.

"He is a handsome child with a great howl," she told me enthusiastically. "I could see my father in his eyes."

"How is Mahasti?"

"Like all new mothers, she behaved as if drugged. I tried to ask her about the Shah, but she was so preoccupied with the baby that I think she has forgotten the name of his father."

We laughed together.

"How is Koudenet?"

"Full of envy. She wishes she had borne the first son. She is also peevish because the Shah isn't visiting her as much as he used to."

"I imagine he wishes to be with Mahasti right now."

"I don't think so. Mahasti mentioned that he won't return to spend the night until the child is sleeping through the dark hours."

"When is the celebration?"

"Tomorrow, and it will last for three nights. The first night is for the Shah and his closest retainers. The next night will include all the noblemen. The third night is the public celebration for the citizens of Qazveen."

Our eyes met and we did not have to say much.

"The third night?" I asked softly.

"Yes. If God is with us, we will succeed."

Pari sent word to a groom to order the horses that would carry Fareed to safety three nights hence, and I sent a message to the physician ordering the digestives. As I went about my tasks, I felt the enthusiasm of a soldier primed to meet his enemy on the battlefield. We had been planning our assault for a long time. At last, victory seemed close at hand.

That night, I fell into a deep sleep, a luxurious blackness in which I would have liked to remain. But some time very early in the morning—too early—I heard a noise near my door. It must be my little radish coming to bring me some news, I thought fondly, smiling a little, but then came the sound of iron ripping wood. Before I had time to leap out of bed, the door split open, its lock broken, and four eunuchs armed with daggers and swords burst in. Ya, Ali! I didn't recognize them, but from their engraved shields and metal helmets, I knew they were part of the Shah's guard.

Balamani opened his eyes. "What is all this noise about?" he asked almost lazily, and I realized he was hiding any sign of concern.

"Get up. You have been summoned by the Shah," the captain announced to me.

I acted as if I had a clean conscience. "It is my pleasure to be of service," I replied, getting out of bed.

"The work of a loyal servant is never done," Balamani said. "Wake me when you get back."

He rolled over, and before long, a believable snore escaped from his nose.

As I wrapped myself in a dark robe, placed my turban around my hair, and put on my leather shoes, I silently inventoried all the things that could have gone wrong. Had the physician betrayed me? Had Sultanam laid a trap for us? Had Fareed blabbered to someone? Had I made the same mistakes as my father by talking to too many people?

"Follow me," said the captain, and when I did, one of his soldiers hugged closely behind. Massoud Ali came speeding down the corridor, but when he saw the soldiers, he wisely continued elsewhere, his eyes wide with worry. The other soldiers remained in my room, which meant they would be searching my things. I broke out into a sweat.

We walked through the still-dark gardens, which were heavy with dew, and entered the Shah's birooni. Its ceiling was decorated with plaster carved into the shape of icicles, which made it look as cold as a cave. A mosaic of tiny mirrors on the walls reflected every detail of my frightened face and made me imagine that the Shah's eyes and his spies were everywhere.

I was called in right away, a terrible sign. My heart fell further at the sight of Pari, who had dressed hastily in a plain robe, with no jewelry, her hair loose over her shoulders except for a white kerchief holding it in place. I tried to discern from her eyes what to say or do, but she made no sign. Sweat leaked from my armpits into my sash.

The Shah was seated on a low throne covered with cushions on a blue silk carpet. There were hollows under his eyes, and although he wore a fine silk robe, he had not bothered to put on his turban, and his hair stood on end. I pressed my hand to my chest, bowed low, and waited.

"Let's hope your servant can explain himself," the Shah said to Pari, with no preamble. His voice rumbled with rage. "Why have you been visiting my servant Khadijeh? Remember that you lie to your shah on pain of death."

I saw Nasreen Khatoon sitting by herself at the back of the room. I would have to be as smooth as perfumed oil.

"Light of the universe, I have visited your servant on several occasions to request charity. She has been very generous."

"Charity for whom?"

"For unfortunate women who presented themselves to my lieutenant, Pari Khan Khanoom, and begged for help."

"That is ridiculous. My sister has enough money to help anyone who asks."

"Yes, but the need is great, and often other women wish for an opportunity to help their fellow Muslims."

He stared at me skeptically. "Tell me about every visit."

I looked at Pari for a sign that I was on the right track, but she gave no clue.

"Certainly. I will try to remember. The first time, a lady had come to my lieutenant after losing her house because she needed assistance in the form of clothing for herself and her child. She was from Khui. The second time, the lady had recovered her house and sent a thank-you gift of embroidery, which I delivered to your servant. It was very fine, with poppies and roses."

"You can omit the florid descriptions."

"I beg your pardon. On another occasion, a lady that my lieutenant knew was ill needed medicine to quiet her grieving heart. I had heard that your servant was skilled at such things—"

"Skilled indeed!" interrupted the Shah, looking around at his assembled staff. "But not as skilled as she had hoped!" His laugh was loud and horrible. All the eunuchs and the women in the room looked chastened, as if the subject were too ghastly for words. A pit of fear opened in my belly.

"That is three visits. What about when she was making jam?"

"Jam?" I said, to give myself time to think. Nasreen Khatoon had seen me with Khadijeh that day. Delivering a gift from Pari seemed like a flimsy reason, especially since the two women hardly knew each other.

"Answer me!"

I feigned embarrassment. "Forgive me, lord of the universe, but I went to see her because I was ill. Since she is famous for her medicines, I asked for some."

As Nasreen Khatoon hadn't stayed in the room, she wouldn't be able to contradict my assertion. I only hoped I wasn't laying a trap for Khadijeh.

"That is a stupid excuse. You have use of the palace apothecary."

"I needed it right away," I said. "I was having trouble with something I dare not mention in the royal presence."

"Give me an idea."

I hoped that the Shah might have a shred of sympathy for a roiling stomach, since he had a bowel problem of his own.

"Something I couldn't stop from pouring out of me—"

"Diarrhea? Don't mince words."

"Like water, lord of the universe."

"Is the medicine in your chambers?"

"No. She didn't give me any."

His eyes were cold. "If you have nothing to fear, why are you so nervous? You are sweating."

"I am afraid I may have somehow offended the royal radiance. Nothing pains me more than that idea."

The Shah turned to Pari. "Did you know he asked one of my women for medicine?"

"No," she replied angrily. "It is not correct for my vizier to make personal requests of the women close to you. He will be reprimanded for his transgression."

I assumed a fearful look and threw myself at the Shah's feet. "Light of the universe, I beg your forgiveness!"

"Get up," said the Shah, and I rose slowly to my feet, my face crumpling out of concern. I was frightened in a way I had never been before—for myself, for Pari, and for Khadijeh.

The Shah called in the captain who had broken my door. He entered and bowed low. "Did your men find anything in his room?"

"Nothing but a book of poetry," said the eunuch. "But a messenger has just arrived for him from a physician."

I realized with a jolt that the messenger had come to lead me to the poison in the bazaar. My mind became clear and cold as I began to think of what I might say to justify buying poison, and I decided that although I would lose my life, the only way to protect Pari, and maybe even Khadijeh, would be to swear that I had decided on my own to poison the Shah.

"What did he want?"

"His stomach medicine is ready," the guard replied.

"What is it with you eunuchs?" the Shah demanded. "You always have problems at one end or the other!"

"Please forgive me for my unworthiness."

Someone whispered in the Shah's ear, and he turned his attention on me once again. "Ah. You are the self-gelder, aren't you?"

"I am."

"What a freakish tale. I expect you think you have proved your loyalty once and for all. Know that I will require further demonstrations of it."

"Chashm gorbon," I replied, my head bowed.

The Shah turned to Pari. "Do you understand now why I have to be so thorough? You never know when a murderer will strike."

His words threw another arrow of fear into my liver.

"The light of the universe is wise," Pari replied.

The Shah looked pleased. "I intend to root out every would-be killer in the palace," he added.

His courtiers' faces blanched with fear; the silence in the room felt suffocating. For a moment I caught Nasreen Khatoon's eyes, which were like ice.

The Shah waved his hand to dismiss me. "Your servant has leave to go," he said, not bothering to use my name. "But you had better keep a closer eye on him in the future."

I walked to Pari's home and gave my heartfelt thanks to God that I had survived. It was just becoming light, and birds had begun singing in the trees. Their cheerful tune filled me with sweet relief.

When Pari arrived, her face was closed. She called me into her private rooms and slammed the door. Rather than sitting down, she stood so close to me I could smell the sharp scent of fear emanating from her body.

"Javaher, have you lost your reason?"

I didn't care for her angry tone. "It was for the sake of getting information."

"Why didn't you tell me about her?"

"I gave you an idea of my source. I thought ignorance would protect you, and her, too."

"Was she the person who gave you the digestive?"

"Of course."

"What else were you trying to discover?"

"The Shah's personal habits."

Her frown was so deep it made her face look like a weapon. "You could have gotten us killed. Now he is going to be more careful than ever, and it is all because of you."

"What do you mean?"

"I mean you have overstepped your authority."

"By the fires of hell! How did you think I procure such excellent information for you?"

She pointed her finger at me accusingly. "You need to tell me when you take such risks. You have violated one of your own rules by keeping your activities secret from me all this time."

"I wanted to keep everyone safe, including myself. That is my job."

She guffawed suddenly, but the sound was devoid of mirth. "Okh, okh! You donkey! You have behaved like a know-it-all."

I was in no mood to be accused of things, even if they were true. I turned my face away as if from a bad smell.

"Fortunately, I knew enough to tell the Shah that you had requested charity for my petitioners. When he pressed me for more details, I told him I had so many cases I didn't know which ones you had brought to which ladies. It was only luck that you had mentioned charity to me not long ago—pure luck. We need a better strategy than that."

"It seemed to work well enough," I retorted.

Pari glared at me as if I were a worm. "By God above, don't you understand what has happened?"

"No." My belly clenched with pain.

"Last night, the Shah was awakened by suspicious noises. He noticed that Khadijeh was standing near his flask of water and fumbling with something. When he jumped up and grabbed her around the waist, she screamed. Crushed in her hand was a clay vial, which she claimed bore amatory musk. She told him she hoped the potion would work its magic and allow her to bear a child.

"The Shah was almost convinced until he decided to order her to drink it. She argued that she didn't need it to feel amorous. When he insisted, she tried to rid herself of the vial, but he forced her to drink its contents. Before long, she began clutching her stomach and writhing in agony. Just before she died, she told him she had acted on her own to avenge the death of her brother, but he didn't believe her. All this morning, he has been interviewing her ladies and her visitors to discover who else is to blame."

The room around me had grown dark and suffocating. I clapped my hands against my chest and held them there.

Pari stared at me. "Javaher, why do you look as if you have lost the light of your eyes?"

"I have!" I exclaimed, but stopped myself there. I couldn't admit to Pari that I had been in love with one of the Shah's wives. She would consider it an unpardonable transgression.

"If only I could take her place!"

Pari's lips turned down in surprise. "Why?"

"Because," I continued, half-choking, "because this means the Shah has proven himself willing to kill a woman, and now you are no longer safe, either."

I couldn't stop angry tears from dampening my eyes, so stricken was I by the news.

"Javaher—you are truly frightened for me—is that it?"

"Yes, my lieutenant," I replied, wiping my face and trying to collect myself. "I am truly frightened."

"Don't worry about me. Very few people know of our plans: only Gowhar and Sultanam, who are on our side, plus Fareed, who needs money, and the physician, who is compromised by his own past. Is there anyone else?"

"No," I said, because I did not want to implicate Fereshteh or Balamani. And then I was filled with fear: Would they betray us?

"All right, then. We will curse Khadijeh's name and express righteous pleasure that the Shah has foiled a slave's plot against his life."

"It was brave of her to make the attempt," I insisted.

"I can't approve of a slave deciding to poison the Shah. It was overstepping her station."

"Overstepping? Then why is it right for us to do so?"

"I have royal blood."

I was flooded with rage. She should be praising Khadijeh's name, not condemning her.

"Javaher," Pari said, looking at me strangely, "you are shaking. Did you have anything to do with Khadijeh's plan?"

"Nothing at all," I replied, and it was the one true thing I had said all morning. "But I am sick over it. I only wish I had known so I could have stopped her."

"By God above, I have never seen your heart so inflamed. What are you keeping secret from me?"

I remembered Khadijeh offering me a taste of jam, her eyes sweeter than the sugared quince. Now those eyes were sightless forever. Fervently I wished I had never revealed our plans; what a fool I had been!

"We were good friends," I confessed. "Now she is dead, and it is all because she wanted to help."

I fell to a squat, my arms dangling brokenly between my knees. I felt as if my skin had peeled off, leaving all my organs bare to the elements and every nerve pulsing with pain. I longed from the depths of my soul for the extinction of all my senses. Had I been near a high mountain pass, I would have leapt with gratitude to my death. For a long time, I forgot where I was.

When my head finally cleared and I stood up, shaken, a tray had appeared beside me with one of Pari's handkerchiefs and a vessel of something. I wiped my face.

"Javaher, drink the mixture. It will soothe you." Pari's voice seemed to come from far away.

I smelled bitter herbs and honey, which I consumed in a single draft. Dullness flooded through me.

"I am sorry about your friend."

I could not speak.

"How I wish that even one of my brothers could boast the kind and loyal blood that sparkles like rubies in your veins! I deeply regret that your service to me has caused you so much grief. Oh, Javaher! If you only knew how much I wish I could shield you from the ugly business of the court, how I long to make our lives shine as bright as gold. How can I ever thank you enough for the risks you take for me every day?"

Her moist eye and anguished lip revealed the depth of her concern. How caring she was in that moment of my most crushing sorrow! Was it even—could it be—the tenderness of filial love that I saw blossoming in her regard? She had virtually said so, had she not? As I walked back to my quarters in the harsh morning sun, I felt as if my heart would shred with feeling, like a peony swirling its bloody skirts.

For the rest of that week, I was at pains to assume the expression that I must wear when Khadijeh was mentioned, one of grim satisfaction that justice had been served at the palace. But when I allowed myself to think of her, I remembered the delicacy of her brown body under her orange robe, and I drew courage from knowing that she had needed nothing to guide her but her determined heart. Had there ever been a man who could claim to be as fearless? She had never even held the heavy swords and sharp daggers that gave soldiers their swagger. Khadijeh may have been a slave, but in her heart, she was a lion-woman.

CHAPTER 7

AN END TO
THE CHASE

As soon as he was old enough, Fereydoon began learning the arts of horse riding, swordsmanship, and military strategy. Once he had mastered these endeavors, he began training an army in the desert to combat Zahhak's tyranny. For good luck, he asked a blacksmith to make him an iron mace topped by an animal's head. Some say it was a cow, but I like to think it was an ox—a castrated bull.

One day, from his camp, Fereydoon saw Kaveh marching to him with his leather apron flying high in the air and his army of protestors behind him, and he knew that the time to liberate Iran had come. Fereydoon gave Kaveh a hero's welcome and decorated his humble apron with jewels, gold brocade, and fringes until the banner glittered in the sun. Then, when all was ready for battle, Fereydoon's soldiers carried the banner on the front lines as he led his army to the city to fight Zahhak.

Upon arriving, Fereydoon discovered that Zahhak had left for a campaign of pillage in India. He stormed his empty palace, liberated those who had remained, and took possession of the women.

Before long, Zahhak returned with an army to reclaim his city. His men surrounded the palace, only to find that the local population had sided with Fereydoon. Enraged, Zahhak broke away from his army and used a rope to lower himself over his palace walls to try to take Fereydoon by surprise. But Fereydoon recognized him right away by the snakes slithering on his shoulders, and he struck Zahhak with enormous blows of his mace until the tyrant was subdued. Then Fereydoon claimed Zahhak's throne and declared himself the ruler of a new era.

That is how the brains of the men of Iran were saved from destruction, and justice returned to the land.

When my father died, it was as if I were being pulled deep into a lake of grief; it seemed impossible to swim to the surface. After Khadijeh's death, I sorrowed just as deeply, but not with the helplessness I had felt as a boy. Instead, what grew inside was a sharp coldness like the edge of a sword. I became unswerving and vowed to carry out my mission even unto my own death.

To keep strong in my purpose, I began visiting the House of Strength at the palace and training with the heavy wooden clubs that athletes swing over their shoulders to tone their bodies. As the weeks passed, the muscles in my arms, chest, and thighs became as dense as the clubs themselves. My neck became even thicker than before. I developed a ravenous appetite for meat and ate lamb kabob daily, even as the excess weight on my body began to fall away. When I caught a glimpse of myself in a mirror, I realized I looked more like a normal man than I ever had.

For some time after Khadijeh's death, Pari and I struggled to reestablish the solidity of our relationship. We still met daily and she delivered assignments to me, but they were minor and I could see in her eyes that despite the affection she had expressed for me, she wasn't certain she could trust me. This new veil saddened me. I longed to feel as if we were comrades in arms again.

One night, I dreamed that Isma'il Shah had discovered our plot and that we were about to be executed. I woke up sweating with fear, my sheets damp. In the dark, I admitted to myself that I had been wrong not to tell Pari about Khadijeh, especially after I had taken the princess to task for not keeping me informed. As the sweat on me cooled, I shivered at my foolhardiness, which could have doomed us.

The next day, I told Pari about the dream and begged her forgiveness for jeopardizing our lives. I had been too stricken with grief to admit that I had erred, I told her, and I promised to modify my approach. Pari accepted my apology graciously; but more importantly, it lightened her spirit. A smile appeared on her lips the next time she greeted me, and I began to feel that she was enjoying my company again. As the weeks went by, we found a new way of working together, and trust grew quietly between us like that of an old married couple.

Pari and I didn't discuss how we would rid ourselves of the ongoing scourge. It was too dangerous to mention any plans; security had become tighter than ever, and anyone around us could be in the pay of the Shah. But we both knew our goal remained the same. When no new murders came to light, we thought it prudent to bide our time until our sleuthing revealed an ideal time to strike.

While we were engaged in this dangerous business, it would have been folly to bring my sister to court. I took Balamani aside and gave him a sealed letter with my final instructions. If anything happened to me, he was to use all my means—including my precious dagger and my *Shahnameh*—as a dowry for my sister and make certain that she was settled in a good family in Qazveen. I did not trust my mother's cousin to treat her well in the event of my death.

Six months passed, and life returned to its accustomed patterns. The snows gave way to spring, the New Year, and a hot summer. We commemorated Moharram and the martyrdom of the Imam Hossein with ceremonies recalling his immense suffering on the battlefield, and we thought about all the other injustices that we had yet to tackle.

Gradually, the palace hierarchy began to shift in our favor. Shamkhal Cherkes won a few high postings and land concessions for the Circassians. Mirza Salman managed to get himself appointed grand vizier, through a relentless campaign of sabotaging the reputation of Mirza Shokhrollah, who was ultimately dismissed in disgrace. We hoped that Mirza Salman's appointment as second in command meant that Pari could be rehabilitated one day, even though he must now keep his distance from her.

Ramazan arrived that year in the second month of autumn. For weeks in advance, preparations were made at the palace for the fact that day was about to become night, and night day. Tradesmen brought in plenty of oil, since lamps would burn all night while we were awake, as well as all the necessary supplies of food that did not need to be fresh—rice, beans, dried fruit and vegetables, spices, and the like.

On the eve of Ramazan, I stayed up late with Balamani, a few of the other eunuchs, and Massoud Ali. We took a walk near the mountains and sat in the open country, wrapped in wool blankets, to drink hot tea that we made over a charcoal brazier. I watched the night light up with stars and imagined that I saw Khadijeh's eyes there. When the night grew late, Balamani suggested we recite some poems. The flasks of wine and much stronger *aragh* came out and all of us grew emotional as the night wore on and we recited the lines that were dearest to our hearts.

I stood up and addressed the moon, calling her beautiful, but in my heart I was speaking of Khadijeh. The poem I declaimed was about a lover whose love had gone to another, leaving the flower of his soul withered forever.

Then I recited a poem about a young man lost in battle, while thinking of Mahmood. The other men shouted, "Bah, bah!" when I recited an especially beautiful line, and I wiped dampness from my eyes. It was safe to weep together over the beauty of the lines of poetry, even though all of us were no doubt thinking of our own losses.

Massoud Ali, who had stayed by my side all evening, begged to practice a few submission holds he had been learning in his one-on-one combat class. Gleefully, he wrapped one arm in front of my neck and one arm behind it, locking me in a deadly embrace. I praised him and showed him a few tricks to increase his power.

Even though it was very late, he asked me to finish telling him the story of Zahhak and Kaveh. I sat up on a cushion and began where I had last left off. When I reached the part about how Fereydoon struck down Zahhak with his great mace, I emphasized the role of the hero's great strength. Massoud Ali's eyes lit up with joy.

"How can I be just like Fereydoon?" he asked. Before I could answer, he yawned, curled up against me, and sank into a deep sleep. From the lively, changing expressions on his face, I had no doubt that he was playing the role of Fereydoon in his dreams.

All of us ate a large meal before dawn, returned to the palace, and performed our morning duties. Then we returned to our quarters to rest. When I awoke in the afternoon, Balamani was still asleep on his bedroll, a pillow cradled in his arms. During the month of Ramazan, many of our official duties took place after the cannon boomed and lasted well into the night. There was no need to disturb him yet. I got up quietly and went to the baths, where I saw Anwar and another eunuch through a veil of steam. Both had pendulous breasts and flat pubic areas, which made them resemble women. In another corner of the bath, a younger, sylphlike eunuch flirted with an older one, displaying his pretty, smooth body as if it were for sale. I was glad I had not developed such feminine traits, due to being cut so late. My chest was still hairy, square, and manlike, God be praised, and my arms bigger than before due to lifting the heavy wooden clubs.

When I was clean and dressed, it was still too early to go see Pari. Alone in the quiet afternoon, I felt the heaviness of the loss of Khadijeh. If I had had a mother or a sister close at hand, I would have gone to one of them for comfort, but now I had no one nearby. So I left the palace and walked toward the well-tended neighborhood where Fereshteh lived. People were just starting to open their shops. I passed a fruit seller whose bright red pomegranates made my stomach growl loudly at the thought of their sweet juice.

When I was shown in to see Fereshteh, I noticed that her pillow had left a mark on her face. She looked fresh in a pink robe with a purple tunic underneath. I removed my shoes and sat down on a cushion across from her.

"Your visit brings happiness," she began.

"Thank you. I came because problems continue at the palace. I am wondering if you have heard any news about the Shah's habits."

"Nothing important. What is new?"

It took a moment before I could continue. My voice seemed to have stopped deep in my chest. When I could speak again, I told her what had happened to Khadijeh.

"I couldn't save her—"

Fereshteh's large eyes filled with concern. She reached over and cupped the top of my bare foot with her warm palm, which was hennaed a beautiful shade of red. I remembered how the mere touch of her hand used to send desire jolting from my toes through the rest of my body.

"Ah!" I exclaimed, surprised through and through. I felt it again, my missing limb, just as clearly as if it were stiffening against my clothes. How could it be? I hadn't expected that feeling to surge through me.

Fereshteh could read the signs in a man's body as easily as others read the written word.

"Is this the reason for your visit, then?" Her tone was cold. Abruptly, she pulled back her hand.

"I admire you as much as before," I said, "but I didn't come as a client."

"Then why did you come?"

I reached out for her hand and held it between both of mine. It trembled. I felt as if I were enclosing a butterfly that demanded the greatest gentleness.

"I need a friend. I have lost many, and you are one of the few people I remember with affection."

"I will always be your friend," she said evenly.

"And I yours. In addition, when it comes to matters of the body, I am not the same man as before. I remember being very demanding, but now I will only lie with a woman if she both desires and demands it."

Fereshteh looked surprised. "I don't know if I desire such things anymore. I do them so often that they have fallen out of the realm of desire."

"I understand. As for myself, I don't proceed in the same way."

"What do you do without those parts?"

"I know what to do," I said with a smile, "but I reveal my knowledge only if invited."

Fereshteh looked as if she was pondering something, and I wondered if I would be invited. The silence between us lasted a long time, until finally she said, "You look as though you could use an embrace."

I felt embarrassed at being so transparent.

"I could," I admitted.

"In that case," Fereshteh replied, "I invite you to embrace me as a friend. No one ever does."

I opened my arms and wrapped them around her, and she leaned the weight of her body against mine. I felt the gentle rhythms of her breath, like an ocean spreading its waves out onto a shore. I watched her eyes close, her dark eyelashes fringing her white cheeks.

"Aw khesh," I said in satisfaction, knowing that the embrace was for my sake.

We stayed that way for a long time without speaking, and I thought about how differently I felt from when I knew her before. Rather than being possessed by an urgent animal desire, now I simply wished to give whatever comfort she needed and to take whatever she offered.

The room darkened as the autumn day faded, and the cannon boomed, signaling that it was permissible to eat, drink, and love. I held Fereshteh until a servant knocked and announced that one of her clients had arrived. Reluctantly, I released her.

Fereshteh rearranged her clothes and tightened her sash. "It is good to be cared for, even though it is so fleeting."

Something in her tone made me bristle. "Because I am a eunuch?"

"Because long ago, you disappeared."

We were both silent, remembering those days. I thought about how confused my feelings had been. Because I had spent so many nights with her, she had meant more to me than someone to be used and discarded, yet I had not permitted myself to think of her as anything more than a prostitute.

"Regardless, I will send a messenger to you if I hear anything useful."

"I would like to visit you again whether you discover anything or not."

"All right."

Her tone was cool, but it reminded me that some people become cruel when they say goodbye because it is the only way they can bear to part.

Fereshteh's maid showed me out into the courtyard, where a man dressed in a fine brown silk robe appeared to be dallying for a moment by the fountain. He turned around at the sound of our voices.

"You are supposed to show him out through the back door," he complained to the maid, who blushed in embarrassment.

"I beg your forgiveness," she said. "I won't be so careless again."

I wondered why the man cared so much until I realized that it was none other than the Shah's companion, Hassan Beyg. We stared at each other, mutually surprised. Hassan Beyg had unusually elegant eyebrows that looked as if they had been shaped to match the contours of his turban. They set off his high cheekbones and smooth brown skin. Although probably in his late twenties, he looked younger because his skin was so flawless. The haughty way he kept his chin lifted suggested he was well aware of his status as a handsome trophy. Introducing myself as a servant of the court, I signaled to Fereshteh's maid with a nearly invisible flick of my hand that we were to be left alone. She scooted away, a quick learner.

"I serve Pari Khan Khanoom," I said, and when he showed no reaction, I made my lips jerk downward as if in an involuntary sign of resignation.

He smiled, revealing small, perfect white teeth. "I have heard all about her."

"No doubt, but I am not sure any man alive knows what it is really like to work for such a woman. What have you heard?" I raised my eyebrows as if to indicate there were plenty of confidences to be had from me that Isma'il might want to hear.

"That she is a power grabber."

I laughed. "And what royal woman isn't! But you wouldn't believe what I have to go through sometimes. I don't know what it is like for you, but her petty requests make me wish I worked for a man. The other day I was sent back to the bazaar three times until I delivered the right face powder. What a waste of time!"

"I prefer to serve men," he replied.

"I understand."

The door cracked open and the maid indicated that Fereshteh was ready to see him.

"What is the rush?" I said, turning back to Hassan.

"Didn't you enjoy yourself in there?" Hassan replied, and then he stopped for a moment. "Wait a minute. You don't even have a . . . What are you doing here?"

"It is true I didn't come here for the usual reasons," I replied swiftly. "The business I conduct is confidential. Today it has nothing to do with face powder, thank God."

"What is it?"

"I really shouldn't say."

I knew he would feel better if he forced it out of me. His opportunities for subjugating men of my rank were few.

"As Isma'il's companion, I demand that you tell me."

I acted as though I had been humbled by one of my betters. "W-w-ell," I stammered, "the t-t-truth is, I came to ask about a certain charm that makes people fall in love."

"For whom?"

"I am not allowed—"

"The princess wants a man to fall in love with her?"

"But of course," I replied disingenuously. "Doesn't every woman?"

"Her brother will kill her."

"I don't think so," I replied. "The charm is intended for him. She longs for his brotherly love."

He laughed. "I see. I will let him know."

"I beg you not to reveal the business of my princess," I pleaded. "I will get in trouble."

"I won't," he said, but I knew he was lying.

He had his tidbit, and now I wanted mine.

"No doubt you came here on business, too. I am certain you are not here for yourself."

"No, of course not." Hassan rubbed his fingertips across his pretty lips. I was certain he found it easy to distract others by doing that. "If you tell anyone you saw me here, I will deny it."

"Of course I won't," I said. "Like me, you must need an occasional reprieve."

A look of relief crossed his eyes at being understood, but he did not let it linger.

"But surely you are taking a risk. Given all the murders around the palace, don't you fear for your life?"

He looked frightened; he was as soft as yogurt. "Don't you?"

"Every day. Serving the royals is like gambling one's life on a game of backgammon. Some days I think it will either make my fortune or dig my grave."

He laughed. "So it might."

"Where do you find relief besides here? I have no way of taking advantage of what Shireen offers."

He held my eyes with his sugary brown ones. "During Ramazan, it is not so bad," he replied. "The celebrations put him in a good mood." But rather than look overjoyed at the prospect of entertaining the Shah, he appeared weary. As he adjusted the gold chain he wore around his neck, I caught a glimpse of his seal, which filled me with foreboding.

"Well, then, I hope you enjoy yourself," I replied. "Perhaps, like me, you are happy enough if the prospect involves drawing in another breath. Yet sometimes I wish I could take a breath like an ordinary man. Do you know what I mean?"

The veil dropped from his eyes, and he looked as lonely as the goat who had been unable to escape his tormentors in the bazaar.

"How do you plan to celebrate?" I prodded.

He hesitated for a moment, and then he said, "Tomorrow night after breaking the fast, we will gallivant around the bazaar in disguise, just as if we were ordinary men."

I stared at him, surprised. His revelation seemed like just what an unhappy man might let slip to try to change his circumstances. He said a hasty goodbye and entered the house.

Pari had just come back from visiting Mahasti and Koudenet, who remained coy about revealing anything useful about the Shah. When I told her about the Shah's plans, her eyes glowed with hope. She opened a book of poems by Hafez to take an augury and read the poem she chanced upon out loud:

> *Seeing but himself, the Zealot sees but sin;*
> *Grief to the mirror of his soul let in,*
> *Oh Lord, and cloud it with the breath of sighs!*

"It is as if the poem had been written about Isma'il," she remarked. "A more committed zealot I have never seen. I will take that as an augury in our favor."

She closed the book. Her forehead was smooth and calm, her bearing decisive.

"Proceed!"

"Chashm."

I sent a message to the physician to let him know I was finally ready to receive the digestives. The next afternoon, I fetched them from his man in the bazaar, placed them carefully into their individual compartments in the octagonal box, and returned the box to the passageway. Pari summoned Massoud Ali and ordered him to tell Fareed to await our summons. He departed on fleet feet.

"It is time to renew your vigil on my roof. Once you are certain they have gone out, Fareed can make his delivery."

"If I am discovered, what is my alibi?"

"Say that you can't resist the urge to dress up in a woman's chador. It is hardly worse than claiming diarrhea."

I laughed so hard my turban loosened, and so did something in my heart. This was the first time that Pari had joked with me about the excuse I had made in front of the Shah. At last, she had forgiven me completely.

Covered in a chador, I climbed the steps and sat on Pari's rooftop watching the Ramazan revelers make their family visits. Each time I heard a door open, I thought it might be Hassan's. After the cannon boomed, Azar Khatoon brought me hot milk and bread with cheese right away, followed later by lamb kabob with a generous serving of rice. "How lovely you look with your body obscured by your chador, like the moon by a cloud!" she teased.

"Don't the poets describe the fairest men and women in exactly the same way?" I teased back. "They have rosebud lips, cheeks as red as apples, large, soulful eyes, dark velvety eyebrows, curly black hair, and a beauty mark just like yours."

Her long, throaty laugh kept me company as she descended the stairs. As it faded I wondered, if boys and girls were so similar as love objects, both in painting and in poetry, why were they treated so differently when they grew into men and women? What was the difference between having a tool and not having one? Even I could not say.

I had just finished my meal when the heavy wooden door to Hassan's house creaked opened, and Hassan, the Shah, and their men, all in disguise, entered their courtyard and walked toward the wall with the secret door. I rushed downstairs to tell Pari.

"They have gone out," I said, hearing the excitement in my own voice.

"I will summon Fareed," Pari said, her hands trembling as she smoothed the hair at her temples.

"I will go to the passageway to await him."

Just then my stomach roared nervously.

"Wait!" Pari commanded. She bent down to a tray and wrapped some bread and cheese in a cloth. "At least take this."

I opened my palms and bowed to accept her offering, touched to the core of my heart. No doubt Pari had never handed food to a servant before. Her kind gesture acknowledged the risk I was taking on her behalf.

From the Promenade of the Royal Stallions, I found the small park, disappeared behind the trees, and descended into the dark with the key to the passageway's doors at hand. For a moment, I felt I had lost my sight, and not knowing the way as well as Pari did, I groped around the passageway and its many offshoots, but soon my feet remembered our previous walks and carried me along until the ground sloped upward and I felt the bag of money against my toe.

Once I had assured myself that no one was near, I removed the tile and placed the box of digestives and a bag with half the money on the floor of the pavilion in the next room. Descending again, I pulled the tile into place above me, sat down in the passageway, and listened for footsteps. If there were more than one pair, I would know that we had been betrayed, and I would flee through the passageway and warn the princess.

I ate my bread and cheese and prepared for a long night. The damp underground air seeped into my skin, as if I had been buried in my grave. I went over every detail of our plans in my mind, plagued by the one thing that could mean our doom: The box would not bear Hassan Beyg's seal. I began thinking about what would happen if we were to get caught. Of course we would be killed, but before we died, we would be tormented in ways too terrible to contemplate. I imagined how the soles of our feet would be beaten until they bled, our eyes burned with hot irons, our backs broken.

The sound of running made my hair stand on end, and my ears went on full alert. A deep scraping noise made me worry that someone was trying to remove the tile. Something brushed my knee, and I leapt to my feet, stifling a cry. Pulling my dagger out of its scabbard, I thrust it before me, determined to strike first. My dagger made contact with something firm, and I grunted with satisfaction and relief. I groped for my prey, but my fingers found only the dirt wall. Angry squeaks in the distance made me realize that I had been startled by rats.

I don't know how much time passed before I heard footsteps. They paused in the room where I had left the box. The coins jingled, then fell quiet. Wood scraped against the tiles. Then the footsteps retreated.

I waited until the only sound I could hear was my own pulse before I lifted the tile and looked around. The box and bag were gone. I descended back into the passageway to await Fareed's return. Now my agitation came back. Would Fareed perform his mission as he had promised? If he were caught, how quickly would he betray us? Had he already sent someone to investigate the pavilion? The scuttling of small animals in the passageway sounded to me as loud as an army of soldiers sent to hunt me down and kill me.

It seemed like a long time had passed before I heard footsteps above me. I paused, hot with nerves. Fareed could easily have told soldiers to wait at a distance from the pavilion. I listened for voices and footsteps in vain until I had no choice other than to proceed. Lifting the tile gently, I stepped outside, leaving the passageway uncovered in case I had to run. Tiptoeing into the next room, I said, "Salaam aleikum."

Fareed jumped to standing. "By God above! You *are* a jinni."

"Were you successful?"

"The servant who opened the door was bleary-eyed from lack of sleep. I thrust the box into his hands, and he took it without asking any questions."

"All right, then. Let's go."

"Where is the rest of my money?"

I handed him a bag, which he stuffed in an inner pocket of his robe. Pulling a long cloth out of my robe, I covered his eyes. I walked him around the pavilion to try to make him lose his bearings, guided him down into the passageway, and quietly replaced the tile.

"Hold on to the back of my robe," I said.

"It smells of death."

"Don't worry, I will lead you."

"Is this a grave?" he said, his voice rising with panic.

"Of course not."

"I don't believe you!" he cried. "I will see for myself."

He let go of my back and, after a moment, began to shriek. "I can't see! I can't see! You have thrown me into a hole."

He was yelling so loudly I was afraid he could be heard aboveground.

"Choke yourself!" I commanded. "We can't walk out through the palace gates in full view of the guards, can we? Now grab my robe and hold on so that we can quit this place."

He began reciting passages from the Qur'an about protection from evil, and I felt his hand on my back again. It was trembling, and I knew he had understood the enormity of what we had done. I tried to soothe him.

"There are horses waiting for you," I said. "Your work is finished, you are rich, and you will soon be free. I envy you."

More verses issued from his lips, but he grabbed the back of my robe, and we stumbled slowly through the dark.

"I don't like this at all," he said. "How can it be right to kill? Is God already punishing me for my role in this?"

"Of course not. All you have done is deliver a box," I said. "And what else are we supposed to do? Shall we act like sheep until we all get murdered?"

"May God protect us," he murmured.

"Listen," I said. "Let me tell you a famous story. Once, long ago . . ."

I began telling him a tale from the *Shahnameh,* throwing in the actual lines of poetry where I remembered them, to soothe his nerves. To my relief, the tale worked its magic. Fareed stopped whining and seemed eager to follow the thread of the story.

When we finally reached the end of the passageway, I covered my body in a chador and my face with a picheh and led him outside into the small park. Nearby, I saw the groomsman waiting with two horses, just as Pari had promised. Fareed couldn't stop himself from breaking into a run. I accompanied him to the Tehran Gate and made sure that he left the city.

The princess's face beamed like the sun bursting out between the clouds. Her gaze warmed me to my very core, making me feel that all my hard work was worth it. I knew not to speak until she sent Azar Khatoon out of the room for tea and dates.

"All is in order," I said simply.

"Did anyone notice the lack of a seal?"

"No. Not yet, anyway."

"Fareed?"

"Gone. He is so frightened I don't think he will ever leave the imprint of his foot in Qazveen again."

She let out a long, deep sigh. "May God always keep you safe."

We discussed our movements during every hour of the last two days and agreed that if either of us were challenged, we would say she had been in her rooms writing letters to her female allies at other courts.

"The Ottomans still haven't sent an emissary to congratulate Isma'il on his coronation," Pari said. "It is such a breach of protocol that I need to write to Safiyeh Sultan, Murad III's wife, to express my concern about maintaining the peace treaty, and naturally I will also send a gift. If questioned, I will say that I hired the horses and groom to send the items on the first stage of their journey."

"What shall I say about my whereabouts?"

"You have been assisting me. If someone saw you in the bazaar fetching the digestives, you will say that I gave you permission to go in search of a new medicine for your stomach—which by now has been well established as a vexing problem."

I smiled.

"Now, before you return to your quarters, I wish to read you a poem I have written."

"What a welcome surprise."

"Sit down."

I stared at her. Sit down, while she was still standing? It would be the first time I had ever violated this protocol.

"Go ahead."

I lowered myself carefully onto one of her cushions. Pari picked up the burnished cotton paper on which she had written her poem and read it out loud.

> *"At first you would think he was a mouse*
> *Scuttling discreetly through the house*
> *He could make himself seem to disappear*
> *In quietness and stealth, he had no peer*
> *Like an honest woman, he listened well*
> *His selfless words could comfort you in hell*
> *You might be tempted to think him soft as gruel*
> *As if weakened through lack of some tool*
> *Yet inside he was made of damascened steel*
> *His heart was a lion's; his roar was real*
> *He proved the truth that a man's fragile skin*
> *Gives no hint of the white fury within*
> *That a man of the pen schooled mostly in poems*
> *Can rise to a height surpassing the greatest domes.*
> *Was he a man? A woman? A bit of each?*
> *I would argue the third sex has plenty to teach*
> *From now till eternity, one name holds this key:*
> *It is Payam Javaher-e-Shirazi!"*

"May your hands never ache! It is beautiful."

"You say that because your ears hear only beauty," she replied demurely.

"I mean it," I said, feeling myself soften. To think that the princess would write me such a loving poem! It was more than I had ever hoped for. Men would always think of me as lesser because of my missing tool, while women would imagine that I was exactly like them. They were both wrong. I was indeed a third sex, one more supple than those stuck in the rigid roles handed to them at birth. Pari had understood. Rather than seeing me as defective, she chose to celebrate the new thing I had become. My birth as a eunuch had finally been recognized and recorded with as much fanfare as the moment a male child enters the world.

I was a man, so I wanted to embrace her; yet as her soldier, I must only salute her. The conflicting feelings made me leap to my feet in an effort to pursue the right course. Then I just stood there, not knowing what to do next, until Pari's smile told me that she knew what was in my heart.

The palace was quiet all that day. I was as skittish as a cat, wondering if every noise in the corridors announced that the deed was done. But all was calm. Late in the afternoon, I told Pari I wanted to return to my vigil on her roof to try to discern whether the digestives had been eaten.

"You may go," she said. "I will send one of my ladies with a platter of food for you."

"Thank you, Princess."

I removed my turban, borrowed one of her ladies' chadors, covered my body, and ascended the staircase to the roof. A white chill pervaded the air. I covered my head and stared at the sky, watching the first few stars appear. When one winked at me, I imagined Khadijeh was signaling her approval.

After the cannon boomed, Azar Khatoon brought me a blanket and my meal. Pari must have told her to spare nothing. I ate roast lamb falling off the bone, several types of rice, stewed lamb with greens and tart lemons, chicken with sweetened barberries, cucumber with yogurt and mint, and hot bread. When I had finished, Azar brought me a large vessel of tea flavored with cardamom.

"That black garment brightens your coffee-colored eyes," she teased, and her smile showed off the pretty black beauty spot near her lower lip.

"Only a rose like you would be so gracious even to the humblest of flowers," I flirted.

"What are you doing on the roof?" she asked as she descended the stairs.

"Studying the stars," I replied. "The princess has asked me to improve my astrological skills."

I hoped not to see the door of Hassan's house opening, because that would mean the Shah had survived. But when the moon rose high in the sky, the door creaked open and Hassan exited with a man swathed in ordinary robes—the Shah—and a few well-armed bodyguards. I burned with disappointment. Obviously, he had not eaten the digestives yet. But what if he had, and they had not been strong enough?

After they disappeared, I didn't see any reason to stay outside in the cold. I went downstairs and found Pari.

"They have just left for their celebrations," I said, feeling anger in my teeth.

"Very well, then," said Pari coolly. "Why don't you help me with these letters?"

My body was tensed for action. I reminded myself what Balamani had once told me about cheetahs. They are the fastest animals on earth, but they don't eat very often. Sometimes, in a matter of seconds, they run out of energy and give up while their prey dances away.

I forced myself to relax. "Of course."

While Pari finished her letter about maintaining the peace treaty, I voiced similar sentiments to other notable women, writing as her scribe. My pen flew across the page. All my nerves were so alert, I felt as if I would never need sleep again. We drank tea and ate sweets to keep our strength high. Pari called in her servants regularly so they could witness us at work and provide an alibi. The only sign of how the princess felt was that from time to time she dribbled ink onto her letter and had to start over.

Deep into the night, she turned to me and said, "I think I have finally understood why my father didn't designate an heir. He was only too aware of the problems each man would have brought to the throne and couldn't settle on any one of them."

Her eyes were thoughtful, her face soft. I decided to take a risk and reveal some of what I longed to know. "Perhaps he wanted fate to reveal who would be the greatest Safavi leader."

Pari stared at me, surprised. "So you know about your chart? How did you find out?"

I smiled. "I have my ways, Princess."

"I know you do."

"But I don't know everything, of course. Is that the reason you and your father decided to employ me at court?"

"It is one of the reasons, yes. But don't think for a moment we would have kept promoting you if you didn't deserve it."

"Thank you, lieutenant of my life. May I know why you didn't tell me about my chart?"

"We were advised not to. When people hear such a prediction, they try to fulfill it. We wanted you to be a vessel for truth."

Tahmasb Shah had followed the guidance offered by his dreams, and they had never failed him. It didn't surprise me that he had taken the prediction about me so seriously.

Azar Khatoon entered the room and asked Pari if she wished for more refreshments. I waited impatiently for them to be done. Sweat gathered at my temples where my turban hugged my head.

When they had finished talking, I said, "May God grant that I fulfill the prophecy you mentioned! But right now something else troubles me. For a long time, I have been trying to unravel the story of my father's murderer, Kamiyar Kofrani."

I thought it was safe to tell her now. She needn't worry that a quest for revenge would split my loyalties.

"I understand you have kept the court historians busy with your requests."

"Deh!" I should have known her spies would report me to her.

"What is it you still wish to know?"

"The histories say he had powerful allies."

"Really?" Pari's forehead puckered, and her eyes looked puzzled. "As far as I know, the man was an ordinary accountant. You might ask Mirza Salman. He employed him a long time ago in Azerbaijan."

Why hadn't Mirza Salman ever mentioned that?

"Do you know why he wasn't punished?"

"Yes."

Panah bar Khoda! I stared at her, my eyes full of questions.

"Javaher, I can't tell you the reason just yet. Have patience, and I will reveal it to you when it is safe for you to know."

Now my concentration disappeared entirely. Seeing me so flummoxed, Pari told me to return to my quarters and rest. The lines at her mouth looked deep with worry. I didn't blame her.

I went to my room, making sure to mention to a few eunuchs how tired I was from assisting Pari with letters all night. Balamani was already asleep. I lay on my bedroll with my copy of the *Shahnameh*, but instead of reading, I found myself thinking of the cord at Mahmood's young throat, the poison in Khadijeh's belly, and the dagger in my father's chest. Why couldn't Pari tell me what she knew?

I lit a lamp and opened the *Shahnameh* to the page about how Kaveh had stood up to Zahhak and chastised him for his bloodthirstiness. Kaveh's boldness in the face of injustice had so surprised the tyrant that he hadn't been able to stop him. One man had to stand up to Zahhak so that others would finally gain enough courage to fight for justice.

I marveled at the bravery of that humble hero of old, who had neither nobility nor money nor friends—nothing but his sense of justice to guide him.

Well before noon, I arose, dressed, and went to see Pari. When I arrived at her house, she was wearing the same blue robe as the night before, and the hollows under her eyes were even darker. She was just where I had left her.

"Princess, what ails you?"

"I couldn't sleep. Every time I heard a noise, I expected news. Just now, Mirza Salman sent a message that he needs to speak with me urgently. I must discover the reason."

"Could he have unearthed our plans?"

"No. He would have sent the royal guard instead, and he wouldn't have asked permission."

It didn't take long for Mirza Salman to arrive. He came with only one servant rather than the usual large retinue that accompanies a grand vizier. My pulse quickened when I noticed a few stray hairs hanging out of his normally impeccable turban. I showed him to his side of the lattice in Pari's birooni and stayed to better observe him.

"Esteemed servant of the realm, your visit is welcome." The princess's low, sweet voice filled the divided room.

"Princess," Mirza Salman replied in a sober tone, "an unprecedented situation has occurred at the palace. Your brother, the light of the universe, hasn't shown the sunshine of his face this morning, and everyone at the palace is worried."

My heart soared with hope.

"Indeed?" Pari said, sounding surprised. "When did he go to sleep?"

"A few hours before dawn. By midmorning, his retainers had gathered outside his rooms as usual to await his emergence, but there has been no sound. They don't know what to do."

"Has someone knocked at his door?"

"No. They have been fearful of disturbing him."

"For God's sake!" said Pari, her voice rising in what sounded like distress. "What if he has fallen ill? You must knock on his door immediately."

"And if there is no answer?"

"Break it down, and tell him you did so at my command. Go now without delay, and take my vizier with you. He will report to me what has happened."

"Chashm," Mirza Salman replied, and said his farewells.

I followed Mirza Salman and his man out of Pari's door. He hadn't said where the Shah had gone to sleep, but he crossed the courtyard, marched toward Hassan's house, and banged loudly at the wooden door. It was opened by the servant who usually attended to tradesmen. We passed into the courtyard, which I had observed so many times from Pari's roof. The servant showed us deep into the house's andarooni, the most private quarters. The furnishings were opulent, but I could not focus on them.

When we arrived at the rooms that adjoined the bedroom, we greeted the Shah's physician, Hakim Tabrizi, as well as two of the most esteemed qizilbash amirs, Isma'il's uncle Amir Khan Mowsellu and his new Ostajlu chief, Pir Mohammad Khan. The Shah's bedroom lay behind a thick carved wooden door, which even the amirs did not dare approach.

After greeting the men, Mirza Salman said, "Has there been any sign?"

"No," said Amir Khan.

"Is it possible the light of the universe has already departed through another door?"

"That is the only one," replied Hakim Tabrizi.

"In that case, by order of the highest-ranking woman of Safavi blood, I am going to knock."

The men's eyes widened with awe; probably no one had ever dared to disturb Isma'il Shah before. Mirza Salman strode to the door and rapped on it with two polite taps.

We waited a long time with no reply. He knocked on the door again, this time more firmly, and when all remained quiet, banged with his fist. I was filled with hope and fear.

"What now?" asked Amir Khan.

"Hush!" replied Mirza Salman. "Listen."

A weak sound reminiscent of a sheep's bleats emerged.

"Help!" I thought I heard. Was it the voice of the Shah?

"Hassan Beyg, is that you?" asked Mirza Salman.

"The d-d-door! H-h-help!"

Mirza Salman directed a "four-shouldered" soldier to take charge of the door, and he swung a metal mace at it until it groaned under his attack. The wood began to splinter and crack. When the door was finally breached, the soldier bent his arm inside and released the bolt. The broken door swung open, and Mirza Salman and Hakim Tabrizi rushed inside. Two forms were huddled under bedcovers.

"Light of the universe, can you hear me?" Hakim Tabrizi asked. When there was no reply, he pulled the covers gently away from the

Shah's face. His eyes were closed, his mouth slightly open. The physician bent over him and placed his ear against his chest.

"His heartbeat is weak."

My own heart sank in my chest like a boulder falling into a river. How could the poison not have worked?

Mirza Salman gingerly lifted all the bedcovers off Hassan's side of the bed. He didn't dare do the same for the Shah, who might not be in a proper state of dress. Hassan lay on his side, dressed in pale yellow pajamas.

"By God above, what happened?" Mirza Salman demanded of Hassan, who hadn't moved.

"Can't m-m-move . . . l-l-legs," Hassan slurred. The skin over his sculpted cheekbones looked dull and slack.

It took a long time to get the story out of Hassan because he could barely talk. He related that he and the Shah had gone out the night before and had eaten several pills of opium, as well as a large meal and a few servings of halva. When they returned home, the Shah asked for his digestives. The box had been refilled, but it didn't have Hassan's seal. Hassan advised the Shah not to partake, but he was insistent, so Hassan ate one first to make certain that they were safe. When he experienced no ill effects, the Shah ate three of them, and they went to bed. Hassan didn't wake up until he heard the pounding at the door.

"What a ridiculous story," said Mirza Salman. "Who else but you could have poisoned him?"

"Why? I would f-f-fall from the firmament faster than a shooting star. Do with me as you like, but that is the t-t-truth."

Mirza Salman crept around the bed to where Hassan couldn't see him. He removed a small dagger from his sash and poked the tip of it into the back of Hassan's thigh. Blood welled out and stained his pale yellow pajamas. Hassan did not move.

"He tells the truth," the physician declared.

"What about the Shah?" asked Mirza Salman.

"All we can do is pray for his recovery," the physician said.

Silently, I cursed the physician Halaki, who had promised to provide a perfect poison.

"Is he comfortable?" asked Mirza Salman.

"He feels nothing at the moment," replied Hakim Tabrizi.

"Let's check the digestives. Where are they?"

"C-c-cushions," replied Hassan. Mirza Salman fetched the box and opened it.

"Four are missing, as you have said. Now I need an animal."

A servant was dispatched to the street and returned quickly with a scrawny cat with yellowish eyes and long matted gray fur. It purred loudly as if hungry. By God above! If it ate one of the digestives it would surely die, and then they would know it was poisoned. I wiped my forehead as I watched, although the building was cold.

The men put the digestive on the ground and pushed the cat toward it. The animal sniffed it and walked away. Even when coaxed, the cat refused to eat it.

While the men were occupied with the cat, I kept my eyes on the Shah, hoping he wouldn't open his eyes or speak. By God above! I felt as if my life hovered in balance with his.

Hakim Tabrizi still had his fingers on the Shah's pulse, but after a few moments, he suddenly cried out. "May God be merciful. His pulse is fleeing!"

The Shah's faint breathing sounded ragged, as if he were trying to grab air and failing. He began to make choking sounds that were horrible to hear.

The physician patted the Shah's face, but there was no response. Amir Khan and Pir Mohammad rushed into the room to see him for themselves. I remained outside since I did not hold such high rank.

"Alas!" the physician cried suddenly. "I can no longer feel his breath!"

Mirza Salman bent over and put his ear against the Shah's nose, then moved it to his lips and back again to try to detect breath.

"Woe to us, great woe!" he cried.

Amir Khan, who stood to lose a great deal because of his status as Isma'il's maternal uncle, bent over the Shah, then arose with a grim expression.

"By God above, his life has fled!"

Pir Mohammad began reciting lines from the Qur'an.

"Who is the culprit?" asked Amir Khan with a snarl. "I will kill him with my own hands."

My knees grew tense underneath my robe.

"We must find him as soon as possible," Pir Mohammad replied, but he didn't sound equally upset. Some of the Ostajlu were still in prison, after all.

"Wait a minute. Hakim Tabrizi, what is the cause of death?" Mirza Salman asked.

The physician looked uncertain. "I will have to examine his body and issue a report."

"Is it poison?"

"I don't know yet."

The physician and the qizilbash leaders stared at the Shah's corpse and then at each other, not knowing what to do. Only Mirza Salman looked as crisp and efficient as ever.

"We must not let the news of the Shah's death leak outside the palace," he said. "Remember how the city sank into lawlessness when Tahmasb Shah died? I will ensure that the Ali Qapu gate is closed so that the news can't penetrate into the Promenade of the Royal Stallions. Then we will convene the top-ranking amirs immediately and discuss how to guide the state through this crisis."

"What about the killer?" asked Amir Khan Mowsellu.

"Is there one? Hakim Tabrizi, let us know if you find poison in the Shah's body."

"I will."

The men left Hakim and Hassan in the room with the dead Shah. Hassan still had not budged. Pir Mohammad and Amir Khan departed to convey the news to the noblemen. When Mirza Salman came out of the Shah's bedroom, I affected grief.

"What a world-changing calamity. May God show mercy on us all!"

"Insh'Allah," he replied.

"I only wish I didn't have to inform my lieutenant of this terrible news."

Mirza Salman leaned close to me. "Surely there was no love between them!" he whispered.

I squelched my surprise at his provocative words. "Siblings may quarrel and still love each other," I replied gravely. It would only harm us if he spread the rumor that Pari was her brother's enemy.

"But not these two. In any case, please be sure to tell her I am at her service for anything she needs. She knows of my loyalty: I will not fail her even if people say the deed shows her hand."

"I will let her know."

As I rushed across the square to Pari's house, my heart felt lighter than it had in more than a year. For the first time since Isma'il had become shah, justice had finally been done at the palace.

When I arrived, I told her servants I had an urgent message. She was sitting on a cushion in her private rooms with Azar and Maryam, who was massaging her hand. A cast-aside letter suggested to me that her hand had cramped from all the writing she had done lately.

"My lieutenant, I regret that I come to you with a message of woe, one so grave I wish my tongue could turn to stone rather than utter it."

"But speak you must."

"The light of the universe didn't emerge from his bedroom this morning. Suspecting illness or foul play, his noblemen broke down the door and discovered that he had breathed his last. One of his doctors believes he may have consumed too much opium."

I thought I should launch a plausible rumor about Isma'il's death as soon as possible. I would urge Azar Khatoon to spread the rumor far and wide.

Pari let out a terrifying scream and collapsed forward, while her ladies bent forward to comfort her. In her scream I heard not woe but rather the ferocity of her relief, like my own. Her ladies began to keen with her. Now, I thought with satisfaction, everyone can scream with joy.

"The gates to the Promenade of the Royal Stallions are being closed while the nobles decide what to do," I added.

"I understand. You may leave me to my sorrows."

I went back to my quarters, lay on my bedroll, and closed my eyes. My body pulsed as if I had just left a victorious battlefield.

Whatever happened, even if my eyes should open to the sight of guards poised to kill me, everything would be different from now on. One disordered man would no longer terrorize us. We would no longer fear the cold blade of execution. Zahhak was dead.

At every moment, I expected the Shah's guard would come for me and call me to account. Someone would betray me: Fareed would be unable to restrain himself from confessing, or the physician would rule that poisoned digestives had killed the Shah and tie them to me, or Pari would be questioned and tortured, since even the person I trusted most could be broken through her body. But what actually happened surprised me even more.

That afternoon, black cloths were draped from the windows and balconies of Hassan's house. The Shah's wives hosted a mourning ceremony, and from everywhere in the palace arose the sounds of lamentation. Sultanam's sorrow was real; she had more of a right to it than anyone else. A few other people who truly loved the Shah or stood to benefit from association with him looked grief-stricken. All of us had donned black mourning robes and our faces were sober, yet there was an irrepressible feeling of relief in the air, like the one that precedes the first temperate day of spring after a cruel winter.

I caught a glimpse of Haydar's mother, Sultan-Zadeh, whose green eyes looked as unclouded and as radiant as a summer sky, even as she pretended to wipe away tears. She had received her revenge at last on the man who had displaced her son. The Shah's sisters, many of whom had lost their favorite brothers to his murderous hand, were at pains to suppress their feelings. They kept their eyes downcast, but the corners of their mouths lifted spontaneously with joy.

A woman with profound religious knowledge came to the grieving ceremony in the harem and spoke of the tremendous sadness of a man taken too soon. When a man was loved, such speeches would bring tears to the eyes of everyone in the room. This time, the official mourners howled frenetically as if to make up for the fact that the relatives couldn't summon much grief. Sultanam's face was grave, but she was not weeping. Only Mahasti's eyes were red with sorrow. As the mother of the Shah's firstborn son, she would have enjoyed high position all her life had the Shah lived. Now her future was in doubt.

Afterward, I went to see Pari. She invited me into her most private room, the one with the mural of the unabashedly naked Shireen, and shut the door. I remained standing until, to my surprise, she gestured to the cushion to indicate that I should sit. I lowered myself onto the peach velvet pillow, feeling as if I were about to have tea with a friend.

"My loyal servant," she said, "the physician has just issued his report on the cause of death. It suggests several possibilities: Either the Shah ate too much opium, consumed so much food that it cut off his ability to breathe, or he was poisoned."

"Do you think our efforts produced the intended result?"

"We will never know for certain."

"Is that a comfort to you, Princess?"

She thought for a moment. "I suppose it is. I had to force every nerve in my being to hew to this task. Nothing could have been more unnatural to me."

"Only a lord of orders like yourself would have dared to be so bold."

Pari smiled. "If not for you, this terrible task could have foundered. I am pleased I decided to promote you to be my vizier. I wasn't certain you were ready, but you have earned your promotion in seventy-seven different ways."

"I thank you, Princess."

"In gratitude for our good fortune, I have manumitted a dozen of my slaves, all of whom have chosen to remain in my service. They will be given employment for as long as they wish to stay with me. I have also promised to arrange for the adoptions of any girl orphans presented to me from the city of Qazveen. Finally, I have sworn to go on a pilgrimage to Mashhad and to endow a new seminary there."

"Your munificence makes your name shine bright!"

"But now we have much to face in the days ahead. I refer to the future of this country."

"What do you anticipate?"

"Iran needs a just leader," she said. "The remaining princes are too young and inexperienced to rule. The only suitable person is me, even though no woman can rule officially."

"True. What do you desire now?"

"I wish to be made regent to Isma'il's son Shoja. I will rule in his name until he is old enough to rule for himself. When I am finished with his education, he will be a leader of excellent character."

I was awestruck. "That means you would essentially serve as shah until he is of age."

"Yes! At last, I will claim my rightful sphere. I will rule this country with a loving hand and bring justice back to those who have lost it."

I was filled with pride at the sight of her in her dark robe, her intelligence bursting from her pearly brow, the very pinnacle of learning and grace produced by three thousand years of Iranian civilization. No one would be a better ruler! She had proved herself once, and now she would finally receive the opportunity to show all she could do. My heart soared with joy for her.

"May God shower His blessings on you!"

"As my devoted servant, your position will become more exalted," she added. "I will provide a good title for you when I organize the men of the Shah's inner circle."

"Princess, it is my life's greatest honor to continue to serve you."

I had good reason for hope. I would finally be able to bring Jalileh to Qazveen and to provide her with a sumptuous dowry. If she married one day and had children, their laughter would echo all through the house. At last, I would be part of a family again.

A messenger knocked at the door and announced Shamkhal Cherkes. It had been months since we had seen him. I stood up before he entered and positioned myself in my usual place near the door. There were more lines on his face and more gray hair in his beard than I remembered; it looked as if his service to Isma'il had been hard on him. He sat on a cushion across from Pari, his powerful body tense.

"Princess, I came as soon as I could to offer my condolences about your brother Isma'il," he said. "Not to mention all the other princes who died during his reign."

"Thank you," Pari replied, then lapsed into silence.

"May I speak with you in private?"

"My servant Javaher is like one of my own limbs."

My heart bloomed under the sun of her words.

"Of course," he said, not bothering to glance at me, so great was his desire to please her. "I came to tell you how much I admire your courage."

"No doubt it comes from our family," Pari said, returning the compliment, but with only the thinnest of politeness.

"Really, I mean it."

There was an awkward silence, which Pari refused to fill.

"I have come to ask whether, in this difficult moment, there is any service I can provide for you." There was a pleading look in his eyes.

"No, thank you."

Shamkhal adjusted his large white turban awkwardly. Pari didn't bother to offer tea or sweetmeats or other comforts.

"It is difficult to explain how trying it has been to live under the constant threat that the Shah might decide to kill me."

"You, too?" asked Pari sarcastically.

"I deeply regret not helping you more," Shamkhal continued. "We were all paralyzed by fear, as if caught in a fog through which we could not see. You alone weren't afraid."

"I *was* afraid."

"But you didn't permit your fear to stop you from taking care of the problem."

"Uncle, whatever do you mean?" she parried, wisely refusing to admit to anything. "My poor brother died from an opium overdose and extreme indigestion, by God's will. The important question at the moment is what will happen next."

"That is why I am here. I want to assist you."

He was too vital an ally to dismiss outright, yet how could she trust him? Her eyes were full of reproach.

"I haven't always done what you wanted," he said, "but have always kept you in my heart."

"Indeed? What I am to do with someone who promises loyalty to me, then gives it to someone else?"

"What else could I have done? I couldn't say no to the Shah's promotions without offending, and I couldn't countermand his orders without getting in trouble."

"Did you advocate for me?"

"I tried, but he wouldn't budge. I suspect that someone powerful has been speaking out against you, Pari."

"Mirza Shokhrollah?"

"I don't know. At one point, Isma'il mentioned a reason for his animosity. He said that you had thrown your support behind Mahmood Mirza before he was crowned."

"You know I never did."

She spoke the truth.

"I wonder if that rumor originated with Mirza Salman," he continued.

Pari looked unconvinced.

"His promotion to such a high post was a surprise. What did he do to earn it?"

"He is good at his job," she said. "He is also fiercely loyal. He even came to visit me after the Shah had prohibited it."

Shamkhal looked abashed. "Pari *jan*—my life, listen to me. We are family. I will always advocate for you, unless the Shah orders otherwise. At least I am willing to admit to the truth of things, unlike others who walk a tightrope of loyalties, hoping that neither side tugs too hard."

"I require more than such a tentative vow. Say or do what you must regarding the next shah, but I don't want your help unless you swear yourself to me."

"I understand. What do you wish to do now that the Shah is dead?"

"I want to be Shoja's regent, with your advocacy."

"How bold you are! No woman is like you, and no man, either. With deep humility, I swear my allegiance to you."

To my surprise, he bowed and bent to kiss her feet as if she were shah. Then he looked up in the hope of receiving her acceptance of his pledge.

"All right, then. I will think about it."

"You will think about it?"

"That is all."

"But, Princess—"

Shamkhal looked as if he might burst out of his robe to convince her of his goodwill.

"That is all that is possible at the moment."

I was glad that she disciplined him. How could she trust him otherwise?

A messenger knocked at the door and announced Mirza Salman. "Here, now, is the grand vizier. Let's hear his news."

In her birooni, Pari seated herself on one side of the lattice with her uncle while I joined Mirza Salman on the other side. He was still wearing the same robe as the day before. Judging by the darkness of his upper lids, he hadn't slept.

"Salaam aleikum, Grand Vizier. I am here with Shamkhal Cherkes," Pari said through the lattice.

"Salaam. I wish to report to you on the emergency meeting that I called to determine the future of our country. Alas, the amirs almost came to blows."

"How unusual," she said archly. "Over what?"

"Each group wants influence. I implored them to withdraw their swords until a new shah is named."

"Thank you, Grand Vizier. As always, you are as effective as a sharpened blade. I wish to congratulate you on your recent promotion."

"It is an honor, but one that didn't last long. Please accept my condolences on the loss of your brother."

"And please accept mine in return. Some things . . . can't be helped."

His eyes were untroubled; he was one of those courtiers who float over every wave.

"Nothing has been settled yet. The amirs have inquired as to your wishes."

"Why didn't they come to my quarters?"

"Having been prohibited from seeing you by the Shah, they felt honor-bound not to flout his command. As I promised you earlier today, I proposed that you should be regent to Isma'il's son."

"And?"

"The men didn't like the idea."

"Why not?"

"They were adamant that Isma'il's son shouldn't rule. One of them stood up and recited a section of the *Shahnameh*."

"Which one?"

"It went like this:

> *"My noble lords, no man has ever seen*
> *A king as wicked as this king has been:*
> *He hoarded all he'd stolen from the poor,*
> *His reign was murder, rapine, grief, and war.*
> *No one has heard of any former reign*
> *That was so evil, or that caused so much pain.*
> *We do not want his seed here on the throne*
> *And from his dust we turn to God alone."*

"Indeed? They fear baby Shoja?"

Her tone was barbed, implying that the men did not like the idea of her ruling so unencumbered.

"They suggested that the natural leader of Iran is your late father's son, Mohammad Khodabandeh, who is after all the eldest."

"But he is blind! Why did that disqualify him only a year ago, but not now?"

"For one thing, his mother Sultanam is qizilbash, and the qizil-bash like to support their own. Also, he has four young sons who could succeed him, which gives them comfort. When his name was mentioned, the unanimous refrain of 'Allah! Allah! Allah!' was spoken and everyone swore to support him."

"What role shall I have then?"

"You will be his chief advisor, since he cannot rule on his own."

"Mirza Salman!" exclaimed Pari. "Tell the truth: The men feel that Mohammad Khodabandeh will be easier to influence, isn't that so? Everyone knows he has no interest in being ruler. The amirs will be able to get him to agree to whatever they propose."

"No one said that," Mirza Salman replied.

"But that is the reason, no doubt."

"I can't report on words that weren't spoken."

"Regardless, it is your duty to anticipate what the amirs are thinking and to be strong in the face of their demands."

"I will, I promise. And I assure you that I fought fiercely for you and did as much as a lone voice could do. But now the men are waiting for a word from you. They won't inform Mohammad Khodabandeh until you agree. They recognize all you have done."

There was a long silence; Pari wasn't pleased and neither was I. Shamkhal's deep voice boomed from the back of the other side of the lattice.

"You are the grand vizier. Why can't you bend them to your will?"

Mirza Salman rolled forward on the balls of his feet as if to make himself taller.

"You don't know how hard I tried."

"But you haven't been successful."

"That is a strange thing for you to say."

"What is your meaning?"

"My meaning is that no one has been more loyal to the princess than myself."

"You should have done more."

"If any man believes he can do better, he is welcome to try."

Shamkhal was in no position to force the qizilbash to do anything. His bluster was an attempt to win Pari's love.

"Why are you trying so hard to convince her that Mohammad Khodabandeh is a good choice?" Shamkhal asked. "Is it because his wife's a Tajik, like you?"

Mirza Salman looked offended, but his words were calm. "My concern is for the safety of the realm. We need to decide on the succession quickly to prevent invasions and to avoid another spate of lawlessness."

"I agree," said Pari.

"By the way," Mirza Salman added, "I also argued that we shouldn't waste any further efforts trying to determine if Isma'il Shah, may his soul be at peace, was poisoned."

"Why not?" Pari asked in a sharp tone.

"I argued that he is in God's hands, and it is our job to think of the future."

"They should be grateful that Isma'il's death has shielded the surviving princes from his sword—not to mention themselves," the princess said.

Mirza Salman's forehead creased a hundred times. "True. One of the men admitted that he had been ordered by the Shah only a few days ago to execute Mohammad Khodabandeh and his boys."

Pari drew in her breath so sharply we could hear it on our side of the lattice. "All of them?"

"Yes. He delayed as much as he could because he was so loath to carry out his task. By the grace of God, he didn't have to do so."

"How narrowly we have escaped a terrible fate! My dynasty would have crumbled."

"I reminded them of that."

So Pari had changed the course of history once again. For that matter, so had I. Was this what my stars had meant? Who, then, was destined to be the greatest Safavi leader? Could it be Mohammad Khodabandeh?

"Why didn't Isma'il's nobles bother to do anything about the injustice he imposed on those around him?"

"They had sworn their loyalty to him."

"I see," she said. "So I am correct that the amirs did nothing."

Her condemnation hung in the air for a moment before she continued. "Everyone acknowledges that a royal princess has saved the realm and deserves a reward. I want you to convince them to make me regent instead of what they suggested."

"I can't. Not a single man spoke in favor of the idea after I proposed it. This was the best concession I could get after arguing with them for a long time."

I believed him. He had every reason to make a deal for her that would make him her most trusted ally.

"Please consider, esteemed princess, that you will be performing that very role when you are Mohammad Khodabandeh's chief advisor."

"Unless, for some reason, he doesn't wish it."

"As you have pointed out, he is known to be malleable."

"Which amirs spoke in favor of the idea that I should advise him?"

"All of the leaders agreed it is a good idea. They believe that you are fair and make good decisions."

"So they will support me as his advisor?"

"They will."

There was a pause while Pari discussed with her uncle something that I couldn't hear.

"In that case, you may tell the men these exact words: I accept their decision that I shall become chief advisor to Mohammad Khodabandeh, but only if every one of them agrees to stand behind me in that role. Will you get their word man by man? And tell them there is no longer any prohibition against meeting with me. If they fail to appear at a meeting after the third-day mourning ceremony for the late Shah, we don't have an agreement."

"Chashm. Thank you, princess, for ensuring that this transition will be more orderly than the last one. May I convey the news to the elders?"

"You may."

Mirza Salman took his leave, and when he was gone, I rejoined Pari and Shamkhal. Pari looked angry.

"What did he mean about you?" she demanded of her uncle.

"Nothing," he replied. "Can't you see how he tries to manipulate you by pretending to be the most loyal of all?"

"Isn't he?"

"I have my doubts."

Pari looked at him quizzically. I too was wondering whether he was trying to make Mirza Salman look deceitful to advance himself.

"How well do you know Mohammad Khodabandeh?" Shamkhal asked her quickly, changing the subject.

"Not well. He has served outside the capital ever since I was a child. But since he has no interest in ruling, I will take charge."

"What if the situation is like the last one?"

"Mohammad Khodabandeh is much weaker than Isma'il ever was, and more reasonable."

"His wife is fiery, I hear."

I remembered how Khayr al-Nisa Beygom had knocked over the tray of pudding when Isma'il had been crowned.

"She will arrive with very little standing in the palace. I will put her in her place if needed."

"Too bad Mirza Salman wasn't able to be more effective," he said with a dismissive sneer.

"What do you think?" Pari asked me. It was rare for her to solicit my opinion in the presence of her uncle.

"Serving as a blind shah's chief advisor is a reasonable compromise," I said. That was the truth of politics: A compromise was the best we could hope for.

Shamkhal looked from me to her and back again, as if he could feel his influence draining away.

"How can I help?" he finally asked.

"I will let you know. Forgive me, Uncle, but now I must attend to other things."

"I see. May I call on you again soon?"

"Yes, yes, of course."

Shamkhal stood up, clearly disappointed at being dismissed, and took his leave. Pari remained seated for a moment after he left; she looked lost in thought, and then she sighed.

"I miss my father. Little did I understand, when he was alive, that no other man would ever match the constancy of his love."

An inadvertent protest escaped my lips. Pari added softly, "I meant no other relative."

As was customary, Isma'il Shah was interred on the day he died. Before the official ceremonies late that afternoon, I met Balamani at the baths. After giving my robes to the bath attendant, an old eunuch who was missing a few teeth, I washed myself all over with soap and buckets of water, then eased myself into the hottest tub beside Balamani.

"Aw khesh," I exclaimed as the heat warmed my bones.

"Hello, my friend," Balamani replied, as the waves I made splashed against his chest. "What surprises have greeted us! The thirteenth of Ramazan is a day we won't ever forget."

"God is great."

My affirmation echoed through the room. Balamani lowered his voice so that only I could hear him.

"He is, but it is difficult for people to understand why this cataclysmic event occurred. A rumor has been circulating that the Shah was poisoned."

"Indeed?" I said, turning to Balamani, whose large body looked whitened by the steam. "And who is to blame?"

"They say it is his sister."

His words alarmed me. "Does anyone believe that rumor? I happen to know she was writing letters all night, since I was with her."

"That is good to know," he said. "I will pass on the information. In the meantime, I hope you are satisfied."

His tone wasn't entirely friendly. I had closed my eyes, enjoying the heat, but I opened them to look at him.

"I believe everyone is satisfied," I said.

"Not me."

"Why not?"

He lifted water to his forehead and cheeks, smoothing away the lines for a moment.

"I am thinking about Tahmasb Shah. He certainly sent his share of men to their execution, even his own kin. The problem comes when a man starts to believe that he is entitled to do such things all the time."

"True."

"I would hate to think you might become such a man," he added.

"Me? Are you joking?"

Balamani ignored me. "Your lieutenant will become very powerful now. These rumors about her won't hurt, as long as they can't be pinned on her. In fact, they make her seem as tough as the men, if not tougher."

"She is fierce," I agreed proudly.

"Pari has proved herself willing to do something they were too afraid to do. They will fear her for it."

"What is wrong with that? It seems to work."

"Things could be tricky if she decides to take such action again. In that case, she will ask those closest to her for their help."

"That will never happen. Just because we have gotten rid of a Zahhak doesn't mean we have to become one."

He poked my forearm the way he used to do when I was young and missing his point.

"I would keep my eye on the question if I were you. Remember, others will now be watching you, and if they wish to bring her down, they will start with you."

I had expected praise from him, the man who had been like an uncle to me, but his words were harsh.

"Balamani! Aren't you my friend?"

"Always," he said, "but I am a friend of this court's, too. If the point of your actions was to bring about the return of justice, don't become uglier than what you destroyed."

His words offended me. I lifted myself out of the bath and signaled to the attendant that I needed a towel.

"You have hardly begun to soak off the dirt," Balamani said.

I glared at him.

"Listen, my friend," he said. "Don't make any mistakes that would require you to make a lifetime of amends."

"Of course I won't," I said as I dried my back.

His expression was so full of something like remorse that it stopped me from leaving as quickly as I had planned. I wrapped the towel around my middle and sat down on the ledge above the water, immersing my legs again. Balamani slicked water over the crown of his bald head. His eyes were clouded as if he were remembering something.

"Did that ever happen to you?" I finally asked.

"Yes."

"How?"

His face twisted with regret.

"You still don't know why I took such an interest in you?"

He was like a big angel with his smooth charcoal-colored skin, lilting voice, and generous belly. He had been an angel to me many times. The ghosts of my past rose within me all of a sudden, and I shivered.

"I thought you felt sorry for me."

"Yes, that is part of it."

"What else?"

"You might dislike me forever. I know things that I couldn't tell you—until now."

Looking into his dark eyes, I felt as if I were falling into a deep pit. Suddenly the image of a bloodied white sheet scalded my vision.

"My father," I said softly.

"Yes."

"Why was he killed?"

"You know why. He was accused of diverting money from the treasury."

"Who made the allegations against him?" Challenge roughened my voice.

"What have you deduced?"

"I have come to suspect that someone else gave the order to Kamiyar Kofrani to kill my father."

"Well done," said Balamani, his almond-shaped eyes filled with appreciation for my sleuthing. "Have you figured out who it was?"

He was ever the master pushing me to make discoveries on my own. My heart began pounding; my voice tightened in my chest.

"I suspect Mirza Salman."

"No. Look higher."

Higher? That left only royalty and the handful of men closest to Tahmasb Shah. I thought about each one of them. Mirza Shokhrol-lah? The Shah's previous grand vizier? The qizilbash nobles? I had no evidence against any particular courtier.

"Here is your towel, my good man. Would you like a shave or a massage, gorbon, from the man with the golden hands? Surely an exalted fellow like you . . ."

The voice of the bath attendant welcoming a new bather shattered my concentration. How fawning he was in the hopes of earning tips! Even the littlest man had his fiefdom to maintain, just like a shah. My father had lost his life to someone who was determined to protect his own. Who could it have been? Who, back then, would have been most passionate about the throne other than the Shah himself?

Balamani's eyes were full of encouragement, as they had been when he was first training me. All of a sudden, I shouted out loud.

"Isma'il?"

"Yes."

I was incredulous. "From his prison in Qahqaheh?"

"That is right."

"Why?"

"The last thing he wanted was for another man to usurp the throne while he was incarcerated. He didn't think Tahmasb Shah would believe his allegations, so he hired an assassin of his own."

"In that case, why didn't Isma'il have me killed when he became shah?"

"Why should he risk incurring Pari's wrath when he was so afraid of her? You were neutered in his eyes—though he was wrong about that."

"How do you know all this about my past?"

"Isn't that my job?"

"Answer me."

Balamani shifted in the tub, sending a current of water to the other side. "Years ago, I was charged with taking messages between Isma'il and his mother. Hidden within one of his letters was the order for your father's murder."

"Wasn't the order sealed?"

Balamani laughed. "Of course."

"Once you had read it, why did you deliver it?"

"I had to. A courier who destroys royal letters can be executed."

I felt as if a lightning strike had scrambled my thoughts. "Why didn't you tell me all of this after I came to the palace?"

"When you were a hotheaded young man, I feared you would try to take revenge on Isma'il and get yourself killed."

I cast my hand over my forehead. Had all of that been written there?

"And so I have."

"And so you have. Little did you know how I prayed for the success of your mission. There is justice in the world, although it takes unpredictable paths."

"May God be praised."

"Your father's murder is one of the reasons that Tahmasb Shah kept his son locked away at Qahqaheh. After that episode, the Shah was doubly certain that he couldn't trust him."

"Now I understand why you looked after me so well. But why did the Shah take me in to begin with?"

"He decided to make it up to you."

"You mean I didn't have to get myself cut?"

Balamani grimaced, and I was pierced by a sensation as extreme as the one that had followed the removal of my parts. I had to clap my arms around myself to keep from crying out.

"I don't know. The Shah paid attention to your plight only after you requested an audience. That is when he told Anwar to investigate the matter, and Anwar reported his belief that your father had been falsely fingered by people who wished to bring him down because of the favor he enjoyed. When the Shah discovered that you became a eunuch out of a desire to serve him, he was doubly moved by your story."

"If the Shah thought my father was innocent, why didn't he admit the mistake and give restitution to my family?"

Balamani laughed ruefully. "How often does a leader admit someone has been killed in error? Besides, he wasn't the one who ordered the killing."

"How strange my fate has been!"

"One of the strangest. That is why I wished to help, as did others, like Tahmasb Shah. He thought highly of you."

"How do you know?"

"I heard him tell Pari that your intelligence and loyalty made you one of the jewels of the court. He made her promise to treat you well."

Balamani sighed deeply, creating ripples in the bathwater. "I wish I could have told you all of this sooner. You are like the nephew I never had. I hated to have to withhold the truth from you for so long."

I looked at Balamani's thick, knotted fingers and thought about how those very hands had carried the order for my father's death. Yet the same hands had also massaged my temples when I was ill with a fever and had intervened for me whenever I needed help. Blaming him would be like attacking a messenger who happened to bring bad news.

"Balamani, I owe you nothing but thanks," I said in a congested voice. "How can I ever repay you for so many years of kindness, oh wise, fearless, and loving friend! You have taught me what it means to be a complete man."

Tears sprang to Balamani's eyes. He rinsed his face with the bathwater, his broad shoulders shaking. How lucky I had been that God had sent me to him!

The heat of the bath was making my head swim; the steam in the room obscured my vision. I felt as if I couldn't breathe. Easing my legs out of the tub, I called to the bath attendant to bring my clothes and handed him a generous tip.

"Javaher, are you all right?" Balamani asked.

"I need air."

As I left the hammam, I felt a strong urge to visit my father's grave. I hadn't been there in years, and now the things I had learned made my spirit long to commune with his.

I passed through the Ali Qapu gate and turned down the Promenade of the Royal Stallions toward my old family home, remembering the day my father's body had arrived wrapped in a bloody cotton sheet. I didn't know who lived in the house now and didn't want to know. After leaving the Friday mosque behind me, I arrived at the cemetery at the southern outskirts of town where my father was buried. At the entrance, I bought rose water from a peddler and went in search of my father. The cemetery had grown since the last time

I had visited, and it took me time to find the granite slab marking his grave.

I called one of the graveside attendants to sweep away the dirt and wash the slab with buckets of water. While he did his work, I heard the cry of birds above me. I looked up and saw a flock of white geese that were leaving on the vanguard of winter for warmer climes.

An old man in a tattered cotton robe approached me. "Shall I recite the Qur'an for you?" he asked in a hoarse voice.

"No, thank you, I will do it myself," I replied, and gave him a coin anyway.

"Blessings on you and all your children."

"Thanks, but I don't have any." I heard the bitterness in my own voice.

"Trust in God, my good fellow. You shall."

He sounded so sure of it I almost believed him.

Once he and the grave washer had gone, I closed my eyes and recited prayers for the dead, losing myself in the rhythm and the rhyme of the words. They rolled off my tongue in the crisp air, softening my heart and everything around me.

I crouched on my heels and gazed at my father's gravestone. He had only been about ten years older than me when he was murdered. It was one thing to be felled by God, through illness or an accident, which we all expect one day or another; it was quite another to be felled by a man.

I sprinkled the rose water on the stone. "May your soul rise to heaven, and may you revel in the reward you deserve," I whispered.

The flock of geese soared overhead again, crying out as they passed. Looking up at their pure white bodies, I was filled with lightness, as if my father's soul had just then been freed. In the vastness of the sky, I could feel his warm brown eyes smiling on me.

I heard the call to prayer from a nearby mosque and felt moved to communicate with God. I beckoned to the grave washer and asked for water, a prayer mat, and a tablet of clay from Mecca. After spreading out the mat near my father's grave, I washed my hands, face, and feet. As I bent low to pray, my heart was full of more things than I could say. I thanked God for His protection and prayed for His judgment on my soul to be light. I asked Him to look kindly on me because I was a strange creature, one that He had not designed and perhaps did not countenance. Feeling the caress of the tablet of dried earth against my forehead, I prayed for the tenderness and mercy that He showed all his creatures, even the most humbled.

In the bazaar there were always strange creatures like the one-eyed goat that were derided and jeered at, yet I always tried to stroke their noses for a moment or two, because how could they have come to be, without God's hand? Soldiers returned from wars with missing parts—limbs torn off or eyes gouged out. The old lost the powers they had had as youths, becoming as gnarled as branches and as sedentary as trees. My mother developed a fissure in her heart and was felled by sorrow. God had created perfection in man, but time on earth ate away at him, part by part, until finally nothing remained and he vanished into spirit. Yet there was glory in being half, not whole, glory in the task of it. I thought of a blind man who had recited poetry at court and how he cried out the lines of the *Shahnameh* as if they were seared into his heart, as if the loss of his eyes had allowed him to see more clearly into the soul of the words. He spoke true, truer than a man with eyes could ever speak, and he cracked open the hearts of those who heard his call.

The lines of a poem suddenly blazed within me:

> *Praise, oh praise! Praise for the not-whole*
> *Praise for those who stumble along*
> *Though wounded in body or soul*
> *Praise for the one-legged man*
> *Who runs races in his mind*
> *Praise for he who sees truth as clear*
> *As light, though he is blind*
> *Praise for the deaf man who hears nought*
> *But the voice of God all the time*
> *Praise for the woman forced to trade*
> *Her dearest possessions for bread*
> *Praise for all who have been cut or lamed*

Twisted, wrenched, battered, or torn
Within or without, whatever the wound
Oh praise! For when the soul's mirror is cleaned
Then man becomes spirit while still man.

When I stood up from prayer, my heart finally felt at ease for the first time in twelve years. No doubt it had been my fate to become a eunuch. If I hadn't, I would never have gotten close enough to Isma'il Shah to avenge my father.

CHAPTER 8

A STAR PLUMMETS

When Faranak heard that her son had unseated Zahhak, I am certain she threw herself down in prayer and thanked God for his blessings. No doubt she opened her home to the less fortunate and offered a feast to them every day for a week.

If I had been present at the festivities, I would have called the crowd to attention and said this: "Kind Khanoom, there is more to this story than you in your modesty have revealed. If you had not been clever enough to find the cowherd and his glorious cow, Fereydoon would have perished before he started to walk. If you had not taken him to India to be trained by a sage, he would have failed to learn wisdom. If you had not demanded justice for the murder of his father, he would not have burned for revenge. If you had not prevented him from attacking Zahhak before he was ready, he would have been killed. If you had neglected to share your kind heart with him, he would never have learned mercy. Praise, oh praise for Faranak the wise!"

Word was sent to Mohammad Khodabandeh in Shiraz that he had been chosen as the new shah. Like Isma'il, he didn't believe it at first. He had been under house arrest for so many months, it was no surprise he thought it was a trick to test his loyalty to his brother. At first, he ordered that the envoy be executed to avoid the plot he was certain was being laid for him, but the envoy saved himself by suggesting that he merely be imprisoned for a few days until the truth about Isma'il's death could be verified. Eventually, when the evidence was overwhelming, the envoy was released and Mohammad agreed to come to Qazveen and take up his new post.

At the palace, no serious attempt was made to discover who had poisoned Isma'il. After the physician's final report deemed the cause of death unclear, Mirza Salman had worked hard to convince the amirs that running the country was more important than chasing a plot that may not have existed. Since it was uncertain what had killed the Shah, he argued, it was senseless to seek reprisal. They had enough to do.

Naturally, I was relieved when it became clear that no one would be punished, yet surprised the men relinquished their duties so easily. They seemed to me to be the worst kind of cowards: cringing under their leader's demands, mouthing the right words to win his approbation, hating him in their hearts, yet doing nothing to stop his evil deeds while he was alive—nothing. These were the nobles of our land, the men whose presence had filled me with adulation when I was a child. Now I knew that despite all their gold and titles and weapons, they quaked with fear. Brave men were rare indeed.

After three days of mourning, the noblemen were summoned to the princess's house for their first meeting with her. On the appointed day, her servants set up the blue velvet curtain that would conceal her from the men at her home. Pari secreted herself behind the curtain, and we tested whether I could hear her voice from every corner of the room, just as we had long ago. But this time, she delighted me by reciting a section from the *Shahnameh* about how the great hero Rostam had tamed his ferocious steed, who became his most loyal companion. From every point I listened, her voice was loud and strong.

Soon after the cannon boomed, everyone sat down to their first meal of the day, as it was still Ramazan. Hands reached eagerly for drinks, and once the first wave of thirst was satisfied, we settled down to enjoy bread, cheese, nuts, and fruit. I was still chewing my food in the company of Pari's other eunuchs when Shamkhal Cherkes arrived. I leapt to my feet to attend to the princess.

After greeting Pari, Shamkhal said, "I came early to ask if you wish me to be your representative to the men, as before."

The princess thought about it for a moment and then said, "Thank you, Uncle, but you won't be needed."

Shamkhal looked as if he wished he could fold into his own large body. In that moment, the cowardice shown by Pari's own kin struck me with full force. Court life had made them fearful and changeable. Even as they swore loyalty, they were peering over their shoulder to see who could boost them higher.

"Are you certain?" he asked.

"I have been on my own all this time, haven't I?"

He looked chastened. "If I may assist you, I will do so gladly."

"Perhaps another time."

I had never seen her look more like a princess than at that moment.

"Actually," she added all of a sudden, "I have already asked Javaher to lead the meeting."

She hadn't asked, but I was pleased by the faith she showed in me. Of course I wanted to represent her to the nobles.

Before the men began to arrive, Pari seated herself behind the curtain. I was gratified to see a dozen of the leading noblemen and palace officials, notably Amir Khan Mowsellu, Pir Mohammad Khan, Anwar Agha, Khalil Khan—who had been Pari's guardian when she was a child—Morshad Khan, Mirza Salman, and several others take their places according to rank. They were as quiet and respectful as if meeting with the Shah. How different from when the princess had called them to order before Isma'il had arrived!

Standing on the platform in front of her curtain, I looked out with confidence on the sober nobles, their silk robes impeccable, red batons erect in the qizilbash's turbans. "Prepare to pay heed to the princess, lion of the Safavis, lord of orders," I instructed them in a firm voice.

The men heeded me in a way they had never done before, my changed status reflected in their very posture. When they were so still that we could hear the footsteps of someone walking through the square, the princess began to speak from behind the curtain in a low, melodious voice.

"My good noblemen," she said, "welcome. Once again in little more than a year, we face the necessity of keeping the country intact until our new shah arrives to claim his throne. My goal is to deliver to him a functioning government and a capital city where law prevails. All of you will be asked to assist me in avoiding the problems we had last time."

"It is our duty, princess," Mirza Salman replied, speaking for the men.

"Our shah-to-be will arrive soon. First he will travel to Qom to pay his respects to his mother and to thank God for the safety of his sons, except for the much-lamented Sultan Hassan Mirza. Then he will enter the palace according to his astrologers' recommendations for an auspicious arrival. If everything is to be ready, we have much work ahead of us."

"Mark well the words of royalty," said Shamkhal Cherkes proudly, even though Mirza Salman now outranked him and should have been the one to speak.

"Anwar Agha will be in charge of organizing the coronation ceremonies within the palace," Pari continued. "He and I will be consulting daily, and he will inform you of your responsibilities in this matter."

"When shall we go to Qom to pay our respects to our new shah?" asked Mirza Salman.

"Not until the palace is completely in order," Pari replied. "No one has permission to leave his post unless it is given directly by me. Is that understood by everyone?"

"We shall obey," the men replied.

"Good. That said, let me remind you that the principal duty of a leader is to provide justice. Remember Nizam al-Mulk's story of the poor widow and Anushirvan the just? One of Anushirvan's nobles expropriated the land of the widow because he wanted to expand his estate. After the woman complained to Anushirvan and he verified her story, the nobleman was skinned and stuffed. All of his property was bequeathed to the woman, but even more important, Anushirvan's subjects learned he would be uncompromising about enforcing justice. That is the kind of court we will aspire to in the future."

The noblemen looked at each other, wondering, it seemed, what exactly Pari was going to hold them responsible for. But then she added sugar to the stew.

"Accordingly, my first act as the new shah's representative will be to restore justice. Many noblemen have been sent to the palace prison because they fell out of favor. I hereby order that those men be released to their families."

A great shout of approval burst out from the men. "May God be praised!" said Khalil Khan.

"Are you including those who supported Haydar?" asked Pir Mohammad Khan.

"I am. Sadr al-din Khan Ostajlu will be one of the first to be set free."

"May God rain his blessings on you!" he replied. "How sweet is this day."

"Before celebrating, I need to hear from all of you about the problems in the realm. Mirza Salman, you may speak first."

He cleared his throat. "Many provincial governorships still remain empty, threatening our stability. They include the posts vacated by the tragic demise of the princes."

"The delays have been inexcusable," Pari replied. "You and your men may develop a list of recommendations in consultation with me. I will present the list to the new shah and urge a quick decision, especially where our borders are most vulnerable."

"Chashm," said Mirza Salman.

I could already see some of the men looking hopeful; they would be sure to petition her for their sons and retainers to be granted those posts. For Pari, it would be an excellent opportunity to put her own men in powerful positions, men who would then owe allegiance to her.

Morshad Khan, the noble in charge of the palace guard, asked to be recognized next.

"I am concerned about the treasury. Isma'il's men are still on guard, but with a change of shah at hand, they may not be trustworthy. In addition, if our enemies hear the news and suspect we're vulnerable, they could attack."

The treasury was located in a low, fortified building near Forty Columns Hall. It was hidden behind thick walls and guarded by soldiers. Very few people were permitted to enter, and every entry was recorded in a book.

Pari's answer was immediate. "Shamkhal Cherkes, organize a retinue of Circassian guards and make sure they don't stint in their duty to protect the treasury day and night."

"Chashm," he replied, smiling broadly now that he had been honored with such an important task.

"Princess, wouldn't it be better if the guard consisted of several groups, including the qizilbash?" Mirza Salman asked.

"Don't you trust us?" Shamkhal shot back.

"That is not the point. A mixed group will require everyone to take responsibility for protecting the country's wealth."

"Answer my question!" commanded Shamkhal.

"It is not a real question," said Mirza Salman, holding his ground. "Moreover, it seems to me it would be easy to prove which one of us is the most loyal."

"Are you threatening me?" Shamkhal's eyes bulged with his over-eagerness to do something.

"I am merely stating a fact."

Two weeks before they had barely been speaking to Pari, and now they were ready to come to blows to prove themselves!

"Stop this unseemly sparring," Pari commanded from behind

the curtain. "Mirza Salman has a point. I will ask the Takkalu to join the Circassians in guarding the treasury."

The Takkalu had become her allies, ever since the Ostajlu had returned to Isma'il's favor.

"That would be the only fair thing to do," said Mirza Salman.

Shamkhal looked enraged; he had lost almost every battle so far. Mirza Salman smiled at him, taunting him. All of a sudden, I remembered how hard Mirza Salman had worked to take Mirza Shokhrollah down. It had started just like this, with a sneer at a meeting.

"The princess has closed discussion on this issue," I told the assembly in a firm voice. "We will proceed to the next topic."

"What about our revenues? Are we receiving the monies owed from the provinces?" Pari asked.

"We have a shortfall from the southwest," replied the eunuch Farhad Agha, whom Isma'il had put in charge of treasury revenues.

"Why?"

Khalil Khan asked to be recognized. He had a formidable nose and was known for playing backgammon with masterly deception. He would appear to lose for a long time into the game, then score point after point until his enemy was crushed.

"There has been an earthquake in my province, and many harvesters have been killed. We need time to recover."

"It is granted," Pari replied, "but I will expect a thorough report on the status of the harvest in the next month."

Hameed Khan, a young nobleman, asked to be recognized next. "I wish to report a success. After Badi al-Zaman died in Sistan, we endured a full-scale rebellion in my province, but the conspirators have been unmasked and vanquished, and now our border is safe and strong. I thank the esteemed princess for understanding the severity of the danger we faced before anyone else did."

"That is what a leader is for," Pari replied.

"We honor you for it. You have been a lion where others might quake."

"After this meeting, everyone should contact their retainers and ask if there are any threats of revolt or invasion in their provinces.

Report to me as soon as you receive an answer. Don't forget that our enemies will soon learn about the Shah's death and will be eager to take advantage."

"Chashm," the men replied.

"I continue to be concerned about affairs in Van. Rumors abound that the Ottoman governor there, Khosro Pasha, is poised to attack us. Ali Khan Shamlu, I want you to lead an army to Khui to show our strength and discourage his plans. Nothing is more important than preserving my father's hard-won peace with the Ottomans."

"Al-lah! Al-lah! Al-lah!" chanted the men, and Ali Khan looked pleased that he would finally get to carry out the mission that Pari had assigned before Isma'il had stopped him.

"Are there any other concerns?"

Khalil Khan stood up. "There have been rumors of irregularities at the palace," he said, wagging his finger at the curtain. There was a long, uncomfortable silence.

"State your business," I demanded.

"Some have gone so far as to claim that the Shah was murdered," he charged.

Since Khalil had been Pari's guardian long ago, which usually resulted in a lifelong bond, I wondered why he had decided to challenge her so publicly.

"The physician's report was inconclusive," I reminded him.

"It is my duty to let the princess know about rumors that a murder plot was hatched in the harem."

I stiffened and frowned at him.

"That is preposterous," said Shamkhal, leaping to his feet. "What are you implying?"

From behind her curtain, Pari said, "Curious rumors are always circulating among you men about the royal harem. You seem to imagine it as an opium den full of connivers, but it is more like an army regiment organized by rank and task. How could you know what goes on in the harem? Have you ever been inside?"

"Of course not," said Khalil Khan.

"Then I think you are best off leaving such concerns to me."

The men laughed, and Khalil Khan's face reddened. "Now wait a minute. If Isma'il Shah was murdered, what is to prevent the same thing from happening to the next one? We would all be fools not to fear a murderer on the loose."

Some of the men actually looked disquieted. Amir Khan's mouth pulled down into a frown. God be praised, they were afraid of her!

"It is difficult to imagine things will worsen, after all that has happened in recent months," Pari replied. "Still, I give you my word that as long as you obey orders, I will stand by you. As you know, I never abandoned you. Even when I was forbidden to participate in palace affairs, I argued for clemency for the condemned at great cost to myself."

"She speaks the truth," said Shamkhal.

"In exchange, I ask for your loyalty now as I assume my new role as Mohammad Khodabandeh's chief advisor. Men, what is your verdict?"

"Make all your voices heard," I instructed the nobles.

"Hail to the best graybeard a country could have!" shouted Pir Mohammad Khan, whose enthusiasm no doubt reflected the news about his imprisoned relative.

"Al-lah! Al-lah!" yelled Shamkhal, starting up the chant.

The rest of the men joined in the roar. "Al-lah! Al-lah! Al-lah!"

The sound echoed the joyous pumping of my heart. I rushed behind the curtain to find Pari already on her feet. She looked, all of a sudden, exactly like her father, tall and slender in a saffron robe. She was neither smiling nor cowed, but completely at ease with being in charge. Though the men would never admit it, her bravery had tamed them. It seemed to me that the royal farr had penetrated her so completely that it illuminated her from within. Some would say it was in her blood, but I knew she had earned every glimmer of it, and my heart swelled with pride.

Organizing the upcoming coronation occupied everyone for the next few days, including the lowliest errand boy. The noblemen arrived to receive their orders early in the morning, eager to show their loyalty. Everyone took a long rest in the afternoon. After breaking the fast at night, Pari and I continued working on the essential tasks of running the palace. Then she and I often consulted until shortly before dawn, when we would take a break to eat another meal. Pari was finally being permitted to do the work she had trained for at her father's side, and she glowed with satisfaction. Even her mother remarked that she seemed as radiant as a new bride, and she no longer bothered her about getting married.

As for me, I had become a man of significance. When the nobles assembled in her waiting room, they arrived early to get my ear. They told me their problems, begging for my intercession. I did what I could to help those who seemed honest and who could aid the princess.

On the last day of Ramazan, the Day of Feasting, we were all in the mood for a grand celebration. Excessive indulgence was forbidden because the Shah had died so recently, but Pari prepared a respectful celebration for her ladies and her eunuchs to mark the end of the fasting month. A woman schooled in religion recited to us, reminding us that the Qur'an was revealed to the Prophet Mohammad, peace be upon him, during Ramazan. I prayed fiercely, asking for forgiveness for my recent deeds and hoping they would be judged justified in the eyes of God.

Right after the new moon was sighted, we were served a festive meal beyond our imaginings. There were haunches of roast lamb, long skewers of kabob, rice studded with herbs, beans, or dried fruits, and countless stews. I started with one of my favorite dishes of lamb stewed with parsley, fenugreek, coriander, and green onion, flavored with the small tart lemons that gave the dish its special bite. I ate it with a cooling serving of yogurt mixed with cucumber and mint, enjoying the way the flavors married each other on my tongue. The errand boys, who were especially attentive to me now that I was Pari's closest confidant, came by repeatedly offering me drinks and hot bread, and to satisfy them, I accepted their offerings. Massoud Ali sat with me for a few moments until the lure of games called him into Pari's courtyard, where the other boys were lighting fireworks and shouting with excitement. I went outside and watched the children play for a while.

"Oy, defective!" I heard all of a sudden. "Are you man enough to play a game of backgammon with me?"

It was Ardalan taunting Massoud Ali. I squelched the urge I felt to jump up and defend him. I had worked for months to strengthen him in body and mind, and now I must let him test his own resolve.

The taunts continued. Massoud Ali's small fists tensed at his sides. "You talk big, but you are nothing but a coward!" he yelled back.

Ardalan's face reddened. Massoud Ali charged toward him and poked him in the sternum with the knuckles of his left hand.

"Are you man enough to lose?"

"What?"

"Well, are you?" Massoud Ali demanded, bristling like a cornered cat.

Ardalan stepped back and raised his open hands. "Of course. Let's set up the board."

I made sure that Massoud Ali saw my proud smile. Then I left the boys to their game and returned inside.

It was time for the poetry recitation. The princess had found a blind man who used to perform for her father, and since he could not see, there was no problem admitting him into the ladies' quarters. Once we had all eaten our fill, she asked him to recite for us from the *Shahnameh*. As he tuned his six-stringed *tar*, Pari turned to me. "Tonight my dear father is much on my mind," she said. "So much has happened in the year and a half since he died."

"You speak the truth. It is as if we have lived two lifetimes in that short period. How proud he would be to see how well you rule!"

Her smile reflected something more noble than pride; it was the certainty of how well she now fulfilled her role. "Yet my plans are different from his," she said. "He gave up the arts of the book and most kinds of poetry because he wished to be pious. I want to bring all those things back and make this court the paragon of its age. We will hire artists, calligraphers, gilders, painters, and poets, and we will create competitions and prizes to encourage talent both old and new.

Men's hearts will soar again from contact with the joy of poetry and the beauty of art. Instead of simply honoring masters of the past, we will create the lights of the future. Javaher, I want you to help me achieve this dream."

After all we had endured, to be able to create a court celebrating beauty, learning, and dignity! How glorious!

Pari smiled and I felt her radiance, strong and true, as the reciter began. The birooni became quiet and we listened to his melodious voice bringing to life Ferdowsi's words. Although written five hundred years before our time, they still stirred my blood with the desire to fulfill Pari's dreams.

> *Noble and valiant warriors, see that you*
> *Act righteously in everything you do—*
> *If you would have God turn your present night*
> *To dawn and victory with His glorious might*
> *See that in darkness when trumpets sound*
> *You leap into the saddle from the ground*
> *And ride as if the sun itself arose*
> *At midnight to do battle with our foes.*
> *Don't dream of rest until the battle's done*
> *Rest is for when our victory is won.*

I looked at Pari, who was listening to the reciter as if he were the only person in the room, and I imagined her as Fereydoon liberating the people from an evil force. I thought it was no accident that Ferdowsi's greatest tale made heroes of three different types of people: a mother, a blacksmith, and a noble. Without all of them working together, how would victory ever have been achieved?

The end of the month of fasting was always a time of high spirits and generosity. I took the opportunity to ask Pari if I could send for Jalileh, and she graciously granted her permission for her arrival after the New Year holiday, when new recruits to the harem would begin receiving their training. By then I would also have received a substantial portion of my increased salary. Since the New Year was more than three months away and the succession of the new shah could disrupt all promises, I decided not to share the specifics of the news with Jalileh until it was a certainty. She had been so disappointed by the last delay that I did not want to bruise her again. Instead I wrote to say that things were settling down at the palace and that I was hopeful for a resolution in the spring.

Right after Ramazan, Mohammad Khodabandeh sent a group of his men to ready the palace for himself and his family. They met with Anwar Agha, who permitted the eunuchs among them to examine the buildings on the harem grounds, scrutinizing the residence for sharp corners, unexpected flights of stairs, or open balconies that could prove dangerous to a blind man. The eunuchs suggested modifications after consulting with the palace architects.

The next time that Mohammad Khodabandeh's retainers came to the palace, they arrived in a much bigger group that included soldiers. Pari and I were told that they had been sent to check on the status of the modifications to the palace. Late that afternoon, however, Anwar Agha sent a message to the princess that there was conflict brewing at the treasury, and she dispatched a message to her uncle and sent me to the birooni to determine what was happening.

As I wrapped myself in a warm robe and rushed toward Forty Columns Hall, I remembered the soldiers tearing the hearts out of the rosebushes when Haydar was killed and hoped I wasn't about to witness another clash. It was a cold, wet day, and the trees I passed looked burdened with snow. In front of the treasury, Shamkhal's Circassian soldiers stood guard along with the Takkalu, as I had expected. They stamped their feet and shuffled from side to side to stay warm. But there was also another group of armed men facing them.

"The shah-to-be commands it," their leader was saying, his breath visible in the air. I recognized him as one of the Ostajlu.

"My orders are to stay here," replied the head of the Circassian guard.

The men glared at each other, their hands on their weapons.

"Salaam aleikum, my good soldiers," I said in my most commanding voice. "Shamkhal Cherkes is on his way. You must respect the palace grounds until then. Have you already forgotten what happened the last time a group of soldiers brought their squabbles here?"

I gestured meaningfully in the direction of the prison. That quieted them for a moment, and they agreed to wait for Shamkhal. I ran back to tell Pari the news. She and her uncle were meeting with Mirza Salman.

"Princess, I beg you to change your mind," I heard Mirza Salman say from his side of the lattice.

"What is your reasoning?"

"The first thing the new shah will want to know is whether you are bowing to his wishes."

"But his idea is terrible."

"I think that disobeying will bring even worse results."

"Don't you see this as the tribal conflict it is? The Ostajlu are trying to dominate the court again. We can't permit that."

"But the Shah can favor whomever he likes."

"Do you obey an order even when it is stupid?"

Shamkhal guffawed loudly. "Obviously he does."

"What idiot said that?" asked Mirza Salman.

"It is Shamkhal, and you are the idiot now."

I wished Shamkhal and Pari would be more diplomatic. Mirza Salman had become too powerful to offend.

"Your question brings to mind one of the stories in the *Shahnameh* about the ruler Kavus," he replied in a neutral tone. "Do you remember how he decided to invent a flying machine and tried to soar in it like a bird? His men thought it was a stupid idea, but they assisted the king until Kavus injured himself in the failed invention. The lesson of that story, I think, is that when you are in service, you must stand by your leader's decisions, even if they are wrong."

"So I should put our country's finances at risk and allow the tribes to clash just to show Mohammad that I am at his service?"

"Yes, princess. That is my opinion."

Pari turned to me to ask what I thought. "He is right," I whispered. "Let us make sure the new shah loves and trusts you before opposing him."

Pari's face darkened. "Mohammad is too weak to oppose anything," she whispered back.

"What about his wife?"

"She is only a woman," she said, which made her uncle laugh.

In a louder voice, she said to Mirza Salman, "I am grateful for your counsel, but for the good of the country, I can't agree. Mohammad's men will be sent away."

There was a long silence on the other side of the lattice while Pari waited, pulling impatiently at a loose thread on her sash.

"Esteemed princess, I implore you not to countermand his orders. Don't get shunted aside like the last time," Mirza Salman said.

"But I am right about this!" Pari replied, her voice rising in frustration. "If the Ostajlu succeed, they will feel entitled to concessions. Moreover, how do I know they can be trusted as guards? I refuse to risk my country's wealth."

"Princess, what if the treasury is placed under the control of all three tribes—the Circassians, the Takkalu, and the Ostajlu?"

I thought this was a good solution. Pari could claim to have obeyed the order while still retaining a lot of control. "It is an excellent idea!" I whispered.

She ignored me. To Mirza Salman, she said, "They will squabble among themselves."

"Your refusal could expose the palace to an internal war," Mirza Salman argued.

"My answer is no."

"How, then, do you plan to pacify the men?" he asked.

"I will take care of it," said Shamkhal. "There are some things a Tajik administrator just can't do."

The insult was as harsh as the taste of metal.

"Uncle!" Pari exclaimed. "Tajik and Turk commingle in the blood of the Safavis, as you know! How can one live without the other?"

Since I had the veins of both, I had to agree.

"And what of the Circassians?" Mirza Salman charged, but

wisely didn't say more. All of us knew that the Circassians and the Georgians, being newcomers to the court compared to the qizilbash, were trying to force their way into better positions.

"What of them? We are as fierce as anyone," Shamkhal said.

"We are *all* Iranians," Pari pointed out.

"If only the tribes saw it that way. Everyone is working for the advantage of his own group: Ostajlu for Ostajlu, Circassian for Circassian. Must it always be so?" Mirza Salman asked.

In other words, would Pari take her uncle's side against him from now on?

"No," she replied. "But my decision about the treasury stands."

There was a long, aggrieved pause. "For God's sake, princess! It is a mistake," he said.

"I agree with Mirza Salman," I insisted in a whisper, although it felt peculiar to do so, given that he had failed to tell me how well he knew the accountant who murdered my father.

Pari's eyes shot flames of disapproval at me. "Shamkhal, go quell the men," she ordered. "Mirza Salman, you are dismissed."

Had she learned nothing from her experience with Isma'il? Why must she insist on maintaining control when it might cause her to lose her battle of influence over the new shah? I could only hope that Mohammad was as willing to be swayed as she seemed to think.

"Javaher, I told you long ago that I won't always agree with your advice," she said when we were alone.

"Yet I must give it. I fear you are being swayed by your desire to rule."

"You are quite wrong: My decision is entirely strategic. Mohammad must understand that he cannot wrest anything away from me. I will not repeat the mistakes I made when I trusted Isma'il to reward my efforts. I failed to maintain any leverage, which made it easy to shunt me aside. This time, I will meet power with power of my own, and the fiercest lion will win."

Her eyes blazed as if she was ready to fight then and there. I stared at her, awestruck.

"I am risking everything with this strategy," she continued, "but I am doing it for Iran. Think of the people who will suffer if the

Ottomans or the Uzbeks invade! Think of how our land will be bloodied by our own soldiers if there is another civil war! I must act for Iranians who can't act for themselves. Royal blood flows in my veins, and this is my duty, whether I live or die."

Her impassioned words sounded like a battle cry. I was silent for a moment, contemplating the weightiness of her declaration.

"Do you mean to rebel?" I asked quietly.

"If I must."

I stepped back in surprise.

Her eyes sought mine and held them. "If it comes to that, I will need your help more than ever."

Was this what loyalty required? Had my father felt similar doubts about his leader?

Of course he had.

That evening, Balamani told me that Anwar had witnessed Mirza Salman and Shamkhal Cherkes arguing in front of the treasury. Mirza Salman urged the Circassian and Takkalu guards to obey Mohammad's orders by disbanding, while at the same time, Shamkhal threatened the Ostajlu with reprisals if they didn't disperse. When Mirza Salman wouldn't back down, mighty Shamkhal drew his sword and brandished it.

"You may be the grand vizier," he shouted, "but you are still a weakling!"

Mirza Salman flushed to the top of his forehead and stormed away, his face as red as if he had a sunburn. What a humiliation for someone who fancied himself in the role of a soldier!

After that, Shamkhal threatened the Ostajlu until they backed down. The Ostajlu didn't like it, but Shamkhal was a powerful nobleman, with the intimidating girth of a bear. The only other choice would have been to fight him, the Circassians, and the Takkalu, which they decided wasn't worth the likelihood of relinquishing all the pleasures of this earth.

When Pari heard about Mirza Salman's behavior, she was greatly displeased that he had inflamed the situation rather than obeying her orders. She called him in to explain himself, and I joined him on the visitor's side of the lattice, the better to watch him.

"I am sorry, princess. I was deeply afraid that Mohammad might consider your opposition an act of treason," he said. "I was trying to protect you from being branded disobedient."

"How dare you suggest treason?" asked Pari, her voice shaking with fury.

"Princess," said Mirza Salman, with desperation in his voice, "I feel it is my duty to warn you of consequences, however unpleasant."

"Don't you understand? Nothing is treasonous unless it is treason against me!"

It was tantamount to declaring herself shah. Mirza Salman looked as astounded as I felt. No matter how angry, she couldn't make such claims without the risk of being declared a traitor.

"Princess, all is being done as you ordered. The treasury is being guarded as you wish. The royal armies have been sent to the northwest to protect our borders. The palace runs according to your desires. And yet—a new shah will take over very soon."

"Leave me to manage that."

"The situation is very delicate."

"Did you hear me?"

"Yes, my lieutenant."

There was a long silence, during which Mirza Salman paced around the small room. "Princess, may I speak? There is something else that concerns me greatly."

"Well?"

"It is your uncle. Will he ever be reined in?"

"He was protecting my desires. I don't approve of his behavior toward you, but neither do I condone yours toward me. You were disobedient."

"Rose of the Safavis," said the grand vizier, "I expect that family ties will always bind you two together. But how do I stand now in your eyes? Will you advocate for me with the new shah?"

In other words, would she recommend that he be retained as the grand vizier? Most servants wouldn't have dared ask so directly. I sensed so much urgency in the question that I left the room abruptly to tell Pari I thought she should hear him out.

When I arrived on her side of the lattice, the princess still sounded angry. "There is always a place for obedient servants," she was saying. "Are you such a servant?"

"I do my best," Mirza Salman replied. "Right now, it is difficult to avoid being caught between your desires and those of the shah-to-be."

"Princess—" I whispered, but she held up her hand to silence me.

"I should like you to prove your loyalty to me in coming weeks."

"God willing, I shall."

"Do that, then. You may go now, and return when you have found a way to show the depth of your obedience."

Her tone was quite cold.

"Princess," I said after he had left, "let's not make the mistake that your brother did by refusing to show favor to his best servants. Let Mirza Salman know that you still value him and give him a reason for hope."

Pari's fury evaporated so quickly I realized that she had been playing a role. "Don't worry, I will. Mirza Salman must not think, just because he is grand vizier, that he can take his position for granted or that he can tell me what to do. When he disobeys, he must be chastised, otherwise he will do it again. I am testing him right now to see whether he will be a faithful servant, and whether he has the ferocity of character to stand with us to the end."

Shortly after the incident at the treasury, Mohammad Khodabandeh and his family arrived at the holy city of Qom. They lodged at the home of his mother, Sultanam, who had moved there because she could no longer bear court intrigue, and they paid their respects to God at the local mosques. The noblemen at court began to agitate to be allowed to visit him in Qom, hoping to begin the process of winning his favor, but Pari insisted that they remain at the palace to finish their duties. They chafed under her rules, but so great was her power that most obeyed.

Mirza Salman was an exception. He called on her and asked her permission to pay his respects to Mohammad, arguing that he thought it would be wise if he explained the incident at the treasury as well as her decision to send armed men to shore up the country against Ottoman invasion.

Pari and I heard him out on her side of the lattice.

"Princess, I wish to smooth the way for your first meeting with the Shah. I will ensure that there are no malicious tongues sowing seeds of conflict between you and your brother. You asked me to prove my loyalty to you. I will do so."

"What is the hurry?"

"I am a cautious man. When the Shah arrives, he will be over-whelmed with visitors and it will be difficult to make an impression on him. I wish to tell him of all your successes, starting with how you helped Isma'il to power and ending with your efforts to put the palace in good order before Mohammad's own arrival. I believe I can convince him how much he needs you."

"Is that the sum of what you plan to do?"

"No," he said. "Naturally, I wish to be retained as grand vizier. If he agrees, I will continue to be of service to him and to you."

Pari whispered to me, "At least he admits to his own desires."

Shamkhal had been terrorizing Mirza Salman whenever he saw him around the palace. He would draw his dagger and slit the tip of his finger to show how sharp the weapon was or make grue-some comments about enemies left on the battlefield as fodder for vultures. He kept threatening Mirza Salman as if to make up for the fact that his own position at the palace was now inferior to the grand vizier's. Mirza Salman wanted to leave, I suspected, because he felt threatened. I was of two minds about whether he should be let go.

"Mirza Salman, you have my permission to leave under two con-ditions. You won't announce your departure, and you will write to me shortly after you meet with my brother to let me know his views of my actions. You are being granted an exception because of my faith in you."

"Thank you, esteemed princess. I am honored by your confidence in me."

"What are you planning to say about the treasury?"

"That you had the best interests of the country at heart."

As I showed him out, a brief smile brightened his features. He looked like a man who had gotten something he wanted very badly.

Pari and her uncle Shamkhal had become close again and strategized together every day, although they often disagreed. Despite Shamkhal's role in Mirza Salman's departure, he thought Pari had made a grave mistake by letting the grand vizier go to Qom. During one of the times that they sat closeted together in her private rooms, Shamkhal argued that Mirza Salman would be free to say whatever he wished about her to Mohammad.

"Advancing his own position is his greatest skill. Look how he rid himself of Mirza Shokhrollah."

"Uncle, do you have evidence of his disloyalty?"

Shamkhal equivocated, his eyes flicking around the room. "Why not wait until the Shah arrives and explain your decisions to him yourself? No one can do so better than you."

Pari paused to think for a moment. "I don't oppose Mirza Salman advancing himself. If he convinces Mohammad to retain him as grand vizier, that will serve my interests. The three of us will be an excellent team. Mirza Salman and I will strategize, and the Shah will tell the nobles what to do."

"You don't know him the way I do, from all the times we served Isma'il together."

"What exactly do you know?"

"He is not trustworthy."

"What is the evidence?"

"His behavior. I have seen him flatter a courtier one day as if he were his best friend, then scheme to bring him down the next. By God above, child, why don't you heed my words?" Shamkhal sounded exasperated.

The princess gave him a cold stare. "I think it is time for me to follow my own counsel," she replied.

The big man wilted under her gaze, her royal farr too bright for him to withstand. I decided to visit Fereshteh. Perhaps one of her clients would have heard something about Mirza Salman's true intentions.

I walked to her house one morning feeling heavy in my heart for a reason I didn't understand. It was the middle of winter, and the city looked cold and frozen in the early light. I counted the months since Khadijeh's death and realized that the better part of a year had passed. My single-minded pursuit of the shah had allowed me to squelch my grief. Now that the terror of Isma'il was finally gone, my grief for Khadijeh surged afresh. I didn't know where she had been buried—no doubt in an unmarked grave—so I couldn't vent my sorrows there. Fereshteh had had sorrows enough of her own to be able to understand.

When I arrived, Fereshteh's maid showed me directly into her private room. Today it smelled of frankincense, and there were bowls filled with red apples, whole walnuts, and dates. I removed my shoes, leaned against a silk cushion, drank tea with cardamom, and felt myself beginning to relax. The lady painted on the wall still sported with her amorous lover, and I tried not to think of Khadijeh.

When Fereshteh came in, I caught my breath. Her eyebrows looked like brown velvet, and her eyes were as huge in her face as a doe's. Her cheeks and lips shone red, and her skin was as unblemished as ivory silk. Her long, thick black hair hung unbound over her turquoise robe. How lovely she was!

"Salaam aleikum, Javaher. Your presence brings happiness."

"And yours, too. Fereshteh, you were good enough to invite me to visit you again. I have come because I need your counsel."

"I am always happy to help an old friend."

I folded my legs under my robe. "As you know, the new shah will arrive soon. In the meantime, I need some information about the man who hopes to be his grand vizier."

"He too has been one of my clients," she said.

"Mirza Salman?"

Her wry smile said it all.

I was surprised, but I shouldn't have been. "Have you learned anything about his views of Pari?"

"No. What do you wish to know?"

"If he is loyal."

"And if he isn't?"

"Pari could be in grave trouble with the new shah."

She paused for a moment. "Given the rumors about Isma'il's death, wouldn't Mohammad be afraid she might try to poison him? As a blind man, he is especially vulnerable."

"It is possible. That is part of the reason I need to know if Mirza Salman will speak well of her."

"I will let you know if I learn anything."

"When will you see him again?"

"Not until he returns from his voyage."

"I see."

Mirza Salman had been instructed not to discuss his trip, but he had already told Fereshteh.

There was a silence, during which I realized that I needed to talk about something else. Since I had first found Fereshteh, I had been remembering our times together and I realized that I had loved her. I had not understood this at the time: I was too young and too full of myself. She was a prostitute, and I had thought she wasn't worthy of my love.

Fereshteh's eyes didn't leave my face. "My friend, you look sad."

"Lately, I have been thinking about when we were young," I said, "and what it was like to be in each other's arms. I don't know what you felt for me, but I have come to realize how much I wish I had been able to save you from the streets."

Her eyes were skeptical. "Really?"

"At the very least, I wish I could have told you that I longed to save you—because I did."

"You were confused," she said. "Although you were passionate in my arms, when our lovemaking was done, I could feel your heart turning away from the very idea that you might love a woman of low standing."

She had understood me correctly, and I was mortified.

"I was still a nobleman's son," I replied. "I thought such liaisons were beneath me. I expected to marry a pretty, sheltered girl who would serve me all of my days. What an irony that I became a servant of women."

She smiled. "And I became a servant of men. I would have preferred that my body remain my own territory, but I haven't been so fortunate."

Neither had I.

"Do you blame me?"

She sighed. "I wish you had been courageous enough to admit that you cared for me and wanted to help me."

She was right; back then, I had not had the wideness of heart to admit to loving her or to acknowledge the severity of her suffering. I had assumed, with childish disgust, that a woman in her position was forever tainted by what she had done. But look what I had done to myself! At least she had not lost her ability to bear a child.

"I apologize from the depths of my heart," I said. "I failed you because I was a child of privilege, but I no longer feel as I did. I understand now that life requires sacrifices, many of which are bitter."

Fereshteh's eyes were sympathetic, reminding me of how she had comforted me in my struggles when I was young.

"Your own sacrifices have changed you," she replied. "The bird of your understanding has spread its wings, and now it flies free."

Something in my heart lifted at her kind words.

"Perhaps we won't always be caged," she added. "I shall escape as soon as I can, and you will do the same."

"Insh'Allah. If Pari succeeds with her plan, I will be closer to realizing my independence. If she falls from grace, I will, too. That would ruin all my plans."

"What plans?"

I told her about Jalileh and my worries about her future, which was so dependent on mine. By the time I had finished, my voice was thick.

"Poor child. Why didn't you tell me about her earlier? There is a small chance I can help. Before Mirza Salman left, I gave him the name of a lady of high price to visit in Qom. I will send a messenger and ask her to tell me if she learns anything useful."

"I would be very grateful," I replied. "Would silver help?"

"She will help as a favor. I have a web of such friends in all the major towns."

When I returned to Pari's side, I told her about our conversation and suggested that she dispatch a gift to Fereshteh. The princess sent a pair of pearl and filigree earrings beautiful enough to loosen any tongue.

A few days later, Mohammad and his entourage traveled from Qom until they were only a few *farsakhs* from Qazveen. They set up a camp while awaiting the astrologers' determination of an auspicious day to enter the city. Looloo had recently been rehired by the court on my recommendation. I hoped he would be consulted.

Mohammad summoned Pari to his camp to pay her respects. I helped organize her entourage including her ladies, her eunuchs, and Shamkhal's soldiers. Pari and I agreed that it was essential to demonstrate her strength through the size and grandeur of her guard.

On the day of our departure, everyone expected that the princess would be riding in a gold-domed palanquin, but I had sent it on its way earlier, and it was awaiting her outside the city. Pari wished to exercise her horsemanship. It was against the rules for her to ride unaccompanied by an entourage, but we had achieved it with a bit of subterfuge.

Soon after the city gates opened, the princess and I emerged in the small park near the Promenade of the Royal Stallions, met the horses that awaited us, and rode out together in the chill air. She was mounted on her favorite Arabian mare, Asal, so named because she was the color of forest honey. She wore a long, fur-lined gray robe, with slits designed for riding, plus thick woolen trousers, leather boots, a fur hat into which she had put all her hair, and a gray woolen cloth wound around her face for warmth that covered everything but her eyes. A little boy, seeing her pass, exclaimed to his mother, "I want to be just like him!"

We proceeded at a dignified pace toward the Tehran Gate. Its large central archway was flanked by two smaller ones so that traffic could proceed in both directions. The white, yellow, and black tile patterns on the gate made me think of butterflies and filled me with the optimism that accompanies a much-anticipated journey.

Not far behind us were Pari's eunuchs and errand boys, led by her still-retired vizier Majeed, as well as chests containing her clothing, personal necessities, and the gifts she would present to her brother. Behind them rode a large contingent of Circassian and Takkalu soldiers organized by her uncle, as well as servants bearing the necessities for setting up camp.

As we rode through the gate, the princess looked back toward the long procession that would accompany her and said, "May God be praised. Isn't it a fine sight?"

"It is, indeed!"

The procession would be slow and stately because of the amount of baggage it carried. As soon as we left the gate, she said, "Let's go!"

Pari spurred her horse and rode off into the distance, following the spine of the snow-covered mountains. The glorious land around us was wide open, and the frozen road was empty. I tried to keep up with Pari, my breath steaming around me, but couldn't. As her horse sped farther away, I admired her grace as a rider: I had had few opportunities to witness it. She rode as if sitting on air. After a while, she began to disappear into the landscape, and it seemed to me that she might never come back. If only there were somewhere for her to go! Her responsibilities inside the palace consumed her every breath. No wonder she thrilled at the sight of open country.

After a long gallop, Pari turned around and returned to me, and then we rode together.

"How good it feels to be unencumbered!" Her skin was flushed with the joy of the gallop.

"You look happy, princess. It is a pleasure to see."

"A new shah and a new era are at hand. This time, everything will be different."

"Insh'Allah."

We rode together until we reached a river near the mountains, where I had sent the gold palanquin earlier that day with Azar Khatoon inside. When we arrived, Azar spread out a warm blanket and Pari threw herself down in front of the river near a crackling fire. She untwisted the cloth that covered her face, shed her big warm robe, and sat for a moment in the free, open air. More color flooded her cheeks, and her brow looked relaxed for the first time in months.

"Bah, bah!" Pari exclaimed. "Who needs more joy than this? I wish I could live like this every day of my life."

Azar Khatoon shelled some walnuts and handed them to us. We ate them contentedly, watching the birds overhead, while Azar poured steaming cups of tea. I stretched out my legs. Soon, very soon, I would be with my sister again, and I would show her all the things I loved about Qazveen. On our free days, I would take her for walks in the countryside and bring a picnic of her favorite foods. How glad I would be to know her at last!

A thick cloud of dust in the distance stirred me out of my happy thoughts. "Princess," I cautioned, "I see your guard approaching."

"So soon?"

With a sigh, Pari picked herself up and reluctantly concealed herself in the gold palanquin.

When her men arrived, Pari's palanquin was placed at the head of the procession, and we continued on our way. We proceeded very slowly now that her bearers had to go on foot. I walked alongside the palanquin. It was a clear, cold day, and the frozen ground crunched under my feet. We passed fields that would be alive with wheat and barley in summer. Shepherds tending to their flocks greeted us and asked us if they could offer us milk. We thanked them and continued to the camp.

In the distance, I saw a cluster of large black tents, and before long, the individual soldiers guarding them. When we reached the entrance to the camp, Pari's palanquin was greeted graciously by one of Mohammad Khodabandeh's eunuchs, while his groomsmen took charge of our horses. Pari and Azar were escorted to the tent that would be theirs in the women's section of the camp, and I followed closely behind.

The tent was made of a thick, coarse fabric to protect inhabitants from winter winds. When the eunuch lifted the flap of the tent and we stepped inside, Azar gasped with delight. The interior had been furnished with ruby-red rugs and cushions, which made it seem warm. The walls were hung with crimson satin embroidered with whirling flowers and other twirling forms dancing within them. Soft cushions were arranged into seating areas and a bedroll was placed behind a long embroidered cloth. Wooden trunks had been brought in for Pari's clothing and cosmetics.

We were admiring the tent when another eunuch arrived promptly with steaming vessels of tea and pastries. We refreshed ourselves, then unpacked Pari's things. By the time everything was set up, it was the hour for the evening meal, which was brought to the princess by Mohammad Khodabandeh's servants. They spread out a clean cotton cloth and served a large platter of roast lamb on hot bread, which soaked up all the meat juices, as well as yogurt and greens. I left Pari and her ladies to their meal and walked to a tent used by Mohammad's eunuchs. Before I entered the tent, I heard some of them talking.

"Have you seen that woman's retinue? It is as if she thinks she is shah!"

"With an armed guard like that, he will have to think twice about offending her."

I chuckled. When I walked in, I was welcomed like an old friend. Together we supped and conversed and celebrated late into the night.

The next morning, Pari was summoned to meet the shah-to-be. A eunuch led us to his tent, which, for his safety, was not identified in any way from the outside. Inside, though, it was even more opulent than Pari's. The carpets on the floor were deep indigo wool with white silk patterns that sparkled like stars in a twilight sky. There were porcelain vessels for water and wine that had been transported all that way, despite their value, and porcelain cups and serving platters. Fruit and sweets and nuts were piled high on engraved silver trays.

Mohammad Khodabandeh was seated on cushions, his wife, Khayr al-Nisa Beygom, on his right side. His dark eyes were blank, and he sat with his head thrust forward as if to better position his ears for listening. He wore a brown robe, a gray sash, and a white turban, subdued attire that made him look like a man of God. Next to him, his wife glittered like a peacock. Her pink robe seemed bright over a green tunic, which matched a triangular headdress made of pink and green silks. She wore gold bangles on both wrists, rings on every finger but her thumbs, a chain of pearls on her forehead, and large pearl and ruby earrings. Her full lips glowed red from madder, as did her cheeks. While her husband gave the impression of being thoughtful and retiring, she threw off sparks like the jewels she wore. Her eyes swept across us and around the room with frequency, as if to make up for the fact that her husband could see nothing.

"Welcome, sister. Your arrival brings us happiness," Mohammad said to Pari.

"Yes, welcome," added his wife in a voice that was high, nasal, and loud. "I have rarely had the pleasure of seeing you, but all of us have heard your father's praise of you as a paragon among women."

Pari dropped gracefully onto a cushion facing them, while I remained standing near the door. "I am unworthy of your generous words, but I thank you for your kindness. How are you? How are your children?"

"All are well, except, of course, for my husband's son Sultan Hassan Mirza, whose loss we still mourn," she replied.

"The loss of a child is worse than anything that can be described," Mohammad said. "Truly it was as if the light of my eyes had been extinguished."

"May God comfort you in your sorrow. What a terrible affliction you have endured."

"Your losses have been equally great," he said.

"I hope that God has granted you good health during this difficult time."

"Since we last saw you, my husband's eyesight has worsened," Khayr al-Nisa replied. "It is a calamity for a man so gifted at reading and writing poetry."

"It is the will of God," he interjected, sounding resigned. "Now I compose my verses in my head, and my scribes write them on paper. By then I have committed my poetry to memory anyway."

"Shall we exchange verses?" Pari asked. "It would be a joy to hear your words."

"We will organize that when we are settled in the capital."

Mohammad Khodabandeh ordered some refreshments, including tea and rice pudding made with saffron and cinnamon, which warmed us on that cold day. I was very pleased with how the visit was proceeding so far, yet I was on my guard, since nothing of substance had been discussed yet. After the refreshments, the talk finally turned to the business of the palace.

"Sister, we have heard much about the goings-on at court. You must tell us everything."

"Of course," Pari replied. "I have worked closely with Mirza Salman these past weeks. I gave him leave to report to you, but haven't heard from him since then. Has he told you all that has happened?"

There was a moment's pause before either of them answered.

"He told us everything," Khayr al-Nisa Beygom said in a flat tone.

"Did he tell you about why we sent the army to Khui? Did he explain about the treasury guard?"

"Yes, everything," Mohammad Khodabandeh said, echoing his wife.

Their responses were odd. I had expected them to praise her for her excellent service.

"It has been my duty to serve you," Pari said, filling the empty space. "After you are crowned, I will spend day and night by your side implementing your commands."

She sounded just right: confident, yet humble.

Mohammad Khodabandeh sighed. "You should know the truth: I am not a man who has ever aspired to be shah, and I doubt I will change my ways."

Pari smiled in anticipation of fulfilling her new role. "Put your mind at rest," she replied. "The men are used to me now, and they will do what I command. I will make sure your orders are carried out."

Khayr al-Nisa Beygom's eyebrows shot up. "That won't be necessary."

Pari looked surprised. "I mean no offense, but the palace is a complicated world. Someone without intimate knowledge of it will find it difficult to gain obedience."

"We are glad you have such knowledge," said Mohammad Khodabandeh. "After you tell us all that we need to know, daily affairs will be handled by my wife."

"By your wife?"

"That is correct."

Pari's lips drew down. "I really don't understand why the mother of four children would wish to add to her burdens by trying to manage the affairs of state. It is too much for someone who has not been raised with this life, as I have."

My heart sank at the implied insult.

"Yet that is what I shall do," said Khayr al-Nisa Beygom haughtily.

"I have spent all my years studying such things, from even before the time I became my father's advisor when I was fourteen. These matters aren't trivial."

"No, they aren't," said Mohammad Khodabandeh. "That is why you will train my wife, and she will implement my wishes."

"Brother, I beg you to consider, given all my learning and experience, that there should be a permanent position for me in your court. Even the nobles have agreed that I am the best choice for this job."

"If the two of you can find a way to work together, that is fine with me," Mohammad Khodabandeh said placidly.

The fine embroidered bands at the edges of Pari's robe trembled. I chafed at the injustice of it.

"The noblemen are nothing to be trifled with. If they suspect hesitation, they will take advantage. A weak person will be crushed. It is not just for myself but for your own protection that I make this demand to be your chief advisor. I have, after all, risked my life for you."

She meant by removing Isma'il, but of course she couldn't say that.

"What do you mean, risked your life?" Khayr al-Nisa Beygom asked.

"Living under such a murderous rule, we didn't know whether we would remain in possession of our lives. If not for Isma'il's death, and if not for the fact that the nobleman assigned to kill your family found excuses to delay his visit to Shiraz, you would be a childless widow now—or worse."

"That is certainly true, but what did you have to do with that? I thought Isma'il's doctor said he died of too much opium and too much food, which twisted his organs into a fatal knot."

Khayr al-Nisa Beygom looked triumphant, which made me uneasy.

"I meant that I did all I could to persuade him and those around him to call off the murders," Pari said, "including those of your children."

"The fact is, God didn't decree such a fate, so it didn't happen," Mohammad Khodabandeh replied. "Why fight about such things? The hour is getting late and my books are calling. I will leave the two of you to work things out."

By God above! It was even worse than I had feared: He wouldn't even stay long enough to keep his wife in check.

Khayr al-Nisa's smile was like ice. "Yes, indeed. We will work things out. You may begin by kissing my feet to show your fealty."

It was such an insult to make this demand of a Safavi princess that I had trouble masking my shock.

Pari stood up, her chin high in the air. "You are asking a woman of royal blood to kiss the feet of a child of the provinces?"

"I am asking you to acknowledge she who is first among women."

"If you knew court protocol, you would understand that my status is higher than yours."

Khayr al-Nisa Beygom batted at the air as if waving away a fly. "Not for long."

"Now, Pari," said her brother in a mild tone. "You must respect my wife at all times."

"I have respect for sensible people," Pari said angrily. "If you insist on toying with matters of governance, you could lose not just the court but the country. Let me remind you of what we face. In the north, the east, and the southeast, the people have sickened of our rule and rebelled. In the northeast and northwest, we face invasions by the Ottomans and the Uzbeks. Our land is ringed with troubles. Our people are threatened with suffering. Remember, without justice there is no prosperity and no country. Take heed!"

Mohammad Khodabandeh sighed. "We will see what needs to be done after the coronation. Thank you, sister, for coming to visit us."

"It is my duty," she replied, "as it is to speak unpleasant truths when necessary."

Khayr al-Nisa's pretty red lips puffed out as if she had eaten something sour, an expression that her husband could not see. I was proud of Pari for having spoken the truth, yet concerned about what her sharp words boded for her future.

"Don't worry, Javaher," she said as we left them and began walking back to her tent. "I will find ways to master her. She is no match for me."

Her breath steamed in the cold air. Rather than looking daunted, her eyes sparkled as if she was excited by the prospect of a new battle. Conflict always spurred her to fight harder, but was it the best strategy?

"I think you should visit your brother in private, drop to the ground and swear your loyalty, and prove it every day until he trusts you with his very soul."

"And if he still denies me my right to rule?"

"Then accept your fate as God-given."

She laughed. "Javaher, you have the perfect servant's heart, but I don't. If that happens, my uncle and I will be ready to take over."

"Take over? If Mohammad learns what you are planning, he will surely destroy you! No shah can permit rebellion within his own palace."

"Not necessarily. If he understands our strength, he may be more willing to make concessions, like the ones he has already made to the Ostajlu."

"It is a dangerous strategy," I said. "Why not compromise instead?"

"I have come to despise that word," she said. "I am nearly thirty years old and have never been able to rule, even though I am more knowledgeable than most about Islamic law, the mathematical and physical sciences, the customs of the court, the rules of poetry, and the art of governing. Even my dear father, may God bless his soul, had eccentricities that led to poor decisions I had to accept. Now, at last, the noblemen have recognized that I have earned the right to rule, and I won't let Mohammad or his wife spoil my plans."

I stared at her in awe and terror, remembering Balamani's words in the hammam. I had thought of the decision to remove Isma'il as a one-time necessity, while by contrast, it had emboldened Pari to demand her entitlement to rule. Deep inside her beat the vigorous heart of a shah.

"I suspect you find me intransigent," she said as we arrived at her tent, "but I have earned the right to be that way. Are you with me, Javaher?"

She gazed at me as if to pierce through my secrets.

"I swore to be your faithful servant always," I replied, but for the first time, I wasn't sure I meant it.

While we were at the camp, messengers arrived from the palace with letters for the princess as well as one for me. The letter was from my mother's cousin. It was brief and cutting, like a hot knife:

Greetings and I pray that this letter finds you well. Thank you for continuing to send the money for your sister's upkeep, although it is difficult for us to make do, given how much she imposes on our slim budget every day. We regret that due to financial problems of our own, we cannot wait for you to fulfill your promises any longer. Thanks be to God, we have found a solution. A man in our neighborhood has his eye on her. He is older, to be sure, but he is willing to take her without a dowry. Trust me, speedy acceptance is a good idea. Men with means don't choose impoverished wives very often, and we must take care of this problem before Jalileh is pickled. We imagine you will be overjoyed at this news. All we need is your permission and we will proceed with the marriage. If we do not hear from you soon, we will assume that you have given your assent, and we will proceed.

I felt hot with shame at the tone of the letter. Even less did I like the one I received an hour later.

Salaam Javaher jan. I have paid one of the scribes in the market to write you this letter so that no one learns about it. Our mother's cousin has just introduced me to the man she wishes me to marry. He is an old fellow with only four teeth who has already outlived two wives and whose children are older than I am. When I met him for the first time, he chastised me for not serving his tea as dark as he liked it, as if I ought to know. I think his mind is addled by memories of his dead wives. I suspect he wants a servant, not a wife. I know that I have been nothing but a burden to you, but have mercy on me, I beg you. Save me from his flaccid hands.

My heart burned in my chest. What kind of man could I claim to be if I could not rescue my sister from a life that would make her young eyes dim with grief? I wrote back to my mother's cousin and promised to send money as soon as I could, explaining that I had been promoted to an exalted position and that rivers of silver would be forthcoming. I reminded them that palace servants were paid a lump sum twice a year, and that the next payment was due in a month. In addition, I forbade the marriage, swearing that I would provide a rich reward for all their services as long as they did not give my sister away.

When there was a lull in our business, I explained to Pari that my mother's cousin was threatening to marry off Jalileh and I needed a large advance on my salary so that I could pay them back for her upkeep and bring her to Qazveen as soon as possible.

"Of course I will assist you," she replied. "We will discuss the specifics when we have returned to the palace."

I clapped my hand to my chest and bowed to express my gratitude, and her eyes told me that she understood.

The camp astrologers were busy making forecasts to determine whether it was an auspicious time for Mohammad and his wife to enter the city, at which point we would accompany them as they rode into town. In the meantime, I received a messenger from Fereshteh, who had been sent by Massoud Ali to find us at the camp. The messenger told me that Fereshteh had such urgent information for me that I shouldn't delay even a moment to receive it. I rushed to the princess's tent to tell her the news.

"I have been summoned by Fereshteh. I suspect she has vital information about Mirza Salman."

Pari smiled. "Ah, Javaher, you are a master of unlocking secrets. I hate to send you away from my side."

"I promise to return as soon as I can."

"Fereshteh has been very helpful. Commend her for me, will you?"

"I will."

"You shall ride Asal," she said, and instructed her eunuch groom to make the mare ready.

"Thank you, princess, but an ordinary horse will do."

I had already donned my heavy cotton riding trousers, my thick wool vest, and a warm robe, and had wrapped a wool cloth around my neck and face.

Pari smiled. "But you are no ordinary eunuch. You are a jewel, like your name. I know that well. You will shine always, even after I am gone."

I was taken aback. Her bright eyes, smooth olive skin, and gleaming black hair made her look immortal, yet her words sent a shiver through me.

"If that is so," I said, with the expected reversal of flattery, "it is only because I reflect the sparkle of the greater jewel that I serve. But, Princess, your words worry me."

"Don't trouble yourself. I am prepared for whatever lies ahead. The only judge of me, flaws and all, is almighty God."

"Is there any human who isn't flawed?" I asked, and Pari gave me a wry smile.

The ride to Fereshteh's house took much of the morning. The roads were frozen, and Asal was skittish. I tried to strategize about the future, but I had to coax along the horse, and my enthusiasm was dampened by the weather and by feelings of gloom. Wet, sticky flakes of snow blanketed the fields and my outer robe. By the time I rode into Qazveen, even the street vendors had deserted their usual posts.

I handed Asal to Fereshteh's manservant, who promised to have the horse fed and groomed at the royal stables. Fereshteh's house was pleasantly warm. She wore a green robe that reminded me of a field of grass, and the pale tunic underneath was as softly lit as the bellies of clouds at sunset. Her dark hair was pulled away from her face.

"Come in, Javaher. I see from your wet clothes that you have had a cold, hard ride. Would you like refreshment?"

"Yes, please."

I removed my boots while Fereshteh called to her servant to bring sour cherry sharbat and tea. I remained standing, eager to hear her news.

"Mirza Salman visited my friend in Qom the day before yesterday," she said. "The news is so dreadful I had to tell you in person, to avoid any possibility of being betrayed."

Dread coursed through me. "What happened?"

"Mirza Salman was preening like a peacock. He told my friend that although the royals think they're superior, they can be brought down as easily as anyone else."

"Okh, okh!" I said, my stomach burning.

"My friend plied him with bang, and when he had nearly lost his senses, she coaxed the details out of him. He told her that he had visited Mohammad and his wife, asking if they wished to be made aware of the happenings at court. Then, under the guise of being an honest servant, he argued that the person they should fear the most was Pari Khan Khanoom. He terrified them by hinting that she had been responsible for Isma'il's death, despite the safeguards over his person, and suggested that if left unchecked, she might put an end to them as well."

"What a traitor! I presume they will retain him as grand vizier?"

"That is correct."

"Shamkhal Cherkes was right about him after all."

To my surprise, Fereshteh winced as if in pain, and her hands clenched at her sides. "Javaher, I have more news, and it is even worse."

I braced myself. "Mirza Salman told my friend that Shamkhal has been executed at the request of the Shah."

By God above! It was as if the stars in the sky had been extinguished all at once, except for the star I cared about the most.

I strode to the door and shoved my feet into my riding boots. "Thank you, Fereshteh, for everything. The princess asked me to express her gratitude as well."

"May God keep you and your commander safe," she replied.

I rushed to the royal stables to get a fresh horse and rode it through the Tehran Gate in the direction of the camp. As soon as I left the city, I spurred my horse faster and faster until we were both heaving with effort. What would we do now? Shamkhal was dead. How would Pari bear it?

Looking back on Mirza Salman's actions at court, his tendency toward treachery seemed evident. He had taken two men down in order to advance himself; then he had done the same to us. I cursed myself for not understanding him sooner.

When I approached the camp, I thought I must have lost my way. Only a few tent stakes remained in the sky, like a body reduced to bones. Large trunks had been packed, awaiting the donkeys that would haul them. An errand boy told me the astrologers' readings that morning had been so favorable that Mohammad had thought it foolish to delay. He and his wife and Pari had ridden back to town on a road that was slower than the one I had taken but easier on caravans. After their arrival at the city gates, they planned to ride ceremonially through town. Pari would be taken to her home in her palanquin, and the new shah and his wife would be housed with Mirza Salman's family until the right moment came for entering the palace.

Mirza Salman again!

I turned my weary beast around and headed back for the city, this time on the road that led to the Shah's Gardens Gate. The day was growing grayer, and it started to snow again. My horse's breath steamed in the cold air. High above, a flock of ugly crows blackened the sky. I spurred my horse faster, trying to catch up to the royal procession. After a while, I could see the gate in the distance, a mere speck at first. The royal party was nowhere in sight.

When I arrived, the gatekeeper told me the royal procession had already gone through. I urged my horse, who was now wet, in the direction of Pari's house. Many people thronged the streets, having been alerted that their new Shah had entered Qazveen. It was difficult to get through the crowd. Finally, though, I came upon the end of the procession and saw the gold-domed palanquins. I suspected that the one in front must house the Shah's wife, and the one behind was probably Pari's. I thanked God that she had almost reached her house. Turning down a side street, I galloped ahead.

When I emerged, the lead palanquin was no longer in sight. Pari's had gone through the Ali Qapu portal into the palace and had halted near her house, but she hadn't been carried through her front gate. The bearers must be waiting for something.

Her palanquin was borne by soldiers. At their head I recognized Khalil Khan, Pari's former guardian. Behind them were all of Pari's supporters, notably the Circassian guard. I resolved to open her gate myself and speed her return home. Dismounting from my horse, I knocked loudly, and when the gate opened, I handed the reins to a servant.

"Make ready for your princess," I said.

I approached Pari's palanquin and identified myself. "Lieutenant of my life, I bring world-shattering news!" I whispered.

The brown velvet brocade curtains stirred slightly, and Azar Khatoon slid out, fully covered by her chador.

"Jump in."

I hoisted myself into the palanquin, and the men who were holding it cursed out loud when they felt the extra weight. Pari was sitting cross-legged in the small domed space, framed by a canopy of saffron-colored velvet.

The palanquin was small enough that my knees almost touched Pari's. Her face was so close to mine that I would only have had to lean forward to touch her lips. My heart beat faster, no doubt from my hard ride.

"Princess—" I began, still panting. Pari's furrowed forehead, which fate had distinguished with so many rich stories, told me she could see how bad the news was.

"Tell me now."

"Mirza Salman has convinced Mohammad and his wife that you are a murderer. But that is not the worst of it: Shamkhal has been assassinated."

Pari reached out for my arm. I felt the warmth of her grip penetrate the sleeve of my robe, and wished that I could put my arms around her and comfort her against my chest like a child.

"The dirt of the universe is on my head!" she exclaimed.

All of a sudden, the palanquin jerked abruptly and we started off, but the bearers seemed to be heading away from her home.

"Where are we going?" I shouted. When there was no reply, I opened the curtains and confirmed that we were traveling away from Pari's house. Deh! I called out for help from the Circassian guard. They surrounded the palanquin, shouting at Khalil Khan's men, who held us on their shoulders, and began to struggle for control of it. Pari and I slid around inside, bumping into each other as we were tossed back and forth. For a moment I felt her shoulder against my chest and smelled the fierce piney perfume in her hair.

"May God protect us," Pari said.

At last the palanquin stopped jolting and jerking. From outside came the voice of a Circassian soldier. "Princess, you are safe now. We have you and we are taking you home!"

The Circassians must have managed to wrest the palanquin away from Khalil Khan's men. I put my head outside the curtain again. Khalil Khan, who was still mounted on his horse, addressed the Circassian guard, who protected us now.

"Listen, soldiers. I am acting under orders of the new Shah himself. Oppose me only if you wish to explain yourself to him."

The Circassians hesitated, not knowing what to do. A chill froze my blood as I closed the curtains. "Lieutenant of my life, say something to your men so they defend you!"

Her dark eyes looked as if all the light in them had been extinguished. "No."

"What?"

"Tell them to go home. Otherwise, many will be killed in vain."

We could not give up the fight, not after we had endured so much. I stared at her.

The palanquin shifted and jerked again; there were shouts and sounds of struggle, and we were thrown around inside until Khalil Khan's men reclaimed us. The men began arguing over who had the right to the princess.

Had the sun emerged from behind the clouds, or was it Pari's royal farr that seemed to illuminate the inside of the tent? She put her hand over mine before I could speak.

"Javaher, our game is finished. Hush and listen:

"Weave not, like spiders, nets from grief's saliva
In which the woof and warp are both decaying

But give the grief to Him, Who granted it,
And do not talk about it anymore.
When you are silent, His speech is your speech,
When you don't weave, the weaver will be He."

I recognized the poem from Maulana Rumi and felt touched to the depths of my heart when I realized that Pari was committing both of us to God's care.

"I will never abandon you. You are the star that I follow always."

Pari's eyes misted. "Yes," she said softly, "you alone of all my servants have truly loved me."

"With all my heart."

The palanquin jerked again, and clarity returned to Pari's eyes. "Open the curtains for a moment and tell me what you see."

I parted the velvet curtains and put my head out. Suddenly I felt Pari's strong hands pressing against my back. I slid out feet first, bumped into one of Khalil Khan's soldiers, and landed in the street. Pari had tricked me; now I had no choice but to obey.

"What does she say?" asked the captain of the Circassians, a burly man with bright blue eyes.

Out of loyalty to her, I forced myself to say the most difficult words I had ever spoken. "The princess orders you to disassemble so you come to no harm. Go home now and await further orders."

"But she is being taken away," he protested. "We won't leave unless we hear the command from her lips."

He didn't know yet that Shamkhal Cherkes was dead. If he had heard, he would not have dared to be so bold.

"How lucky you would be if she graced you with her speech! But it is not for you to demand it."

The velvet curtains of the palanquin stirred. The men took note, knowing a royal hand had touched them.

"Hear the words of your princess," commanded Pari from inside.

The men stood still, their faces transfixed. It was so rare for a princess to address a crowd of ordinary men that it was like hearing a voice from heaven.

"I thank you for your excellent service. You are dismissed to your wives and children, and that is an order. May God bless you with good luck!"

The men's eyes softened, as if they had received a blessing from a saint. "We obey you with gratitude!" replied the Circassian captain.

Without further protest, his men left the palanquin in the care of Khalil Khan's soldiers, who held it gingerly, wondering what to do now that they, too, had heard the princess's deep, lovely voice.

"March," shouted Khalil Khan. "Hurry! Hurry!"

"No!" I yelled, not caring that I was risking my life. "You may not cart away a princess of Safavi blood!"

Khalil Khan's small eyes narrowed, and his lips curled with scorn. "How dare you challenge me, you gelding! Get out of my way before I strike you down."

I drew my dagger and rushed at his chest. The fear that entered his eyes only encouraged me to attack. From close up, his skin looked white with panic. When I was near enough to smell the fenugreek on his breath, I raised my dagger in the air, feeling the muscles of my neck stiffening. I am certain I snarled, anticipating the pleasure of feeling the dagger plunge into his undefended skin. When I saw him raise a long sword to defend himself, I blocked the maneuver and broke his nose with the heel of my hand. Water sprang into his eyes, and his sword arm grew limp. But then the side of my head seemed to slam into something hard, and the dagger slipped from my hand.

Everything around me went black and quiet. I must have remained that way for several minutes. When I awoke, the captain of the Circassians and a few of his men were standing around me, dabbing my face with a cloth and holding a vial of rose water under my nose. The strong scent revived me.

"Good work," the captain said, chuckling. "Not one of us will ever forget the fear in Khalil Khan's eyes. It isn't often that a nobleman gets humiliated like that. He wanted to kill you, but when he saw that we were ready to fight, he gave up."

I put my hand on the place under my turban that ached. It came back covered with blood. White spots danced in my vision.

"What happened?"

"One of his soldiers flattened you with the side of his sword. I imagine your head is burning like an oven."

The square was quiet now except for a few onlookers. I had been down for longer than I realized.

"Where are they?"

"Khalil Khan gave them orders to go to his house. They marched the palanquin down the Promenade of the Royal Stallions."

He handed me my dagger, which I slipped back into its sheath. "May your hands never ache, Captain."

I got up and ran toward the Ali Qapu gate in the direction of Khalil Khan's house.

"Agha, wait! Are you sure you are well?" I heard behind me as I left, but I did not stop. My head was pounding as if I were banging it against a wall with each step. Warm blood trickled into my ear.

When I arrived at Khalil Khan's, some of Pari's supporters were still milling around his door demanding that the light of the Safavis be released. Khalil emerged from behind the gate holding a bloodied cloth over his nose and yelled at them to disperse, threatening that he would take a sword to them otherwise. Then he slammed the heavy wooden door in our faces.

In despair, I called out to a boy in the street and told him to go to the palace and tell Daka Cherkes Khanoom about her daughter's whereabouts. Placing a small coin in his hand, I promised to double his money when he delivered a reply.

I walked around the perimeter walls of the grand home and tried to find another way in; there must be an entrance for the servants. Before long, I saw a young maid laden with cloth bags full of fruit stop in front of a small door that probably led to the kitchen.

"Excuse me, kind Khanoom, do you work for Khalil Khan?"

"I do."

"A great lady has been taken inside the house, and I would give much to see her. A small fortune, in fact."

She looked carefully at my expensive riding attire to gauge what I might be worth.

"How much?"

I showed her a heavy silver coin. It was probably the most money she had ever seen, and she dropped her bags and reached for the coin with both hands. I eluded her grasp.

"If you want me to sneak you into the house, forget it. They would have my head."

"Then how about if you tell her I am here and bring me a message from her. My name is Javaher."

She reached out for the money again.

"It is yours as soon as you bring me news from the lady."

After she went in, I crossed the street and stood in an alley where I could see the kitchen door but not be easily observed. The day grew colder, and my head pounded. I found one of Pari's handkerchiefs in my robe and stuffed it into my turban to absorb the blood.

I waited a long time before the door opened and the maid came out and looked around for me, her face covered now with a picheh. I stepped out of the alley and called softly, "Over here."

She approached and lifted her picheh. Her dark eyes were as troubled as a river whose muddy bottom had been stirred up by a stick.

"It wasn't worth the silver you promised. Never would I wish to see such a sight again."

I felt my heart clutch in my chest so tightly I could not breathe. "What sight?"

"That great lady in her bed." She turned away as if to banish the thought. I grabbed her arm, too tightly perhaps, and said, "Tell me."

She shook off my hand.

"The other servants told me that a group of soldiers had brought a lady into the courtyard in a palanquin. When Khalil Khan ordered her to come out, she cursed him and refused. He reached inside, took hold of her legs most disgracefully, and pulled her out. Her curses filled the air. Two of his men grabbed her body and forced her inside the house. She was yelling all the while, but soon after they closed the door behind them, the house grew deadly silent. No one wished to know what was happening. After only a few minutes, the soldiers departed. Khalil Khan gave orders that no one should enter that room, and no one dared. By the time I returned from shopping, the house was as quiet as the grave. After the master retired for his afternoon rest, I slipped inside."

Here she paused and put her hand against the mud wall to steady herself.

"Is she alive?" I asked, feeling the breath freeze in my throat.

"No," she replied. "Her eyes were open and staring at the ceiling. Her neck was bruised and bloodied, and the cord they had used to strangle her was still wrapped around it as if she were nothing more than chattel. Her forehead was creased with agony and her teeth were bared, as if she wished to maul those who had murdered her."

"Say no more," I said. "No more."

"I wish you had never asked me to look. What I saw will haunt me until the end of my days. No amount of money could be worth such a sight."

Nonetheless she stretched out her hand. I steadied myself against the wall and fished out the coin.

"You have received the better deal," she said, turning to go. "May God be with you."

My heart felt as if it had turned to shards of ice. I grabbed at the wall behind me for support, but it crumbled in my hands. I drew the dirt on my fingers over my face and head as if it were the dirt of my grave. Pari dead? It could not be. It could not be!

Racked with sorrow, I stumbled through the streets, drawing stares.

"Agha!" an older man called as I passed. "What pains you? Are you all right?"

I don't know how long I walked, or where. All I know is that I ended up at a tavern in a low part of town, which stank of men's feet. I sat on a cushion covered with a tattered, stained cotton cloth. A few men welcomed me as their new drinking companion. I called for spirits, and after a few glasses of a foul cinnamon-flavored concoction, I switched to bang. It was very strong. Whatever was put before me, I drank, and then I consumed some more.

Before long, I lay on the floor of the tavern and began speaking to the angel who was ministering to me. She appeared in a blaze of light, her long hair like a comet whose tail turned into sparks. As I spoke, she hovered over me, her eyes filled with compassion. I told her the story of my life, starting with how my father had been killed and how I had been chopped at the middle. Then I described Pari and our times together.

"I don't have royal blood," I told her, "but we two could have been twins. It was as if we swam in the same fluids in our mother's womb, so that some of my maleness became hers and some of her female-ness mine. That made us strange in the eyes of the world, which does not care for in-between beings. We have both taken blows because of it. She was protean, as am I. She was fierce and affectionate and smart and unpredictable. That is why I loved her . . . that is why!"

I told the angel what had happened in the streets. When I reached the part about Khalil Khan, I could barely speak. "She pushed me out of the palanquin. She wouldn't let me try to save her!"

The angel hovered over me, and I felt wrapped in a heavenly embrace. "My child," she said, "don't you see? She pushed you out so that you wouldn't come to harm. She loved you, too."

God be praised! Pari loved me, too. Tears flowed from my eyes. I pulled out a handkerchief to wipe them away. Its perfume bore the pungent scent of pine—her scent, which I would smell no more. I wept so loudly that the tavern grew silent for a moment and my fellow drinkers clustered around to ask about my sorrows. I told them I had lost a treasured woman, and then they all wept with me, for who hadn't? Mothers, sisters, wives, and daughters—we had all lost someone dear.

Early in the morning I awoke on the tattered cushions, my head burning. My hair was matted with blood. All the other men were gone, and my money purse was gone, too. I lay there for a moment, wondering if I could arise without pitching over, and then I remembered the furtive maid and her account of what had happened to Pari. Oh my esteemed lieutenant! Oh my battered heart!

I arose unsteadily, found my feet, and walked back to the palace in the cold. My turban had been stolen along with my warm outer robe, but the men had not wished me to freeze to death, as they had left me my shoes. The snow was thick and white on the ground. I hurried through the frozen streets. When I arrived at my room, I opened the door and was surprised to see that although Balamani was gone, a tiny figure was huddled on my bed. It was Massoud Ali. He woke up, rushed toward me, threw his arms around me, and howled, his tiny face collapsing with grief. I deeply regretted not having been there to comfort him.

"My child, my child!" I said. "Don't swallow so much sorrow."

"What will become of us?" he asked between sobs. "Where will we go?"

I did not have an answer.

"Who will take us into their service now?"

"Her mother," I replied promptly, trying to comfort him.

His sobs became huge.

"She has been killed as well."

I felt as if I had been stabbed with a sword. No wonder the boy messenger had never returned.

"May God protect us. An old woman!"

Massoud Ali sobbed harder all of a sudden. "And a little child has been killed, too!"

"Who?"

"Shoja."

By God above, they had not even spared an infant. Poor Mahasti! Pari had offered to send her child away from the palace to protect him, but Mahasti had refused.

"Don't worry," I said. I wanted to sound calm and to reassure the poor child, who was quaking with fear. "We will find a new protector, I promise you."

"The princess was kind to me," he said, still weeping. "Who will be kind to me now?"

"I will," I replied. "I promise to be kind to you always. Now come sleep, and we will sort all of this out later."

I led him to my bedroll, tucked him in, and held his small hand until he fell asleep. As I sat listening to Massoud Ali breathe, his mouth slightly open, his cheeks salted white from his tears, I knew that he had reason to be scared. We had been the closest servants of a princess who had fallen into the deepest disgrace. Would the new shah look upon us as traitors? We could not know. Our survival depended on being thought humble and powerless, but what if Mohammad and his wife judged us otherwise?

My father's death came to my mind as freshly as if it had just happened. I had become, once again, the closest servant of someone whose star had plummeted into the sea. My heart was torn anew, and I wept as if I were a young man again facing the rest of my life all alone.

CHAPTER 9

BREAD AND SALT

Fereydoon trussed Zahhak, threw him onto a donkey, and rode with him to the foothills of Mount Damavand. He intended to kill him there, but an angel instructed him to stay his hand. Instead, Fereydoon climbed the mountain until he came upon a cave populated by boulders. Slinging Zahhak over his back, he scaled the tallest boulder, threw Zahhak onto the rock, and pounded nails into his arms and legs until he dangled over the middle of the cave.

I suspect that Zahhak did not die. He and his snakes are eternally suspended, awaiting the moment when the forces of evil unleash their powers again.

After Massoud Ali fell asleep, I bathed at the hammam, dressed in a black tunic and trousers, black robe, and black and brown sash, and walked to Pari's house near the Ali Qapu. My head was pounding from my excesses of the night before, and the wound near my temple had swollen. Azar Khatoon opened the door clad in a dark mourning robe, her eyes red from weeping.

"I take refuge in almighty God," she said, her voice trembling. A tear slid down her cheek and coursed over her beauty mark.

"Alas!" I said, stepping inside. "What can be said?"

We went into Pari's birooni, which was large and empty. A hard white light poured through the windows, making me wince. Some of Pari's ladies wandered in and out of her rooms like ghosts who could find no rest.

"How can they expect women to serve such a brutal court?" Azar asked, looking as vulnerable as if she had been struck. Her face crumpled, and she reached for me and cried into my robe.

Hearing steps behind us, we turned and saw Maryam, whose body sagged within her clothes. Her tangled blond hair hung limply near her face, and she had wept so much that the lower half of one eye looked full of blood.

"My poor, dear lady!"

"Was there a braver woman? A fiercer flower?" Maryam asked. Angry tears fell onto her cheeks.

"The loveliest roses are always plucked first," said Azar.

The three of us were quiet for a moment, paralyzed by woe. Then Maryam's lips split into a ghastly laugh. "Anwar told us earlier today that the shah-to-be has prohibited a ceremony for Pari. Neither will there be an official burial. We will never know where her body lies."

She put her fists to her cheeks, and tears flowed over them. "I won't ever be able to visit her grave, sweep off the dirt, and adorn it with flowers and my tears. It will be as if she had never existed."

"By the skull of the Shah!" I swore angrily. "Before they erase the woman we loved, let's collect her letters, her poems, and her papers, and try to save them so that others may know her as we did."

"What about her heirs?" asked Azar.

I thought for a moment. "Since she has no children, the law stipulates that her possessions must be divided among her brothers and sisters," I said, realizing all of a sudden that Mohammad Khoda-bandeh would be included. "What a grotesque violation of propriety that the man who ordered her murder will inherit her property."

I shouldn't have spoken so forthrightly about the new shah, but in my grief, I didn't care.

"Her poems will be valuable to those who loved her. Let's work quickly," I added.

The three of us occupied her writing room and began looking through her papers. We left untouched the copies of her official correspondence—the letters she had written to the wives of other rulers, receipts she had received or given, deeds of ownership. When we found a scrap of anything personal, such as a poem or a personal letter, we hid it in between the pages of a *Shahnameh*. But we had barely begun when we heard a ferocious banging on the knocker for women, which felt like nails being driven into my pounding head. Maryam started and grabbed Azar Khatoon's hand, and the two women looked at each other in alarm.

I went forth and faced a group of eunuchs bearing shields and swords.

"Who are you?" I growled.

"We come from Khalil Khan," said their leader. "Pari's things now belong to him, so get out, and make sure the women leave with you before we invite the soldiers in."

I tried to slam the door in his face, but he and his eunuchs pushed their way into the house. Their eyes came alive with greed when they saw the fine carpets, silver samovar, and antique luster-ware there. I rushed to tell Azar, Maryam, and the other women, who looked terrified at the thought of Khalil Khan and his soldiers.

They covered themselves quickly and followed me out, and I accompanied them back to safe quarters within the harem, leaving the soldiers to plunder.

I was deeply aggrieved that I had not even been able to save Pari's personal papers. Almost nothing would be left, not only to those who had loved her, but to history.

I went to Balamani in search of consolation and told him everything that had happened, including what I had learned about Mirza Salman's betrayal. I was the only person at the palace who knew about it, other than the new Shah and his wife, and I wanted Balamani's advice on how to discredit Mirza Salman.

"But first I would like to slash his neck like a chicken's."

Balamani eyed me as if I were a deranged dog. "Has someone smacked you in the head? He is the second most powerful man in the realm. You had better look to your own neck instead."

"Am I in danger?"

"I don't know. God be praised, as a clever vizier you are worth your weight in turquoise. Now our job is to convince those around Mohammad Khodabandeh that you are loyal. I will speak with Anwar. You need to do your part by singing the praises of the new Shah."

It was exactly the type of thing I had advised Pari to do, and it filled me with dread.

"Don't let your feelings for the princess impede what you must do," Balamani chided. "What is wrong with you? Why is your heart so bruised?"

"It is a matter of justice," I said angrily. "It riles me to see men winning high position because they're bullies and blackguards, while they send Pari to an early grave."

"She played a man's game and fell with honor. Your only mistake was that you loved her."

"A man has to love someone."

"Perhaps you are no longer suited to palace life."

"What else is there for me? I have no male family and no other employ."

"I know."

"I miss her. I keep thinking I hear her voice."

"Are you forgetting your place? Your job is to serve the shah, no matter who it is."

"Balamani, please stop. You sound like a sycophantic slave." I turned away in disgust.

Balamani grabbed my sash, bringing me to a halt.

"I intend to say whatever is required to save you," he said, and in his eyes I saw the goodwill of a longtime friend.

Because there was to be no public mourning ceremony, there was no place to grieve. Nor could I speak about Pari except in whispers because it was dangerous to show such partisanship for an executed princess. My grief felt as explosive as gunpowder packed in a cannon. Now I was mourning two treasures, Khadijeh and Pari, and thoughts of one would lead me to thoughts of the other until my heart felt pounded blue.

The palace women asked me repeatedly to describe what had happened to Pari. I told the story without sparing the details so that everyone would know how the princess had been butchered.

The younger women were frightened by the story. "That is what happens when you act like a man," Koudenet said, a shiver running through her. "She should have married and contented herself with raising a family."

Sultanam, who had come from Qom for her son's coronation, was more thoughtful: "If she hadn't been so powerful, they would have sent her into exile. She terrified them."

To compound my grief, the loss of Pari's patronage meant that my plans for bringing Jalileh to court had turned to dust. I suspected that if I wrote my cousin the truth—that my patron had died—she would give up hope and sacrifice Jalileh. Instead I gathered all the money I had and sent it as a gift, describing it as a foretaste of the reward I would provide when I was able to bring my sister to Qazveen. I wrote to Jalileh separately, hinted at my difficulties, and urged her to resist their marriage plans.

This fresh defeat upset me deeply. If Jalileh were to suffer more bad luck, there would be no reason for me to awaken in this world. But I had no idea what I could do to save her.

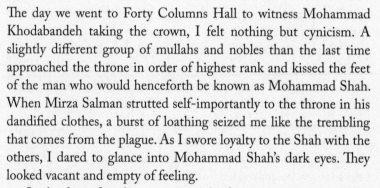

The day we went to Forty Columns Hall to witness Mohammad Khodabandeh taking the crown, I felt nothing but cynicism. A slightly different group of mullahs and nobles than the last time approached the throne in order of highest rank and kissed the feet of the man who would henceforth be known as Mohammad Shah. When Mirza Salman strutted self-importantly to the throne in his dandified clothes, a burst of loathing seized me like the trembling that comes from the plague. As I swore loyalty to the Shah with the others, I dared to glance into Mohammad Shah's dark eyes. They looked vacant and empty of feeling.

In the days after the coronation, the few remaining princes, the nobles, and the highest-ranking palace employees began to be summoned one by one to see the Shah and given their posts and promotions. Anwar instructed me to report to him until it was my turn, which was likely to take weeks. He told me that my interim assignment would be to read the princess's mail, which was still arriving at the palace in great quantities, and to inform him of any important news. For the sake of courtesy, I was also to write to correspondents of significant rank and announce her death; otherwise, they would be insulted that their letters had gone unanswered. "She was unparalleled," Anwar whispered to me sympathetically, "and all of us who served her know the truth, even if it must die with us." He told me to work in the company of the palace scribes, where I would find abundant supplies of paper, ink, and reed pens, and would be spared the grief of working in the princess's old quarters in the palace, which in any case were about to be occupied by members of Khayr al-Nisa's family.

I arrived at my posting the next day shortly after the morning prayer. Once I had conveyed my orders from Anwar, I was welcomed into the large, light-filled office by Rasheed Khan, the chief of the scribes. He gave me a wooden lap desk and showed me how to request supplies. I thought I saw sympathy in his weary, red-rimmed eyes.

Massoud Ali fetched and delivered all the letters that had come for Pari after her death, which had been held by the chief palace courier. Although it had been only a few weeks since her murder, it took Massoud Ali several trips to bring them in. He still looked wan with grief.

"Want to play backgammon later, my little radish?"

"All right," he said in a dull voice, and I knew he was just trying to please me. How it pained me to see him suffer! I swore to myself that I would try to get him assigned to me permanently at my new posting so that I could watch over him every day.

I stared at the pile of letters. The dry white paper made me think of Pari's bones whitening somewhere under the earth. I could hardly bear to touch the pulverized linen and hemp, but as I was now under the scrutiny of Rasheed Khan and his staff, I assumed a workman-like demeanor and began my task.

The first letter I opened was from a prostitute Pari had met once when she had gone to the shrine of Fatemeh Massoumeh in Qum to honor that holy sister of the Imam Reza. The letter, which had been written by a scribe that the prostitute had hired, reminded Pari where they had met and that the princess had given her money to start a new life. The prostitute had spent the money on felt and tools and had started a business making felt blankets for horses. After two years of hard work, she had developed a small stream of income that allowed her to quit her old profession. She thanked Pari for her belief in her goodness, and promised to say prayers for her every week at the shrine.

Yes, I thought, that was the princess I knew. Not the scheming Pari that tongues wagged about in the palace, but the Pari who would never let a request from a poor woman go unanswered, no matter how shameful her profession.

I began composing the response to the prostitute in my mind. "Dear Friend of the Court, I am very sorry to have to convey to you the earth-destroying news that the princess Pari Khan Khanoom, the most celebrated and revered flower of the Safavi women, has . . ."

I dropped the letter, my hands shaking.

"What is the matter?" asked Rasheed Khan, who happened to be passing by my station. "You don't look well."

"It is nothing," I said. "I need some tea and sugar."

"Ask the tea boys; you can't drink anything in here."

I went into the next room, away from all that precious paper, and a boy served me a glass of tea with a date before I had even asked for it.

My new job was ghastly. To have to convey Pari's death in formal courtly language made me feel as if I were reliving her murder. I imagined her bruised neck, gaping eyes, and bared teeth, and wished that Khalil Khan's maid had spared me.

When I returned to my task in the main writing room, I noticed a letter with a swooping, intricate royal seal indicating its provenance from the Ottoman court. I opened it carefully, certain that it must bear news of political import. Murad III's wife Safiyeh wrote that she was eager to ensure that the long-running peace treaty between the two countries be maintained, but had been discouraged by friction between Safavi and Ottoman troops near Van. Were the reports true? She begged for a reply before the soldiers escalated the fighting. The tone of her letter was polite but not warm, which alarmed me since she and Pari had enjoyed friendly relations in the past. I put the letter aside to show to Anwar; it would require an immediate reply by the scribe in charge of political missives.

I read a few more letters until I came upon one from Rudabeh, Pari's correspondent from Khui. Rudabeh also wrote of skirmishes on the border between Safavi and Ottoman troops, but added that she had heard that Khosro Pasha, the governor of Van, had decided to teach Iran a lesson by organizing a fighting force of Ottomans and Kurds against the Safavis. She knew this because one of her family members had been solicited to be one of the soldiers. She thought the princess would want to know.

I set the letter on the desk, alarmed. Pari had been right; the peace between the Safavis and the Ottomans had been based entirely on strength. The minute we looked weak, the countries on our borders became predators.

I sought out Balamani immediately and gave him the letters, which he promised to bring to the attention of Anwar, who had Mohammad Shah's ear.

"But don't expect much," said Balamani. "The Shah is too busy emptying out the royal treasury."

"What?"

"He has been heaping bags of gold and silver, as well as silk robes of honor, upon his new appointees. He is trying to buy loyalty."

"So he is desperate?"

"His lavishness reveals how weak he is."

"Just like Haydar. What a pity."

It seemed to me then that the royal court would never reward honesty. It would breed sycophants eager for treasure; it would require capitulation. No truthful word would be spoken to the royals in power. Those who succeeded would slither like snakes to earn their rewards; those who protested would be struck down.

"That is the least of it," Balamani continued. "The Ostajlu and Takkalu are at each other's throats again along with their allies, which makes me fear another civil war. Disgruntled citizens in the north and south are organizing revolts. The Ottomans and Uzbeks are threatening invasions on our western and eastern flanks. No corner of the country is safe."

Panah bar Khoda! Were we to live under the rule of yet another incompetent? Working for such an inept court was not just maddening—it was perilous.

That night, I had a dream I will never forget. It was as if the *Shahnameh* had come to life and swept me into its stories. The blacksmith Kaveh appeared at my door and asked me to join him on a mission. His face was ruddy from the forge, his forearms as strong as steel. Together we stormed Zahhak's palace, and Kaveh shredded his lying proclamation before his eyes. At the city square, Kaveh lifted his leather apron on the point of a spear and rallied the people against the evil leader. I marched with him, my heart bursting with pride.

"Long live Kaveh!" I chanted. "Death to the tyrant!"

The crowd swelled and yelled, their cheers like thunder. Surely our liberation was at hand! But when the cheers were at their loudest, Kaveh turned toward me.

"I am born in every generation," he whispered. "I protest and die, but still the tyrants prevail."

His black hair was flecked with gray, his leathery face creased with worry. I could not believe that he looked so despondent, and I was stricken with dread.

"How much longer must we endure injustice?" I asked.

But even Kaveh had no answer.

Defying Balamani's advice, I went to see Mirza Salman on the pretext that I needed to tell him what I had learned from Pari's correspondence. He kept me waiting until I was the last person who wished to see him, and then he couldn't put me off anymore. He was dressed in yet another magnificent robe, this one made of rose silk with paisley patterns, with a matching turban and sash. The opulence of his garments disgusted me.

"I am sorry to hear the news about your lieutenant," he said as he motioned from his cushion for his scribes to leave us. "Please accept my condolences."

I couldn't conceal my outrage, despite all my years of training to be the perfect servant. "Condolences? From you?"

"Of course. What a tragedy, a princess in her prime."

I laughed with such scorn that he put his hand on the dagger in his sash.

"Leave it be. I have no fear of your blade."

"Did the blow you took addle your brains? What is the matter with you?"

"With *me*? You are the one who spun tales to entrap the princess."

His face went white for a moment; I could see his mind buzzing over all the possible ways that I might have found him out. "Spun tales? I don't know what you are talking about."

"How good you are at saving yourself—as good as a flea who jumps to dry land from a capsized boat."

"You are a fantasist. I didn't give the order for her execution."

"But no doubt your propaganda made it seem like a good idea."

"I have never said anything different from what everyone else said about her thirst for power."

"You encouraged her to try to become the Shah's chief advisor, remember? You arranged it with the nobles yourself."

"That was before I talked to his wife. She is just as fierce as Pari was, but has the advantage of being her husband's main confidante. How could Pari fight that?"

"She would have been a better ruler."

"Not as far as the Shah is concerned."

"He will be sorry one day."

"You fool! How dare you speak out against your new leader? You could get pitched out of court and thrown into the river."

"Through one of your campaigns of sabotage?"

"You are one to talk. After all, you helped plan a murder."

"I don't know what you mean."

He laughed. "I wouldn't be surprised if the new Shah decided to get rid of you."

"A talented eunuch like myself shines brighter than gold. Remember, I am the crazy fool who cut himself to join the court."

"I doubt the new Shah cares much about what you did to your cock."

His language infuriated me. "I may not have a cock, but at least I am not a prick like you."

"Get out before I inflict a mortal wound on the parts of you that are still intact."

I laughed at him. "From what I have heard, you wouldn't have the balls to do much."

He leapt off his cushion, his dagger drawn. To show him how concerned I was, I turned my back on him and strolled out of the room. As I expected, he didn't follow.

Shortly thereafter, Mirza Salman began a campaign of sabotaging my name. It started with small comments made in passing about my loyalty, which Anwar heard and mentioned to Balamani. Then it escalated to open accusations that I couldn't be trusted. Mirza Salman even spread a rumor suggesting I had been affiliated with a physician who was suspected of poisoning Tahmasb Shah's orpiment.

I was in grave danger.

Balamani's creased forehead told me that he wished my situation at court were resolved, but neither of us could do anything to speed along my new posting. Nor could I leave palace service of my own accord: No servant was permitted to depart, even for a vacation, without permission. In any case, I didn't have funds to support myself on the outside.

Worse yet, my attempts to placate my mother's cousin were not successful. I received a letter from her demanding a firm departure date for Jalileh and money for the caravan. If they did not see an end to my excuses soon, they would permit the old man to marry Jalileh. I was plunged into despair as dark and deep as the bottom of a well. Although now I had the means to bring my sister to Qazveen, I had no place to house her and no way to keep her. By God above, what was I to do?

While I waited to be summoned to see the Shah, I continued my job of reading and responding to the princess's letters. Because all the correspondents wrote to Pari as if she were still alive, I began to feel as if I could see her pearly forehead, smell her piney perfume, and feel her arm guiding mine as I selected letters and wrote my responses.

I had been focusing my attention on the letters sent on the best paper with the most exalted seals, knowing that the writers would be demanding. One morning, however, a letter written on simple paper fell away from the rest of the stack. I picked it up and opened it. It was from one of Pari's *vakils,* a landowner in Qazveen. He wrote as follows:

> *Esteemed princess, I received the letter you sent from the Shah's encampment and wish to inform you that I have fulfilled your request and have transferred the deed of the mill near the Tehran Gate into the name of your servant Payam Javaher Shirazi. It is now legally his property. I will keep the deed until he comes to claim it and will hold the revenues from the mill for him until then. Please let me know if I may be of service in any other way.*

I dropped the letter in surprise and then snatched it up again before anyone else could see it. Balamani had been right: Pari had wished to take care of me! She must have written the letter on the very morning of her death.

I hid the letter in my robe when no one was looking. As soon as I could get away, I went to see the mill, which was located in a residential neighborhood in sight of the Tehran Gate. Donkeys walked in a circle around the mill to turn its heavy stone wheel, crushing sheaves of wheat into grain. Each person who used the mill paid a fee for this service. After watching for more than an hour, I determined that the mill was in such constant use that it would provide a steady stream of income. May God be praised! Sometimes fortune rains down from the sky.

"Who owns this mill?" I asked the man in charge of the donkeys, who was skinny and wiry. I was eager to hear my own name. With what pleasure I would introduce myself as the new owner and claim all that was my due.

"A generous patron. During the last holiday, poor people lined up here to receive free grain. May the gates of paradise open wide for him when the time comes!"

I was puzzled. "What is his name?"

"Khalil Khan."

The man halted his donkeys abruptly and rushed to my side. "Agha? Are you all right?"

I hurried back to the palace to tell Balamani the news. He was leaning against cushions in the guest room in our quarters reviewing some documents for Anwar about the new Shah's plans for religious endowments.

"Balamani, you were right about the princess," I said. "She did not forget me. She has left me the mill near the Tehran Gate."

He dropped the documents onto the wooden desk on his lap. "May God be praised! How much money does it bring in?"

"I don't know yet."

The relief in his eyes made me realize how worried he had been about me. "Now you can take good care of your sister, and maybe even of yourself."

"Perhaps," I said, but my voice sounded gloomy.

"Javaher, what is the matter? This should be one of the most joyful days of your life. You have been favored beyond imagining, even though your patron is dead."

"I know. My heart is full of gratitude toward her. How kind she was to remember me! Little did she know what problems would ensue. Khalil Khan has claimed the mill. How can I wrest it away from him?"

Balamani looked puzzled. "You know how. Go to the grand vizier, show him the proof, and ask for his help in transferring the property into your name."

"Mirza Salman won't help me."

"Why not?"

"He despises me."

Balamani scrutinized me closely for a moment. "What have you done?"

"I had an altercation with him."

"About what?"

"About a few things that were bothering me."

"For example?" His brow furrowed, making him look like an avenging angel in his pale blue robe.

"I lost my temper. I couldn't help it." Embarrassment crept through me; it was the last thing an experienced courtier was supposed to do.

"What did you say?"

I looked away. "I accused him of instigating Pari's murder."

Balamani was stunned into a long silence. He stared at me, the skin between his eyes knitting into such fierce lines of concern that I felt as if I had disappointed my own mother.

"And that is not all—I smashed Khalil Khan's nose. It points to the left now."

He snorted. "It is a wonder you are still breathing. You are going to need the help of a power greater than any here on earth."

I did not reply.

"Javaher, you have been a fool," he added, his voice rising. "How do you think you are going to get the mill now that the grand vizier—who has the last word on all property documents—is set against you?"

"I don't know. All I can tell you is that I felt like the reed that has been torn from its bed. How can I play a sweet tune when all that pours from my heart is sorrow and loss?"

"You know the rules at court. Why have you sabotaged all my hard work in your favor? What good do you do Pari if you destroy yourself? What a donkey you are!"

I felt the blood rush to my forehead, and my hands balled into fists at my sides. "By God above, I couldn't bear it anymore! Are we not men? Do we not have tongues? Have they been so severed by the tyrants who rule us that we have lost our ability to speak?"

Balamani tried to interrupt, but I continued.

"For the first time in my life, I stood up like a man. I may pay the price of my life for my words, but at least I said them. I don't care that I made an enemy. I don't care that I may lose my posting. For once, I did not feel as if what was true in my heart was as different from what was on my lips as day to night. I became like hot white light, pure and clean. I felt as if my testicles had grown to the size of mountains and I had earned the right to shout out, 'I am a complete man!'"

Balamani's eyes softened, and he looked older and sadder than I had ever seen.

"I have never dared to do what you describe, my friend. I still think you are a fool"—he opened his palms to the heavens in won-der—"but I am proud of you."

A mist clouded my vision. I shook it away angrily and gratefully. "Balamani, what can I do now?"

The skepticism in his eyes indicated that he didn't think I had much of a chance. "What are your desires?"

I thought for a moment. "I want the mill so I can leave court with an income, and then I want to learn what it means to be my own master."

"And how do you expect to achieve all that?"

"I will go to Mirza Salman and ask for the mill because it is my right."

Balamani's laugh was long and sad. With regret, I remembered all the time he had spent drilling me so that I would never slip at court.

"Your behavior has been so provocative that he will refuse to help. At least accept one morsel of advice."

"Of course."

"Apologize. Explain that grief unhinged you. Swear to be an ally. That is the way of a smart courtier, and you have been one of the best."

I grew hot with anger. "So I am to return to subterfuge, is that it?" I barked.

"Calm down," Balamani ordered. "How badly do you wish to win?"

Mirza Salman wouldn't even allow me to be shown in to see him, although I waited all day. When I rushed past his servants into his rooms, insisting that I had urgent business, his face puffed out with rage. I was hardly able to get the request for the mill out of my mouth before he called me an illiterate fool and had me thrown out.

I decided right then to visit Fereshteh with the excuse of wanting to exchange information with her about the court's new personalities and plans. I needed her advice. Even more than that, I longed to see her and unburden my heart.

When I arrived at her house, I was told Fereshteh was occupied and would admit me when she could. I drank some tea, ate some small cucumbers, and admired a new painting on her walls of a noblewoman serving wine to a smitten courtier. The day dragged on, and I realized that Fereshteh was probably servicing a client. What if it was Mirza Salman? I was filled with loathing at the thought.

When I was finally shown in to see her, she didn't rise to greet me. Her large eyes looked weary, her robe creased and tired.

"What is the matter?"

"My daughter has been vomiting," she said. "I gave her some medicine and now she is finally sleeping."

"I hope she gets better soon."

"Thank you."

"I have come to thank *you*. You have helped me with many things."

"I only wish my intelligence on Mirza Salman had arrived soon enough to save your commander."

"I wish the same," I replied. "It is strange, but I believe Pari knew in her heart that she was going to her grave."

"Why?"

"She spoke to me about death and judgment even before she knew about her uncle's murder."

"Alas! What a tragedy. Was she as fierce as they say?"

I thought back to Pari's meeting with Mohammad and Khayr al-Nisa Beygom. "She was so bright that her light could burn. She was one of those people who neither compromise nor hold their tongue. She made people angry enough to want to destroy her."

"Because she was too outspoken?"

"And because she had too many allies. Now that Mohammad Shah and his wife have also executed her mother and her uncle, they have uprooted Circassian power at court and made room for their own supporters. To me, though, it is as if they hacked a limb off their own tree."

My cheeks felt wet all of a sudden, and I wiped them with the cloth that I still kept tucked inside my sash. It was Pari's silk handkerchief, and the sight of it only made me feel worse.

Fereshteh's eyes searched my face. "Did you love her?"

"Yes," I said, "in the way that a soldier loves a good commander or a nobleman loves a just shah."

"I understand. May this be your final sorrow!"

"Thank you."

"It is a terrible loss. What will you do now?"

"I don't know. I must wait to see what plans they have for me at the palace. Balamani said he would try to help me."

"I hope you receive favor. In the meantime, I have heard some useful news," Fereshteh continued. "Mirza Salman has just gotten married."

"Oh?" I said.

"His wife's name is Nasreen Khatoon."

I snorted with disgust. "She spied on me and accused me of wrongdoing, which could have gotten me killed. Have she and Mirza Salman been working together all this time?"

"I presume so."

"They deserve each other."

"Mirza Salman doesn't expect to be faithful to her, of course."

Everyone knew that a nobleman could have several wives and keep as many other women as he could afford. Why had Fereshteh bothered to mention that?

"Come now: What are you saying?"

She was watching me very closely. "He has made me an offer."

"Of marriage?"

"Of upkeep. He has promised to pay all my expenses if I serve him alone—in which case I could see you no more."

I felt a violent surge of anger in my chest. "Does fate strew the man's path with nothing but roses? A high posting, the removal of Pari, a well-placed wife, and now all your beauty? Good God! Why doesn't he offer to marry you?"

"You know very well that noblemen don't marry prostitutes."

"He is a princess-killer, and he has tried to thwart me at every turn. How could you even consider him?"

"What other options do I have?"

"You said you wished to retire."

"This is the only form of retirement I have ever been offered."

I couldn't stand hearing about him anymore. I leapt up, strode to the door, and thrust my feet into my shoes, hard with anger.

"How is his offer different from prostitution?"

"How is any marriage different?"

"That is ridiculous."

I stopped in my tracks and turned to look at her, a cruel comment on my lips. She raised her hands as if in protection. The warning look in her large eyes stopped my tongue.

"Javaher, I must think about what is best for my daughter. More than anything, I wish to relinquish my profession."

I paused. "What would you do if you had some money?"

"I would set about making myself respectable by learning a craft so that I could earn money another way. When my daughter is grown, I wish her to marry a kind man from a good family. There is no chance of that unless I can show the world a new face."

She looked sad, and I thought about how no one had been able to save either one of us from our fate. What if, through the blessings of good fortune, we were able to save those who came after us? Only then would it seem as if our lives had been redeemed. What happiness we would feel if we could shelter our young ones from the lives we had endured!

I kicked off my shoes and sat down again, sighing.

"Fereshteh, I apologize for my outburst. Perhaps there is a way we can help each other. Pari left me a mill, but Mirza Salman won't allow me to claim it. I need something damning about him in order to force his hand. If I can get ownership of it, I promise I will help you. The mill does well, and people always need its services. Its income would help you get started in a new life. I would like to be able to thank you for all your help, and I know that Pari would wish to do the same."

Her whole face brightened with hope. "How grateful I would feel to be in charge of my own person! I would never have to touch one of those things again."

I couldn't help a wry smile.

"Why don't you ask the Shah for help with the mill when you are called in about your new posting?"

"Mohammad Shah gave Khalil Khan all of Pari's money as a reward for her murder. I doubt he would feel compelled to fulfill any of her last wishes."

Fereshteh thought for a long time. I watched her face and was surprised to see what looked like strong emotions playing over it, but I couldn't read them.

"I know of one person who might have the information you seek."

"Who is it?"

"I can't tell you," she said.

"If we are to be partners in this, I need to know who it is."

"Never mind. Leave this to me."

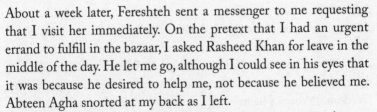

About a week later, Fereshteh sent a messenger to me requesting that I visit her immediately. On the pretext that I had an urgent errand to fulfill in the bazaar, I asked Rasheed Khan for leave in the middle of the day. He let me go, although I could see in his eyes that it was because he desired to help me, not because he believed me. Abteen Agha snorted at my back as I left.

When I was shown into Fereshteh's private guest room, she was completely veiled; I couldn't even see her face because she had covered it with a white silk picheh.

"You may leave us," she told her maid, who shut the door as quietly as if it were a shadow.

"Fereshteh, is it you?" I said lightly. "I have never seen you so covered."

She did not reply. A chill froze my heart as she slowly removed the picheh from her face. Her right eyelid was the color of a rotten pomegranate, and the area underneath it was yellow and black. Her bottom lip was swollen to twice its normal size and cleft by a dark scab. Her eyes glistened with what could only be tears.

"By God above!" I roared. "Who did this to you? I will kill him."

Her hands were shaking, I suspect, from the pain. "Remember how I met Sultanam the first time?"

I thought for a moment before recalling that a client had beaten her so badly that she had gone to the royal mother and demanded her help.

"You went back to that terrible man?"

"Yes."

Slowly she removed her outer robe, revealing that one of her pale arms and the top of her breasts were covered with eggplant-colored blotches.

"Fereshteh, who would do such an ugly thing? Tell me and I will petition to have the monster punished."

She shuddered as one of her long sleeves grazed a tender part of her forearm.

"I feel much better today than I did a few days ago. The pain has hardly been the worst of it. It was what he insisted on doing while having sex. I will omit the ugly details. I have paid very dearly for the information you wanted."

The pit of my stomach filled with bile. "I would never have asked you to sacrifice your person, not even to save my own life."

"I know," she said. "That is why I didn't tell you my plans. I decided that a week of pain would be worth the chance to win my freedom. Perhaps I have."

A smile of triumph illuminated her face and made her look almost beautiful again despite her ghastly injuries.

"Fereshteh! I would rather have sacrificed myself for you instead."

"Never mind that now. Here is what I have learned," she said excitedly. "When Mirza Salman was wooing Mohammad Shah and his wife, he was also working on a plot to elevate their eldest son, Hamza Mirza, to the throne instead. In short, he was betraying them."

I was seized with hope. "Is there proof that would allow me to get Mirza Salman dismissed?"

"No one will come forth and admit it. The best thing you can do to get the mill is tell Mirza Salman you have proof without telling him from whom. I know enough details about the plot that he will realize your source is impeccable."

"How do you know it is impeccable?"

"The nobleman I saw was in on the plot with him. He is angry at Mirza Salman because he relinquished the plan to elevate Hamza Mirza when the Shah and his wife offered to keep him as grand vizier. I shall not reveal the nobleman's name for fear that he would kill me if it came out."

A shiver of fear went through her. She shook it away and began narrating the details of the plan, which I committed to memory. When the pain became too great for her to bear, she ate a few poppy seeds to relax and rubbed some liniment onto her poor bruised body.

"Thank you, Fereshteh. Your sacrifice has been far greater than any I deserved. I will do everything in my power to live up to what I promised."

"A silken cord has bound us since we were little more than children," she said gently.

I gestured toward a glass vase shaped like a tear-catcher that adorned one of her shelves. "I don't want you to collect any more tears for me, though."

She smiled. "So you know the story about the origin of the tear-catcher?"

"No."

"Once there was a shah who was jealous of his queen and uncertain of her love. One morning he went off on a hunt and told his men to report to the queen that he had been torn apart by wild animals. The queen was sick with grief. She ordered her artisans to design a glass tear-catcher in which to collect all her tears. A few days later, the Shah's spies reported that her room was filled with dozens of glass tear-catchers in shades of blue and violet, which glowed with her sorrow. Chagrined by the grief he had caused her, the Shah returned and promised to trust her and love her until the end of their days."

I paused. "I wish that every terrible story had such a happy ending."

"So do I."

When I returned to the palace, I sent Mirza Salman a message saying that I had urgent information that could threaten the very foundations of the court, thereby obligating him to see me. He had just claimed one of the best offices near Forty Columns Hall, one with high ceilings and windows made of rare multicolored glass. I sat in his waiting room filled with deadly calm, thinking how pleased Balamani would be to know how resolute I felt.

When I was finally shown in, Mirza Salman frowned. I noticed that he had purchased a fancy silk carpet, which felt as soft as a baby's skin, and he had positioned himself at the long end of it so that visitors would have to admire it while talking to him.

I didn't waste time on pleasantries. "I have heard you have been speaking out against me."

"So? I say what I think."

"So do I. I am here because I need that mill—the one that Khalil Khan claimed as his reward for murdering Pari."

Mirza Salman shuddered as if I had mentioned something indelicate. "Khalil Khan is one of the richest men in the country now. Why should I challenge him for your sake?"

"Because the mill belongs to me."

He guffawed. "Can't you think of a better reason?"

"Do you really want to make an enemy of me?"

"I am the grand vizier, remember? It is not even worth my time to smash your balls."

I did not raise an eyebrow. "You have to help me," I demanded. "It is the law."

"I don't have to do anything."

I gestured to his eunuchs, who looked ready to grab me and throw me out of the room. "I have something to tell you that you will prefer to keep private."

He sent them to the corners of the room so that they could not hear, but kept his hand on his dagger.

"I know about your plot to bring Hamza Mirza to the throne," I said quietly. "Don't you think that news might upset the Shah?"

Mirza Salman's chin snapped into the air and his back stiffened as if he were riding a horse. "Nonsense."

"Your plan was to bribe the Ostajlu guard inside the palace at the same time that you sent an army of supporters to guard all of its entrances, having learned from the mistakes that Haydar made. Once you had the palace secured, you were going to declare Hamza Mirza the new shah, with yourself as grand vizier."

I began describing the minutiae of the plan, watching his face change from assured to ashen, until finally I had convinced him that I knew everything.

"Enough! I am not to blame, but you are a good enough story-teller to make it sound like a competent rumor. So you want the mill? Very well, then. I will see that you get it, but only under one condition: You must leave the court."

It was exactly what I hoped he would say, but I pretended to equivocate. "You want me to relinquish my post at the palace? Why should I?"

"That is the deal. Otherwise you can fend for yourself."

I pretended to look as if I felt cornered. "This is my home. Where else is a eunuch supposed to go?"

"Out of my sight."

"I intend to stay."

"Then I won't help you."

"Very well, then," I said angrily. "When shall I expect to receive my orders to depart?"

"Right away." He dismissed me with a flick of his wrist, and as

I reached the door, he hissed, "You are very lucky." His gaze was as chilling as the highest peaks of Mount Damavand.

"It is not luck."

A few days later, Mirza Salman contacted Pari's *vakil* and asked to see her letter about the mill. When it arrived, he had an expert at court verify her handwriting and declared the letter sound. I didn't know what form of persuasion he used to wrest the mill away from Khalil Khan, but I suspected he was compelled to demand it as a personal favor. It didn't take long before Mirza Salman sent a messenger to me with the deed. Once I had it in hand, I immediately sent a message to Fereshteh telling her of our success.

> *Kind lady, know that the tears shed by your loving eyes*
> *Have transformed into oceans that rival the skies.*
> *Because of your sacrifices and your pain*
> *Those oceans rematerialized as sweet summer rain.*
> *That rain fell upon my desert of woe*
> *Your waterfall of kindness made things grow.*
> *Allow me to thank you for the gift of your tears*
> *With a shower of good news: Our liberation nears!*

That afternoon, Balamani informed me that Mohammad Shah had commanded me to present myself before him the next day. I was surprised, having thought Mirza Salman would arrange my dismissal and save the Shah the trouble of seeing me. Now I would have to prepare for any eventuality. Would the Shah chastise me for being Pari's servant? Worse yet, would he accuse me of disloyalty or of murder? I hastily penned a letter to Pari's *vakil* instructing him that my sister, Jalileh, was to inherit the mill in the event of my death. Then I gave a copy of the letter to Balamani for safekeeping. After reading it, he tucked it into his robe.

"May God protect you from harm," he said, and insisted on

spending every moment of that evening in my company, as if afraid it would be my last.

The morning of my meeting, I dressed in the dark blue head-to-toe that Pari had given me, hoping that some of her royal farr would protect me, and into my sash I tucked one of her handkerchiefs embroidered with the lady reading her book. Mohammad Shah was too blind to be able to see my attire, of course, but I imagined it would impress his wife. I arrived and waited in the guest room where I had gone with Pari so many times to petition Isma'il. Nothing had changed; the paintings and furniture were the same, only the occupants were new.

When I was shown in, I was surprised to see no sign of Mohammad Shah. Khayr al-Nisa Beygom sat on a gold-embroidered cushion, where the Shah would normally sit, and was surrounded by her ladies and her eunuchs. She was wearing such a bright red robe that it made her skin look as white as a ghost's; her lips were red like a gash.

Now that she was queen, I greeted her as Mahd-e-Olya, the Cradle of the Greats, which was fitting since she had given birth to four royal sons.

"Thank you for the opportunity to bask in the royal radiance," I continued in Farsi, her native language, knowing my fluency would please her.

"You are welcome," she said regally. "It is time for me to decide what to do with you. Before I do, tell me why you are so valuable to the court."

I realized right away that she was making good on her promise to take control. The word around the palace was that her husband was shah in name only.

"I can write a letter in three languages, procure sensitive information, and give sound advice on strategy. No wall stops me."

"I have heard much about your talents. The only question is where you should serve."

I was taken aback. I had expected her to question me and get rid of me.

"Thank you. I thought you should know that Mirza Salman

advised me that leaving palace service would be for the best," I said euphemistically. "He said he would speak with you about it."

"He did, but my decision is the only one that matters." She stared at me as if waiting to be challenged.

"My eyes are yours to be stepped on."

"Good. Let us return to the problem of where you should serve."

Sensing a trap, I struggled to get what I wanted. "Kind lady, I apologize for burdening you with my problems. A grave concern demands my presence away from court, if you are kind enough to grant it."

"What problem?"

"It is my sister, Jalileh. The family members who have been caring for her are old and ailing," I improvised quickly. "I fear for her honor."

"Does she have any talents?"

"She reads well and writes an excellent hand."

"In that case, there is no problem," said Mahd-e-Olya. "Bring her here, and we will find a position for her in the harem."

I stared at her: Now she wanted my sister, too? Such an invitation was a sign of great privilege.

"Is there a special service you wish me to perform?"

"Yes. After we hired Looloo, he told me the details of your astrological chart, which surprised me so much I asked him to calculate it again. Your chart still says you will help usher in the greatest Safavi leader ever. How can I allow you to leave?"

I forced my face into submission.

"Obviously, that leader wasn't Isma'il," added Mahd-e-Olya. "It would be foolish to release you when that leader might be right at hand."

I had the distinct impression that she meant herself, which filled me with scorn.

"I was honored to assist the esteemed princess, Pari Khan Khanoom," I said, hoping lavish praise of her would disqualify me. "She was a great thinker, poet, statesman, and flower of her age, perhaps of all time! She was unequaled."

"It is fitting that you admire the royal woman you served. Now, as to your employment: The court scribes can always use a master of languages such as you."

"The *scribes*?" I replied, the contempt in my voice obvious. It was like telling Kholafa he should be in charge of the royal zoo. Worst of all, I would not be free.

Mahd-e-Olya did not flinch. "It should be an easy job for you. You deserve an excellent reward after your tribulations with Pari."

"It was an honor to serve her," I insisted.

"I appreciate your loyalty. I am very pleased to give you another opportunity to show your worth."

"What a great gift," I replied, the words sticking in my mouth.

She looked toward the door as if she were about to tell her servants that our meeting was finished. I was stuck like a donkey in mud.

"There is just one thing. Is there a possibility I might live outside the palace, if it turned out to be best for my sister?"

"No. When has an actively serving eunuch ever been allowed to live outside the palace? Your lack of other ties is what makes you and your brethren so valuable to the court."

I grasped at the last request I could muster. It was code for "I beg you to release me," and it was almost never refused of good servants.

"Cradle of the Greats, I swore that I would make a pilgrimage to Mecca if your husband was crowned shah. I would feel like a bad Muslim if I didn't fulfill my vow. Would you give me leave to go?"

The voyage could buy me a year or two.

"My husband and I are deeply honored when our servants make promises to God on our behalf. But now is not the time."

I was stunned by her refusal; in my experience, it was unprecedented. But I refused to give up. "In that case, may I petition you again in the future about my sworn oath to make the pilgrimage, so that I don't disappoint God?"

"Of course. At this court, know that your good service will always be rewarded. God willing, one day you will get your wish."

I left the meeting so angry that my body gave off waves of heat. No matter how much I longed for my liberty, it seemed my fate was to remain a prisoner of the court, and I felt caged and thwarted by the desires of others.

The one bright spot in my life was that I immediately began receiving money from the mill, including the earnings I was owed since Pari's death. As soon as I had the money, I went to see Fereshteh and told her I would give her a regular allowance for her living expenses for as long as money was forthcoming. The joy in her eyes was beyond describing. She promised she would learn a craft, and then she immediately visited the shrine of a saint, repented her past, and swore to reform. Her servants were instructed to tell her clients that she had pledged herself to a new life. One of them, a comptroller at the palace, complained about the loss of tax revenue she provided to the treasury. Mirza Salman, rather than promising to marry her like an honest man, told her he would find a woman who would be more grateful.

I wrote to my mother's cousin that my sister had been ordered by the new queen to come to court, unmarried, in order to wait on the royal women, and I sent the necessary fare and a large reward for their services. As long as they had not already married Jalileh to the old man, I knew that they would never dare disobey such a command. I waited anxiously for their reply.

If my sister served the royal ladies well, she would learn how to be a lady herself and would earn the opportunity to make a good marriage. The money from the mill would accumulate until it became a generous dowry for her. Slowly, I hoped, we would form a new bond, and when many years had passed, we would be able to forget all the long years during which we hardly knew each other.

While I waited, Balamani's official day of retirement arrived. We spent his last evening with a group of eunuchs at a picnic by the river. Together we ate lamb kabob and bread made in an oven dug deep into the earth. As the moon rose, we drank strong spirits made of raisins. My heart was very full because of what I was losing. Balamani had been everything to me: mentor, friend, and family. I recited a poem to him from the *Shahnameh* about a kind shah in order to reflect on Balamani's generosity through all the years. When the men yelled "Bah! Bah!" I launched into some verses I had composed myself:

> "Many is the heartfelt poem written
> For mother, father, daughter or son.
> Those whose family includes such treasures,
> Have been graced with a lifetime of pleasures.
> But other gifts can be just as dear
> Like the friendship between you and Javaher
> Sometimes bonds that go beyond blood ties
> Become as precious as the light of our eyes.
> Tell me: 'What is the source of your love?
> Is it learned, or is it a gift from above?'
> No angel was ever more kind or true
> No comrade more beloved than you."

Balamani paused for a moment before answering, looking as if he was lost in thought. Then his warm old eyes sought out mine, and I felt as if he was speaking to me alone.

"Remember I told you about Vijayan, the boy on the boat that brought me here long ago? One day, when the sailors were fighting a storm and most of the other boys were recovering from their operation, Vijayan offered me a stolen fruit. For the first time, I tasted a mango's sweet flesh. How delicious our secret was! Nothing was sweeter, though, than finding a friend when I was broken and alone. Because of Vijayan, I learned to outlive my sorrows."

Tears prickled my eyes. Now I must devote my life to helping those who needed me as much as I had needed Balamani. How joyful it had been to discover that money could save Fereshteh—and, I hoped, my sister—from entanglements they loathed. With Anwar's help, I had also just managed to get Massoud Ali assigned to me at the office of the scribes.

The day after Balamani left for Hindustan, I took up my new duties with the scribes. The work was boring and beneath my abilities. Abteen Agha, the assistant to the chief, made sure to give me the pettiest jobs available, such as writing letters to provincial scribes about the latest methods for registering contributions to the royal treasury. I was able to pen the official edicts in an hour or two of the day, and the rest of the time I chafed at my new, unsatisfying role. It would have been more rewarding to be in charge of the royal zoo, where at least I could have run free with the animals.

I was overqualified for my new job, and they all knew it. I had the brains and, dare I say, the balls to be one of the best political players at court. But I had been emasculated in every way, as had most of the men around me. They served at the pleasure of the rulers, and if the rulers chose to be murderers and liars, or lazy, drugged, or insanely pious, courtiers must make themselves fit their demands the way a cobbler fashions leather around a man's malodorous foot, praising him all the while. Yet at least now I was safe, and I consoled myself that there was a certain relief in being ignored. The old Sufi proverb came to mind: When you are in a cage, fly anyway.

Because it was the start of a new reign, the office of the scribes was very busy. Mohammad Shah's wishes must be conveyed, monitored, and fulfilled, mostly through letters and other paperwork. In addition, his court historians were engaged in documenting the beginning of his rule, while others were being selected to write Isma'il Shah's short history. I decided to take the opportunity to correct the record about the tangled relationship between my father, Kamiyar Kofrani, and Isma'il. I told Rasheed Khan what I had discovered, and after checking the story, he ordered that the relevant pages be rewritten. At least I could do that much for my father.

At this time, the office of the scribes began receiving written reports about various pretenders in different parts of the country who claimed to be Isma'il and who said he had never died. These fake Isma'ils invented stories about how they had been deposed and deserved to be reinstated, and they began gathering disaffected people around them. One of the most powerful among them, I learned, was recruiting rebels among the Lur people in the southwest of the country, where Khalil Khan was governor. Accordingly, Khalil Khan was ordered back to the area to put the rebels down. I caught wind of this from someone whom I had paid very well to spy on him, and I immediately dispatched a loyal messenger to the Lur leaders informing them of the day that Khalil Khan departed from Qazveen and the number of soldiers and weapons he had with him. After that, I waited for news, knowing that if by some chance my plans were to be discovered, I would be accused of treason and executed. But it wasn't long before the court learned that Khalil Khan and his men had been ambushed by the Lur leaders and that he had been killed when an arrow pierced his heart. It seemed fitting, since he had certainly punctured mine.

Mirza Salman would be much trickier prey. I resolved to watch him and bide my time. As Balamani had advised, I would pretend to be a loyal servant in every possible manner. As the years went by, Mirza Salman would lower his guard, and then I would strike hard and deep. He would never even see the blow.

In the meantime, I paid attention to the scribes' gossip with the goal of learning everything I could about Mohammad Shah and his wife. It wasn't long before the men began talking about how much the qizilbash disliked Mahd-e-Olya. She had a firm hand, like Pari, and wouldn't allow them to do whatever they wanted. They had bargained on being able to manipulate her weak husband, but instead they had to submit to the demands of a powerful wife. Once again, the threat of civil war began to blow through the palace like a bad smell.

Since Mahd-e-Olya seemed to have a very good opinion of herself, I thought I could convince her that she was indeed the chosen leader of the Safavis, so she would think my destiny was fulfilled and would be willing to release me. Or perhaps a leader would emerge

whom I wished to serve, and hope would sing in my heart again. I
knew I would have to be patient.

After several weeks, I was overjoyed to receive a letter by express
courier that Jalileh's caravan had departed and would be expected
in about ten days. I visited the guards at the Tehran Gate, through
which she would enter the city, and told them I would pay well in
the weeks following for news of any caravan from the southern coast.

At the scribes' office, I had lately been assigned to write admoni-
tory letters to provincial governors who had failed to pay enough
taxes to the treasury. I enjoyed writing such letters; they were one of
the few assignments that allowed me to vent my aggression. I found
myself achieving new levels of rhetorical effect, sprinkling the letters
with metaphors and with exhortations from the Qur'an to make my
point.

One day, when I was finishing the last of this batch of letters,
Massoud Ali came looking for me, his dark eyes shining, his turban
as neatly wrapped as I had ever seen it.

"A caravan has just arrived from the south!" he said. "The travelers have been taken to Caravanserai Kamal."

I put aside my pen and ink. On my way out, I tripped on the lap
desk of a scribe who was laboring over a hard-earned page, sending
the desk onto a nearby cushion. Massoud Ali stared at me, his round
eyes wide. The scribe sputtered, "What is the rush? Has your mother
come back from the grave?"

"In a manner of speaking," I replied.

Outside, the day was sunny, the sky like a turquoise bowl. I hurried down the Promenade of the Royal Stallions toward the Friday
mosque. The white swirls on the dome seemed to spin, as if it might
lift off to partner with the swirls of cloud. I felt my heart surge at the
sight. At long last, my sister might be here! Would she have a face
like the moon? How would I even recognize her?

As I passed the mosque and walked toward Caravanserai Kamal,

I came upon the entrance to the cemetery where our father was buried. Someday, when Jalileh was established, I would bring her to see our father's grave. We would sprinkle it with rose water together, and we would pray in the spiritual presence of our father, hoping he could see and hear us from the place where all souls await the Day of Judgment. Although Jalileh probably didn't even remember him, I hoped she would be eager to come. I wanted to tell her the story of our father's bravery and of the politics that cost him his life. I would make her understand that he had risked everything because he believed in the possibility of a perfect world. How satisfied I would feel when I told her that his soul had been avenged! Of course, I would not relate my part in it, to avoid putting her at risk.

In the distance, I saw the narrow wooden gate that marked the entrance to the caravanserai, which had high walls so that travelers would feel embraced and safe at night. As I approached, a hot breeze surged off the street and lifted my robe all of a sudden, making me aware of the place where my parts used to swing. They had been gone now for almost half my life. I thought wryly of the nickname mothers used for their baby boys: "Ah, my little penis of gold!"

How horrified my mother would have been to learn of my fate. Would Jalileh understand why I had acted as I had? As soon as she saw me enter the harem, she would know I had been unmanned. Would she love me anyway? Or would she merely pretend to care for me because she needed me so badly? Would our reunion be filled with disappointment, like Pari's with Isma'il? My stomach dropped away.

Inside the caravanserai, the large open courtyard pulsed with activity. Men unloaded their animals, women helped their toddlers descend from camels, and older children fetched water for younger ones. As the loads were removed, the animals were led away and fed, while the caravanserai's owner accompanied his guests to their rooms, followed by a porter who offered his strong back. I searched the crowd for a face that was like my mother's, scrutinizing each person one by one as the crowd diminished.

Too dark, that one. Hair too curly. Face too round. Too old. Wearing a Christian cross. That one lacked an arm, poor thing. The crowd began to thin even further as the travelers were shown to their rooms. Had Jalileh joined a different caravan? I went in search of the caravan's leader, an older fellow with a long drooping mustache.

All of a sudden I heard my name in a voice that sounded ragged with relief. "Payam! Payam!" I turned around to find her, but before I could identify her, I felt two thin arms around me and a head buried in my bicep. Was it her? How had she recognized me? Her body was trembling as she murmured a prayer of thanksgiving. My heart quickened and I could not see anything for a moment, just the top of her faded blue headscarf and the wisps of black hair escaping the fabric at her temples. The noon call to prayer came from a nearby mosque, and as its sweetness filled the air, she continued reciting her thanks.

Finally, the young woman drew away from me and lifted her face. I took a step back in surprise. How strange was my first glimpse of her! It was like seeing myself reflected in a mirror, except that she was a girl half my age. She had my mother's rich, honey-colored eyes, fringed with dark black lashes and eyebrows, and from what I could see of it, my father's looping black hair. She was small like my mother, yet the energy in her tiny frame seemed uncontainable, like a hummingbird's. Was she pretty? All I know is that I was irresistibly drawn to her.

"Sister of mine, may God be thanked!" I began, my voice tangled with emotion.

An old woman whose eyes were buried in wise wrinkles had been observing us all this time. "Happiest of families, how long has it been?"

I looked up. "Twelve years!"

"Voy, she was just a baby. How did you recognize her?"

"I recognized *him*," said Jalileh proudly.

"It is no surprise. You are like velvet cut from the same bolt," the old woman observed.

"In that case, I am glad my brother is comely," Jalileh replied in a teasing voice, "by the blessings of God!"

I laughed out loud at her boldness, then exhaled with relief at it. Though Jalileh wore a faded cotton robe and tunic, with not a single ornament in her ears or around her neck, and though she had not felt a parent's love since she was seven, it seemed that her spirit had not been ground into powder.

I gave Jalileh's few belongings to the porter and sent him off to the palace. Then we said goodbye to the old woman and the caravan leader and walked outside the caravanserai together, side by side for the first time. Her gait was rapid, her eyes alive with interest, but they stayed on my face rather than being distracted by the city's sparkling domes.

"Where to begin?" I wondered aloud. "Our cousin didn't—"

"Our mother wanted—" Jalileh said at the same time. We stared at each other, feeling the weight of all the missing years.

"*Labu!* Hot labu!" a vendor called out, and my stomach came alive with hunger as the syrupy scent of beets filled the air. But then I remembered how my sister had hated beets as a child. I looked at her, wondering. There was so much I didn't know.

"I love beets," she replied to my unasked question. "And I am hungry!"

I laughed and paid for two beets. The vendor served them to us steaming hot in ceramic holders, smiling for no particular reason at both of us. We blew on them and feasted in the middle of the street. Jalileh's lips and fingers grew purple as she ate. She giggled and wiped her mouth.

After we finished, we cleaned ourselves, and then there was another awkward silence. What could we say to each other after so long? Jalileh's eyes were red, and I realized that she needed to rest.

"Come," I said. "Let me take you to the palace so that you can see where you will be living."

"I am to live in a palace?" She could not hide the excitement in her voice.

"Yes, you are. And soon you will wear a fine robe and ornaments in your hair, I promise you."

"But where will you live?"

"Nearby," I said. "I will tell you everything once you are settled. Right now, I want to show you something."

We walked together in the direction of the Tehran Gate until we reached the mill. A group of women were waiting in line to have their grain crushed, while others were purchasing the flour sold there. We stood and watched the donkeys turn the wheel that moved the huge stone, which rolled over the wheat and crushed it into flour. Jalileh was transfixed.

"At home, I had to do that by hand," she observed. I took one of her hands and brushed my fingers across her rough and chapped palm. She had never written anything about work to me; she had never complained.

Jalileh removed her hand from mine, pressing her small lips together in chagrin. "If we buy flour, I could make you some bread," she offered, her voice very small. "I learned all our mother's recipes from her cousin."

Suddenly, it was as if I were back in my family home again watching my mother pull her sesame-sprinkled bread out of the oven, her eyes glowing with pride, while Jalileh and I gathered around to admire the crisp, corrugated loaf and to rip off pieces of it while it was still hot. No baker's bread had been as good. My nostrils flooded with the scent, and my tongue ached with longing for it.

"Jalileh, this mill belongs to us. Someday I will tell you the whole story, but for now you can think of it as a legacy, in a roundabout way, from our father."

As I said this, I realized how true it was. If our father had not been killed, I would never have served Pari, and if I hadn't served her, I would never have received the mill.

"I am glad it is ours," she replied. "Is that why you were able to bring me to Qazveen?"

"It is part of the reason," I said. "Before you were invited to the palace, it was helpful to know that I had a means of supporting you."

Her eyes looked pained, and I wished I hadn't put it that way. She had probably been told all her life what a burden she was.

"I am grateful for all you have done," she said. "But is there nothing I can do for you? Nothing at all?"

A tear of pride welled up in one of her eyes, which she brushed away almost angrily. I saw the loneliness of an orphan there, and her uncrushable spirit, too. I realized what I needed to do.

"Manager!" I called out. He came forward to greet me, wished blessings upon me and my family, and reported that the mill had been doing even more business than usual.

"That is good news," I replied. "Even better news is that my sister is now living in Qazveen. Please fetch a bag of your best flour for her."

Jalileh's smile beamed as bright as the moon on a dark night. Quietly we walked back to the palace, the bag of flour between us.

The day after delivering Jalileh into the care of one of the ladies at the entrance to the harem, I sought her out in her new quarters. She had been assigned a modest room shared with five other young women-in-training in a large dormitory, and when I appeared early that morning, she looked perplexed at the sight of me within the harem grounds. I invited her for a walk in the gardens. Outside, when she asked what I was doing in the harem, I took a breath and blurted out that I had become a eunuch in order to clear our family name. Her eyes flicked to the middle of my robe, then away. For a moment, she looked as if she could not grab her next breath. She asked to sit down. I led her to a bench in one of the outdoor pavilions and we sat on it side by side, staring at the blooming peach trees. When Jalileh finally looked at me again, I expected to see horror in her eyes. Instead she slipped to the ground, wrapped her arms around my ankles, and laid her cheek on top of my feet.

"What you have paid in flesh, I will pay in devotion. I swear it!"

I tried to help her up, but she refused to budge. As her warm tears slid over the tops of my feet, it was as if the deepest rips in my heart were being mended with her tenderness. I lifted her to her feet and embraced her, and the tears in her eyes were matched by those in my own.

Every day from then on, I visited Jalileh to check on her progress. On Mahd-e-Olya's orders, she began a rigorous program of apprenticeship to learn how to serve the ladies. Her days began early with lessons on how to greet women of different ranks and in the daily and seasonal rhythms of the palace. I was gratified when the ladies commended her on her handwriting, her quickness, her desire to please, and her ability to face difficult situations with good cheer.

On our occasional days of leisure, Jalileh made me bread in one of the smaller kitchens in the harem; we ate it together with sheep's cheese and walnuts, just as we used to do when we were children. It was as if I had never eaten bread before, so great was my satisfaction in sitting beside her and tasting with pride what she had baked. Little by little, we told each other the story of our lives, and with every story a new understanding grew between us. Until we began sharing our histories, I had not realized how utterly alone I had felt.

Others could argue with a sibling or an uncle and still have more blood relatives to turn to; they could engage in petty fights and avoid speaking for years, relishing their anger while still being embraced by other family members. But Jalileh and I had no one else, and that knowledge made us treasure each other like priceless pearls plucked from the stormy depths of the Persian Gulf.

While Jalileh labored to master palace protocol, my work continued at the scribes' office in a routine fashion until one morning, I overheard a court historian explaining to his young assistant how they would undertake the work of writing the history of Isma'il Shah's short reign. He told the assistant to deputize a few men to collect details from his closest advisors about his efforts to deal with national and international problems, as well as to interview other nobles about his patronage of mosques and of the arts. The assistant would organize the material and provide it to his master, who would write the official history.

Once those details had been settled, the assistant lowered his voice.

"What are you going to write about that sister of his?" he asked the historian in a near whisper.

"You mean the one who poisoned him?" the graybeard replied.

"I thought he was poisoned by the qizilbash." The young man had an offensively bright red mouth and tongue.

"Who knows? The harem is a mystery. There is no way to be certain about what goes on in there."

"Of course there is," I said so loudly that the men looked up from their pages. "Why don't you ask the eunuchs who work there every day?"

"Why bother? The women hardly do anything at all," said the young man.

I stood up. "Are you a fool? Pari Khan Khanoom did more in a day than you do in a year. Compared to her, you are like an old mule."

The graybeard looked at me as if I were mad. "Calm down!" he said. "We are only going to write a few pages about her anyway."

"Then you will be missing one of the most arresting stories of our age."

"You think that way because you served her," said the young man dismissively.

Memories of Pari appeared so suddenly that they seemed more real than the men in front of me: her challenges on the first day I had met her, the gleam in her eyes as she dropped the peacock bowl, the ringing sound of her voice when she declaimed the poem that silenced Mirza Shokhrollah, the fearless way she had begged Isma'il for clemency for the condemned, the strength of her hands against my back pushing me out of the palanquin. I missed her with all my heart. Her great flaws—obstinacy, arrogance, and fervor— had also been her strengths. Why didn't the historians care enough to find out?

"Illiterate!" I said to the young man. "Don't you imagine you have a duty to the truth?"

He shrugged. Rasheed Khan motioned the young scribe to the other side of the room and told him to get on with his work. From there the scribe glared at me but kept quiet. I realized that not only would the court historians fail to write enough about Pari, but they would not bring her story to life. How could they? They had never breached the royal harem. The women's daily affairs, political efforts, passions, eccentricities, and quarrels would rarely be charted, and if they were, they would be misinterpreted and misunderstood. Worse yet, Mohammad Shah's court would no doubt portray the princess as a monster to justify her murder.

Then and there I decided I must write Pari's life story, under cover of responding to court letters. Not only would I tell the truth of events, but I would beat away misconceptions and help her live for all time. That was the least that she was owed.

As the only chronicler who served her closely enough to breathe in her perfume, I knew better than anyone that the princess was not a flawless gem. I never wished to pretend otherwise, in the way that our historians often try to justify the irregular behaviors of our shahs. I knew only too well about Pari's arrogance, her refusal to compromise, and her temper, but I also understood that her magisterial nature stemmed from the fact that she was more learned and better trained in statecraft than most men. She was right to wish to rule; only the greed and fear of others prevented her from achieving the greatness she deserved.

I began work on my prologue that very afternoon, after most of the scribes had gone home for their afternoon tea. When it became too dark to see, I concealed my pages carefully in a dusty corner of the library. I realized that I had finally begun fulfilling the fate predicted by my astrological chart. My presence at court was ordained so that I could tell the true story of Pari Khan Khanoom, the lieutenant of my life, the khan of angels, the equal of the sun.

AUTHOR'S NOTE

Pari Khan Khanoom lived from 1548 to 1578. Several contemporary court historians suspected her of poisoning her half brother, Isma'il Shah, although other theories proposed that he overdosed on drugs or was poisoned by a group of nobles who were disaffected with his rule. A few months after he died, Pari was assassinated by order of her half brother Mohammad Shah and his wife, Mahd-e-Olya.

After Pari's death, Mahd-e-Olya was the de facto ruler of Iran for about a year and a half, until the qizilbash nobles tired of her command and assassinated her. The grand vizier Mirza Salman, ever adept at judging shifts in the wind, changed allegiance just before the nobles decided to remove her. A few years later, he was assassinated in his turn by the qizilbash, who resented his power. Strife raged for years to come as tribal groups struggled to dominate one another.

During Pari's short life, one of the most powerful empires on earth was that of the Ottomans. Under Suleyman the Magnificent, the Ottomans had conquered territory all the way west to Hungary and had fought frequent battles with Iran and other neighbors on their eastern borders. In 1555, Pari's father, Tahmasb Shah, brokered the Peace of Amasya, a treaty in which the two powers divided up disputed territories and the Ottomans recognized Safavi Iran for the first time. My novel posits that Pari would have worked tirelessly to maintain this treaty, although I found no specific evidence for this in the sources I used. Not long after Pari's death, the Ottomans invaded Iran and hostilities resumed again, with devastating consequences including loss of Iranian territory.

The Safavi dynasty ruled from 1501–1722. The founder of the dynasty, Isma'il I, declared Shi'a Islam the official religion of Iran, with the result that Iran is now the largest Shi'a country in the world. Despite much political turmoil, the Safavi dynasty was stable and wealthy enough, particularly during its first half, to fund the creation of many of the masterpieces of Iranian architecture, weaving, painting, pottery, and other crafts. Among these is an illustrated *Shahnameh* commissioned by Tahmasb Shah that is regarded as one of the finest examples of bookmaking in the world. Tahmasb gave the book to the Ottoman Empire in 1567, along with other rich gifts loaded on the backs of dozens of camels, an inestimable loss to future generations of Iranians.

After years of internal and external power struggles following Tahmasb's death, an able ruler finally took charge of Iran. The greatest leader of the Safavis would turn out to be Abbas—the second son of Mohammad Shah and his wife, Mahd-e-Olya—who was crowned in a palace coup in 1587 at the age of sixteen and ruled for more than forty years. Shah Abbas finally quashed the fractious qizilbash by uprooting old power structures and elevating new groups, especially converted Georgians, Circassians, and Armenians, who owed their loyalty only to him. Perhaps his greatest legacy, however, is the city of Isfahan, which he declared his capital in 1598 and refashioned with the help of master architects, engineers, calligraphers, and tile makers. The central square that dominates the town and the bridges that traverse its river are among the true crown jewels of his rule.

The key members of the royal family mentioned in this book were real people. On occasion I made up first names for women whose names were never recorded. The servants of the palace harem, including Javaher, Khadijeh, Balamani, and Maryam, are invented characters.

ACKNOWLEDGMENTS

I n recent years, several scholars have mined original sources and generated new thinking about the political sophistication of premodern Muslim women like Pari Khan Khanoom. Their work has been invaluable in allowing me to imagine the decisions Pari might have made and the life that she might have lived. In particular, Shohreh Gholsorkhi has written an insightful article about Pari's role in the politics of her day, and Maria Szuppe has written in detail about the extent of the education, wealth, and power enjoyed by some Safavi court women. Szuppe's work suggested to me the complicated relationships that Pari might have had with her uncle Shamkhal Cherkes and the grand vizier Mirza Salman, and brought to my attention the conflict that occurred over control of the treasury in Qazveen. In addition, Leslie Peirce's work on premodern Ottoman women has been extremely helpful in illuminating the organizational structure of a royal harem and the tasks fulfilled by the women residing within it. Despite being sequestered, some Muslim court women had much more power, wealth, and influence than they are usually given credit for.

One of the key primary sources for the historical events mentioned in this novel was a court chronicle written by Eskandar Monshi, who for decades served as historian to Shah Abbas (1571–1629). The first volume of his history sets the stage for Abbas's reign by recounting the stories of his ancestors. Monshi (which means "scribe") writes in detail about Tahmasb Shah's death and about his children's power struggles: Haydar Mirza's attempt to take the throne, Isma'il Shah's murder of most of his brothers and cousins, and Pari Khan Khanoom's participation in politics. However, since Monshi provides little information about what Pari did on a day-to-day basis, I invented many such scenes. And although I followed Monshi in recounting key events (coronations, murders, and power shifts), I changed some details and invented others to suit the needs of my story. Readers interested in Monshi's telling of the events can consult Roger M. Savory's translation, *History of Shah Abbas*, vol. 1, pp. 283–342 (see Key Sources).

The italicized stories that begin each chapter of this novel come from a tale made famous by the great Iranian poet Ferdowsi in his *Shahnameh*, which was completed in 1010. For my retelling of the tale, I used as my sources the translations by Dick Davis and by Arthur George Warner and his brother Edmond Warner. The ancient story of the blacksmith Kaveh's rebellion against a foreign tyrant still retains iconic status in Iranian culture today; the "Kaviani Banner" featuring the blacksmith's apron is a potent symbol of resistance.

For their helpful comments while this novel was being written, I wish to thank Ahmad Amirrezvani, Ali Amirrezvani, Firoozeh Amirrezvani, Catherine Armsden, Genevieve Conaty, Carolyn Cooke, Laurie Fox, Ed Grant, Tess Uriza Holthe, Marshall Krantz, Katherine Smith, and my agent, Emma Sweeney. Sandra Scofield, my mentor and friend, provided detailed suggestions on an early draft. My heartfelt thanks to Alexis Gargagliano at Scribner for being an old-school editor in the best sense of the term: thorough, thoughtful, and transformative.

KEY SOURCES

Ayalon, David. *Eunuchs, Caliphs and Sultans: A Study of Power Relationships.* Jerusalem: Magnes Press, the Hebrew University, 1999.

Babaie, Sussan, Kathryn Babayan, Ina Baghdiantz-McCabe, and Massumeh Farhad. *Slaves of the Shah: New Elites of Safavid Iran.* London: I.B. Tauris, 2004.

Babayan, Kathryn. "The Safavid Synthesis: From Qizilbash Islam to Imamite Shi'ism." *Iranian Studies* 27, nos. 1–4 (1994).

Beck, Lois, and Guity Nashat, eds. *Women in Iran: From the Rise of Islam to 1800.* Urbana: University of Illinois Press, 2003.

Bier, Carol, ed. *Woven From the Soul, Spun From the Heart: Textile Arts of Safavid and Qajar Iran, 16th–19th Centuries.* Washington, D.C.: The Textile Museum, 1987.

Browne, Edward G., trans. *Chahar Maqala* (The Four Discourses of Nidham-i-Arudi-i-Samarqandi). London: Messrs. Luzac & Co., 1921. Printed by the Cambridge University Press for the EJW Gibb Memorial Trust.

Dankoff, Robert, trans. *The Intimate Life of an Ottoman Statesman: Melek Ahmed Pasha.* As portrayed in Evliya Çelebi's *Book of Travels.* Albany: State University of New York Press, 1991.

Davis, Dick. *Epic & Sedition: The Case of Ferdowsi's Shahnameh.* Washington, D.C.: Mage Publishers, 2006. First published in 1992 by the University of Arkansas Press.

Echraghi, Ehsan. "Description contemporaine des peintures murales disparues des palais de Shah Tahmasp à Qazvin." *Art et société dans le monde iranien.* Paris: Institut Français d'Iranologie de Téhéran, Bibliotheque Iranienne, no. 26 (1982).

Farrokh, Dr. Kaveh. *Iran at War: 1500–1988.* Oxford: Osprey Publishing, 2011.

Ferdowsi, Abolqasem. *Shahnameh: The Persian Book of Kings.* Translated by Dick Davis. New York: Viking Penguin, 2006.

Gholsorkhi, Shohreh. "Pari Khan Khanum: A Masterful Safavid Princess." *Iranian Studies* 28, nos. 3–4 (Summer/Fall 1995).

Hambly, Gavin R. G., ed. *Women in the Medieval Islamic World.* New York: St. Martin's Press, 1998.

Hathaway, Jane. *Beshir Agha: Chief Eunuch of the Ottoman Imperial Harem.* London: Oneworld Publications, 2005.

Komaroff, Linda, ed. *Gifts of the Sultan: The Arts of Giving at the Islamic Courts.* Los Angeles: Los Angeles County Museum of Art, 2011; New Haven: Yale University Press, 2011.

Lambton, A. K. S. "Justice in the Medieval Persian Theory of Kingship." *Studia Islamica* 17 (1962): 91–119.

Losensky, Paul E. "The Palace of Praise and the Melons of Time: Descriptive Patterns in 'Abdi Shirazi's Garden of Eden." *Eurasian Studies* 2 (2003).

Marmon, Shaun. *Eunuchs and Sacred Boundaries in Islamic Society.* New York: Oxford University Press, 1995.

Matthee, Rudi. "Prostitutes, Courtesans, and Dancing Girls: Women Entertainers in Safavid Iran." *Iran and Beyond: Essays in Middle Eastern History in Honor of Nikki R. Keddie.* Edited by Rudi Matthee and Beth Baron. Costa Mesa, CA: Mazda Publishers, 2000.

———. *The Pursuit of Pleasure: Drugs and Stimulants in Iranian History, 1500–1900.* Princeton: Princeton University Press, 2005.

Monshi, Eskandar. *History of Shah 'Abbas.* Translated by Roger M. Savory. Persian Heritage Series 28. Boulder, CO: Westview Press, 1978.

Mulk, Nizam al-. *The Book of Government or Rules for Kings.* Translated by Hubert Darke. London: Routledge & Kegan Paul, Ltd., 1978.

Peirce, Leslie P. *The Imperial Harem: Women and Sovereignty in the Ottoman Empire.* New York: Oxford University Press, 1993.

Penzer, N. M. *The Harem: Inside the Grand Seraglio of the Turkish Sultans.* Mineola, NY: Dover Publications, 2005.

Roemer, H. R. "The Safavid Period." *The Timurid and Safavid Periods.* Edited by Peter Jackson and Lawrence Lockhart. *Cambridge History of Iran* 6. Cambridge: Cambridge University Press, 1986.

Savory, Roger. *Iran Under the Safavids*. 1980. Reprint, Cambridge: Cambridge University Press, 2007.

Szuppe, Maria. "Palais et jardins: le complexe royal des premiers Safavides à Qazvin, milieu XVIeme–debut XVIIeme siècles." *Res Orientales* VIII (1996).

———. "La participation des femmes de la famille royale à l'exercice du pouvoir en Iran safavide au XVIeme siècle." Pts. 1 and 2. *Studia Iranica* 23, Issue 2 (1994); 1, Issue 24 (1995).

Tsai, Shih-shan Henry. *The Eunuchs in the Ming Dynasty*. New York: State University of New York Press, 1996.

Warner, Arthur George, and Edmond Warner, trans. *The Shahnama of Firdausi*. London: Kegan Paul, Trench, Trübner & Co., Ltd., 1905.

Wilson, Jean D., and Claus Roehrborn. "Long-Term Consequences of Castration in Men: Lessons from the Skoptzy and the Eunuchs of the Chinese and Ottoman Courts." *The Journal of Clinical Endocrinology & Metabolism* 84, no. 12 (December 1999).

Yarshater, Ehsan, ed. *Encyclopaedia Iranica*. Costa Mesa, CA: Mazda Publishers, 1992.

Yinghua, Jia. *The Last Eunuch of China: The Life of Sun Yaoting*. Translated by Sun Haichen. China Intercontinental Press, 2009.

Zarinebaf-Shahr, Fariba. "Economic Activities of Safavid Women in the Shrine-City of Ardabil." *Iranian Studies* 31, no. 2 (Spring 1998).

ABOUT THE AUTHOR

Anita Amirrezvani is the author of *The Blood of Flowers*, which was longlisted for the Orange Prize, and is a former staff writer and dance critic for the *San Jose Mercury News* and the *Contra Costa Times*. She is currently an adjunct professor at the California College of the Arts in San Francisco.

READING GROUP GUIDE FOR ANITA AMIRREZVANI'S *EQUAL OF THE SUN*

Introduction

In sixteenth-century Iran, the princess Pari Khan Khanoom rules alongside her father, Tahmasb Shah. But when the Shah dies without leaving an heir, the court at Qazveen is thrown into upheaval. Amid the squabbling about who will become the next Shah, Pari is faced with a dilemma—how can she ensure that whoever becomes Shah will accept her as an adviser as her father did? Pari's eunuch and confidante, Javaher—known for his ability to extract information from any source and navigate the tricky hierarchies at the court—comes to her aid. But he has his own agenda: to uncover the identity of the person who accused his own father of treason years before.

Topics & Questions for Discussion

1. In the opening pages of *Equal of the Sun*, Javaher notes: "People say that one's future is inscribed on the forehead at birth—Pari's forehead announced a future that was rich and storied." Does Pari fulfill her prophecy? What about Javaher?

2. Why do you think Pari opposes Haydar and supports Isma'il, even though she hasn't seen Isma'il since she was a girl?

3. How much did you know about Iranian history before reading *Equal of the Sun*? What was the most striking or interesting thing you learned while reading?

4. Balamani calls information a "jewel," and it is from this proclamation that Javaher derives his name. How does information act as a currency in *Equal of the Sun*? Does Javaher live up to his name?

5. There are many different, competing tribes in Qazveen, including the Ostajlu, the Takkalu, and the Circassians. Javaher himself has both Tajik and Turkic blood. How do these tribal conflicts influence Pari's attempt at power?

6. What do you think is the significance of the novel's title, *Equal of the Sun*?

7. Why do you think Javaher agrees to become a eunuch at such a late stage in life? Is it his only option?

8. Excerpts from the epic poem the *Shahnameh* appear before each chapter. How do these passages influence your understanding of the novel? What role does poetry play in Pari and Javaher's world?

9. Javaher attempts to avenge his father's death by discovering who ordered him killed. Does he find closure when he uncovers the truth? Discuss your response.

10. How does Javaher feel about Pari? Romantic? Paternal? Worshipful? How do these feelings change and evolve throughout the course of the novel?

11. Javaher says, "God demanded that his leaders rule with justice, but what if they did not? Must we simply endure tyranny?" Do you think Javaher and Pari come to a moral solution when dealing with Isma'il? Why or why not?

12. Pari describes Javaher as a "third sex." Do you see aspects of both masculinity and femininity in Javaher's character? What about Pari?

13. Javaher says, "Just because we have gotten rid of a Zahhak doesn't mean we have to become one." Are Javaher and Pari ever in danger of using their power too ruthlessly? Do they ever step over the line?

14. Why is Pari so stubborn in her treatment of Mirza Salman and Mohammed after Mohammed is chosen Shah, even when Javaher

and Shamkhal warn her against it? What are the ramifications of her actions?

15. From his relationships with his sister, Mahmood, and Massoud Ali, it's clear that Javaher would have liked to be a father. Do you think he regrets his decision to become a eunuch? How do his feelings change over the course of the novel?

16. Do you think Amirrezvani's observations about power and gender have resonance today? Discuss.

Enhance Your Book Club

1. Find a copy of the *Shahnameh* at your local library. Anita Amirrezvani recommends translations by Dick Davis and Arthur George and Edmond Warner. Have each member read a passage aloud at your book club meeting. Do any of the passages remind you of scenes from *Equal of the Sun*? Discuss the experience of reading the passages aloud with your book club members.

2. Food plays an important role in the court at Qazveen—especially the sweets offered to guests in the ladies' chambers. Prepare popular Iranian desserts—like Shol-e-zard (saffron rice pudding) or Paloodeh (sorbet made of vermicelli noodles)—to serve to members at your book club discussion.

3. In the Prologue, Javaher says of Pari: "When I think of her, I remember not only her power, but her passion for verse." Instruct each book club member to bring in their favorite piece of verse— it can be a famous quote, a sentence from a beloved novel, or a favorite poem. Share with the group and discuss why you choose it. What is it about the sentence structure or word choice that draws you in?

A CONVERSATION WITH
ANITA AMIRREZVANI

What is known about the lives of pre-modern Iranian court women?

Not a lot. We know that court women could be as well educated as men. They composed poetry and letters; went horseback riding; provided charitable donations to mosques and other institutions; employed viziers; served as advisors to Shahs to whom they were related; fought for power "behind the curtain"; and worked to advance their sons. But little information survives to tell us what they did on a daily basis or what their thoughts and feelings were. Those who made an impact on Iranian politics, like Pari Khan Khanoom and Khayr al-Nisa Beygom, were chronicled by Iranian historians, but these men would not have had direct access to the women. Therefore, the histories offer only a filtered view.

How has writing this novel changed your understanding about Iran?

It may seem obvious that a woman with wealth and family connections might wish to participate in politics, but stereotypes about women in the harem have made it difficult to see through the veils of obfuscation on this topic. It appears that women who were related by blood to the Shah were considered almost a separate breed because their family ties conferred upon them a special, almost magical status. New scholarship has revealed much about how influential women could be, but more remains to be done. I am hoping that a cache of documents will be discovered one day that will provide new insights.

What made you decide to tell your story through the eyes of a eunuch?

When I first started writing the novel, I tried using six alternating narrators, including Javaher and the dead Tahmasb Shah. As the writing progressed, I faced reality and whittled down the narrators to the three who interested me the most. Eventually, to my surprise, Javaher's voice emerged as the most compelling. The first time I dreamed about him, I realized that he had become as real to me as a friend, albeit a complicated one.

As a sheltered upper-class young man, Javaher starts out with limited experiences of women outside his family. As a eunuch in the harem, he gets close to power players like Pari, which ultimately challenges his assumptions about society's rigid gender roles. Additionally, the fact that Javaher no longer possesses one of the essential tools of being male makes him rethink the meaning of masculinity. I settled on Javaher as my narrator when I realized that he could offer a fresh, insider perspective on both sexes.

What role did eunuchs play in the Middle East?

They were enormously important for centuries. In the ancient Iranian empire, they served the kings in a variety of capacities, as advisors, sexual consorts, or even military leaders. A eunuch named Bagoi helped lead Iran's charge into Egypt in the fourth century B.C.E. and was later suspected of arranging for the murder of his own king, Artaxerxes III, so that his son could take the throne. After Islam arrived in Iran in the seventh century and unrelated upper-class men and women were increasingly segregated from each other, eunuchs became increasingly vital as messengers, advisors, and go-betweens. For my novel, it was convenient that Javaher could travel easily between men's and women's spheres.

How did eunuchs become eunuchs?

For many centuries, eunuchs were usually brought to Middle Eastern courts as child slaves. In this terrible practice, children from other lands (such as India or East Africa) were captured by slavers, castrated, and sold to courts or to upper-class families who could afford them. Boys and young men (as well as young women) were also sometimes captured during wars of conquest. Mary Renault's 1988 novel *The Persian Boy* imagines the life of such a captured eunuch, who is given as a gift to Alexander the Great, serves as his sexual consort, and falls deeply in love with him.

At court, eunuchs were educated to perform specific important duties: guarding the entrance to a harem, administering its operations, training young princes and child eunuchs, overseeing religious donations by the court, and so forth. Because they had no other family and no other ties, they were thought to be especially loyal to their patrons. On occasion, eunuchs were able to achieve high position, becoming wealthy and influential. For example, Beshir Agha, a eunuch from Abysinnia, was in charge of the Ottoman royal harem from 1717 to 1746. According to scholar Jane Hathaway, he "was arguably the most powerful occupant of that office in Ottoman history." Most eunuchs were not that fortunate, of course, but it's interesting to note that enormous economic and social mobility were possible.

Did men ever become eunuchs voluntarily?

Sometimes. In *The Imperial Harem*, Leslie Peirce tells the story of two Hungarian brothers who had converted to Islam and served at the Ottoman court in the mid-sixteenth century. After being informed by Sultan Selim that they could join his intimate household staff if they were willing to become eunuchs, they submitted to the operation. One brother died, but the other, Gazanfer, went on to have a distinguished career for more than thirty years.

In China, young men or boys also voluntarily undertook castration in order to make themselves attractive as employees. In *The Last Eunuch of China: The Life of Sun Yaoting*, author Jia Yinghua recounts that when a court eunuch came to Sun Yaoting's village in 1908, Sun was so impressed by the man's wealth and prestige that he begged his father to make him a eunuch. His mother objected, but one day when she was away, his father performed the operation using a razor and no anesthetic. Sun spent two months recovering, only to learn that the last emperor of China, Pu Yi, had abdicated. Still, he managed to serve the royal family and others for many years.

What kind of sexual lives did eunuchs have?

It's difficult to say for sure, but in *The Last Eunuch of China,* Jia Yinghua writes the following: "Castration did not always deprive the eunuchs completely of sexual desires. Quite a few eunuchs had an obsession with anything related to sex and would go to extreme lengths to find substitute outlets. They enjoyed looking at pornographic paintings, had endless gossip about sex, and sometimes engaged in homosexual relationship [sic]. Sun Yaoting found himself attracted to pretty women. When first shown some pornographic paintings in Prince Zai Tao's house, he remained sleepless all night with excitement."

Apparently, a eunuch castrated after puberty could retain more sexual feeling than one castrated as a child. Some research on people with spinal injuries, as reported by Mary Roach in *Bonk: The Curious Coupling of Science and Sex,* influenced my thinking about the possibilities for a eunuch's sexual life. Roach wrote about people with spinal-cord injuries who still have sexual feeling and even orgasms in non-genital areas; sometimes they even develop "a compensatory erogenous zone above the level of their injury." This research by Dr. Marcalee Sipski and others suggested to me the idea that some eunuchs might have discovered non-traditional areas of physical sensitivity and unique ways to express their sexuality.

What were some of the biggest challenges for you in writing this novel?

Since poetry was and is so greatly respected as an art form in Iran, I decided that it would add authenticity to my novel if the characters expressed themselves in verse at moments of great feeling or great urgency. I challenged myself to write such poems using a style that sounded courtly and that borrowed the rhyming scheme typical in the poet Ferdowsi's work: aabbcc. As a result of trying my hand at this difficult form, my respect for poets has become boundless.

Why do you write novels?

I'm interested in what-ifs; I love posing questions to myself and trying to answer them. I ask myself things like this: "If you were a woman in a harem who did not have access to public life, yet you longed to rule, how would you exert your power? If you were a eunuch, how might you express your sexuality?" Then I try to imagine the answers.

What is your position on "truth" in historical fiction?

I have tried to stay true to the key events reported by historians about the lives of the royals during this period. That said, I had to invent a lot of material because of the lack of information. Pari's servants, her love affair, her animosities, her preferences, and much of her approach to political strategy all had to be imagined in order to tell the story. It was fascinating to explore how a woman like Pari might have expressed her sexuality and her desire for power in a segregated society.

What do we know about lesbian and gay sex in Iran in the pre-modern period?

The favorite young male consorts of various Shahs are sometimes mentioned by historians without any seeming embarrassment. Then again, they had to be careful when discussing the habits of their patrons. Some pre-modern poetry by men appears to be quite frank about the glories of young men (but because Farsi uses a single pronoun to mean both "he" and "she," it is possible for the writers to be coy about this issue). However, the many poems that glorify the new down on a lover's cheeks are presumably about young men.

As far as the historical characters in my book are concerned, I found little information about their sexual lives other than mention of their marriages or engagements. Pari was engaged to her cousin Badi al-Zaman, but the marriage never took place. Isma'il Shah married the daughters of Shamkhal Cherkes and Pir Mohammad Khan, as well as slept with an unnamed slave (I call her Mahasti) who bore his child Shoja al-din. But it is quite possible that he had other love interests as well. In his *Life of Shah Abbas I,* which was published about twenty years ago in Farsi, historian Nasr'ollah Falsafi described Hassan Beyg as "young and beautiful" and as the "lover and day-and-night companion" of Isma'il Shah.

Lesbianism does not seem to be mentioned much in the pre-modern period in Iran, possibly because writers tended to be men. According to an article by scholar Minoo Southgate (the article is called "Men, Women, and Boys: Love and Sex in the Works of Sa'adi," and it appeared in 1984 in *Iranian Studies*), "while medieval Iranian texts attest to the prevalence of homosexuality, they avoid lesbianism. This writer does not recall a single lesbian episode in medieval Iranian writings, literary or otherwise. The absence of lesbianism in literature, however, is not proof of its absence in life. Sexual segregation encourages lesbianism among girls and married women. Similarly, polygamy encourages lesbianism in the harem, where several wives are forced to share one husband" (p. 438).

What about prostitutes in Iran? Did they really exist, and did they really pay taxes?

Yes on both counts. The great French traveler and writer Jean Chardin, who visited Iran in the 1670s and wrote ten volumes about his travels, estimated that there were 14,000 prostitutes in Isfahan, who paid 13,000 tomans in taxes.

Why do some of your Muslim characters drink alcohol?

Wine-making flourished in Iran long before the arrival of Islam. The custom of wine-drinking was so well established that many people of means refused to give it up. Even today the province of Shiraz is known as an excellent grape-growing region (although alcohol is now forbidden to Muslims). Wine-making and drinking at court went through phases, depending on the piety of a given Shah. Tahmasb Shah became pious and foreswore alcohol, but his son Isma'il Shah permitted it.

Why do so many people assume Iranians are Arabs?

Good question! Iranians are often confused with Arabs because of geography and because of certain historical connections between the peoples. Before the seventh century, the dominant religion in Iran was Zoroastrianism. Arabs conquered Iran in the seventh century, and Iranians were ruled by the Arab caliphate at Baghdad for hundreds of years. Over time, most became Muslims. (That said, in Iran there are still minority populations of Christians, Jews, Zoroastrians, and Bahais.) Starting in the sixteenth century, Iran became a Shi'a majority nation, which differentiates it from most Arab countries, which are Sunni-dominated. Also, Iranians speak Farsi, not Arabic. Farsi is an Indo-European language, whereas Arabic is a Semitic one.

What is the importance of the italicized tale that begins every chapter of your book?

For a long time, I've been deeply inspired by the poet Ferdowsi's tale of Kaveh the blacksmith, who takes a stand against political despotism. Presumably, Ferdowsi had to be very careful not to offend the ruling Shahs of his day; writing about a humble blacksmith challenging a Shah was probably a radical act during such a hierarchical period. I thought that the story of Kaveh the blacksmith could be used to inspire the characters in my book to take action against the injustice around them, just as it has inspired Iranians for centuries. Pari's father, Tahmasb Shah, commissioned a famous illustrated *Shahnameh,* and members of his court worked on it for years before she was born. I think it is likely that Pari would have grown up memorizing Ferdowsi's poetry—and that every literate person at court would have done so. To this day, the *Shahnameh* is still considered Iran's national epic.

Who was Ferdowsi?

Ferdowsi was one of the greatest Iranian poets; his *Shahnameh* is, for

Iranians, like the *Odyssey* for the Greeks. The book consists of sixty thousand lines in rhyming couplets. Ferdowsi completed the poem in the year 1010 after working on it for about thirty years. Not much is known about his life, but the legend goes that when he asked the Ghaznavid Shah, Mahmood, for patronage after he completed his great epic, the Shah refused, and Ferdowsi died in poverty.

The *Shahnameh* recounts the stories of hundreds of legendary Iranian kings, as well as historical kings, all the way up to the arrival of Islam in the seventh century. That was when Arabs conquered Iran, and Islam gradually replaced Zoroastrianism. Although a Muslim himself, Ferdowsi's lament over the conquest of Iran by the Arabs and the changes brought to the culture is one of the most powerful pieces of writing in the book.

Once when I was visiting Iran, my dad and stepmom took me to a traditional Iranian restaurant, where we were entertained by a performer playing the *tar* and reciting poetry from the *Shahnameh*. It was good to know that Ferdowsi's work still has such an important role in everyday Iranian life. There is a beautiful monument to Ferdowsi in the city of Tus in eastern Iran, which is inscribed with verses from the *Shahnameh*, and it is visited with reverence by many Iranians.